ICE ISLANDS

ICE ISLANDS

Humphrey Hawksley

SEVERN
HOUSE

First world edition published in Great Britain and the USA in 2022
by Severn House, an imprint of Canongate Books Ltd,
14 High Street, Edinburgh EH1 1TE.

Trade paperback edition first published in Great Britain and the USA in 2022
by Severn House, an imprint of Canongate Books Ltd.

severnhouse.com

British Library Cataloguing-in-Publication Data
A CIP catalogue record for this title is available from the British Library.

ISBN-13: 978-0-7278-5062-1 (cased)
ISBN-13: 978-1-4483-0751-7 (trade paper)
ISBN-13: 978-1-4483-0750-0 (e-book)

To my brothers, Jeremy and Tom

PROLOGUE

Tokyo

She was out, clear of the death house. She had to get away. Completely. Long distance. Free from dread. From guilt. From paralyzing fear. An airport. Another country. Sara Kato rode in the back of one of the family sedans, her brother Michio beside her, window down, city noise in her ears and drizzle splattering on her face. In the bag strapped around her shoulder was her passport, credit cards, vaccination certificates, a few hundred euros and her phone from London which worked in Japan. She still had the American soldier's phone in her jeans pocket.

Shibuya's lights shone around her, massive futuristic images of gadgets, celebrities, fashion wrapped around skyscrapers. Umbrellas bobbed up and down as people ducked around each other in the rain. It would be so easy to slip away, vanish in the crowds. Easy, if she did it right.

'Why don't we walk?' she suggested. 'And I need an ATM to get some yen. I only have euros.'

'There you are.' Michio peeled off a wad. 'That'll keep you going.'

'Thank you, but no.' Sara lay a hand on his arm, trying to hide a repulsive shiver on showing any affection. 'I need to do something normal, be on the street, go to an ATM, get some money, feel people around me, feel cold.' After the horror in that stifling house, she made it sound believable. First step, out of the car. Second step, run as fast as she could.

'Of course. I wasn't thinking.' He squeezed her hand and instructed the driver to pull up. 'We'll get out here. The rain, getting a bit wet doesn't worry you?'

'It'll be refreshing.' She took her hand off his arm.

The driver turned into a narrow road and stopped behind a green taxi. Sara pulled the handle to open her door. It was locked. The driver glanced at Michio who gave a single nod. There was a click. The door opened. She gripped her bag's shoulder strap and stepped out. She drew in the bustle and buzz, eyes scanning on how best to escape. 'There's an ATM.' Michio pointed to a bank of three along the sidewalk, green and yellow lights glowing from their screens.

She saw two men ahead. She turned. Another two behind. A motorcyclist, engine running, foot on the sidewalk, looked toward her. They would be trained to stop her going anywhere. She needed to slow down and work out how to get past them.

'They're with us?' she asked.

'Sorry.' Michio shrugged. 'If you're a Kato in this city, you can't just go for a walk.' He took her arm. 'Ignore them. Come. Get your money.'

She stood in front of the cash machine, the cordon around her, taking her time, checking her PIN, her balance. Michio was a man she adored more than any other, her brother whom she trusted completely. What she had just seen shook her to the core, even though it wasn't against her. Michio was picking up as if nothing had happened, which made it worse, more confusing. She craved to understand him.

She concealed trembling, fought hard against a choking sense of more despair. She withdrew 50,000 yen. Turning to Michio, she forced a smile, 'Now, at least I can buy my big brother a drink.'

Michio led her into a tiny, winding street with poky counter bars and sushi places crammed next to each other. The same six or seven men trailed or went ahead of them. They were recognized. Bar owners bowed or raised hands in greeting. Not just to Michio, also to the men with him. They moved from place to place. One moment they were in an old red-light district of hodgepodge narrow streets. The next they were guests of honor at a bar decked out like a film set, with cameras, spotlights, fake sand dunes and thumping music.

She let Michio talk. Justifying. Explaining. Most in Japanese. Some in English. About being Japanese. Bloodlines, Family.

They kept moving from place to place, sometimes on foot to a bar or café nearby, a couple of times, a short journey by car. She lost track of where they were. She had never known

Tokyo well, hadn't lived here since she was ten. The security cordon stayed. Even in the rest room, a woman appeared from nowhere to keep watch.

She tried to leave. They were perched on stools in a tiny counter bar, Michio discussing with the owner the outcome of the Pacific War. Sara touched him warmly on the shoulder and spoke in English, 'I'm beat, Michio. We both know why I can't go back to the house. You stay. I'll check into a hotel.'

Michio laid a hand on hers, gently but firmly. 'It's late. We're all tired. There's a hotel just around the corner.'

She was terrified to show anger. To survive, she had to show she supported him in his evil. She felt suffocation. Her mind didn't know where to go. Stop, she wanted to scream. Stop controlling me. Stop giving me surprises. Stop being so bloody nice.

'Let me treat you. Just tonight.' He smiled at her.

'I need to—'

'I know,' interrupted Michio. 'You need to be by yourself. You will be, and early tomorrow morning I want to show you something about our family.'

She didn't want to hear anything more about her family. Her father had banished her from Japan when she was just ten. He was a monster. She knew the Kato family were stinking rich. She had never asked details because she had never felt part of them. She had been smart enough to keep her distance, but not smart enough to stay completely away. She had come back because she loved Michio, her elder brother and her protector. Everyone needs family. Now, she had seen that Michio was a monster, too.

'Our businesses are much more than just hotels, golf clubs, airlines and karaoke joints,' Michio was saying. 'We help people all around the world. I want you to see that, then you can decide what you want to do. Let's all get a good night's sleep.'

Her hotel room was vast with a huge bed, a sunken bath, a rain shower and windows with a surround view of the city. Sara walked around and around, sinking her bare feet into the thick yellow carpet. Michio's men were outside the door. Her brother had taken the room next door with an adjoining door to hers. She knelt and lowered her head to the carpet like in prayer. She let her mind go blank for five seconds, ten, more, until she realized that Michio could be watching her every move. She tried to rid herself of the thought that he would harm her. She couldn't. She had seen his eyes, his determination, the way he wiped blood off his hand. She pushed herself up, went to the bed and, fully clothed, enveloped in exhaustion, she crawled under the covers, pulling the sheet over her head.

She pulled the American's phone from her jeans pocket and scrolled through to see how it worked. She recognized neither iPhone nor Android technology. It was something different. Surely, they could pinpoint where she was. The American had made her register a thumbprint. It worked. She remembered the four-number pass code. The screen lit. Her heart pounded as she typed out a message in capitals. HELP. She thought a moment on how to make it clearer so it didn't get lost in some bullshit American bureaucracy. She deleted it, rewrote the message and sent it. R-A-K-E O-Z-E-N-N-A. H-E-L-P M-E P-L-E-A-S-E.

ONE

One month earlier

Douro Valley, Portugal

'Slow,' said Rake. Their headlights swept across vines on both sides of the driveway.

'You worry too much, Ozenna.' Jo Duarte turned impatiently from the front seat. 'We're here. This is it.'

Duarte had come with the job, a freelance agent hired through Portugal's Security Intelligence Service, its counterpart to the CIA. Rake had been assured Duarte was the best for the job. He knew the players and was raised in the area.

Rake was in Portugal because one of its colonies used to be Macau, an enclave on the southern Chinese coast. Now run by China, Macau was filled with casinos and dirty money. A trail of Asian organized crime that Rake picked up there had led him to the vineyard in the Douro Valley above the northern city of Porto.

A Japanese businessman, who claimed to be close to the North Korean dictatorship, wanted to set up a vineyard in there. He was a pitiful character, a chancer who had stepped on the wrong side of America's anti-corruption laws. In exchange for dropping charges, the Japanese was to give Rake a channel into the network of a far more dangerous and disciplined player, Michio Kato, heir to one of Japan's most dominant crime families. Michio had gone off radar more than a year, and Rake needed to find him.

'Stop,' Rake instructed. They were two hundred yards from the sweeping gravel driveway where there was a white Mercedes SUV. To the left was an open carport with vehicles. 'Cut the lights.'

The track and vines fell into a darkness, lit by a murky moon.

'You're overreacting, Ozenna.' Duarte's right hand was poised to open the door. His left gripped the leather headrest as he turned to face Rake. 'This is Douro, not Syria.'

Duarte had met Rake at an airfield near Lisbon, tall and confident in the way of a military officer clinging to past victories. They had driven through Portugal's dry landscape of red-roofed villages and fields of livestock and crops, and Duarte showed himself to be a man with stories and opinions. He had lectured Rake on many things. Money, which Rake didn't care much about. Marriage, which Rake had almost done, but not. Portugal, where Rake had never been until today. Duarte told him America needed to learn from Portugal which once had an empire that was now lost. Americans were heading that way, too. He had asked Rake nothing.

The mansion was a modern building with a red sloping roof, a whitewashed flat front and outbuildings on both sides. The left side of its double-fronted door hung open, a light shining from within.

'Where are the other vehicles?' asked Rake.

'They came by bus from their hotel. The driver must have gone off for his dinner.'

'And the one there?'

'I don't know.' Duarte looked away. 'I've known this family all my life.'

Duarte had given Rake a Glock 19, standard Portuguese police issue with a serial number scrubbed off. He carried a folding knife, which he moved from his pants pocket to his right hand. He tried to get the Mercedes SUV plate through his compact binoculars, but it was smeared with mud.

'I grew up with them,' pressed Duarte. 'Everything is fine. Or they would have called.'

'We wait,' said Rake. The meal break and vehicles didn't ring right. Portuguese and Italians might give drivers a meal break, but not Chinese, Japanese or Koreans. Anyone cutting a deal with North Korea through black money in Macau would be low trust, the type to keep vehicles close by.

'You wait. You're so jumpy. I'll bring him to you.' Duarte opened his door and got out. Fit and fast for his age, he jogged up the track onto the driveway and had the presence of mind to shine his flashlight into the Mercedes SUV, showing no one inside. He caught his breath on the mansion's front steps, smoothed down his suit jacket, pushed open the door and walked inside.

Four minutes later, a stocky man, not Jo Duarte, appeared at the front door. He looked Asian, athletic, tough, and wore a green T-shirt with a brand-name logo. Rake focused the binoculars on a transparent plastic sack he was carrying, filled with a jumble of phones and documents. Looking around, he walked across to the driver's seat of the SUV. He placed a stubby, folding automatic on the ledge on top of the dashboard. He dropped a magazine from a pistol and put in a new one.

'You go,' said Rake. The driver looked around sixty and had a weathered, sun-washed face. He met Rake's gaze in the rear-view mirror. Rake was certain Jo Duarte would not be coming back out of that house and, if the driver stayed, he would most likely end up dead. Rake gave him two hundred-dollar notes. The driver understood. He flipped a switch ensuring the internal light stayed dark when Rake opened the door. The car was a hybrid. He reversed on the battery with no lights and no engine noise. Rake moved through the vines toward the house and found cover with a garden hedge that formed the boundary of the carriage driveway. He lay flat on damp, irrigated grass with a view to the front of the house. The night air carried a freshness and silence.

The entrance hall light went off. Lamps from the driveway were enough for Rake to be able to make out a second Asian-looking man, tall and more formally dressed in a dark suit, pale yellow shirt, no tie. His eyes swept the landscape. He carried a greater sense of urgency. In his right hand was a pistol with a suppressor attached, which would account for Rake not hearing any shots. He brought the weapon up again, ready for use, reached the SUV within seconds and quickly got inside. The SUV's headlamps stayed off. Its tires crunched gravel stones as it turned. Rake played through scenarios in which he could stop the two men. None came to mind. They were better armed. There were two of them. They were trained. He watched the taillights fade into winter mist down the track.

Rake matched the face of the second man to many images he had studied over the months. There was no mistake. This was Michio Kato, the man he was hunting.

Rake fired up his satellite phone, the military one, separate from his encrypted cell phone. He didn't know what he would find inside the mansion. He had been on enough assignments that had gone rotten to sense it wouldn't be good. He needed Harry Lucas, who was running the operation from Washington, DC, to secure resources to investigate, keep it quiet and get Rake out of the country. He sent Lucas a message, broke his cover and ran across to the mansion.

The large entrance hall had light wood flooring and a high ceiling stretching up three floors. Jo Duarte had been shot just inside the front door, and was collapsed forward as if praying. Rake found others in a reception room which led on from the hall, with a thick blue carpet, rugs patterned with birds and flowers, and oil portraits of the family owners and the Portuguese landscape.

It was impossible to tell how a person would fall when lethally hit by a bullet. Disruption of blood flow, vital organs shutting down, and the brain in its last throes, jerked the body around unpredictably. Sometimes there was blood, sometimes barely a trace. Sometimes, dignity. Sometimes stripped of it. Sometimes, no expression. Sometimes, terror such as never experienced before.

Rake counted the bodies. Three males looked southern European, dark suits, colorful ties, around forty, well-polished city shoes. One female, dark hair, black heeled shoes, one torn half off her right foot in the fall. Another man looked more north European Caucasian, older, around fifty, could be Russian. Four were Asian. A male and a female were formally dressed, wearing pastel pandemic masks. There was a bodyguard whose weapon was buckled into his shoulder holster, a Chinese standard-issue military QSZ-92. Rake left it there. Another younger male, around thirty, expensive pants, shirt, and trainers. He would be the North Korean Rake had on file. He recognized the two Japanese. One was the businessman he had come up here to meet.

The smell of gunshot hung in the air with the smell of blood. With surprise on their side, Kato and his colleague could have eliminated all in seconds. There were no identity documents. They and the victims' phones would be in the plastic sack now in the SUV. Rake used his phone to photograph faces. Two rooms branched off. To the left was a kitchen, empty, untouched. To the right, a more lived-in rumpus room, where he found three more. A woman in her mid-thirties, barefoot, red T-shirt, blue denim jeans, looked more a nanny than a mother. A boy with tousled blond hair, around ten, and a dark-haired girl of maybe five or six.

The woman had died first, sitting on a blue and yellow sofa, two shots, chest and head, like the others. Something gave the children time to start running, hands clasped, managing to get a few feet toward an outside door before being hit by two bullets each, head and back. Even with such sudden, intense trauma to the body, until their last breaths they had had the presence of mind to keep holding onto each other. The brain was like that sometimes.

The killings were not about a vineyard deal. It was something more lethal that needed Michio Kato's personal hand. A message of cold cruelty. About status. A challenge. A warning.

There were no surveillance cameras. It wasn't that type of mansion. Like Jo Duarte had kept saying, people trusted each other in this community. Outside, Rake sent his phone photographs of the massacre to Harry Lucas, who replied straight back that a team was in place to extract him from Portugal.

Rake walked down through the vines, keeping off the track. Killing to send a message was more brutal and absolute than killing to get something done. Which was why the children had to die. To have spared them would have shown a weakness. Rake covered five miles down the hillside against a hard, night wind coming cold off the river. Low gray clouds created a darkness that gave him cover. Two black sedans sped up toward the house. Not far behind followed larger vans, also black. A message came through on Rake's phone with the plate number of a vehicle that would drive him to Porto Airport where a plane would fly him out. Rain began to spit, feeling cold on his face.

'Kato?' Rake asked.

'Negative,' replied Lucas. 'He's gone.'

TWO

Rake Ozenna was safely out of Portugal where he had stumbled upon a bloodbath. A string of tiny lamps flickered back and forth on the top of a screen as Harry Lucas's facial recognition software worked its way through the images Ozenna had sent through. Michio Kato, one step ahead of them, had killed the conduit they planned to put into play to get inside his network. Not only that. By murdering everyone else at the gathering, he had made a point to all crime operations everywhere. Don't mess with the Kato family.

Harry ran a private security company which had enjoyed the trust of the White House through three previous administrations. Now, a new President had moved in, and Harry wasn't so sure. He had not been receiving the positive signals that usually came with the change of administration.

His head office was in Crystal City, five miles to the south, close to the Pentagon and at the heart of the defense and security industries. His home, if anyone could call it that, was this ground-floor apartment close to Dupont Circle in central DC. It had four spacious, high-ceilinged rooms and a secure basement car park. The furniture gave it the look of a hotel lobby, and the bedroom was decked out like a five-star resort. The place was a bachelor pad, business-like, nothing personal, which summed Lucas up at this stage of his life. The personal could wait yet again.

Harry's concentration shifted to his automatic number plate surveillance keeping vigil on the road outside his apartment. It flagged a vehicle of interest. A black Lincoln Town Car pulled up and, once the passenger was on the sidewalk, Harry recognized National Security Adviser, Nick Petrovsky. Harry had thought best to pre-empt any fallout from Portugal by alerting the National Security Council. What he had not anticipated was a five in the morning personal visit from its boss.

Harry opened the door before a Secret Service agent could press the bell and said, 'Is it just you, Nick? Or your security, too?'

The question caught Petrovsky by surprise. He had only been in the job a month, unfamiliar with how a White House security cordon worked.

'Better just you and me,' added Harry. 'They know I'm DV.' DV or developed vetting was the highest form of security clearance. Petrovsky nodded. Lucas asked the two agents, 'You guys want coffee or something?' They shook their heads and stepped back

The National Security Adviser looked around curiously as Lucas showed him in. There were a couple of black leather sofas and matching comfy chairs on one side of the living area and a small round, glass table with three upright chairs in another. An arch led through to the kitchen, from which came a smell of old coffee and microwaved pasta left over from before the Portugal crisis broke.

Petrovsky was tall, fit, slightly overweight and scruffy, his gray suit creased, blue shirt crumpled and untucked around the waistband.

'We met during that—' began Petrovsky.

'Yeah. Baghdad.' Harry wondered why Petrovsky needed to remind him. Petrovsky had been CIA, Lucas US Marine Corps. As they had crossed the apron at Baghdad Airport, Lucas had recognized the whine and sudden silence that came before a mortar strike. He threw Petrovsky to the ground and covered him with his own body.

'You saved my ass.'

'We saved each other's.' Harry rested a hand on the back of a chair. 'It's five in the morning, Nick. We're both awake because stuff's going on. I gave you a heads-up on what went down in Portugal and Ozenna is out and on his way back.'

'No doubt very angry.'

'Ozenna doesn't do anger and he left no US government footprint. Nothing for the President's morning brief. So why the visit?'

Petrovsky drew a short breath. 'Your privilege of working

alone has ended.' That explained the friendly preface of the
Baghdad meeting. Petrovsky carried the drawn look of a man
who had been up through the night and was instructed to
deliver unwelcome news to a man who had saved his life.

'Meaning what?' Harry kept his tone relaxed and conversational. His job was to track international organized crime
networks that posed a threat to the United States and to work
outside of mainstream agencies, away from turf fights and
blockages. He reported straight to the White House, either the
National Security Adviser, the Chief of Staff, or the President
directly. Harry had heard whispers about President John
Freeman moving against him. But the inauguration was barely
a week gone, and he thought he was too far down the food
chain for anything to happen so soon.

'The President is shutting you down,' answered Petrovsky.
'And, before you ask, his decision came before tonight's
slaughter-fest.'

Harry stayed courteous. 'Who's taking the Kato case?'

'Hasn't been decided.'

'Except it's ongoing and tonight is evidence of exactly how
dangerous Michio Kato is.'

'Our view is that this has nothing to do with the US
government.' Petrovsky's skin was pasty, his eyes tired.

Harry tried again, 'Government agencies work in a jungle
of silos. Our bit of it, Security, Defense, Intelligence, are silos
ringed by moats, walls and razor wire. Everyone protecting
turf. That's why I've been hired.'

'Was hired, Harry. I gave you the courtesy of telling you
face to face because you did save my butt in Iraq.'

'Is this your call, Nick, or the President's?'

'His.'

'Leant on by Pentagon, CIA.'

'I guess.'

'Does he know what we do?'

'He's got the brief, I guess.'

'Do you?'

'Same brief.'

'Then I'll fill you in.' Harry gave a stern smile. 'I investigate
transnational crime networks which pose an extreme threat.

The mission came from an incident a few years back that we only just managed to prevent.'

'I read that, but we don't regard Japan as a threat.'

Then neither the President nor Petrovsky had read it properly. 'Presidential Executive Order 13581, clear as daylight, weakening democratic institutions, degrading the rule of law, and undermining economic markets—'

'That's yesterday's world, Harry. Take it on the chin. Everyone's moved on.' Petrovsky took a couple of steps toward the door.

'No, Nick. It's today's world. Yakuza is named. This is the umbrella of Japan's criminal networks.' His body tightened to suppress rising frustration. 'In Russia, China and North Korea, crime networks are extensions of governments hostile to the United States.'

'That's not Japan.'

'Wrong. It is Japan. To survive, Japanese Yakuza need to strengthen links with their Asian neighbors.'

Petrovsky shook his head. 'Japan is our closest ally, the bedrock of our dominance in the Indo-Pacific.'

'With weak laws against organized crime. It's exposed. Networks there are working closely with other Asian networks and all of them, Russia, China, Japan operate close to the heart of government. Last night in Portugal we saw what—'

'The kind of killing a Latin American cartel does every day of the week.'

Harry did not hide his exasperation. 'Japan is even more of a threat because our guard is down. It's not rocket science.'

'It's bullshit, and the President has called it out.'

Harry stepped around the furniture, so he was closer to Petrovsky, face to face. Petrovsky stiffened and took a step back. Harry spoke quietly, with a rock-hard edge. 'Michio Kato did what he did last night because he has no fear of consequences. We're mid-mission in getting him. We cannot afford to stop now while the case gets lost in some inter-agency spat. You know that, Nick. You are the National Security Adviser. So, do your job and advise.'

His words came out more irritated than he wanted, which Petrovsky exploited. 'You sound tired, Harry. That aggressive streak has let you down before and doesn't help your case now.'

Harry's record in the Iraq war had won him medals and propelled him into a flash moment of hero fame. His combat-streaked face became a symbol of American heroism during a mission in which he freed a village from Al-Qaeda occupation. A television news crew happened to be there, and pictures of Harry leading his unit in under fire, then carrying children, women and the elderly to safety made the front pages of every newspaper and headlined the networks. He went from the military into politics and won a seat in the House of Representatives, where he became chair of the House Intelligence Committee. There were whispers about a White House run. He married a glamorous, smart businesswoman, Stephanie Scrivener, who became a politician. In the eyes of the press, they were a dream couple. In truth, Stephanie was English and lived on the other side of the Atlantic and it became a marriage from hell. Stephanie was pragmatic, knew to cut out when there was no way to make it work. Harry tried too hard and got angry. His failure triggered a destructive mechanism inside him, either post-traumatic stress disorder from Iraq or, more likely, something long embedded within his character. A man could wake up one morning and decide that none of the stuff he'd been striving for was worth it. The wife. The job. The home. He didn't want it. He wanted to be a ski bum. And to seal his decision, he had an early morning drink and didn't stop. Harry had picked himself up and returned to ground he knew best: defense, politics, intelligence, deal-making. He was a risk-taker, lucky enough for a slate of finely judged gambles to have paid off, from which he had won the trust of a series of presidents.

'Sorry, Harry. Long night.' Petrovsky drew black leather gloves from his coat pocket and held them loose in his left hand. 'I'd feel the same. But you serve at the pleasure, and it's over. Other presidents loved you. John Freeman doesn't. Take it on the chin.'

Petrovsky began to put on the gloves, then decided against. He crumpled them in his left hand. Harry calculated that neither Petrovsky nor Freeman understood his work. He would not transfer files to another agency where contacts could be burned, and raw intelligence misinterpreted. 'What about you, Nick?'

He relaxed his body language, leant against the back of the sofa, but kept the edge in his tone. 'Do you want your name stamped on the next blow-back against our country, the next Bin Laden, the next Castro, the next Saddam, the next trigger to the next fucking forever war? Your legacy, Nick Petrovsky, the naïve National Security Adviser who sold out his country because he was too arrogant to read a case file.'

Petrovsky lowered his gaze, so his brown eyes hung like two sullen moons. Harry continued, this time softer and more amiable. 'Let's say that something in what I've told you could be right. The presidential executive order I referred to named Japan and cited a national emergency.'

'Let's say that,' Petrovsky agreed, while taking another step toward the door.

'Portugal was about us embedding an asset inside Japan's Kato family operation. Michio Kato was ahead of us and killed him.'

'And others,' added Petrovsky.

'Exactly. As a message to his rivals. But I may have another.'

'Another asset?'

'Yes.' Harry dangled but would not yet reveal who this was, hoping that Petrovsky's CIA instincts of curiosity would win through.

'Go on.' Petrovsky slowed his reach for the door handle.

Harry asked, 'Are you able to keep things running for a while?'

'Keep running, how?'

'My line open to you. My security clearance. Rake Ozenna on secondment.'

'Line open. Sure. Ozenna. Yes. That can take time to work through systems. Security clearance. Cannot. That stuff's immediate.'

Most of what Harry did was self-contained: He could live without a security pass. 'You do that, Nick, and, whatever goes down, I'll have your back. Share what you need to know.'

Petrovsky pulled on the gloves. 'Who is your new asset?'

'Michio's sister, Sara. She was pushed out by the family as a child. Their father's dying. Michio wants her back in.'

Petrovsky's eyebrows arched. 'You want to make her your asset?'

'Not the first choice, as you know, and she may not have the mental rigor. But it's worth checking. She'll be at a conference in Finland. I can shoehorn Ozenna in as a speaker. He'll watch. If it won't work, he'll do nothing.'

'Turn someone against their family? Long shot even for you, Harry.'

Harry moved past Petrovsky to see him out. He opened the door to cooler air and the shadows of Secret Service agents. 'Right now, Sara Kato is the only shot we have.'

THREE

Åland Islands, Finland, Baltic Sea

S now skidded across the parking lot and swirled around and around in strong, cold wind coming in from the Baltic Sea. Rake scraped ice off the windshield of a rental that had been left doors unlocked, keys inside. Two hours before sunrise, too early for inbound commercial flights, it was not worth staffing the hire car counter. This was a small, trusting island community.

Rake had a knack for sensing threat, and he wasn't seeing one around him. Except he was here to assess the sister of the man who had carried out the killings in Portugal, another supposedly trusting community. He didn't share Harry Lucas's confidence that Sara Kato would betray her family, and he gave turning her into an intelligence asset a slim chance at best. But Lucas was a risk-taker who had made his name on gambles others thought would fail. That's why Rake worked with him.

A low-rise terminal stood ahead with white neon lettering reading MARIEHAMN across the top. To the right jutted a squat control tower, low light glowing through the windows. A military flight had delivered Rake ten minutes earlier and fifteen hours late: he was to have checked into the conference the previous evening. The downside of such flights was their unpredictable schedules. The upside was that you could leave and enter a country without leaving a record, which is how Rake needed it to be. You could also carry weapons and make calls on secure lines. He had flown from Andrews Air Force base outside DC with a bunch of senior officers, to Tromsø in northern Norway, where the brass got off. Rake stayed on alone for the ninety-minute journey south to the Åland Islands, which used to be a flashpoint between Finland and Sweden. That got fixed without bloodshed, and the islands were now home to a peace institute which held masterclasses in stopping war. Good luck, Rake thought.

On the flight he had looked through the file on Sara Kato and her family's crime network, set up by her great-great-grandfather at the start of last century when there wasn't much of a line between racketeering, government and business. Her father, Jacob Kato, was the current head, referred to as *Oya bun*, meaning the boss, connected in commerce and politics, and running a conglomerate that seemed to have tentacles in everything: banking, construction, airlines, hotels. You name it. After a near-miss in Europe two years ago, Rake and Harry Lucas had been tracking the family. Michio, the eldest son and heir, had vanished, only to resurface eighteen months later for the Portugal murders. Why had he gone there in person, when he could have sent payroll contract killers; to prove a level of uncompromising cruelty, one that required killing children. In Michio's absence, his younger brother, Kazan, Sara's twin, had been taking a more high-profile role. Sara, herself, seemed to have no connection whatsoever with the family business.

Sara was twenty-nine years old. Her most striking photograph showed her in black denim pants, black button-up shirt, short dark hair, with the purposeful eyes of a campaigner. She worked as an activist with a group that called itself the Global Association of Native People, and specialized in the Ainu, indigenous to Japan and parts of Russia. Sara's profile described her as trying to fill an emptiness in her life. Righting the wrongs of her ancestors and returning land to the Ainu filled that slot. As a native Alaskan, Rake understood the issues. Just about everywhere there were native people dislodged by others and people like Sara fired up about injustice. As he read on, he found out why. She had no lover or partner that anyone had picked up. Sara had been estranged from the family since she was ten, when her parents sent her to an English boarding school, appointed an official guardian and paid them to look after her. After school, she traveled as a backpacker, taking jobs as a translator, waiting tables, cleaning houses, looking after kids. She went around Europe and Asia but did not go to Japan and was now living in London. There was no record of her getting family money. While her two brothers were educated at top places in Japan and America, Sara had been pushed away by her family.

What Rake read in the file about Sara's family matched what he already knew. It was a story of modern Japan, going back to the late nineteenth century, a period known as the Meiji Restoration, when Shogun military dictators were deposed, and the Emperor brought back. It was a decade after the American Admiral Perry pushed his way into Japan with gunboats and a trade agreement, forcing through the first treaty Japan ever signed with a Western government. From then on, Japan learned from America and modernized. The Kato family influence grew in parallel and peaked in the 1930s as Japan was brutally colonizing Asia. Sara's father was born in 1939, two years before Pearl Harbor. Now in his mid-eighties, having expanded his criminal empire further than ever imagined, Jacob Kato was dying. His eldest son, Michio, was the presumed heir and he wanted Sara back.

The last slab of stubborn ice loosened from the windscreen and fell to the ground. Rake knocked snow off his gloved hands and was opening the driver's door when his phone vibrated. It was Harry Lucas. 'Ozenna?' Although they had worked together a long time, Lucas still called Rake by his last name, or simply 'Major'.

'About to head out from the airport.' Rake slid into the inside warmth of the driver's seat.

'We need to recalibrate.' Not usually a word Lucas used. His voice was tense, on edge more than Rake had heard for a long time.

'OK. Recalibrate what?'

'Hold a moment.' Lucas spoke on another line while Rake watched the SUV's GPS automatically light up to show his destination, keyed in by the rental company as part of the service, 5.3 kilometers south in the heart of Mariehamn, a ten-minute drive which would get him there by 06.30, long before sunrise and a couple of hours before the conference started.

Lucas was back. 'There's been a murder.'

'Not Sara?' asked Rake, letting his cadence slip as if he knew her, as if Michio would gun down even his own sister.

'No. Not Sara Kato. Male, mid-thirties, found at 03.43 in his room at the institute.'

'ID?'

'Not yet.'

'But the locals know?'

'Sure, they know. He was a delegate, and it wasn't a crazy drunken dark winter night domestic. It was professional. His throat was cut. Hold.'

This time, classical piano music played on the line. Rake dropped the ice scraper into a small, green plastic bucket left on the passenger seat for him with anti-freeze spray and a cloth. It took skill and training to cut a man's throat. Muscles around the neck were tough and unyielding. The killer needed to be fast and accurate with the blade, giving the target no time to fight back.

The conference was about ending conflict, and the model for this one was to keep it small. It was to last the inside of week with only twelve delegates, each from a different side of six conflicts: Syria–Israel; Northern Ireland, Protestant–Catholic; Iraq, Sunni–Shia; Nigeria, Boko Haram; even the Black left and the White right from the US; and Sara was partnered in a Japan–Russia dispute over islands taken by the Soviets after the Second World War. Rake's cover was good.

In his US Army role, he had become a seasoned conference performer. The military liked him because he kept his sentences short and didn't do emotion. His track record of conflict, Middle East, Southeast Asia and Latin America, made him a credible war-scarred show pony who could offer advice. He was to join a team of supervisors and mentors to help delegates understand each other's point of view, bury instincts for revenge, take peace messages back to their own communities.

'Ozenna?'

'Here.'

'SUPO are sending a team in from Helsinki.' SUPO was the Finnish intelligence agency, meaning the murder had triggered a swift response from the wider security community. 'Once they arrive, we'll have to declare you.' Declare meant Harry telling his Finnish counterparts Rake's real role. Rake adjusted the wing mirrors and seat.

'Do I go in now?'

'Yes. Now.'

FOUR

Rake put the phone on the dashboard, lifted up his rucksack, unzipped his right-hand jacket pocket and drew out a SIG Sauer P226 pistol, then from a left-hand pocket a smaller 938. A Gortex ankle and shoulder holster were stashed in the larger front pocket, together with ammunition. He slipped a ten-round magazine into the 938 and a fifteen-round one into the P226. He fitted the pistols into their holsters.

One voice in his head told him he was overreacting. This wasn't twelve thousand feet up in the White Mountains of Afghanistan, where feuds lasted centuries with guns, knives, and killing everywhere. He was in Scandinavia. Peaceful. Calm. Polite. A quiet airport parking lot. A louder voice told him he was about to join people who had been raised on a culture of suspicion, revenge and violence, and that one of their number was dead.

Had he known he would have changed on the plane. The terminal building was closed. He would have gone there to change, coffee, breakfast. Instead, he switched into full cold-weather gear outside the car, a silk vest, a dark green brushed cotton shirt, a thin wool pullover and a snow-gray jacket, a mix of down and synthetic filling, with a hood and a waterproof cape in the pocket. He put on heavy-duty boots, which had been clipped to the outside of his rucksack. He chose a folding tactical combat knife, securing it in his pants side pocket, adjusted the shoulder and ankle holsters with weapons inside and climbed back in behind the wheel. He pulled out.

Tires snapped fresh ice and crunched snow. He kept the window down with cold wind on his face.

The road was empty. Ploughs and grit trucks had done their job. Rake's wipers brushed fresh falling snow off the windshield. As he crossed a bridge over a wide inlet, a hint of dawn appeared in the sky. Within minutes he reached the town, more like a one-street village, pretty and neat, colorful buildings hugging the water's edge.

The institute was not imposing. It looked like a large old holiday home with extensions built on. Blue and white police crime tape ran around the grounds and a parking area that held one Suburban, two saloons, and a meat wagon for the corpse, which must still have been inside. There were no blue lamps flashing, no weapons drawn, no sense of crisis.

He parked fifty yards to the north, took a third weapon from his rucksack, a Beretta 92 semi-automatic, and slipped it in the glove compartment with the safety on. He got out to a harsh smell of the sea, the air tasting of salt and one hell of an icy wind that sent slanting snow into his face. Crystals splattered against the windshield.

The sidewalk was firm and gritted. As he moved toward the police cordon, a squat figure ran from the building, his right hand waving, his left holding a flashlight that flickered on the ground, pointlessly, because the area was well lit by street-lamps. A uniformed police constable began unclipping the crime tape. The running figure flapped his hand to stop him.

'Major Ozenna,' he panted, motioning to Rake, but staying on the other side of the tape. 'I am Dr John Norquist, head of the institute. Something terrible has happened. Have they told you?'

Rake shook his head. He wanted to hear it from Norquist who said, 'One of our delegates has been killed. It is horrible.'

'Who?' Rake scanned around. Water lapped against the jetty on the other side of the main road.

'The Russian boy.'

That must be the delegate partnered with Sara on the Russia–Japan disputed islands. The only other Russian involvement could be mercenaries in the Syria dispute.

Norquist fiddled with the crime tape as if it were a line of worry beads. He was shorter than Rake, around five seven, a pot belly, with a gray pointed beard, little hair, no hat, his crown damp with melting snow. Norquist's eyes darted around to a tall-masted sailing ship berthed along the shore, then to the other side of the street, two women, two men, and two boys watching, wrapped warmly in colored jackets and hats. 'We were expecting you last night. Your hotel room is ready.'

'Victim's identity?'

'That is the point. It is a matter for the police. I . . . I cannot reveal his name. Never before. Something like this . . .' Norquist pointed the flashlight to the road behind Rake. 'Your hotel . . . just along here.'

On the steps of the building, a senior uniformed police officer in a dark blue jacket and light armored vest spoke to a plain-clothes colleague in a beige trench coat. Rake asked, 'Are the SUPO here yet?'

'They are coming.' Norquist glanced over his shoulder. 'That is not them. That is Detective Leo Virtanen. He is the detective in charge. He is with the commander of police.' Norquist ducked under the tape. 'Come. I will take you to the hotel. The delegates stay at the institute. Our guest speakers stay at the hotel.'

'You go back, John. I'll check in with my boss and wait here. Won't get in your way.'

Norquist wiped his hand across the top of his head, shaking drops of water from his fingers. 'Our guests, so carefully chosen, they are in there. The police have ordered them out of their rooms into the conference hall. What should I do, Major? Continue with the conference. Cancel it, after all this work? Will you stay? It is terrible. Just terrible.' Norquist repeated himself, his English accent harsh and direct.

'The police will need the delegates as witnesses,' said Rake. 'So, continue. Keep them busy.'

Detective Leo Virtanen shouted from the building for Norquist to join him. 'I'm s-sorry,' Norquist stammered. 'Your h-hotel. Just there. Anyone can show you.'

FIVE

R ake moved far enough away from the cordon for the officers to forget about him. A line of police, searching for evidence, crawled on hands and knees across snow on the lawn that ran down from the building. Three dogs sniffed around the trees.

There was little point going to the hotel. Lucas wanted Rake on site for when the Finnish intelligence agents arrived. He would be declared and would work with them on the murder. Until then, he would wait.

Instead of sleeping on the flight, he had fielded messages from his home Alaskan island in the Bering Strait. Rake's fellow islanders wanted him back. He had done his bit for his country. They had officially registered him as a tribal leader of the Ingalikmiut Eskimo village of Little Diomede. The kids needed a mentor, someone anchored to sort out domestic abuse, read climate change, teach new ways of living, keep the old hunting and fishing skills alive. Something nagging inside told him this would be a good life. Community. Purpose. Family. His mother had left after he was born. His father hung around until he was six, then vanished. Rake heard he had gone to Russia, chasing a woman, and that he might still be alive. Little Diomede lay on the border with Russia. Rake had been raised with Russian guns barely two miles away. In the 1990s, as a kid, when America and Russia were sweeter with each other, he went across looking for him. But his father wasn't there.

Just as he was dozing off mid-Atlantic to the hum of the Gulfstream engines, Rake got a call from his sometime girlfriend.

'It's about June.' Carrie Walker started the conversation as if they saw each other every day. But they hadn't spoken for months. June was a young Little Diomede woman who, like Rake, was an orphan, raised by the island community. She was eighteen years old, wore bling stuff of pink and bright blues and enjoyed getting wasted on spice, a synthetic marijuana smuggled onto the island.

'She says Ronan raped her,' said Carrie. Ronan was June's stepbrother, a talented carver of walrus tusk. June had accused him, then withdrew the charge, saying it had been the spice talking.

'I thought that had gone away,' said Rake.

'It's come back again. She wants Ronan jailed.' Carrie had spent time on the island with Rake. She was shifting careers from trauma surgeon to a trauma psychologist. She and Rake had split because Carrie moved to Brooklyn to live with a doctor, someone more stable in their career. Carrie was the best conflict trauma surgeon Rake had ever worked with – fearless, combative, dedicated to the survival of her patient. She was less skilled at her personal life. Maybe this time, with the doctor, living close to her younger sister and parents in Brooklyn, it would work.

'We need to get June formally diagnosed with BPD—'

'What's that?' interrupted Rake.

'Borderline Personality Disorder. Mood swings. Extreme emotion. Processing situations.'

'OK. Let's do that.'

'Can you get Ronan away until things settle?'

'Will do.' Rake's monosyllabic calm balanced Carrie's urgency. Carrie was in the mental health trade so, technically, she could move things faster than going through Rake, which meant there was something else.

'That humming.' Her tone softened. 'You're on a plane.'

'I am.' He wouldn't tell her to where, and she wouldn't ask. 'How's New York?'

'New York is fine. New York is . . .' She let her unstated thought hang for long seconds, then picked up. 'Yeah. New York is New York, like in the song, except I'm not in it. I'm calling you from my apartment in DC.'

'All OK?' Rake's tone was unchanged, low so as not to wake other passengers.

'You know how it is, Rake,' sighed Carrie. 'You of all people know. When are you back?'

'Sunday. Want to get coffee?'

That gave her a laugh. Then she surprised him by saying, since he was busy, why didn't she handle Ronan and find a place that would take him. The conversation had more levels than Rake could work out. Carrie's move to Brooklyn to set up house with the dependable regular doctor hadn't worked out. It might have told her what Rake knew but couldn't say, that Carrie wasn't a settle-down kind of woman, however much she thought she wanted to be. He wondered how that left him and Carrie, back in the same city, easy enough to fall into each other's bed once more until one of them went off somewhere else again. He wasn't sure what he thought about that. Maybe nothing.

His thoughts were broken by the Åland Islands police commander ducking under the cordon tape, while skillfully sweeping the hem of his trench coat away from a puddle of muddy ice. He walked straight to his saloon, which his driver had parked just ahead of Rake's rental. He gave Rake a quick wave of recognition. Rake didn't look Scandinavian. He was dark, not blond, short not tall, his skin was not smooth but creased and leathered, his eyes were not blue and clear. They were dark, hooded and unintrusive. A stare from Rake Ozenna might not even be detected.

The commander climbed into the back seat. The driver leaned out and spoke to the police officer at the cordon, who lifted the tape and indicated Rake should go through. John Norquist emerged from the building just as Harry Lucas sent a message from Washington. 'We have the victim's ID.'

SIX

Rake shielded his eyes from thick falling snow as he read the message. Yuri Mishkin, aged thirty-two, Caucasian, Russian, height five eleven, weight 160 pounds, body mass index 22.3, hair color dark, identifying marks, none. Place of birth, Moscow.

'Major, Major,' enthused Norquist. 'We have a message that you can work with our police. The Americans have asked that we give you clearance.'

Rake acknowledged with a glance toward Norquist and kept reading. Mishkin had come under the sponsorship of the Euro-Russian Friendship Society, whatever that was. He had a research position at the Russian International Affairs Council. That was about it. Nothing about family, education, career path. A thin profile. There was a mugshot, clean shaven, untidy dark hair, beige jacket, blue shirt, no tie, a rounded face, smooth skin, sharp, playful blue eyes. The photograph shone with youth, privilege and protection. The twinkle of a playboy, along for the fun with the aim of having a good time and getting laid.

'Coffee, Major? We can go to my office.' Norquist led Rake through the shabby front door into a corridor that needed several coats of paint. 'They are about to remove the body and asked us to keep the area clear.'

'I need to see it,' said Rake.

'But . . .' Norquist's face filled with anxiety. 'I have to ask Detective Virtanen. I am not sure—'

'I am here, John.' Virtanen stepped out of a door to the left and closed it. He was an inch taller than Rake and had a bleak, tired face. 'You're Ozenna, a guest speaker. I have a note from SUPO to work with you.'

The detective turned to Norquist. 'John, go make coffee. I'll show Ozenna the corpse.' He handed Rake a pair of thin blue medical gloves and covers for his boots. Virtanen opened the door he had just come through into a good size room, part student accommodation, part mid-price motel, with a mirror above a narrow wooden workbench, an upright, light brown plastic work chair, a yellow fabric armchair under the window with a footrest and matching yellow curtains. Through an open door into a bathroom, Rake saw a stainless-steel shower head. In the middle of the room stood a queen-size bed, covers crumpled half on the bed, half on the floor, white sheets soaked dark with blood.

Yuri Mishkin's corpse lay face up, pale, a shocking, familiar expression Rake had seen in other young men, the face contorting as the brain is suddenly injected with sheer terror in the seconds before death.

Starting below the right ear, there was a deep and long cut on the front of the neck that had severed the carotid artery. Mishkin's front was covered in his own blood, now congealing in chest hairs. There was a bruise on his left shoulder where he may have been held down by his killer or killers.

'Murder weapon?' asked Rake.

'Not yet,' Virtanen was in his late fifties. Given his brisk professional manner and the rarity of serious crime on the Åland Islands, he must have worked in some place where people got hurt and killed on a regular basis.

'Who was through there?' Rake pointed to a half-open door on the left.

'There are twelve delegates, one from each side of six conflicts. They share a room if the same gender. Mishkin was paired with a Japanese woman so her room is through there.'

'Sara Kato?'

'Yes. Yesterday evening, after dinner, they had all been at the bar of the hotel you're staying at. The staff reported no altercations. A lot of laughter. Mishkin was killed around three thirty.'

'And found when?'

'Five thirty by Sara Kato. Either she killed him, or she was going to his bed.'

'Or both.'

Virtanen gave a grim smile 'Or both.' He turned to a knock on the open door and the arrival of the mortuary crew with a gurney and a black, heavy-duty body bag. The detective led Rake along the corridor to a cluttered corner room with views over water and sky, where dawn was delivering early light. The wind had dropped. Snow fell straight and heavy. There was an aroma of fresh coffee. Norquist stepped in from another entrance with a tray of pastries, which he put on the edge of his desk.

He handed Rake a cream sackcloth bag emblazoned with Åland Fredsinstitut inside a circular black logo, and in yellow, red and blue the words 'Autonomy, Minority, Security'. 'Everything is in the welcome pack,' said Norquist. 'How do you want your coffee?'

'Black,' said Rake.

'Black,' said Virtanen.

'Help yourself to pastries. We have rhubarb and almond. The chocolate is very good.' Norquist poured coffee, giving himself milk and sugar.

'Did Detective Virtanen explain?' Not waiting for an answer, Norquist repeated the formula of the conference. 'They live, eat, work together throughout the week. Each has a personal experience of conflict. They have either fought or lost family members. The institute was founded after the Cold War in 1992 as a nonpolitical, nonreligious organization drawing on our islands' own story of finding a path away from war.'

On the flight, Rake had read how the Åland Islands became a flashpoint between Finland and Sweden in the early twentieth century. The islands were closer to Finland, but most who lived there were Swedes, and Sweden threatened to take them by force. The British brokered a solution. Bombs and guns were put away.

Virtanen slipped out, as Norquist continued. 'We have six mentors, one for each of the pairs. They explain details of the Åland Islands solution on language, local government, discrimination, national identity, how we have road signs and documents in both languages. We offer that as a template, and they discuss with each other how much could be applied to their conflict. The goal is not to come up with a solution, but to understand how resolution works, and how difficult it is.'

The story of a hundred crazy wars, thought Rake, listening while looking through the delegates' hard copy profiles from the bag. The Israeli with the scar was paired with a captain from Syria's military intelligence directorate, both mid-thirties. The Syrian looked less damaged. He was in light brown uniform with black and gold epaulets. A second photograph showed his wife and young son in front of the Damascus Umayyad Mosque.

There were a Sunni and Shia from Iraq's never-ending civil war. Both wore suits and ties. The Sunni was disheveled, unshaven, reluctant, awkward, eyes drained. The Shia had a sense of theater, pinstripe suit with waistcoat, even a gold watch chain and a colorful bow tie, confident and camera-friendly.

There were two women from British-controlled Northern Ireland, one Protestant, one Catholic, each with lashings of brown hair, huge smiles and bright summer dresses.

From Nigeria came a commander from the Boko Haram militia, a vicious tribal extremist group in northwest Africa, paired with a captain from Nigeria's Special Forces Brigade who had studied at West Point. Both were large, fit, trained men.

From Rake's homeland there were two former US Marine Corps officers, who had spent six months in the same unit in Afghanistan. One was a black female captain who was part of an anti-racist, left-wing movement, the other a white lieutenant from a far-right group. Either would know how to kill Mishkin, but doubtful they would from a bar-room disagreement.

Then came Sara Kato, paired with the murder victim, a photograph of her leading a protest, on some kind of city square stage, dressed in black pants and top, waving a green and yellow flag, her face flaring with passion and energy, a profile of her job with the Global Association of Native People and a line about the conflict, an island chain that the Japanese called the Northern Territories and that the Russian Federation called the Kuril Islands.

'Our delegates have been identified as future leaders,' Norquist was saying. 'All are under forty. We keep the numbers small, and a condition of their attendance is that they advocate compromise over confrontation.'

'Did Sara Kato and Yuri Mishkin know each other?' Rake flipped through the photographs.

'I don't know.' Norquist tapped his cheek to indicate he was eating and couldn't speak. Rake waited while Norquist swallowed the last of the pastry. 'I think not. You must remember, Major, they only arrived last night. The ladies from Ireland, they know each other. The others, I am not sure.'

'How do you vet your delegates?'

'I vet them,' Virtanen stepped back in. 'Helsinki homicide

gives a man an instinct for rot. I match it with intel files from governments, your agencies, the FBI and CIA.'

'Kato and Mishkin?' Rake repeated.

'They came up as clean as any. The week is about conflict. None has a pretty past.'

'But never a murder.' Norquist avoided Virtanen's gaze and stared at the pastries. 'Nothing like this. Terrible. Terrible.'

Virtanen propped his phone against a book on Norquist's desk. 'I want you to be with me when I talk to the delegates, Major. They're in the lecture hall. Before we go in, you need to see this from the bar last night.' He brought up a frozen frame of a blurred bar scene. Rake could make out Sara Kato and Yuri Mishkin in the corner, separated from the rest of the group.

Virtanen said, 'Kato approached Mishkin to come here after he published a paper advocating a solution in the Russia–Japan islands dispute. Mishkin argued that they should become a demilitarized region overseen by the United Nations and run by the Ainu, the indigenous Japanese minority. Sara Kato found his paper on the web and offered to pay for his trip here. This is a clip from the hotel's surveillance last night. He tells her the paper is useless because Russia would never give up the islands. We've merged images from three cameras and enhanced the pixelation.' Virtanen tapped the phone to start the video.

Mishkin sat on a stool looking at an old black-and-white photograph that Sara was showing him on her tablet. A woman's face filled the screen, her eyes narrowed, crows' feet spreading to the edge of her face. A dark blue patterned headscarf covered her hair. Earrings hung in large, crooked circles. The skin around her lips was heavily tattooed so it looked as if she had a wide false moustache. Sara swiped to a photograph of villagers gathered around the carcass of a whale on a shoreline, reminding Rake of his own people in Alaska, the tattoos, the ruggedness, the individualism, the weakness when faced with encroaching American or, in this case, Japanese civilization.

'These are the Ainu of your Kuril Islands,' Sara said. 'The land belongs to them. Not to my country or your country which tried to strip them of their identity.'

Mishkin smiled, his eyes playful, looking back and forth from the photographs to Sara.

'The tattoos are to fend off evil,' she said. 'They begin by rubbing birch charcoal into small cuts around the lips and are cleaned up with antiseptic from boiled ash bark. The tattoo gets bigger every year, with more cuts, until the woman's wedding day. The Japanese had banned the practice.'

'I think we did, too.' Mishkin sipped his glass of red wine while keeping his eyes on Sara. She didn't respond. Her focus seemed to be on the Ainu issue. They spoke in fluent English, Mishkin with a light Russian accent, Sara with an English one like out of one of those period television shows.

'So, don't you think, we could give the islands to the Ainu? That's what you are saying in your paper.'

'You need to slow down.' Mishkin gave her a long, slow smile. 'You're like a lovely galloping horse looking for a racecourse.'

'I'm a what?' Sara was lifting her wine to take a drink, but stopped, glass midair, looking stunned at what Mishkin said.

'I'll make you a deal?' He leant across and turned off her tablet.

Her face contorted in confusion; she didn't try and stop him.

'We work together for this week, righting the wrongs of our ancestors, and draw up a plan to return land to our indigenous people.' His tone was stern, but the smile remained under the spirited eyes. 'What do you say?'

'Sure. Of course.' She sipped her wine and kept her gaze on him. 'This is what I do, Yuri. It is why I am here.'

'And is it the driving cause that fills the emptiness in your life?'

'What. No.' She put down her glass noisily, giving him a sharp full-on glance. 'Of course not.'

'Good.' He slid off the stool to lean on the bar. 'Because there are problems.'

'Of course. There are always problems. But you and I are children of the new generation. Together we can fix them.'

'I love it. Your enthusiasm is infectious.' Mishkin lay his hand on Sara's arm with a gentle squeeze before moving it

away. 'But here's the thing. Those seas need to stay Russian
maritime territory because they link Sakhalin and Vladivostok
to the Pacific.' His smile became a grin, his eyes teasingly on
Sara. 'Unless we hand our Russian Navy over to Ainu, too.'

'Why did you put it in, then? Why did you come here?'
She sounded irritated, but Mishkin's relaxed manner seemed
to absorb her punch. He kept his smile. 'I got to meet you,
didn't I?' He brushed his loose fringe off his face, still the
grin, still the eyes frisky.

Rake knew the type. Crazy, spoilt, cute. A good-time guy
who might well have been as lost and cause-hunting as Sara.
Now, she was focused on him, eyes shining, brow creased,
hand resting on the polished bar close to his. Everything in
her body language suggested she might well head into his
adjoining room in the middle of the night.

'That's it.' Virtanen stopped the video and picked up his
phone. 'The delegates are in the hall. Let's go meet them.'

SEVEN

The lecture hall, with faded maroon walls, old-framed
photographs and a worn green-patterned carpet had been
cleared to take only the twelve delegates. They were
spaced out at dark wooden desks in an area designed for a
hundred or more. Each desk carried a laminated card with the
delegates' names and their conflict. Windows looked out on
the garden being searched by police. There were two entrances,
coats on hooks inside the doors, uniformed police at each. At
one end there was a slightly raised stage with a wide alcove
and a pull-down white screen behind a long table.

Virtanen headed to the table, which was draped with white,
starched linen, like in a dining room. Bottled water, glasses,
writing pads, pens and white folded nameplates in bold black
capital letters. Rake's and Norquist's names were there for
what should have been the opening of the conference.

Virtanen poured himself a glass of water. Rake stood at the

back in the alcove to the right side of the screen. Behind it was a blackboard and the smell of chalk dust. The whole room smelt like an old school.

The delegates were quiet. The Israeli drummed his fingers on the desktop. The Boko Haram commander pushed back hard in his chair, arms folded, eyes erratically circling the room. The Shia from Baghdad rocked back and forth, chin in his hands. The desks were locked in pairs, but at an angle. The partners sat side by side, facing out slightly. The two Irish women spoke in whispers to each other. The military ones, two US Marines, the Nigerian and the Syrian sat outwardly relaxed, as did the Iraqi Sunni.

With Yuri Mishkin's seat empty, Sara Kato was alone on the left of the room. She had round Asiatic features with high cheekbones. She lowered her head, letting hair hide her face as she slowly turned the pages of a book. Taped to the desk was a card stating Russia-Japan, Northern Territories-Kuril Islands and the names Yuri and Sara. A green canvas shoulder bag sat on Yuri Mishkin's chair.

'Thank you everyone for helping out,' Virtanen began. 'We all know why we're here. It is sad and it is shocking. Yuri Mishkin was murdered last night. All of you met him. You might not have known him well, but from the little I have learned, you liked him. My job is to identify and arrest those responsible. Hopefully, I can eliminate each of you from being a suspect.' He spoke in a tone of a discussion, not an interrogation, an atmosphere of being in it all together, a familiar investigation tactic, exuding trust and engagement, that Rake had never managed to get right. His features were too coarse. He was unable to fake a lowered guard or make his smile trusting when it was not. Virtanen was good.

'I will gather general information now, after which I or one of my detectives will interview each of you separately. This will run in parallel with the post-mortem, the forensic examinations, and other information we have coming in about Yuri Mishkin.'

'And information about each of us,' said the Israeli in a hostile manner.

Virtanen sipped water, then looked directly at the Israeli. 'The Åland Islands police are not used to investigating murder.

So please bear with us, sir. I served fifteen years with homicide in Helsinki, during which time I also worked as an investigator in Kosovo, Iraq and Afghanistan.'

Virtanen's tone became as hard as steel. He had the room's attention. 'You arrived yesterday and some of you were with Mishkin in the bar of the hotel. You came back and he was killed, we think, around three a.m. – about five hours ago. Could I first ask if any of you had met Mishkin before yesterday?'

None raised a hand. Sara pushed hair behind her left ear, revealing bloodshot eyes and tear streaks.

'Which of you spoke to him at the bar?' asked Virtanen.

All but three hands were raised.

'I stayed in my room,' the Israeli said quietly.

'We did, too,' said one of the Irish women.

'And the rest of you were at the Hotel Cikada?'

There was a scrape of the chair, and the Nigerian captain stood up. His name was Victor. 'If I may, sir?' He spoke in an American accent with a Southern twinge.

'Go on, Victor,' said Virtanen.

'Nine of us walked from here to the hotel. I bought the first round. We talked in one group and ended up splitting into three. I was with Darul, Simone and Alex.' He pointed out his conference partner from Boko Haram and the two Americans. 'We talked about race and inequality, but more about soccer, football and baseball. The other group were the three Middle East guys, and at the end of the bar were Sara and Yuri. They headed back before any of us.'

'Does everyone go along with that?' asked Virtanen. There was a muttering of agreement.

Sara put up her right hand. 'If I may?'

'Go ahead, Sara,' said Virtanen.

She stood up, wearing a similar black outfit to the one in the file photograph, black pants, tighter and more stylish, the button-down shirt and a matching business suit jacket. 'I had never met Yuri. But we corresponded online, and I did request him for this conference. You say we kept ourselves to ourselves, you are right. We had a lot to talk about. I wanted to get to know him.'

She spoke in a precise English accent, leaning lightly on the desk with the knuckles of her left hand. With her right forefinger, she traced circles on the surface. Her voice was steady, but her face was drained like parched landscape. 'Compared to the others, our issues are small in human terms. No blood has been shed. Yet. I found Yuri by looking through research papers.'

'And you funded this trip?' Virtanen's tone softened, back to being conversational. Rake guessed costs would run into tens of thousands of dollars and channeled through Sara's Global Association of Native People.

Abruptly, Sara stopped circling the desktop with her finger and looked up. 'I didn't know if funding would be available. Mine is a small campaign. Not many people care.'

'Tell us about the campaign,' instructed Virtanen. 'Or how it is through your eyes.'

Sara brushed down her jacket and adjusted her name badge. 'Russia kept Japan's Northern Territories after the Pacific War. They call them the Kurils, fifty-six islands stretching from far eastern Russian to Hokkaido, our northernmost island. Historically, Hokkaido should belong not to Japan or Russia. Japan only occupied it in 1868, after the Meiji Restoration. Before that it was called Ezo, and it needs to be returned to its native people. Our dispute with Russia is over just four islands.'

'Are you native Ainu, Sara?' asked Virtanen.

Sara lifted her hand to touch the edge of her right eye, then began rearranging her hair. 'These are not Japanese eyes. They are too deep-set. And my hair is thicker. My papers say I am Japanese, but I have Ainu or Ezo blood. Many Japanese do, even though they deny it.'

'How did you think you could work with Yuri Mishkin?' asked Virtanen.

Sara sat down. 'He published a paper saying the islands should come under international control. He argued that the disagreement was stopping economic expansion. It was crazy that Russia and Japan had not even signed a treaty to end the war. If they did that and settled the islands dispute, the economic gain would be enormous.' A sad smile spread across her face. 'I liked Yuri. We talked a lot before we came. And yes, I took him aside at the bar because I wanted to develop trust before the week officially started.'

Virtanen let a silence develop. He hadn't mentioned the conversation in the bar. He jotted a note and took another sip of water. 'You haven't told us how Yuri died,' said the Israeli.

'Why should he do that, if we are suspects?' countered his Syrian partner, eyes forward, hands flat and hard on the desk, stiff body language between the two.

'We're waiting for the autopsy results.' Virtanen kept writing.

'We have a right to know,' insisted the Israeli. 'Any of us could be in the same danger.'

'Give us a frigging break.' The Irish woman who spoke earlier, her face taut with annoyance to face the Israeli. 'Not everything's a conspiracy. This is a bum day for all of us.'

The hall door opened. Norquist, head lowered, stepped inside. Virtanen shifted his gaze to his phone, scrawled a line on notepaper, which he tore off the pad and handed to Rake. 'Mishkin's blood traces in Sara's room.'

Virtanen nodded at Norquist, who spoke to a uniformed officer on the door. Virtanen brought out a second phone and made a fast call where he spoke just a couple of words.

'What's going on?' The Israeli was on his feet, arms loose by his side, ready to defend himself. The Irish woman touched her partner's arm. The Americans stayed still and vigilant. The Iraqis tensed, eyes scanning, familiar with a situation in which anything around could be lethal, anyone an enemy. Sara reacted less than the others, curious, not alert like the military trained delegates. Virtanen stood up, beckoning Rake toward him. Static crackled in Rake's earpiece.

'Ozenna, are you with Sara Kato?' asked Harry Lucas.

'Yes, sir,' answered Rake quietly.

'Get her out of there. Now.'

EIGHT

Rake's right hand slid under his jacket. His fingers curled around the small handle of the pistol in there. He had worked with Harry Lucas long enough to know when an order was immediate and non-negotiable. The order came through at the exact moment of the forensic evidence about Mishkin's blood traces, making Sara an automatic suspect. Keeping Sara safe meant with him and secure until a deal was cut. Rake didn't even know between whom. Governments. Police. Intelligence agencies. Gangsters. It could be done in the next ten seconds. It might take ten hours. Ten days. However long, Rake's job was to protect Sara until then.

Rake jumped down from the stage and, in two strides, was with Sara. His was the only sudden movement in the stillness of the hall. A police officer at the far side of the room reached for his gun.

Virtanen shouted, 'No, Johannes. Stop.'

But Johannes kept moving, smoothly bringing out a weapon in a way that would be familiar to a combat veteran but not to an Åland Islands beat cop.

'Johannes, no!' yelled Virtanen again.

Rake judged Johannes around forty. On processing of surprise, his gun mind would be slower than it once was. Johannes's eyes narrowed to intense concentration, first on Rake, then to Sara, which was when Rake spotted the shift of emphasis to his left hand. His jacket fell open. Its loose sides covered a machine pistol, which changed the dynamic, because Johannes could hit Rake and Sara with one burst.

It became a race. Johannes's hand grasped the weapon, Rake used his SIG Sauer. To his left, Virtanen reached for his pistol, an edge of slight movement that threw Johannes off balance. Virtanen was familiar. His boss. A good guy. A complicated target. Enough for Johannes to hesitate. Enough for Rake to make his decision to disable, not kill, with a single shot to the left gun arm, followed by two rounds into the upper right leg. The first hit Johannes's left shoulder, higher than Rake wanted, but it did the job to neutralize the machine pistol. The second and third, put Johannes on the floor. Sara let out a sharp scream, hand over her mouth.

'*Auta häntä!*' *Help him!* snapped Virtanen. Two men sprinted across to their fallen colleague.

Rake held Sara's arm. She gasped a breath. She didn't look at him, didn't resist. She took her shoulder bag and went with him. Pistol drawn, Virtanen had a second to decide which way to go: Stop Rake, risk further casualties. Or let him go. Rake held Sara with his left hand and the SIG Sauer in his right, half lowered, leveled at no target to reassure Virtanen. He moved her quickly toward the doors while sweeping the room for more hazards. Norquist's face was torn with terror. The police waited for orders. The half-dozen trained people in the lecture hall did nothing. They had no orders. Virtanen stayed stone-faced. The faint, faraway siren of an ambulance became louder.

The Irish woman cried out. The Iraqi Shia was half on his feet when his Sunni partner pulled him back into his chair. The Israeli had his gaze on Rake. The Americans turned back-to-back, watching and protecting each other. The two Africans took note and did the same. No weapons were visible.

'*Päästä hänet läpi*,' snapped Virtanen, repeating the order in English so Rake would understand, 'Let him through.'

In any extraction, the drag of a human body, even slight and small, could prove lethal. Sara walked willingly, which meant she had decided she was safer with Rake than where she was. That didn't mean she wasn't terrified. Sweat drops formed on her forehead. Rake felt trembling through her body. She had the presence of mind to point to her yellow, long coat hanging by the door. It was too cold outside to be without a coat. Rake grabbed it. The police peeled away, allowing them to leave.

NINE

Hailstones smashed noisily against windows and vehicles. Wind slanted in from the west. Sara put up her hand to shield her face. She put on her coat as she walked fast next to Rake, unsure, it seemed, but not totally surprised. Police on the crime-tape cordon stood back. They were young family men, islanders with weathered faces and routine lives. They had their orders from Virtanen. They would know what had happened to Johannes.

Options and explanations spilled through Rake's mind. There had been a well-planned professional murder. But was Sara also a target? If so, why was she not killed at the same time? Why implicate her in the murder with forensic blood traces? Why would a Finnish police officer so publicly and dangerously disobey a direct order? Who was he? Who was controlling him? Who wanted Sara and Rake dead? And what did Harry Lucas know that led to his order to get Sara out?

'I've been told to keep you safe. Any idea why?' Rake asked as they approached the rental.

Sara said nothing. She opened the passenger door herself and climbed in, resting her green shoulder bag on her lap. She clipped in her seat belt, then wrapped her arms around herself to get warm. Rake got in, checked traffic, which was light, pulled out and headed north. The sea on his left reflected the yellow glow of streetlamps thrown around in white water whipped up by the wind. Low-rise building on his right gave way to trees and parkland. He kept his speed down. Virtanen's orders might not have reached traffic cops. Sara unfolded her arms, looked sideways into her wing mirror, and saw what Rake was seeing, two police vehicles following.

'Where are you going?' she asked.

Rake didn't know. The road curved inland, heading toward an intersection that led to the airport. There were 6,500 islands in the Åland archipelago, covering 550 square miles, around the size of Los Angeles, but with a population of around 30,000 and barely a handful of bridges. He needed a plane or a boat. He had neither, and the landscape was unfamiliar. Virtanen's orders could get overturned anytime. Lucas was quiet, no voice in his earpiece.

The sun wasn't yet up. The day was heading in the wrong direction. Rake wanted nightfall, not dawn. There would be seven or eight hours of daylight. Bad weather helped. But it was unstable. One moment the wipers cleared a blanket of hail and snow. The next came a clean, quiet sweep of rainwater. An hour from now, the sun could be out, the wind gone and the sky clear and blue.

From the GPS, thirty minutes in any direction and they

would hit the coast. There was no labyrinth of side roads and farm tracks to lose themselves down.

'You don't know?' She looked hard at Rake, eyes squinting, curious, less afraid.

'The situation needed government resolution.'

'What does that mean?' Adrenalin was draining, leaving her olive skin flushed.

'That I keep you safe until things get sorted out by people way above our pay grades.' Rake wasn't great at politics. He hadn't worked out whether the new President leaning on Harry Lucas was connected. Freeman wanted to settle with post-Ukraine Russia so he could focus on reigning in China. Maybe the murder of a Russian citizen was a trigger for something that would throw his policies catastrophically off course. But that didn't explain Sara.

'I didn't kill him.' Sara said it like a non-negotiable statement, her English accent punching through.

'I know.' Rake had protected many killers. One year, in Southeast Asia, it seemed to be all he did. He couldn't imagine the young woman next to him luring Yuri Mishkin to a conference, laughing with him at the bar, cutting his throat, then turning up in the morning while his blood traces were found in her room.

'Are those cops protecting us or chasing us?' Sara looked into her wing mirror.

'Both,' answered Rake. Johannes, the cop he shot, was most likely working with whoever killed Yuri Mishkin. That meant infiltration of police and government. The two police cars followed at a distance, flanking the road on both sides. There was no other traffic. The road was shut off. Rake turned left at the intersection onto the highway toward the airport. His journey into town had taken five minutes. The drive back would be the same, putting the airport less than three minutes away. With a plane, they could be out and safe. If not, if Lucas had failed to arrange things, with one route in and out, the airport would be a trap. His pursuers would seal the road, and they would have no escape.

'It's because they think I killed Yuri.' Sara's voice weakened. Her brain would be grasping for certainty. She looked around to Rake for reassurance. The body's self-protective system moved through stages, from fear to composure, which was the strongest because it was about survival, to questioning, which was dangerous because it could break confidence.

'I liked him a lot.' Her face was desolate, like a beautiful, ruined landscape. 'Why would I murder him?'

'My orders are to keep you safe, ma'am,' assured Rake. 'That's what I'll do.'

She clasped both hands around the seat belt. 'Who are you?'

It was the right question, and Rake wasn't going to answer it. 'Across the bridge, we may take the first right to the airport, about two minutes from now. A lot can happen in two minutes. If I don't get instructions to do that, I keep driving.' He turned to let her see him, make her own judgment on trust. She met his gaze. Her unsettled eyes were blue-brown. Her short dark hair freshly washed and neatly combed. There was urgency in her expression, but not panic. Rake slowed as he approached the intersection with a turn to Highway One that took them either to the airport or on to the west coast.

Lucas's voice broke through. 'Is Sara Kato with you?'

'Affirmative, sir.'

'Location?' Did Lucas not have eyes on him?

'Highway One, approaching causeway, ninety seconds from airport.'

'Go to Berghamn,' said Lucas. 'The port on the west coast. A ferry leaves for Grisslehamn in Sweden in forty-three minutes. Number plate recognition will let you through. A Paul Koskinen will meet you. Allow him into your vehicle. He will instruct you to drive straight on board. He's SUPO. You'll be under his protection.'

'Got it, sir.'

Lucas went quiet. 'We're getting a ferry to Sweden.' Rake glanced across to Sara, keeping his tone light.

'You called him "sir", like a soldier. Are you a soldier? And you have an American accent.'

'I am. Yes.' Rake tapped Berghamn into the GPS. 'I am an Alaskan Native, America's equivalent of the Ainu.'

'Is that why you're helping me?' Sara's eyes flitted back

and forth from Rake to the road, which was rising toward a
causeway.

'No. But I know where your campaign is coming from.'
The GPS put them thirty-one minutes from the ferry terminal.
Lucas had cut a deal. Governments were talking to each other.
It was good. Rake felt confident enough to encroach more on
Sara's trust. 'And, yes, I am a soldier. Like I said, my job is
to look after you.'

'Do you know who killed Yuri?' A blast of wind shook the
vehicle as they joined the higher, unshielded ground leading
to the causeway.

'I don't.' Rake was about to add it being the work of profes-
sionals when, through a blur of sea mist, he saw an obstacle
in front of him. The road gently curved around with snow-
covered trees and scrubland on either side. The causeway ran
across a body of frozen water about a quarter-mile wide.
Through the mist, Rake spotted blue and red flashing lights
of emergency vehicles. He slowed to snail's pace.

'I thought you said . . .' Sara pressed her lips together and
drew in a breath.

At the entrance of the causeway, two police cars were parked,
hood to trunk, across the highway. Behind them were two
SUVs and an ambulance. All had lights flashing.

'Police blocking road,' Rake told Lucas. 'Clarify.' A hail
squall streaked across the windshield, blurring his view. Oil
drums or some kind of barrier stretched from the vehicles to
the edges of the causeway.

'Are they friendly?' he prompted Lucas.

'They are not,' came the answer. 'That's a negative.'

TEN

There were two red STOP signs in the road and two blue
ones stating POLIS and POLIISI. Swedish and Finnish,
each language required by law, even at a roadblock.
Rake slowed. He was three hundred yards away. At five miles

an hour, he had two minutes before he reached it. Wipers streaked across ice melting on the windshield.

'Your orders remain. Keep Sara Kato alive.' Lucas's voice was unhesitating, the line clear, as if they were in the same room. Lucas would know he was instructing Rake to go head-to-head again with the Finnish police. Rake found it hard to believe that Sara's life would be in danger with them. If he were to carry out his orders, there wasn't the time to question them. He needed to get closer to see if they had spread spike strips across the road to puncture the tires. He needed to gauge the angles of the police vehicles and the space between them.

'Confirm, I am to run the block, sir,' Rake asked.

'Affirmative. Get to Paul Koskinen, SUPO, in Berghamn.'

Rake put on the hazard lights. Slowed to three miles an hour. Sara's right hand clasped her bag. Her left was hooked around the top of the seat belt. Her legs were pushed tight together. She looked scared, but not frozen, as if figuring things out, which pushed an unwelcome thought into Rake's mind. Why was she with him? She had come without a fight. She had seen Rake shoot a man with skill. Why did she think she was better off with Rake than the police? If she hadn't murdered Mishkin, the police would sort it out quickly. At five miles an hour, she could have tried opening the door to get away. Nothing in her body language suggested she was about to do that.

He counted three police with pistols leveled toward him, out of range, a moving vehicle a near impossible target. A fourth crouched behind the hood of the saloon on the right, likely with something more powerful. He was too far away to see for sure.

Rake's gaze shifted to three fifty-five-gallon oil drums, spaced between the trunk of a police car and the edge of the road. Oil drums were fast-tracked blockade devices he had used all over the world. Filled with sand, each drum would weigh almost half a ton; filled with concrete, well over a ton. With water it would be less, maybe four hundred pounds, but enough to stop his vehicle. At the edge of the road there was a drop several feet to the causeway, meaning he couldn't go around the blockade, which would be why the police chose this spot. He flitted his gaze to the wing mirror. The two police cars following had stopped, blocking the road behind. He could not go back. Technically, he could not go forward.

An empty oil drum weighed around thirty pounds, which the Volvo SUV rental could knock aside like a skittle. Barely an hour ago, when Rake drove in, the road was open, no drums in sight. Beyond the blockade were the two SUVs and the ambulance, nothing that could carry half-ton oil drums of sand, concrete or water. A truck could have delivered empty oil drums. But why? To block the road to the airport or the ferry port. For whom? Not Rake. The block would have been in place before he got his orders to extract Sara. Best guess was a turf fight between SUPO and the police, with Sara the target. Lucas wanted Sara. SUPO wanted Sara. Michio Kato wanted Sara. But why? What did she have? And how much was all this connected to Yuri Mishkin's murder.

A wind gust caught his eye. He followed it. If he hadn't been looking, he would have missed a drum shifting a fraction across the meridian strip on the southern edge of the causeway. Yes. They were empty. He was guessing it right. They could get through.

'Get down,' he ordered Sara.

She didn't move.

'Right, down.'

Sara turned sharply to look at him. 'We can't.'

'DOWN.'

A police public address flared up with a warning to stop, but the wind covered most of the words. Rake grabbed Sara roughly by the neck and pushed her head below the dashboard. Electric vehicles were better than gas ones on acceleration. Rake hit the pedal. Four seconds later, almost at the blockade, the Volvo was traveling sixty miles an hour. He began by heading for the right edge, glimpsing the police following his line. Except he wasn't going there. He spun the wheel into a sharp left turn, misjudging the cold damp on the road. He felt the back wheels launch into a corner skid and corrected with the front wheels as they hit the meridian strip. The vehicle pitched into the air. He eased right, aiming the hood at the first barrel spaced just three feet from the trunk of a police sedan.

A gunshot blew out the right headlight. Sara gasped. Rake

braced himself for a wrong judgement, the dead-weight impact of smashing into a half-ton rusting metal drum that would tear through his fender, wrench the engine from its bolted sockets and throw him and Sara forward against seat belts and airbags with a force they might not survive. He tightened his grip on the wheel and guided the speeding vehicle to the edge of the drum, which it hit like a fist going into a curtain. Empty. Yes. He'd calculated right. As it flew away, the left side of the vehicle struck the second drum, which skidded into the third. The drums rolled and scraped and slid. Rake swung the wheel to the right to stop going into the water and straightened up.

His foot stayed down, taking them up to seventy, eighty, ninety. Muzzle flashes appeared like firefly dots in the rearview mirror, pistol rounds going nowhere. The police ran toward their vehicles. Visibility was skewed by sea mist from the water. On the dashboard, emergency lamps lit. He was a hundred miles an hour as they left the causeway. The road stayed straight. There was a superstore on the right and a rotary ahead. There was no traffic.

'Ozenna?' said Lucas.

'We're through, sir. Twenty minutes out from Berghamn.'

'Casualties?'

'None. Can you straighten this?'

'It's straightened. You've got a clear to the ferry. Messages hadn't got through.'

As Rake slowed for the rotary, a single police sedan entered from the right. Its blue light started up. The siren yelped to life. The driver pulled up, blocking Rake's carriageway. A uniformed cop got out the other side, shielding himself behind his open door. He signaled Rake to stop.

'Message still not through,' Rake told Lucas. 'We're being flagged down,'

'Ignore.'

Unlike the causeway, this would be a straightforward run with plenty of space on either side. One police car. No traffic. A wide road. No need to hit anything. He guided the Volvo to the left, then saw the cop raise a weapon that wasn't a pistol, but an assault rifle with a long curving magazine, at least thirty high-powered rounds, enough to stop the soft-skinned rental in its tracks.

He pressed his hand on Sara's shoulder to keep her down and picked up speed. He swerved left to right to throw off the aim. The first rounds slammed through the door into the back seat. By then, Rake was past him, a smaller target. The rear window shattered. Bullets tore into the soft white fabric on the roof. The cop was a controlled shooter. His range would be around 300 meters and Rake was traveling at sixty miles an hour; he had less than ten seconds to stop Rake and only thirty rounds, no time to change magazines.

'We're through,' Rake told Lucas. He took the speed to just above ninety along a smooth, straight road. There was no answer. Trembling all over, Sara pushed herself back into her seat.

'Are we safe?' Her voice quivered.

'Are you OK?'

'Who are they? What's happening? Why are we running away?' Her eyes were filled with fear, looking to Rake for answers he didn't have.

'What the hell is going on?' Rake snapped at Lucas, knowing he was going way above his own rule not to question orders. 'We need to get a grip, Harry. You need to rein it in.'

'Your orders stand, Ozenna.'

Rake said nothing.

Sara leant sideways against the door, one hand on the seat belt, the other on her bag on her lap. 'What do we do now?'

'We catch a ferry.' Rake's voice reflected the uncertainty he felt.

ELEVEN

The route to the ferry terminal showed a wide highway, a handful of houses, no towns, nothing that looked like a police station. The weather cleared, enabling Rake to keep to between ninety and a hundred miles an hour. The GPS put him in Berghamn in fourteen minutes.

Sara pulled a black woolen hat from her bag. examined it and unrolled it over her head. She tucked loose strands underneath. Shifting in her seat, she put her hands back to where they were, one on her canvas bag and one holding the seat belt. She was badly shaken. But Rake sensed something else. She was not civilian scared, not an innocent bystander. She knew things she hadn't said. Or hadn't had time to say.

'Why are they after you?' he asked.

Sara adjusted her woolen hat again and didn't answer.

'Fifteen minutes from now we could be safe and on that ferry,' Rake said. 'Five minutes from now we could be in another shit-storm. Share anything you might know that can help you.'

'I don't know.' Her voice was soft, defensive. A freezing draft blew through the smashed back window. She tensed her knuckles as if he were about to attack her.

'Finding Yuri dead was bad, really bad.' Rake turned to look at her, trying to reflect the empathy of his words in his face. 'Any idea why he was killed?'

'I don't know. Really, I don't.' She squeezed her fingers around her scarf.

'Why did you choose to bring him to this conference?' Two saloon cars, one white, the other blue, passed from the opposite direction.

'Because . . .' She lowered her eyes. 'No. It's complicated. You're a soldier. This is not for you. Follow your orders and I'll be gone. You'll never see me again.'

Two trucks passed them and a mix of vehicles behind. The ferry must have been in. They had opened the road. Behind, there was nothing. No sirens, no racing police cars, no helicopter as far as he could see and hear. On this single highway, they could not have lost the cops. The police must have been called off.

'Is there anything I need to know that will help keep you alive?'

'Nothing.' Her voice was a whisper. She tightened the cord around her bag. She didn't question why her own life might be in danger.

Rake let his hands hang loose on the wheel, moving to a relaxed, casual tone. 'Where'd you get that accent?'

'What do you mean?'

'English. Like the royal family.'

She gave him half a smile, a fast mood-switch. 'I was sent to boarding school in England. They all talk like that there.'

'Your brothers and sisters, too?'

'No sisters. My brothers went to Gakushūin. It's a posh school in Tokyo.' She turned to him again. Her eyes stayed shot through with worry. 'Thank you. But you don't need to small talk with me. I'm fine. I wasn't expecting . . . I mean, it's been a horrible morning.'

A black SUV cut out in front to overtake a truck. A blue sedan followed, causing him to brake. There was only one carriageway in each direction. Sara brushed her right hand over the fake brown leather of the glove box, like she was making a decision. Trauma triggered a need to talk while her sense of survival told her to keep her mouth shut. They passed a golf course and a roadside café. The SUPO agent should be waiting to usher them on board. Or the way things were going down, they could be driving straight into a trap, Sara and he taken in. Rake charged with attempted murder of a cop, Sara with killing Mishkin. Rake had never known Lucas to operate with so many contradictions.

The weather was clearing, blue sky, settled white clouds, no wind, and a flat, snow-laden landscape. Steady traffic headed east from the ferry terminal. 'Five minutes out,' Rake told Lucas.

'Ozenna?'

'Five minutes out, sir.'

'Ozenna?'

'Here, sir.'

'You need to abort. Repeat. Abort.'

Fuck you, screamed through Rake's head. *Enough. Get your fucking act together.* Gears of options spun through his mind. He could not go back. Abort meant he could not go forward. Rake replied calmly, 'Confirming, sir, that we change our plan.'

'Sorry, Rake. It's a shit-show here.' Lucas rarely called Rake by his first name and only when things were bad. Lucas had no back-up plan. If he had, they would be on it by now. The problem must be in Washington, not Finland. That didn't make

it any less dangerous. He had less than four minutes before
he reached the ferry terminal. The rental would have trackers
which exposed them, as would Sara's phone. They had
hours of daylight ahead of them, good weather, and Lucas,
his controller, the guy running the mission, far away in
Washington and out of options.

'What do you mean change of plan?' said Sara.

'That was my boss. The ferry terminal is out.'

'Why? How?' Sara bit her bottom lip hard.

Rake didn't answer. He followed the gradual curve of the
road and saw the opening of a track off to the right. He braked
to a crawl, waiting for a gap in the oncoming traffic. He turned.
There was a pile of snow-covered logs on the verge, and up
ahead trees and a single farmhouse. He drove past the farmhouse, saw another ahead, kept going until he was clear of
both and stopped. 'You need to do exactly as I say without
question. Do you understand?'

Sara nodded.

'Take out everything you have that's electronic. Put it on
my seat.' Rake got his rucksack from the back and brought
out a slim steel case covered with black leather skin. Inside
was a device that located trackers. He got out and stepped
back far enough for the scanner to cover the whole of the
Volvo. It took ten seconds to locate a tracker in the rear fender,
one on the battery and one in the GPS. There could be more.
Whoever they were up against could easily have put extra ones
on the rental.

He took a flashlight from his jacket and slid under the
chassis, feeling the cold of the snow and the hard edges of
ground ice. The thin beam picked up a black magnetic tracker
on one axle casing. Another silver circular one was on the
other. He plucked off both, checked more of the chassis, saw
nothing and slid back out. At the rear he felt around the fender
and found an oblong tracker.

Sara laid two phones, a tablet and a watch on the seat. She
pulled each apart, separating casing, battery, SIM card.
She knew what to do. Rake took the SIG Sauer from his holster
and smashed the butt through the screen of the dashboard
GPS and kept smashing until the electronics were pulverized.

The scanner picked up no more. It was far from conclusive. There could be trackers in the roof, under the hood, anywhere; ones that only gave out a signal once they had been motion-activated. He took his earpiece and the phone which was encrypted but not hardened. He slipped out the SIM card and battery, exactly as Sara was doing. He swept up Sara's stuff and placed everything behind each of the four wheels. He drove back and forth, crushing them into the ice. He smeared dirt and ice over the plates, back and front, to avoid detection by automatic plate recognition.

He drove back a quarter-mile the way they had come, dropping the destroyed equipment and shattered electronic pieces out of his window like a trail of confetti. Then, he made a U-turn and headed fast toward the ferry. The first track where he stopped was now compromised. The GPS had shown another side road, just over a mile ahead, which would be better because it led to coastline where there would be boats.

A container truck was coming toward them and, like before, a black sedan pulled out to pass, causing Rake to brake. A second green sedan stayed behind the truck. By the time they passed, Rake was at the intersection which led off a rotary. He drove through a village of low-rise houses, mostly red with black roofs, a school, a sports center, and further along a campsite and a full-blown holiday resort with flags and cabins.

'Is this right?' asked Sara.

'It's right.' Rake didn't know. But he needed Sara's trust. He didn't want houses and people. He needed emptiness and forest, a place to figure things out, a shelter that wasn't a vehicle. He needed to avoid whatever video surveillance was in the village. He wanted a situation that didn't exist.

The metal road turned to a gravel track covered in overnight snow and ice. The Volvo slipped and Rake righted it and slowed. This was better. There were trees stretching back from both sides, and a couple of miles on they crossed an old bridge over a fjord. Another mile and the coastline came into view. No houses. No people. Just forest, harsh rocky landscape, and the sea.

TWELVE

Sara's coat was only light. The temperature outside showed minus five Celsius. Wind-chill through the blown-out window felt colder. They needed to be under cover and get warm. The track toward the sea was more like a skate rink, thick ice packed like solid rock on which the tires had little grip. He pulled up.

'Keep watch,' he instructed Sara. 'Directly behind us.'

Sara walked the few steps to the intersection and looked back the way they had come, exactly as Rake had asked. He scoured the ground for tracks. There were fresh animal prints. One had two small round marks for the rear of the hoof and a pair of long curved oblong ones for the front. A deer. Nearby, a fox had crossed, two large front paws, two smaller side ones and a triangular-shaped heel. That was it. No evidence of recent human movement, no footfall, no vehicle, no motorcycle, no snowmobile.

He collected a black Gortex bag from the vehicle with two yellow snow chains of hard, durable rubber. He laid them flat on the ice, clearing knots and tangles, then wrapped the chains around the wheels, fastened the clips and tested tension.

From his rucksack, Rake took out a military-standard satellite phone inside a hardened steel case that made it undetectable. Its signal was encrypted and shielded. He turned it on. The signal was 5G. Of course. This was Finland, the home of Nokia. He unpacked a small, basic surveillance kit of six cameras which, with 5G, would not need a Wi-Fi hotspot. Each measured barely an inch square and had dual use of a wide-angle lens and rudimentary thermal imaging. He secured one to a tree branch, concealing it as best he could. He turned on the phone which activated the camera, giving him a wide-range view far down the track.

He beckoned Sara back. As they moved off, the chains cracked and crunched and held well. He kept the speed slow, barely ten miles an hour. Sara took a long, gray woolen scarf from her bag, wrapped it around her neck and tucked it down inside her jacket. Harry Lucas would know Rake's satellite phone was turned on. If Lucas were compromised, he wouldn't use it. But Rake needed to get Sara off the Åland Islands. As of now, he couldn't see a way to do that, not without Lucas's help.

A clump of snow fell loudly from a tree onto the roof. Sara flinched. Rake flipped on the wiper to clear the windshield. He eased the vehicle through a gaping pothole. Sara's gaze concentrated on the white-speckled wooded landscape ahead. The track was straight. There was forest on the left and, on the right, a mix of pine trees and iced-over rock and still no markings of anyone else there. Rake glimpsed the sea less than half a mile away. Sara traced her finger over the door of the glove box. She seemed to be assessing, not in a hostile way, something practical. She took off her hat, pushed up her hair, put it on again and flattened her hands against the side of her head. 'That might have killed me.' She turned to look at the hole in the back window, the jagged glass at its edges, the torn fabric in the roof.

'It might have,' agreed Rake.

'Who?' A tremor ran through her words.

'I'm hoping you might help me figure that out.'

'Will it happen again?'

'My job is to make sure it doesn't.'

To his right, through a gap in trees, about a hundred yards off track, he saw a small weatherboard hut with a corrugated metal roof and a circular steel chimney. There were no foot-prints or tire marks. Rake got out and walked toward it. The ground was thick with freshly fallen snow, flat, treeless, sloping up. There was a pile of logs, a bench under a window where glass was cracked and taped over. Icicles hung from a rope stretched between the gutter and a stake, like a washing line. Down toward the shore lay a wrecked cabin cruiser and a rusted steel rowing dinghy. There was an uninterrupted view from all sides, which was good and bad. They would be less hidden, but he would see anyone long before they got there.

He told Sara to get out with her gear. He drove two hundred yards back down the track and swung to the right into thick forest. He fixed a camera onto a tree at an angle that would pick up anyone coming up the track to the vehicle.

He walked back. The unlocked hut door swung open, solid on oiled hinges. Inside, the air was damp, cold and stale. There was a concrete floor and a wood-burning stove with a flue going up through to the roof. Dry logs were stacked on either side. There was a wooden table with four metal folding chairs around it. A steel workstation was fastened to the wall with hooks for cleaning fish and fixing gear. There was no running water, no sanitation, no power. A torn leather three-person sofa was pushed against a wall. Yellow stuffing protruded from the tears. It was dry.

Rake put his rucksack on the floor and pulled out a thermal survival blanket, white-gray camouflage pattern that would retain body heat while allowing the skin to breathe. In cold conditions, sweat turned dangerous if it froze. He wrapped it around Sara like a cape. 'Curl up and get warm,' he said.

'Is this safe?' she asked.

'For now.' Rake set up three cameras outside the hut, clamping them over gray plastic guttering. Even in half an hour, the weather had changed from the bright winter's day; now a strong westerly wind was bringing cold rain with the strong, harsh salt taste of the Baltic. High wind and lower visibility would obscure smoke. They could safely light a fire. Back inside, he tested the cameras, 360-degrees of protection around the hut, back up from the camera at the start of the track and from the one by the vehicle. He adjusted thermal imaging to 37° Celsius which would trigger an alarm for humans, but not for fox and deer which have a higher body temperature.

Sara took off her boots and lay on her side on the sofa, her feet tucked beneath her. She kept the blanket around her, gripping the sides, like she had with her scarf. She watched Rake crushing ice into a steel container, half cup, half bucket, another thing cramped into his rucksack. He used his long-bladed Fairbairn-Sykes knife to take strips off a log for kindling, and laid the pieces in the fire over a firelighter and cotton wool.

'I can do this.' Sara swung her legs to the floor. 'I'm good with campfires. It's one thing they taught us at that bloody

English school.' The way she pronounced 'bloody' emphasized her English accent.

Rake eased back and allowed her. He needed Sara to speak, best in her own time. She rearranged the kindling, took out the cotton wool, inspected it and put it back in a different place. She broke the firelighter into smaller bits. 'What about the smoke?' she asked.

'The weather's whipping up. It'll be fine.' Rake handed her a pack of matches. She riffled through, inspecting them. She struck one and lit the fire, touching it on firelighters and cotton wool in five places before tossing the match into the flames. Her face filled with new color, she turned to face him. 'Who are you, Ozenna? Tell me that and I'll tell you something you want to know.'

It was quicker to agree than argue and telling her was an offer of trust. 'My full name is Major Raymond Ozenna. My home unit is the Alaska National Guard. I grew up on an island in the Bering Strait that is on the border with Russia, just south of the Arctic Circle. South of there come the Aleutian Islands, which lead down to Japan.'

Sara looked intently at him, assessing, curious. He had her attention.

'I don't have brothers or sisters I know about. I don't know where my parents are. It happens a lot in those island communities. And, yeah, I look more Chinese than European American because I am like the Ainu. I am a native, an Eskimo – indigenous, or whatever white people want to call us. I don't care because I know who I am.'

'That's it? You know who you bloody are so everything's all right?'

Rake flashed a quick smile. 'It means I don't have to screw around with this identity shit.'

'You're funny,' Sara returned the smile. 'And you're scary.' Each of her hands held a side of her scarf, which she pulled tightly down from her neck. 'You risked your life for me.' Her face filled with new color, she turned to face him. 'I think I should tell you about Yuri Mishkin. Who he was and why he was killed.'

THIRTEEN

As Sara talked about Yuri Mishkin, she became excited, hesitant, vulnerable, layers of protection peeling away. She tightened the thermal blanket around her. Rake squatted on his heels, arms resting on his knees, hands warmed by a mug of coffee. If Sara were right, every dynamic changed. It could explain Harry Lucas's flip-flopping instructions, the professional manner of the killing, the brutality, not unlike the violent messaging left by Michio Kato in the vineyard mansion in Portugal. Sara sucked in her cheeks and warmed her hands around her cup of coffee.

'You're certain?' Rake asked. 'Yuri Mishkin was son of—'

'Yes. Yuri was the son of the Sergey Grizlov, President of the Russian Federation, who everyone thinks is a childless bachelor.'

'How did you find out?'

'Before he came, we talked a lot. We liked each other. We set up a special line just for us on one of those new social media platforms. I told him about my family and, one day, out of the blue, he told me who he really was.'

'And you believed him?'

'I did because I trusted him. But I checked some things he told me about his mother and he sent me an old newspaper cutting of her dating the President. Yes. I did believe him. He was smart, kind of lost and, with the island thing, it made sense.' Curled up on the sofa, Sara sipped her coffee and put the mug on the floor. 'For a long time, his father knew nothing about him. His mother is Tatiana Mishkin. You can look her up. She is a virologist who specializes in diseases under the Arctic permafrost. But she's also deputy speaker of the Duma. She's quite famous.' Sara cast a glance at the window, where new clouds blocked sunlight. 'Are we all right?'

'We're fine,' said Rake. 'Bad weather makes us safer.'

Sara nodded, seemingly reassured. 'There's nothing on

Google about Yuri and his father. Tatiana told no one until
Yuri insisted that she contact President Grizlov, who agreed
to a meeting. He must have been lonely in that bleak old
Kremlin castle all by himself. He and Yuri met, and they got
on well. Yuri was a good-time guy. Like his father, he loved
women. He knew how to enjoy himself.' Her gaze darted up
toward Rake with a sad smile. 'In the bar that evening, last
night, my God, just last night. In the bar, Yuri told me how
his father had said . . .' She set down her coffee mug. 'It was
difficult at first. Yuri didn't know what his father thought
about him. They never hung out together and, one day, they
were in one of those massive rooms with statues and murals
in the Kremlin and Sergey Grizlov tells Yuri that he's going
to get him a proper job. If his son had enough time to track
down his miscreant of a father, then the least his father could
do was to get his son on a career ladder. That was when Yuri
knew his father cared about him.' Sara fell silent, her eyes
on the fire. 'Yuri was offered his research job and he was
asked to do a paper on the Kuril Islands, our Northern
Territories. His brief was to find a way through, a win-win
for Russia and Japan.'

Rake moved a log in the stove and felt a soft waft of warm
air and new flames lighting up his face. Grizlov was using
his son to open an initiative on the islands dispute which,
if successful, would change the power canvas of Northeast
Asia. Sooner or later, Yuri Mishkin's identity would have
become public knowledge.

'If you search the Kuril Islands, you won't find much,' said
Sara. 'Actually, I didn't find it. A friend of Michio's sent me
the link. I looked at the paper. It wasn't very good.' Sara
picked up her cup. 'Yuri filled it with naïve conclusions. He
wasn't a scholar. But he was advocating a solution, so I
asked him about coming here and he said "yes" straight away.'

Rake could see why Yuri would agree, a good-time guy invited
for a week away by a beautiful Japanese woman. Sara was alerted
by Michio, suggesting that he did know who Yuri was and that
he used Sara to set up the killing. 'How long after making first
contact did you find out Yuri's true identity?'

'Several weeks. We got in touch August. It's now late

January. Must have been November.' Flecks of hail hit the windows and were loud on the roof. Sara flinched. She slid off the sofa and sat on the floor, near Rake, in the arc of the fire's warmth. Glass shook against a blast of weather. 'Are you sure it's OK here?' she asked again. 'Sounds like we're getting blown away.'

Rake studied each of the surveillance images on his phone. The cameras were holding their positions even against the havoc of the new weather. The landscape blurred and cleared, part hailstorm, part fog, part clarity, all moving like a kaleidoscope, shapes and colors, light and darkness, merging and separating within seconds, gusts howling like a bad orchestra. In the worst squall, his visibility would be less than twenty yards, no time to react. Like he had anticipated, the hut was both shelter and a trap.

'For now. We're good,' he reaffirmed.

'I didn't kill him.' Sara lowered her head. Her fingers played with loose scraps of wood fallen on the hearth. Her voice was suddenly drained of energy. 'I didn't. I couldn't. I liked him. You have to believe me.'

Rake's phone lit up, meaning Harry Lucas. He needed to speak with him, but not with Sara listening, because he would land Lucas with hard questions that needed answering. Did Lucas know about Yuri Mishkin? Had he sent Rake to the Åland Islands knowing shit was about to go down?

'I'll be back in a moment,' he said casually.

He opened the door to screaming wind coming straight in from the sea. It flung hailstones into the cabin. The fire flickered. Sara put her hands over her ears like a child afraid of noise. Rake stepped out, head bent, and edged his way to the back of the hut to a patch which was loud but shielded. He connected his earpiece.

'Yuri Mishkin?' began Lucas, as if in a briefing room.

'Did you know?' snapped Rake.

'You know?'

'Step back, Harry.' Rake barked Lucas's first name, breaking usual formalities and making sure his hard tone made it through the wind. 'The son of the Russian President has been murdered at exactly the same place and time that I am assessing a new asset who happens to be the sister of a target you and I have been tracking.'

'Did Sara kill Mishkin?' broke in Lucas, his calmness contrasting with Rake's sharpness.

Rake didn't answer. 'This is no fucking coincidence, Harry. Either you didn't know, or you sent me into a shit-fight which is still going on. Before I say anything, you tell me what the fuck is going on.'

'Freeman is trying to shut us down. My authority is compromised. SUPO withdrew their support as you were heading to the ferry. The White House has instructed you and Sara to give yourselves up.'

Lucas spoke in short, factual sentences which made sense to Rake. If Lucas was shut down so was Rake, except he didn't plan on handing Sara over to anyone until he had a clearer picture. He had shot a cop and run two roadblocks. A Finnish prison cell wasn't on his schedule for the day. Giving Sara and himself up wasn't going to happen without guarantees.

'I am on assignment to you, Harry. What are your orders?' He would decide whether to obey them.

Lucas answered with another question. 'Is Sara talking?'

'In bursts. She's frightened and protective.'

'Did she kill Mishkin?'

'No. She wouldn't be capable.'

Wind drowned out Lucas's next words. Rake asked him to repeat.

'How secure are you?'

'Could hold until nightfall.' Loose snow swept low across the landscape. Through fog, Rake saw white water whipped up between ice floes on the sea. If they came, now, it would have to be by land. No boat or aircraft could make it. 'Could be exposed in the next five minutes. You need to get Sara and myself passage out of Finland. I can't fix this in the field.'

In a second, the wind vanished. Fog swept away. Hail stopped. Rake felt the warmth of winter sun on his face.

'Ozenna, you've gone quiet.'

'Do they know where we are?' The new quietness around him was enough for Rake to hear Lucas tapping keys.

'Not that we've picked up.'

'Your weather reading?'

'You'll have forty minutes of this, an hour max. Then back to cloud and snow.'

Forty minutes was enough time for Rake and Sara to be captured. He examined the expanse of the rock he was on, the edge of the forest, the sea with white-water waves subsiding and gulls wobbling in flight with the weather change. He let a plan formulate. 'I'm taking orders from you, Harry. If the White House or army tells me different, then I'll comply.'

'Appreciate that, Ozenna. Our focus remains Michio Kato. Get Sara to open up, and about her twin, Kazan. Anything on the family.'

Rake had left the hut in a storm and, minutes later, stood in clear sunshine under a cloudless sky.

'A helicopter can get in here,' he said. 'Right where we are. Get one, Harry or they'll come for us, and it'll only take minutes.'

FOURTEEN

Rake scraped ice off the windows, identifying blind spots. The brilliant clear day was vanishing, visibility patchy again. A person could cover ground from forest to hut in seconds. Sara Kato busied herself around the hut as if it were her new home. She found a drawer filled with old, scratched kitchen utensils, including a torn white T-shirt which she used as a cloth. She was settling, less darting eyes, more accepting, more trust in Rake. He began checking his weapons, a routine military process that a soldier goes through in down-time, casually, a second nature thing to do, reminding her he was there as a soldier who could keep her safe. He started with the SIG Sauer, dropping out the magazine. She looked across, curiously, and Rake asked her firmly, straight out. 'I need to know about your family, Sara.'

The eyes darkened in on themselves like an armored wall. 'What about them?'

'Your father is a powerful businessman.' He paused to gauge her reaction. She concentrated on cleaning the tines of a bent fork with the old T-shirt, hair falling over her face.

'Could there be any connection to Yuri's murder?'

'How the hell would I know?' Sara polished hard.

'Anything at all come to mind? Any deal with Russia that has gone bad?'

She looked up angrily at Rake, 'I have nothing to do with my bloody family. Got it. Zilch. They don't want me. I don't want them.'

Rake said nothing. She set her gaze on the fork and rag again. 'They sent me away to school. They rejected me because I was a girl. Not just anywhere, but to that boring English countryside, about as far away from Tokyo as you can get. My parents didn't tell me. They were too scared. Michio told me. He's my older brother.'

He was in, and Michio was in play. In those few sentences her cadence went from angry to brittle to beginning to talk. The situation in the hut gave them a short decompression, the adrenalin drains when the mind brings in a different world, thoughts of loved ones, memories, sanctuary.

'Michio. Your brother. What did he say?'

'The first time just that I was being sent away to boarding school in England and that our father had appointed a guardian who would take me into his family. I couldn't really take it in. We were at my Shichi-Go-San. Do you know what that is?'

'I don't.' Rake added three rounds to the SIG Sauer magazine to replace those he had used.

'It's a celebration day for children to have a healthy life. First at three, then boys at five and girls at seven. My ceremony was held at the Yasukuni Shrine. Do you know that?'

Rake did. The shrine commemorated Japanese military heroes, including war criminals, the sort of place the Kato network would feel at home.

'A bit,' he replied quietly. 'What happened there?'

Sara abruptly stopped cleaning cutlery. Had he used the wrong tone? Too fast? She left the fork on the workbench, squatted down and opened a cupboard underneath. 'Ah! There it is.' Reaching inside, she brought out a yellow plastic dustpan and floor brush, stood up, looking around for an area to sweep. Rake pointed to the hearth, strewn with wood chips.

'No, not Michio.' She held the brush in the air like a flag. 'Kazan told me first. He's my twin and he is always horrible to me. He ran up to me, yelling, "Goodbye, stupid sister. You're going away, and I never have to see you again."'

Rake stayed quiet. She sank to her knees and began sweeping. 'Yasukuni means peaceful country. But it's about war. So, it's twisted from the start, names and names and names of dead people killed in wars. More than two million. It's like a palace with rooms, and open spaces and gardens. My father took me there for my ceremony but ignored me. He didn't speak to me once. Not once.' Sara dropped the brush on the hearth. Her hands trembled, her face flushed red. 'I should stop. I'm saying too much. It makes me angry, and I don't even know you.'

'Keep telling,' Rake said gently. 'Then I'll tell you how I get angry about my father.'

'All right.' Sara's eyes lit. 'On your island? What about your father?'

'Yes. We'll share.'

'Deal. I want to know about anyone who has a father as shitty as mine.'

'You'll get chapter and verse.' Rake checked each of the surveillance cameras. Thick snow. A deer ambling. Nothing else.

'I began bawling my eyes out,' said Sara. 'I didn't know what Kazan meant. I didn't know then how some Japanese families are. No hugging. No show of affection. I was still a child with all the love to give and receive, and my brother was sneering at me. He was so nasty, and he called me a cry baby and he was glad I wouldn't live in Japan anymore. My mother came over, not to me, but to Kazan. She reprimanded me, saying that this was my special day and I had to behave and not cause problems for people. She took Kazan back to her group. Michio was with my father. He saw me all alone, crying, ran across and gave me a big hug. He was so warm and nice that I cried more. Really cried. He took me to a food stall and bought us both a red and white *manju*, that's a sweet rice wrapped in bamboo leaves and a lychee *ramune*. That's a soft drink. See how well I remember. We sat on a bench, and he asked me what was wrong. I didn't want to say because I didn't want to know. He asked if Kazan had told me about my new school. I remember sucking through the straw even though it was just air left in the bottle.'

'What did your brother say?' Rake brought his Beretta 93R machine pistol out of his rucksack, for which he had three twenty-round magazines.

Sara watched as he stripped down the weapon. 'Michio told me I was being sent away. I asked him why, and he said they wanted me to understand Western culture. I asked why he and Kazan didn't need to know about that, too. Even at seven, I knew that Western culture was in America and not England. Kazan and Michio went to Gakushūin, the school for the elite I told you about, where the imperial family goes. Gakushūin takes girls. So, I could have gone. So, I asked him again and he said he didn't really know. Our father had commanded it, and no one dared question him. Michio thought it might have been because the old man hated the way women were becoming more powerful. He couldn't handle the thought that his daughter might be able to run his family business. But it might have been because of this.' She cupped her hands around the sides of her face. 'Like I described. That Ainu bloodline has come through prominently in my features.'

'We all got blood from somewhere else.' Rake worked the Beretta's mechanisms.

'So, for whatever, I was sent to England.'

'You didn't enjoy it?' He was getting close, but unsure how much to press and when she would bring the shutters down.

'The school was OK, sometimes fun. It was my parents. I hated them because they didn't want me.'

'Families get like that sometimes,' Rake shifted concentration back to his surveillance feed. Mist swept across the sea which was getting choppy. The deer had gone. The track they had driven in on was clear, as was the wide arc view from the SUV two hundred yards away. The view to the forest was the most dangerous. 'Have you made up with your family?' he asked.

'No. I rebelled. I didn't know who I was or what I was. My family wanted to turn me English. At school I was called a "Chink". They couldn't tell the difference between a Chinese and a Japanese person.'

She moved past Rake to the door to sweep up melting ice and grit from the floor. 'I traveled. I worked as translator, waited tables, cleaned houses. Europe and Asia. Michio stayed in touch, kept saying I should come back and go to university. I said I would if my father asked me, and he never did.'

She opened the door to a blast of cold air and threw out the contents of the pan which scattered in the gale. She turned back in, pulled the door shut and held the pan close to her as if protecting a child. Underneath her conversational swings and erratic movements, Sara had steel. Many would have collapsed by now, drinks at the bar, liking Yuri Mishkin, creeping into his room, finding his body, the blood, then the shit in the lecture hall. Wound up as tight as it gets, Sara Kato had the grit to keep going.

Rake lightly held her shoulders. 'It's OK, Sara. We're going to eat something, get some sleep. We'll get out of here—'

'I don't want to get out of here,' she broke in. 'Don't you understand? Haven't you ever been on a train and never wanted it to get to the station because the train is safe and nowhere else is.'

Lucas's voice came into Rake's earpiece. 'We have a helicopter flying in from Sweden. Thirty minutes. A Westland A109. Can it handle?'

'Yes.' The A109 was a twin-engine light utility helicopter. A good pilot could deal with this weather, even the harsher stuff they had earlier. 'I'll mark a landing zone.' Rake ended the call and said to Sara, 'I'll be outside for a few minutes. Stay tight here. I'll be watching. You'll be fine.'

She threw a crumpled tissue into the fire and nodded. Rake hooked his rucksack onto his shoulder, slipped the SIG Sauer into his holster and the smaller one onto his ankle. He carried the Beretta loose in his right hand. He had lived through the sort of morning when a sane man keeps his guns close, and his antennae finely tuned. Sooner or later, someone would be out there to get them.

'We're leaving, aren't we?' said Sara.

'In about half an hour.'

'Where?'

'Sweden.'

Color drained from Sara's face. Rake imagined her mind spinning. She cherished their short sanctuary. She resented the need to move. She knew she had to.

'Here.' Rake handed her one of his phones, black in a steel casing, a protected keypad with a number punched in which would connect her straight to him or Harry Lucas.

'You trashed my phones.' Sara bunched up her nose in disapproval. 'So, thank you.'

He turned it on and held it flat in front of her. 'Right thumb on the screen.'

Sara wiped her thumb as if cleaning it of dust and pressed it onto the phone. Rake put his hand on hers, holding it there until a green light came on. 'Your hands are so cold,' Sara said. 'And rough.'

'Put in a four-digit passcode? Nothing you've used before. One you'll remember under stress.'

Sara keyed in 0607 which Rake remembered were her and Mishkin's room numbers. Not great, but he let it go. 'It'll work anywhere,' he said. 'If we get separated, it'll take you straight through to me or to my boss.'

She slid it into her back pocket. 'Thank you, Mr Soldier Man. I mean it, Rake.' She gripped his elbow. 'For the phone and for letting me talk.'

Rake gave her a small smile. He liked her. He wished they could have the day and he could tell her about his father. She smiled back. 'It's like we've known each other forever. Your face is so hard, but you've got a lovely smile, even with all your guns.'

Outside, the wind was quieter, but enough to whip sea water into spray which reached the hut. No more hail. Snow fell thick and straight. Dark clouds blocked sunlight. The weather was changing, sooner than Lucas had forecast.

FIFTEEN

The landing area would not pass civil aviation standards. But it was good enough for an A109 and a competent pilot. Rake paced out fifteen yards square for the makeshift helipad. At each edge, he pinned a flashing LED lamp.

'Are you seeing this weather?' he asked Lucas.

'In a minute or so you have fog. But the heat is off. The Finns are with us and on their way. A Detective Leo Virtanen in charge.'

Good. Virtanen had made a brave and right call to let Rake leave with Sara. He liked the way Virtanen handled things, how he talked to the delegates – like he had seen worse and stranger a hundred times before.

The hut stood on ice-covered rock that sloped sharply down to the sea and more gradually the other way toward the forest. On three sides, the landing area was clear with rock and water. On the other, with the pine tree forest, Rake allowed forty yards, which would give plenty of room. He didn't want the aircraft coming down in a burst of bad wind and skidding down the steep incline into the water. Nor did he want rotor blades slicing through pine trees.

The aircraft would have state-of-the-art sensors. Rake would stand forest-side with a flashlight signaling the hazard of the pine trees. As he walked across to that edge, he heard the sound of metal clicking against rock. It was faint, barely audible in the loud weather. But Rake had been raised in snowstorms and howling wind. He had learned to listen out for danger, which he heard now. This would not be an animal because none would be out in these conditions. Nor was it a human in trouble. They would be crying for help. It was hostile. Rake broke into a run toward the wooded area. As he reached it, snow sprayed up at the base of a tree in front of him. He heard the snap of a bullet breaking the sound barrier, around a hair's breadth from his skull. Rake made a forward roll like a somersault and readied the Beretta. A second shot slammed into ice an inch in front of him.

Rake ended flat on snow, twisting so he faced the forest where he judged the firing came from. He fired three shots into the trees, then looked quickly back toward the hut. He saw the glow of the fire through a window, but no one approaching, no grab for Sara. There was quiet from the forest. He ran to the steep incline where the rock dipped down toward the sea, thinking it would protect him enough to work out what was going on. He got it wrong. He ran straight into his enemy, taking his assailant equally by surprise. The man fired twice and missed. Rake was too close. His enemy was white with a strong face. But his movements were erratic. The angle of the ice slope was lethal, but a familiar danger to Rake, the ice rough, pockmarked over winter months with crevices and sharp edges.

He saw a second person running from the forest toward the hut, skewing Rake's immediate concentration because visibility was enough for him to see she was female and black. His attacker fell on him, hand raised with the pistol butt. Rake had an option of getting away by sliding down toward the sea. The risk was that he would not be able to break his fall and end up in the freezing water, either hypothermia and drowning or a clear target for a killing. It was better to block the blow. He tilted back. His assailant's strike glanced off the back of his head with enough force to wrench around his neck. Sea spray from rocks hit his face. His assailant towered above him, pistol raised. A man about to strike in conditions like this would be receiving a constant stream of messages from his inner ear about his body's position, forces pulling it in different directions and how he needed to adjust his balance for accuracy of aim. A trained man worked all that from muscle memory. Rake needed to inject something totally unexpected into the process. He was sure this was the American Marine Corps officer from the conference, most likely a veteran who would have a grudge.

'John Freeman. The new President?' Rake yelled. Wind from the sea was quiet enough to carry his voice. The question bought a hesitation. Rake whipped the SIG Sauer from his shoulder holster. The attacker leaned forward as if failing to hear properly. Rake spoke again, 'Freeman's shitting on us veterans.'

Two things happened simultaneously. Rake fired and missed. The attacker lost balance, sliding down, his full body weight crashing into Rake, who landed a pistol-whipping blow onto his attacker's right temple, making him go limp. Rake staggered to his feet. The man was out cold. Rake peeled off the woolen hat. The unconscious face in front of him was indeed the white American US Marine Corps delegate. A fog cloud began enveloping the hut, but not enough to stop him seeing the door opening and someone going in to get Sara. 'Ozenna!' Lucas in his earpiece. Rake blanked him out. Sara was his focus. He clambered up the ice. A search light snapped on, its beam splaying through the fog cloud, mounted on the back of what looked like a black-and-white police truck. There were red flashing lights, blue lights on other vehicles. Rake ran toward the hut. Two police were there before him. A third blocked his way with his hand raised to halt.

'Major Ozenna. Stand down.' A command through a police public address system. The hut door opened. Sara came out with a policewoman. Rake's thermal blanket was wrapped around her. Behind her was the female US Marine Corps delegate, in police handcuffs.

'The helicopter is two minutes out,' said Lucas. 'You and Sara Kato need to be on it.'

'Copy that,' shouted Rake over the wind.

'The pilot can see your LZ. Bring him in. Get on that bird.'

'This is Detective Leo Virtanen from the Finnish Police.' The police vehicle public address system again. 'Everything here is under our command. Everyone do exactly as I say.'

The engine of the A109 became louder, lights piercing fog. Two police officers took positions on the landing area with orange aircraft marshaling wands. Virtanen held a microphone attached to the dashboard of the police vehicle. Police led Sara toward the landing zone.

The approaching helicopter became a roar. Loose ice skidded across the ground. Downdraft shook snow from trees. Rake

sprinted back to the sloping shoreline. His assailant was still
unconscious. He photographed the man's face. Pulled off his
right-hand glove and took a print by pressing the finger on a
laminated card from his pocket. He found a wallet with photo
ID, credit cards and, with it, a passport.

The helicopter's skids settled on the icy rock. Pine trees
swayed. A side door slid open, and a crewman leaned out and
gave a thumbs-up. Rake ran across to Sara, who shouted
through the noise, 'Who are they?'

Rake took her elbow. The police officer with Sara radioed
to confirm the handover. But Virtanen did not respond. His
public address was silent when it should be emitting clear
orders. Rake pulled Sara toward him, covered her with his left
arm, held the SIG Sauer in his right, his grip weak because
of a muscle torn by a fall on the ice.

The police officer escorting Sara yelled something in her
ear. Her expression transformed completely. She began to resist
Rake, struggled to free herself. Against the rain, it was impossible to see what had changed. There was a blur of lights and
activity around the police vehicles. There was static and sharp
chatter on the police radio with Sara. She had come willingly
with Rake since the lecture hall. Now, she was pulling away.
Why? She looked back to where the police officer was pointing.
Three men walked quickly toward them.

'Ozenna,' Lucas said. 'Get on that bird.'

Police officers dragged him back from Sara. She quickened
her pace, toward the men who wore civilian clothes but moved
with military body language. One broke into a run.

'Leave her, Ozenna. Get out of there.'

'What the—?' began Rake.

'NOW. That's an order.'

Strong arms gripped his shoulders. He could resist. But
what for? This wasn't Sara's decision. Something was going
down in Harry Lucas's back-office mess. Rake had been on
operations with bad orders and conflicting ones. But nothing
like this. He was charged with looking after Sara and so close
to getting her to safety. Without warning, she didn't want him.
Police frog-marched him toward the helicopter. They shoved
him forward, as if pushing him into a prison cell. The crewman

wore the yellow and blue insignia of the Swedish Air Force. Rake stepped on the skid and a gloved hand came down and hauled him on board. The engine pitch changed as the aircraft lifted toward low-lying cloud. Medics were with the assailant Rake had knocked unconscious. Virtanen stood by the police vehicle, microphone hanging loose, giving no orders, a detective who knew when he was outflanked. Sara faced the man who had been running toward her. A helicopter light, skewed by rain, swept across the scene, clear enough for Rake to recognize the man he had last seen walking away from a massacre in Portugal. Sara flung her arms around Michio Kato. She turned to look up at the helicopter, her face wet with rain, her expression unreadable.

SIXTEEN

Washington, DC

Experience and age told Harry Lucas to suppress fury that raged inside him like scalding water from a kettle. Turn down the heat and seal on the lid. The Finnish, Swedish and American governments had agreed to guarantee safe passage out of Finland for Rake Ozenna and Sara Kato. In the last minutes, as the helicopter was coming in, Petrovsky reversed the order: Ozenna left; Sara Kato stayed. In his final words from the helicopter, before the line was cut, Ozenna yelled that Michio Kato was at the scene. Sara had gone to him. One new President and years of work flushed down the toilet. No fucking way.

Until a day ago, Harry's high-level security clearance had given him unfettered access to a slate of federal security agencies. Now, passwords and barcode scans weren't working. One-time codes were rejected. As Petrovsky had said, Harry had been shut out, and more. Long-time contacts, whom he had thought were friends, were not picking up. Word was being spread around the intelligence community that Harry Lucas was tainted. He needed to get it stopped, and to achieve that he needed leverage.

He opened a link to London, where his large high-definition screen became filled with an empty office, flooded with light from three sides. He adjusted the contrast to get a view down the River Thames towards the Houses of Parliament, the London Eye and Tower Bridge. He topped up his coffee, which was hot but stale, and that didn't worry him.

'Harry Lucas as I live and breathe. What an undying pleasure!' The slim face of Stephen Case appeared close to the camera. He flapped down his right hand in a half wave, slipped off a bright green rain jacket and walked behind a long, glass-topped desk at the end of his penthouse office in the inner suburb of Hammersmith.

Case was unorthodox, phenomenally intelligent, and a product of the changing world of defense and intelligence. Decades earlier, government inventions had given the world e-mail, GPS navigation and satellites. Much of that now lay with private sector giants who were pioneering cyber, artificial intelligence and more. While trawling for information on Yuri Mishkin, Harry's system had uncovered footage of the actual murder, sitting on the dark web, in dreadful detail like a snuff video.

'I need your dark web expertise,' said Harry.

'Of course. I am the recipient of a generous Harry Lucas contract.' Case wore a pastel orange shirt and beige pants. He moved with the elegance of a ballet dancer, taking a seat in a large white leather chair behind the desk. He slipped off brown leather shoes and picked up a pale green vape pipe made from jade, which he had told Harry was flown in illegally from Myanmar. Case said he had had it carved to show a man, woman and serpent entwined, to remind himself that all good things end with sex, the fang of a serpent and expulsion from paradise. 'Word was that you were out, Harry. Given the boot by the new kid in the White House, and you look like shit.'

Harry had gotten used to Case's flippant humor and theatrical English turn of phrase. He found it a refreshing change from Washington double-speak and deception. Case was on his personal payroll, with allegiance to no one but Harry. Different as they might be, the two got on well. Harry paid. Case delivered. They bantered and got the job done.

'Long night.' Harry answered. He added an extra encryption level and sent through the dark web video file on Yuri Mishkin. By acknowledging the new security layer, both knew their small talk would need to continue for the few seconds it took to transfer.

'I mean it, Harry. You look dreadful.' Case took a drag from his pipe. 'You need to get a better woman, one that looks after you, the type that makes the man the plan.'

'You're right. Need to find the time.'

'It's not about scheduling, for Christ's sake.' This wasn't the first time Case had goaded Harry about his incomplete personal life. 'You're crap with women. You think of them as friends. You need to see them as sirens lying somewhere between sex and the serpent.' He held up the pipe like a mascot. 'Someone who cares for you. I'll send you Emily. Bright as a button. A mountain of love to give and she adores you.' Emily was a thirty-something tech wizard who worked for Case.

As Case spoke, cheerfulness drained from his face. He went quiet, lay the pipe on the desk, pulled his keyboard toward him, studied the screen, then said, 'This is it, right?'

'It is.'

'Do we know whose throat is being cut?'

'Later. Is it genuine?' If it were, it meant two people at least in the room: one killing, one filming.

'I can find out.'

'And the provenance?' Quality doctored videos were made through artificial intelligence platforms which went by names like generators, discriminators, encoders and decoders, each with a specific task. They ran millions of images, choosing, compressing, changing and building them into a composition.

Case worked the keyboard. 'For provenance, I'd say we're looking at Ghana or North Korea.'

'Governments?'

'No, private. But blurry lines, my friend. Am I government? Are you government? Not governments, but hired by governments.' Case typed in a series of codes and leant back, waiting for a result. 'As for genuine, a work in progress.'

'Meaning?'

'The pixelation around the knife and the arm. Whoever's behind this is planning to fabricate a murderer and show the face, which also means there was a face on there that's been wiped.'

'Can you reconstruct it?'

'Like stripping back an oil painting, then redoing the Rembrandt again. Possibly.'

'And can you stop it getting out?'

'As in "going public"?'

'Yes.'

'That I can do.'

'And can you help with this one?' Harry sent across a portrait of Sara Kato. Case screwed his face into an exaggerated frown. 'Is this the one they wanted to frame for the murder.'

'Her name is Sara Kato.'

'Do I know her?' Case flopped back into his chair, hand on his chin, eyes looking out through the window, across the London skyline.

'We've been tracking her family.'

'Ariga? The Nevrosky case?'

'Connected, yes.'

Case had made his name ensuring that Britain left the European Union in a long-ago referendum. His first job for Harry was to assess voting patterns in Eastern Europe. He boasted that he would never take on an election he couldn't win. He expanded to embrace changing technology, using it to master every level of political manipulation, the dark web, social media, bots, trolling, cyber and more. He examined the human brain for areas of exploitation, neuromarketing, neurolinguistics, patterns on how people thought and acted. He called his company Future Forecasting and built teams of loyal, brilliant people, harvested data and created software to feed his growing army of artificial intelligence machines.

'Sara Kato is very pretty,' mused Case. 'Clever, too. What am I to do with our lovely Sara?'

'Find her?'

'I presume, you want that five minutes ago.' Case's fingers

moved back and forth across his keyboard like a piano player. 'And I am not asking why the great Harry Lucas, with all the resources of the world's most powerful governments at his disposal, is coming all the way across the pond to little old Stevie Case for this hunt job.'

'She was last seen down a coastal track near the Finnish ferry port of Berghamn on the Åland Islands thirty minutes ago.'

Case lifted his hands and rested them on the top of his screen. He stared straight into the lens, wearing a quizzical smile. 'Oh, Harry. My good friend, Harry. What a tangled web you bring me!' He pressed an intercom on his desk. 'Emily, tell everyone to stop what they're doing. We've got something.'

SEVENTEEN

Nick Petrovsky's Lincoln Town Car pulled up again outside Harry's apartment, the second unannounced visit in as many weeks.

Two Secret Service agents stayed outside. Petrovsky's worn expression showed that the early days of the Freeman presidency had not treated him well. A man who enjoyed his job could work hard on little sleep, look motivated and stay in shape. His pale, wan appearance belonged to a man whose job left him constantly fighting against his better judgment.

'What the fuck happened on the Åland Islands, Nick?' Harry let Petrovsky in and closed the door.

'The President's decision, Harry. I'm his messenger.' Petrovsky kept a contrite, hangdog look on Harry, making out he didn't want a fight, but a friend.

Harry kept up the pressure. 'Why is the President micro-managing something like this?' He had left the door to his workstation open. Usually with a security-cleared member of government, it wouldn't matter. But he found himself in an alien situation of doubting the President and his messenger. He slid the door shut.

Petrovsky raised his eyebrows. 'So low trust?'

'You fucked me, Nick. Years of work. And we had a deal.'

'That's not why I'm here.' Petrovsky rested his hands on the back of the leather sofa.

'That's why I let you in.' Harry linked his hands together in front of him to control his temper.

'I might fuck with you. But don't fuck with us, Harry, because we're bigger. Let's try to work amicably.' Petrovsky lazily waved his hand toward the entrance of Harry's work area. 'One call and I could have the Secret Service come in here and rip all this apart, analyze everything you have, find stuff that would wrap you in lawsuits and congressional investigations for the rest of your life.' He was right because this was how Washington worked, similar conversations taking place a hundred times a day; leverage, the euphemism for blackmail.

'What do you want?' Harry responded flatly.

Petrovsky unfolded himself onto one of the sofas. 'Freeman believes your work risks our relationship with Japan and Russia, his two foreign policy priorities.'

'What's new?' Harry took a hardbacked chair opposite Petrovsky. 'Bolster the alliance with Japan. Forge one with Russia. Keep China in its box.'

'A Russian citizen murdered in Finland. A Japanese citizen suspected of the crime. An American soldier helps her escape. Moscow will be jumping up and down. We need to get this whole mess sorted before Sergey Grizlov finds out that his son has been murdered.'

'He doesn't know?'

'The Finns have agreed to keep it under the radar.' Petrovsky pursed his lips and lowered his voice. 'Which is why I need you to reach out to your ex-wife.'

'Stephanie?' Harry wasn't expecting that. He didn't even know where Steph was.

'Only one ex-wife, isn't there?'

Harry leant back, hands hooked behind his head. 'You come in here threatening me, then plead for my help.'

'Don't take Freeman on,' said Petrovsky. 'The man's got tentacles all over the place. He destroys people like slapping mosquitoes. Check how many investigations against him have been shut down, no explanation.'

Freeman's reputation swirled around favors and influence peddling, but nothing had been made to stick. 'Then why work for him?'

'So, ride with us, for Christ's sake,' answered Petrovsky.

'Yes, Stephanie is my only ex-wife,' he answered tightly. 'And yes, she does know Sergey Grizlov.' Harry understood the rawness of power that emanated from any White House, particularly a new administration. Petrovsky was as much advising as he was threatening.

Petrovsky said, 'She's currently a visiting professor at Harvard and a fellow at a Washington think-tank. She met Sergey Grizlov in her twenties and, with Grizlov's help, made her fortune in wild post-Communist Russia.'

'All right, you've read the file,' interjected Harry. 'What do you want with Steph?'

Petrovsky continued. 'Her friendship with Grizlov. She has kept in touch with him throughout since they dated, when she was a member of the British Parliament, when she married you, when she abandoned politics to be ambassador to Moscow and Washington. Briefly, Grizlov was Russian Foreign Minister and Stephanie was Foreign Secretary as Baroness Lucas of Clapham. She is currently here in Washington, and the President needs her.'

'You make it sound like conscription.'

'It is.'

'Then call her?'

'No trails. No red tape, and you know her, Harry.' Petrovsky got to his feet. 'The Finns will hold for a couple of days. We need her to get to Grizlov before then. He doesn't know that his son is dead. Let him hear it from Stephanie.'

Harry understood, and it could work. He hardened his next question. 'What about Sara? You cut a deal with her, too?' Sara knew Yuri Mishkin's identity. She was with Michio. Her silence would mean a deal done with Michio Kato.

'I talked to Habiki Saito. He says he'll handle it.' Saito was Japan's National Security Adviser, Petrovsky's direct counterpart.

'And Saito talked to Michio Kato who said he would handle it.' Harry's tone was rich with sarcasm. 'I can't fucking believe it.'

'Yeah. It stinks. But think carefully, Harry. Sergey Grizlov, the urbane, cosmopolitan Moscow insider won the Kremlin on a pro-Western platform. Russia is sick of antagonism. No more Ukraines, and it trusts Washington more than Beijing. Grizlov is lonely. In his sixties, he discovered a son he never knew existed. Yuri Mishkin became a hinterland of his life. Youth. Hope. Legacy. How is he going to react when he learns Yuri has been murdered?'

Harry stood, hands on hips. 'Michio Kato ordered the murder.'

'Let's assume he did it to screw over Grizlov, mess with his mind, weaken the Kremlin, weaken a recovering Russia.' Petrovsky stood up and ran his hands around the waistband of his pants, tucking in his crumpled shirt. 'When that comes out, Grizlov will rightly kick shit, and we would have to side with Japan. Freeman's foreign policy out the window in less than a hundred days.'

Petrovsky's analysis made big picture, global strategy half-sense. But the details didn't add up. Why would Michio kill Mishkin only to be silenced by his government? And did Michio really have the muscle to buy off half the Finnish police force?

'Who in Finland tried to stop Ozenna?' asked Harry. 'Who sealed off the road? Who countermanded the ferry extraction?'

'Names, I don't know. We'll get there eventually. The Finns have an election around the corner where their big neighbor Russia is a divisive issue. Michio Kato tapped into that. The shooter in the lecture hall. The road block. Those guys all came from one unit. The Finns are dealing with it.' Petrovsky tightened his belt a notch. 'I'm to the Oval and need to bring an answer with me about Steph.'

'You're not getting one, Nick. Until I'm a lot clearer about the mess you and Freeman have got us into.'

'I've told you what I know.' Petrovsky adjusted his yellow patterned tie. 'There's a bond between Stephanie and Grizlov. Time to use it for the greater good.'

'Whose greater good? Explain exactly the deal with the Japanese government and Kato.' Harry posed the question as an accusation. Michio Kato was a killer. His family ran a crime network that threatened America. What Harry had not yet revealed to Petrovsky was the exact level of that threat. Nor had he decided when or if he should.

'Sara Kato is innocent,' answered Petrovsky. 'She's on her way home to Japan.'

'Her home is in London.'

Petrovsky ran his hand down his front to flatten the tie. 'This big, rich crime family is like a prosthetic limb to the Japanese government. But we can't have Sara shouting her mouth off. For the next few days, we need her to be under the control of her family.'

Harry let out a sigh of resignation. The aim had been to bring Sara in and turn her to inform against the family. Instead, his own government had made sure she would keep her mouth shut under her family's protection. 'And the killers,' he asked more amicably. 'They were delegates, planted there.'

'The Finns gave us prints and facial. There are two, both decorated captains, both ex-Marine Corps. Simone Tallick, who posed as a Black Lives Matter activist, and James Hunter, who Ozenna knocked out cold, posing as an activist from the far right.'

'Working for Michio?'

'Let's presume.' Petrovsky sluggishly wiped his hand through the air. 'They're not speaking. They are lawyered up. They're pros. No one's holding their breath for a flood of confessions.' He seemed to have laid it out as much as he could. Harry wasn't going to fight him. 'Can you get me back inside the tent, Nick? Access back. Your people at the White House stop trashing me.'

'Done.'

'I'll get hold of Steph.' He stepped toward the door to let Petrovsky out.

'I'll tell the President.'

'Best efforts. No guarantees.'

'Understood. And where is Rake Ozenna?'

'He should be on Swedish soil in ten minutes.' Harry had

arranged for the helicopter to take Ozenna to the Swedish military air base at Uppsala, about fifty miles inland.

Petrovsky stepped into the doorway, knowing his next words would be heard by the waiting Secret Service agents. 'We'll be taking Ozenna from here, Harry. This whole thing is too hot for you to be running wild and alone.' It was a statement not a consultation.

EIGHTEEN

Baltic Sea, Sweden

Rake's thoughts churned as the Swedish helicopter flew low and fast over the Baltic Sea. What could he have done differently? He watched sunlight dance on the gray water, sometimes clear, sometimes through thin mist. He played images back and forth of Sara in those last moments. There had been no fear in her as she walked with him, no resistance, an acceptance that they were leaving until jolted by the unexpected. She saw Michio, missed her footing, regained her step and tore herself away to run to him at precisely the moment Harry Lucas shouted Rake an order to abandon her. There was nothing he could have done. She wanted to be with her brother. The Finnish police had him by the arms, walking him to the chopper. Rake wasn't big on reflection. He had ridden through operations that had gone wrong. Except this one hadn't. He had been given orders. Keep Sara safe. He had followed them until they were reversed.

No words were spoken between Rake and the single crewman in the cabin. He was given no headset to hear communication. His rucksack had not been searched. Nor had he. Close to the Swedish coastline, they flew into low cloud. The pilot brought them down into a washed, blurry landscape of a small airstrip, shut down for the winter. Vegetation grew through ice. There were a dozen civilian light aircraft, their red and blue covers showing in patches through freshly fallen snow. A ragged orange windsock hung from a white rusting pole like a torn dress. There was a low-rise timber hut, more a village sports pavilion than an airfield mess room. Next to it stood a white station wagon, no ice on the windscreen, no snow on the hood, recently arrived.

The crewman slid open the door and beckoned Rake out. Rake hooked his rucksack over his shoulder and followed the crewman's footholds from rung to skid to ground. The crewman walked across to the station wagon, opened the door and took a large, plastic Ziploc folder from the front seat. He handed it to Rake, gave a brief salute and turned back to the helicopter. Inside the folder was an electronic car key fob and a dismantled phone, a Nokia cell, not a satellite, meaning it would rely on a signal from a cell tower. The helicopter scattered loose debris and ice as it took off.

Rake could not see or sense anyone around. Snow chains were fixed to the vehicle's wheels. The single snow-covered road that led out from the airfield carried the tracks of two vehicles, the station wagon and a second, heavier vehicle with a longer wheelbase. Flat open ground running down to a rocky coastline surrounded the runway. Behind the parking lot, there was a steep hillside, mostly covered in snow, with clusters of pine trees and rocks jutting from the ground. Whether snow stayed in place depended on how much sun got through and how protected it was from the wind. In some places on the hillside, snow had not settled.

'This is Ozenna,' Rake tested the line that half an hour ago had carried Lucas's order to abandon Sara Kato. Nothing. Dead. Rake was relieved. Lucas had cut it. Some other agency. He was in a low-trust frame of mind. Sara had been sacrificed in some stinking political deal. There was no way Sara would be safe with Michio. Lucas had let him down. Rake had let Sara down. He had broken his word to her. She was not safe.

He was not going to slot the new phone together, call Lucas, find out what was happening, get in the station wagon and drive to wherever he was ordered. Assembling the phone could be like taking a shortcut across a minefield, the kind of narrow thinking that gets people killed. Whoever made this delivery of vehicle and phone knew where he was now, most likely watching. The station wagon would have tracking sensors. The phone, once on, would shine like a huge spotlight.

A few hundred yards along, the narrow road curved away. Old snow was packed on either side, making it easy to block.

To Rake's tracking eye, a hill trail was visible underneath fresh snowfall where it was uneven with rock, hard ground and scree, not soft undergrowth. The hillside offered good cover. With the advantage of the high ground, he would reset the satellite phone to an alternative encryption. He dropped the Ziploc bag back onto the front seat of the station wagon, shut the door and hooked his rucksack onto both shoulders.

A man with walking boots and a forty-five-pound rucksack could not avoid leaving tracks in snow. Trees and undergrowth came down to the edge of the parking lot, meaning that anyone would have to look closely. Rake began staying with the trail, but soon moved out at a right-angle and back again in a zigzag, all the time looking ahead for an area of ground where snow had not settled. He found it halfway to the top, a thin strip of greenery that branched off like a river tributary. He continued upwards in the snow, leaving heavy prints, until he reached a dense cluster of trees. Then he turned back, exactly placing footstep into footstep the same way he had come up, until he reached the fork, when he jumped out of the snow into the hard, clear, frozen ground.

An experienced tracker would not be fooled. But any standard police or military deployed to bring him in would spend time working it out. Time was what Rake needed. He judged he was a thousand feet up and a thousand from the top. He had a good view over the airfield and its approach road.

He focused one half of his mind on his ascent and the environment and the other half on Sara and their mission with the Kato family. If Lucas had been overridden by the new administration, it would either be something personal, someone wanted to get rid of him. Or it would be on policy. Rake had a hard time matching the dormant island dispute between Russia and Japan with a critical American foreign policy change. Few people had ever heard of the islands, certainly not voters. Yet this was the mix he was in.

A snow clump fell from a tree and splattered in his track, maybe shaken out by the vibrations from an approaching helicopter, a large two-engine flying in from Finland, the same route along which Rake's smaller one had just flown. These were government people. It wasn't a situation to fight his way out of. It could be one to escape from.

Two police vehicles drove down the single-track road to the airfield and pulled up by the station wagon. Rake counted six: four in the dark blue uniform of the Swedish police; two plain-clothed, one with a black trench coat, the other with a green cold-weather jacket and waterproof pants. They were in a hurry, wanting to assess before the helicopter landed. Two men searched the station wagon, taking out the Ziploc bag, holding it up to show it had been abandoned. Eyes shifted toward the hillside, then back as the large aircraft came into land. Three men got out. Rake recognized none from earlier in the day. One strode forward to shake hands with the plain-clothed Swedish police officer in the green jacket. They pointed up toward Rake.

There was a brief discussion before four began following Rake's tracks up the hillside, two from the police vehicles, two from the helicopter. Rake would have ten minutes, possibly fifteen, and he didn't plan to end up in anyone's custody. He switched the encryption code on his satellite phone, turned it on, checked his surroundings, his arc of vision, and made the call.

NINETEEN

Washington, DC

The internal intercom warbled on the wall on Carrie Walker's small studio apartment. It was too early in the morning for visitors. She ignored it; someone must have pressed a wrong button. Carrie was working on the case of Ronan, the young craftsman from Rake's home Alaskan

island of Little Diomede, whom she had talked to Rake about
when he was on a plane to God knows where. Why was she
getting involved, she wondered. Sure, the gentle, mild-
mannered Ronan stood accused of rape. Almost certainly, the
accusation was false, she told herself. But you never really
knew. There was a raft of people, solid organizations, more
experienced than her, that could take up his case. She was
doing it because she hadn't slept well, because Ronan
was Rake's community which, right now, she preferred to her
own solitary, soulless, career-driven one. This was her third
night back in Washington after yet another failed relationship
with a colleague who should have made a perfect husband,
except it didn't unfold like that and she fled.

In the early morning darkness, lamps from the Watergate
Complex shone across quiet Virginia Avenue. Whatever light,
noise, pollution, Carrie liked curtains and windows open, a
rebellion against her grumpy father who savored darkened
rooms with musty air. She had found physical trauma medicine
too disruptive, her work in conflict zones too draining, the
repetitive hopelessness of violence. She switched from trying
to fix broken bodies to fixing broken minds. That's what she
told herself. But, like a million other therapists, she wondered
if it was really to try to understand her own character, work
out what she did and why.

Carrie envied Rake. Fancied him like hell, too. Loved him
even. She had once worn his engagement ring, and that hadn't
worked. Her fault or his? She felt safe and excited when he
was around. His confidence irritated and perplexed her. How
he could live without a shred of self-doubt, where nothing was
questioned? She wasn't even sure if Rake experienced emotion.
Sure, she understood how being raised on a remote, cold island,
cut off from everywhere, with wild weather and a small
community, made a person think in a certain way. She got
why he liked the military, the discipline, the certainty. She
understood why some people sought conflict. But Rake hadn't.
The military was a well-worn escape route from communities
like his, and fighting was what soldiers did. But Carrie herself
had gone looking for conflict. The day they had met in
Afghanistan, she had been treating a patient blown apart by

a car bomb. Rake had physically lifted her away to protect her from a second blast, certainly saving her life. He reassured her that her patient had no chance of survival.

'How the hell do you know that?' she had yelled at him, shaken, afraid, guilt-ridden.

'I know,' he had said. 'And so do you.'

He was right. They dated after that, or, to be accurate, they had sex then dated. There was something she had never pinned down. She didn't feel restless with Rake – that her life was slipping away – as she did in her experiments with affluent doctors whom her mother and her sister wanted her to marry. But she could only ever take Rake so far. At some stage, the human mind reflects and plans. Rake didn't, which was why he infuriated and attracted her so much.

The intercom buzzed again. Carrie stepped across the reindeer-skin rug that Rake had given her long ago and picked up the receiver.

'Carrie, it's Jesse from downstairs.' Jesse was one of the overnight concierges. 'A strange one, so I won't be asking questions.'

'Thanks, Jesse. Go on . . .'

'You know Norman?'

'Yes.' Norman was another concierge.

'Your Rake called Norman on his personal cell. I didn't even know they knew each other.' Rake would know Norman because he was renting an apartment one floor down from her.

'Rake asked Norman to call me, to call you, and patch you and Rake together through the intercom,' continued Jesse. 'If that makes sense, I can do it.'

'Do it.' Her stomach gripped. In a lover's sense, she was excited he was calling her. But the roundabout way he made contact frightened her in a professional way. She poised herself, like in the emergency room, to rapidly process information and make decisions. She loathed herself for liking it, and Rake for calling out of the blue, and because she knew he was about to use her.

'Thanks, Jesse, Norman. We can take it from here.' Rake's voice was measured and clear. He would have had the foresight to set up this system, both simple and complicated. Carrie heard a click. She and Rake had a private line. She heard wind.

'Are you all right?' asked Carrie, a dumb question, but a natural one.

'I need you to do something.'

'OK.'

'Activate a pre-paid. Call Harry Lucas. Link us in if you can. If not, tell him I need orders. Next few minutes.' Rake spoke slowly, made sure he enunciated syllables that would cut through static and background noise. 'Have you got that?'

'Yes. But why should Harry pick up from—'

'He will.' In the locked drawer on the table where she was working, Carrie kept four or five disposable phones, mostly used now to work dating sites. When she had told Rake, he helped her make them more secure. He must also have given the number to Harry Lucas for situations like the one unfolding now.

Where are you? she thought. *What's going on? How much danger are you in?* She fired up a phone, flipped through to Harry Lucas's contact and called his personal number.

Lucas picked up. 'Carrie?' His tone was urgent.

'I have Rake.' Carrie spoke in a measured, familiar, focused tone, set from years of handling up-against-the-clock emergencies.

'Ozenna?'

Rake went straight in. 'What the hell happened?' Every word bulged with restrained anger.

'My orders were overturned. You know that.' Lucas sounded tired and defensive.

'What was the flight plan of the Swedish helicopter that brought me out?'

'To Uppsala, then a plane to RAF Lakenheath, in England.' A roar of static cut through the line.

'Didn't happen. It dropped me at an airfield on the coast. Did you leave a vehicle and dismantled cell phone for me?'

'I did not.'

'A military helicopter has landed. The Finnish and Swedish police are tracking me.'

'How long do we have?' It was an automated question. Carrie sensed Lucas was out of octane. Something had gone badly wrong.

'Five minutes at the most.' Rake's tone was the opposite. He was fired up, and when Rake got like that he could be very dangerous. Carrie knew. She had seen it.

On the coastal Swedish hillside, four thousand miles away, Rake listened to Harry Lucas. He needed the American government to bust him out and expected nothing in the coming minutes. He reached for his pistol, flattened himself in what little undergrowth there was and watched the men tracking him. They were good, moving steadily uphill checking for footfall, snow disturbed on branches, looking for shadows where they shouldn't be. He had hoped for time to reach the summit, get a view, examine escape routes. He sensed that wasn't going to happen, that they had found his trail and spread out to encircle him. He was watching two, but the two others were missing. Then, they came for him.

From outside his arc of vision, a tracker leapt forward, stamping his boot on Rake's gun hand. Pain ripped through his arm, up his shoulder to his neck and throat, making him retch. A blow struck the left side of his face. Men surrounded him. They wore white woolen hats and masks, surrounding him. None was the four he had logged climbing the hill.

Rake had never adopted the mindset that – when cornered – a good soldier takes some of the enemy with him, whatever the odds. His aim was to stay alive. His weapon was kicked away. Arms grabbed his shoulders and pulled him to his feet. Two rounds were fired into the satellite phone. It was flung down the hillside.

One unsheathed a syringe, not the hospital type, but the heavy-duty emergency one designed to penetrate denim and canvas and get to the human body fast. He met Rake's gaze. A professional doing his job. He checked Rake's right hand which had been holding the weapon. Most right-handed people are also right-footed. This was about sedation, not cruelty. He anticipated getting the syringe in his left thigh, where bruising would have less impact. He relaxed the muscles there. The syringe cut through cloth. He felt the breaking of the skin and the insertion. Strength drained from him. His vision blurred. His mind fogged.

TWENTY

Harry tried the line set up with the National Security Council. Silence. He called Petrovsky's direct line only to be told that he was unavailable. He messaged Petrovsky's private cell phone, 'Pick the fuck up and *now!*' He gave it thirty seconds and called.

'We've lost contact with Ozenna,' snapped Harry.

'Are we good with Grizlov?' Petrovsky shot back.

'Did you hear what I said?'

'Russia is our priority.'

Harry wasn't even going there. 'We're not going to be good with Grizlov, Nick, until you fix whatever's going down in Sweden.' He had called Stephanie, his ex-wife and Grizlov's confidante. Detecting the urgency, she cleared her schedule and was on her way over.

'Sweden. Like what?' Petrovsky's tone became hesitant. Harry's speech analysis screen showed undulations of red, green, blue and yellow graph lines, indicating that Petrovsky's hesitancy was genuine: He didn't know about Sweden.

'Gunshots on the hillside. I arranged for Ozenna to fly to Uppsala. They dropped him somewhere on the coast.'

Silence from Petrovsky. A siren in the background. Harry's tracker put the National Security Adviser on K Street, heading east toward the White House.

Harry said, 'You told me you were taking responsibility for Ozenna.'

'Not responsibility. I said we would be taking Ozenna from here.' Lines dipped and rose on the screen. The black one reflected Petrovsky's actual words. Other colors handled emotion. The software's artificial intelligence picked out traits in each syllable: happiness, anger, fear. It processed the information like a human brain, analyzing mood, behavior, veracity. The more the software taught itself about a subject, the more it honed and defined character profile. There was not much on Petrovsky. He had been a surprise appointment, new to the job, and he kept a low media profile.

'Taking him from here, meaning that you would have him gunned down,' accused Harry.

'No. No, absolutely not.' The graphs had Petrovsky fully on the defensive.

'Then, don't mess semantics about responsibility.' Harry's tone was jagged.

Petrovsky hardened. 'The President will mess with whoever he wants, however he wants.'

'Then tell him this, Nick, and listen hard. I will fuck with him, too. John Freeman cut me out in the middle of an operation that is crucial to American security.'

'That's our decision.'

'The government needs to bring Rake Ozenna back home, now, and alive, or I'll tell Steph to turn around and go back to what she was doing.'

'Don't you threaten—' Petrovsky was grasping.

'You want this off tomorrow's PDB, Nick. Your call.' The graphs showed a man way out of his depth. Petrovsky didn't reply, nor did he close the line. Harry said, 'Freeman's predecessor signed off on what Ozenna and I have been doing. There's a White House paper trail which your boss hasn't even asked to see. If what we're hunting goes down badly, the American people will want to know why, and I will tell them.'

'Then tell me what it is?' Petrovsky wavered on each word. He hadn't read the file, probably hadn't had access.

'Are you loyal messenger or useful idiot? I know what you're not, and that's a presidential adviser working in the national interest.'

'If it's such national interest, why are you withholding?' Petrovsky's tone showed some restored confidence, Harry's attack prompting him into a sharper defense.

'I report directly to the President of the United States. I'll tell Freeman. Not you. Set up the meeting.'

'Threaten like that and you'll never work in this town again.'

'I will. But you're on borrowed time. It's your ass that goes down in history. Not mine. Not the President, because he'll cover his ass with sweet-smelling lavender all the way and put his shit all over yours.'

Petrovsky said nothing. Traffic and distant sirens drifted down the line.

'Call whoever you need to and get Ozenna back.' Harry softened his tone. 'Fifteen minutes from now, I will ask Stephanie to go see Grizlov. That's the deal, Nick. Then get me in with Freeman.' Harry stopped abruptly and allowed a beat for Petrovsky to respond. 'Thank you.'

'And, if I'm to handle Stephanie, you need to reinstate my clearance. It's not done yet.'

'We're doing it.' Petrovsky closed the call as Harry's surveillance flashed that Stephanie was approaching the front door. Good for Steph. Impossible to live with, rock solid in a crisis. Harry topped up his tepid coffee, his mind racing from his exchange with Petrovsky. Yes, he had threatened the President of the United States, and he needed to. He tapped a couple of keys that opened up lines to alert him on Rake Ozenna. There was nothing.

Stephanie knew Harry well enough to recognize his mental as opposed to physical exhaustion. She had seen him with both. And that he needed a shower and change of clothes. He opened the door with a smile, a genuine relief to see her. She was wearing a dark blue overcoat with a long, gray cashmere scarf, and her favorite Russian hat made from cat fur with flaps over the ears.

'Yuri Mishkin?' Harry asked as he showed her in. 'Does he ring a bell?'

'No, and not even a peck on the cheek?' She hooked her scarf around a coat stand near the door. 'No, "how are you?" A glance to say how great I'm looking, even if I'm not.' When Harry had summoned her, she had pulled on a pair of denim jeans with a heavy-duty blue cotton shirt and, for the cold, a woolen ski hat and Ugg boots, which she now kicked snow off.

'You're looking great, Steph,' said Harry.

'Thank you.' She gave him a full smile. She was keeping her dark hair short, had lost those pounds put on when holding down big jobs, had taken up a mild gym and jogging routine and won back her figure. She looked around, part ex-spousal, part curiosity. Some years ago, Harry hired a designer to furnish and kit out the apartment. He had asked her opinion, and she reminded him that the last thing he needed was an ex-wife's stamp on the place. She had never been here. It wasn't big. He kept it in fair shape, but not great. There were scuff marks on the walls, stains around the coffee machine. The furniture was sleek, not sexy. The bedroom door was closed.

'You look as if you've had an all-nighter and more.' She stood outside the secure door as Harry opened his work area, with its iris scans, fingerprints and barcodes.

'Mishkin,' he repeated, bringing up a young man's mug shot to a large screen. 'Yuri. Russian academic, early thirties, non-resident fellow at the Russian International Affairs Council.'

Stephanie frowned and stepped closer to the screen. She looked at a carefree, youthful face with hair flopping over his brow, like she might imagine her son, had she ever had children. 'Nope,' she muttered. 'But I'm sure I'm about to find out.'

'He's dead.' Harry pushed his hand back through his closely cropped dark hair. 'He's been murdered at a no-name, no-place peace conference, that won't ruffle hair on a camel's back.'

'Here, in DC? In London, which is why I've been called in?'

'The Åland Islands, between Finland and Sweden.'

Stephanie knew the Åland Islands. 'Britain negotiated a treaty in the 1920s. A think tank operates there, studying conflict resolution.'

'That's the one.'

'And this Yuri Mishkin?'

'Throat cut.'

Stephanie rested her hand on the wall. Work with Harry was never straightforward. 'Then give me ten seconds of your attention and tear yourself away from your bloody screens and tell me what it has to do with me.'

Harry swiveled around, his face glaring with anger, as if

Stephanie was someone else. He quickly mellowed. 'Yuri Mishkin was Sergey Grizlov's son.'

A tremble ran through Stephanie. She sat on a steel office chair pushed against the back wall. Harry's workstation was arranged like an aircraft control panel, with five screens, a large one flanked by smaller ones, two on each side. They showed maps and graphs. There were banks of switches, keyboards, phones, headsets and gadgetry.

'Then, whoever's behind this was trying to kill far more than Mishkin,' she said softly, as much to herself as to Harry. Stephanie had known Grizlov longer than even Harry, since she was in her mid-twenties. They had been lovers. They had become millionaires together. They had remained friends on the way up their career poles. Stephanie had become a household name, and not just in Britain, making it to Foreign Secretary. All that time, through bad moments and good, they had kept their friendship alive.

Over the years, Grizlov had mused about his lack of family, no wife, no children, professional success, price of personal happiness. Stephanie tried to lighten his moods. She was in a similar situation, career above family and all that. She had a cantankerous father living in an annex to her London house, and enough enemies to keep her busy for several lifetimes. They talked, laughed, commiserated, and congratulated each other, and never once in all those long, searching, funny conversations had Grizlov mentioned he had a son. Harry was working his keyboard again.

'Pull yourself away, for God's sake,' she snapped, 'and spell it out.'

'Sorry, Steph.' He shifted his attention back to her. 'I've got a guy missing. Ozenna.'

'Oh my God!' Stephanie cupped both hands around her mouth. 'If Ozenna's involved . . .' She stopped herself saying that if Ozenna was involved, there was bound to be a body count. Harry and Ozenna were close. She also liked the rough-and-tumble Alaskan islander. More so, she liked his sometime girlfriend, Carrie Walker, and felt for the impossible, unworkable relationship she had with Ozenna. Stephanie and Carrie had met in different places around the world, usually with Carrie in town speaking on trauma medicine, and Stephanie on one of her diplomatic postings, Moscow, Washington, London. They enjoyed gossipy, bitching, bar-hopping nights.

'Is Rake OK?' she asked softly.

'I don't know.' Harry spun around his chair and rolled across to her on its wheels. He rested a hand on each knee, giving her a look, which even now melted something deep and undefinable inside her. It wasn't love. It wasn't sexual attraction. It was something the magazines would find a name for one day.

Harry looked drawn, worried, unslept, but his eyes were filled with energy. Stephanie listened quietly as he gave her the background. The tracking of Sara Kato to get inside her family's empire. Sending Ozenna to the Åland Islands. The killing of Yuri Mishkin. The fabrication of evidence against Sara Kato. His decision for Ozenna to pull her out. The cross-current of orders which led to losing Sara Kato. Ozenna missing, gunshots on a Swedish hillside. And the discovery of the murder video on the dark web, which could be doctored, with Sara Kato as the killer.

'You want me to talk to Sergey, explain that Sara didn't kill his son.'

'More than that.' Harry kept his hands on her knees. 'There's a plane at Andrews to take you to Moscow. Can you go see him, Steph? Be with him.'

'Does Sergey know?'

'Not yet.'

'And my mission is to assure the Russian President that America is on his side?'

'Got it in one.' Harry pushed back his chair and stood up. They didn't need to say more. Stephanie would do it. She stepped out into the living area and unhooked her scarf and hat from the stand. Harry opened the door and leant against the jamb, not bothering to hide his tiredness.

'Send stuff through,' said Stephanie. 'Anything on Mishkin. Anything about this mess on the Åland Islands? I'll head to Andrews. You've got my vehicle plate for ID into Andrews?'

'I do.'

Stephanie embraced him, smelling sweat and stale, strong coffee on his breath. She pushed back, affectionately. 'And get a bloody shower, before your next guest arrives.'

TWENTY-ONE

R ake sensed icy damp seeping through his pants and jacket. He couldn't feel it. The sedative numbed his nerve ends. His mind was too much of a fog to think about how long he had before hypothermia crept in. It might already be there. He could barely move. Commanding the muscle of a finger was like wading through a sea of treacle. His vision was hazy. There was a glare of sunlight. There were greens and white around him. He thought there were red lights. He couldn't be sure. His eyes stung and tingling jabs ran through his body, overriding the deadening of the sedation. He could hear birdsong, engines, voices, distorted, screeching, muffled. He thought Sara was there, watching out for him, standing next to the guy with the syringe, telling him how to do it right, like she had rearranged the fire in the hut. She was vivid and real. He could see her expression, her flinching against a cold gust. He knew it wasn't true, the drug playing tricks with him.

They carried him and dropped him on the ice. He was aware of the bump, his own body weight against the ground. It would be bad, but there was no pain. Someone pried open his right hand. There was a smell of rust and copper which he knew to be blood. Close to him. Familiar. Rake had been with blood on snow many times. He tried to concentrate. He thought Ronan was there, the kid from his island, who carved walrus tusk like Leonardo da Vinci. The focus was good. He made himself picture Ronan, then June who accused him of rape in her crazy pink T-shirt, then Carrie, solving problems, getting Ronan away, calming things.

There was quiet. No more voices. No more engines. The

colored lights had gone. He was left with birdsong and the glare of the sun. He pictured Sara back when the helicopter arrived, forcing himself to think hard. Detail. Her face in a spotlight from a police car, filled with excitement, except at that last moment, something changed that made her realize things weren't as she thought they were. Her safety was not Rake Ozenna, but Michio Kato.

A hand covered his eyes, gently, hovering, brushing his thick eyebrows. Rake tried to speak. His lips wouldn't move. He had no voice.

The hand lifted. 'Major Ozenna.' An American male voice. 'Signal if you can hear me?' Rake slowly blinked. 'And again, if you can understand me.' Rake blinked again.

'OK. Good. I am from the US embassy in Stockholm. We're going to get you out of here, first to RAF Lakenheath in England and then to Andrews. Do you understand?'

Rake blinked. They put a monitor on him. They sat him up, removed his jacket and injected him with an antidote. They wanted him out of sedation. People needed to talk to him. They lifted him onto a stretcher. Sunlight, shade, leaves and sky danced around him. They carried him down to the airfield where there were lines of vehicles. They slid him into an ambulance. The embassy guy climbed in next to him. Rake believed he was who he claimed to be. Harry Lucas would have pulled something. His mind was clearing. Lakenheath was a base in England. Andrews was near DC. The ambulance set off.

'We have a plane waiting at Uppsala, about an hour's drive,' said his escort.

'Who . . .' Rake struggled, but he got the words out. 'Who did this?'

'I can only say, sir, that you are now secure and under the protection of the US government.' The embassy guy sat over him like a nurse. He was a kid, no violence in his eyes. A diplomat. 'You want a drink, sir? We can fix you—'

'Coffee,' Rake managed.

'Coffee might not be the best—'

'Black.'

*   *   *

Rake woke in his Washington apartment. A cold breeze blew across his face from an open window, and he imagined the woman with him was Sara. There was a fading smell of fresh paint and of antiseptic, and somewhere in that mix he detected the perfume Carrie used when treating patients. She'd had it on when they had first met during that bombing in Afghanistan, a mix of peppermint, lemon and something feminine and fashionable. She explained it was good for covering the bad smells of conflict. He couldn't remember the name; wasn't sure she had ever told him.

'How you feeling?' Carrie touched his forehead with the back of her hand. 'Your fever is subsiding. They whacked you with one hell of a dose of benzodiazepine. Then we whacked back with a flumazenil antidote. You've been sleeping that off, and I just gave you a local to stitch up that cut in your hand. Looks like you ripped it on ice.'

A lot of words. What cut in his hand? Rake had forgotten.

Rake's apartment was one floor down from Carrie's, two bedrooms with a corner view out across Foggy Bottom. Carrie owned her studio. Rake's was a short-term rental. Harry Lucas's company held the lease. He propped himself up. Carrie had her hair styled differently, still blonde, but scruffy and short, when it used to be flat and long. He remembered he hadn't seen her for the best part of a year, when she went off to build a future with the type of man that Rake wasn't, to tell herself she was adapting, trying to fit into a life she thought she wanted. Unsettled people tried to change who they were, thinking if they moved enough things around – like a house, a lover, a haircut – that life would fall into place. Rake felt for Carrie. She was from divided parentage, her father Estonian and her mother Russian, from a country that no longer existed, and they had ended up in Brooklyn, New York. Unlike Rake, Carrie had no speck of an island in a wild, remote sea that she could call home.

'What's that?' He pointed across the room to a tattered red golf bag with a light brown bone curving out the top.

Carrie smiled. 'It's Ronan's. Or it will be Ronan's.'

'Walrus?' Rake pushed himself up further and lifted his feet off the bed, so he was sitting next to Carrie.

'Mammoth.' Carrie held his arm to steady him. 'Turns out the Smithsonian has an Arctic Heritage project. I got Ronan a slot to carve a mammoth tusk into something spectacular.' The Smithsonian Institute was a massive museum and research operation. The mammoth, a little smaller than an African elephant, became extinct more than ten thousand years ago. Melting ice was now exposing skeletal remains. The indigenous people of North America had special permission to carve walrus and mammoth ivory.

'Ronan's here?' Rake's foggy mind danced with mixed images: Ronan, Sara, police searchlights.

'Mikki's bringing him.'

Rake saw Mikki as his brother, orphans, raised together, Mikki ten years older and his mentor, who had got him to join the Alaska National Guard. Mikki was now a state trooper. He remembered the rape allegation Carrie had explained to him on the plane into the Åland Islands. 'June?'

'She's being looked after in Nome. Ronan has three months here. Mikki thinks that's long enough for the rape accusation to go away.' Carrie pulled in her cheeks, showing two dimples, the way she did when she knew she might have got ahead of herself. 'Is it OK? I told Ronan he could stay here with you. I've got forms to sign you in as temporary guardian.'

Carrie had walked out of his life and was walking straight back in again. She had said nothing about the man she had dumped, nor about resuming some kind of a relationship. Nor their long, tangled history, where Rake had introduced Carrie to his island community and she had loved it, and they her. There were the few months when they were engaged to be married, until she declared them incompatible. Rake, a soldier, killed people. Carrie, a doctor, saved them. How could that ever work? Rake didn't argue. She would do what she would do. Like telling Ronan, a Little Diomede orphan, to stay in his apartment. As if preparing for Rake's disapproval, she gave him a longer, hard-assed look to signal what's done is done. Except Rake didn't mind. He was glad. People had cared for him when his parents abandoned him. He did the same. 'You fixed it good. Thank you.'

She looked at him strangely, blinked, shook her head, and

let out a small private laugh. She kissed him quickly and spontaneously on the lips. 'God, I'm sorry. I've been getting myself uptight working out how to tell you. I was so stupid with Peter, you know, the doctor, whose whole purpose in life seemed to be to find fault. Why did you ever let me end up with a prick like that? Now, with something really complicated like Ronan and June, because of Peter, I am terrified how you'll react, and I forgot you are Rake, lovely, lovely Rake, and you say it's all fine and—'

She stopped her flow and kissed him hard and longing, pulling him to her, arms wrapped around his back. 'God, how I missed you!' She trembled as she held him, Carrie, urgent, physical, demanding, impulsive, persuasive. She slid her hand under the blue medical smock she had put on him. Rake's fog clouds rearranged themselves. He and Carrie had a way of using sex to bust through complications. Rake wasn't sure he wanted it. Which brought Sara to his mind. With Sara, yes. The unknown. Newness. Discovery. With Carrie? Her going off to Brooklyn had changed things. He had never asked himself. Never thought it through. As he felt the warmth of her body, he realized how much her leaving had shaken him up. He didn't resist her. He enjoyed her hands and her touch, until Carrie hurriedly untangled herself. 'Sorry. Sorry, Rake. I don't know what came over—'

Sitting on the bed, she drew her hands down her face. 'When you went missing, I thought you were dead. That your luck had run out. I thought . . . I don't know . . . how I had screwed up. How good we were together.'

Rake lightly tapped her lip with his finger. 'No need to speak.'

'Yes. Yes. We do need to speak. I don't just want to fuck you. I want to talk to you for days and days. I want to understand us because we have something that won't go away.'

Her phone lit up. 'Yes,' she snapped and listened for a couple of beats. 'It's Harry.' She handed the phone to Rake.

Rake stood up. He was wobbly, his balance not yet right. 'How you feeling, Ozenna?'

'Feeling good, sir.' He had had nothing from Lucas. There had been no debriefing, no messages. A car from Andrews

had delivered him to his apartment block where Carrie had
been waiting.

'Carrie looking after you?'

'Yes, sir.'

'Good. Get your uniform on. I'll pick you up in ten. We
have a meeting at the White House.'

TWENTY-TWO

Tokyo

Michio was family, and Sara loved him more than
anyone. For her homecoming, he gave her an old
heirloom kimono that had belonged to her great-
grandmother and had been in the family for generations, white
and pink, woven from heavy crepe Omeshi silk.

Sara and Michio stood outside the downstairs bedroom of
the family house set up to accommodate the terminally ill
Jacob Kato. They were waiting for Sara's twin brother, Kazan.
She and Michio had flown on Michio's private plane straight
to Tokyo. She had her own cabin and slept and dreamed with
dark, twisted nightmares which woke her up gripping her
blanket and short of breath. She was shaken from finding the
body of Yuri Mishkin. She was scared by the violence and
confused from her hours with the strange American soldier
called Rake. She would have stayed with him. She had felt
safe with him and then she had seen Michio and run to him.
All in a few seconds. With the different lights, the noise from
the helicopter and her surprise; how was Michio there? Out
of the blue. When she asked, he said he had come to get her
because their father was dying and wanted to see her. She had
been easy to find. He could have called. Michio gave her a
protective smile. 'I could have called, and you wouldn't have
come.'

She had tried to talk to him about Yuri Mishkin, but Michio
brushed it aside and told her about the kimono. It had been

designed to mark the first birthday of Emperor Akihito. Sara's great-grandmother had worn it for the Imperial Court celebrations in 1935. Ten thousand tiny silk cocoons, each the size of a child's finger, for just this one garment. Although their father had yet to be born in 1935, seeing his daughter in the beautiful family heirloom would make him very happy.

Sara understood Michio's duty as the oldest son. But her father had ignored her for twenty-nine years. Why did he even care to see her? She doubted he would even recognize her.

Despite the family's wealth, the house had always been a modest, three-story building of unexceptional brickwork, a square block in an expensive Tokyo suburb. There were no features of architectural worth, no artwork of note, but there were cultural relics, symbols of Japan's bygone days, and a large, torn, framed flag from 1941 showing the red circle symbolizing sun against a white background, underscoring how dramatically the sun rises over the sea to the East. The flag had flown on the deck of aircraft carrier *Akagi* during the attack on Pearl Harbor, and had been given to Sara's great-grandfather by one of the pilots.

The house itself was laid out as functional living space. As his health deteriorated, Jacob Kato had instructed that his ground-floor study be turned into his bedroom, with its windows overlooking the tranquility of the back garden. An extension ran out from the side, creating a spacious room where Sara had been only once when she was about seven. She remembered a wall covered in swords, old ornaments and a kamidana shrine carved in light brown cypress wood. In one of the very few times he had spoken to her, Kato told Sara he used the room for solitude and reflection.

Kazan appeared. Sara found herself holding the arm of Michio, who was quiet and thoughtful. He didn't look up as Kazan walked briskly toward them. He stopped in front of Sara, too close, right in her space. She smelt his aftershave.

'Don't cause trouble.' Kazan took off his thin, round, gunmetal glasses and tilted his head inches from her face. 'Japan doesn't want you. The family doesn't want you. Go back to Europe.' He spoke harshly, but there was worry in his eyes.

Michio firmly pulled Kazan back. 'I asked her to come. Father wants to see her.'

Kazan let Michio move him away. He polished his glasses with a gray handkerchief bearing his initials in Roman characters, and looked out the window toward the garden covered in a light frost. There were tiers of waterfalls and a pond filled with colorful Koi carp, with a wooden bridge across carved with emblems from Kato family history. The garden gave the old man tranquility and their mother something to fuss over. There was silence among the three siblings as they waited. The atmosphere was familiar to all three, remembered from childhood, Kazan and Sara squabbling and a summons to their father's office.

Kazan was dressed in a dark, formal suit with a collarless jacket and a white pleated linen shirt. The suit was custom-made for his slight frame, with four buttons on each sleeve and four on the front of the jacket. The buttons bore the Kato family crest, an intricate and unique arrangement of rare Japanese flowers. Kazan had a thin, stern face. Laughter did not come easily to him. Nor did spontaneity. Although only twenty-nine, his hair was receding far beyond his forehead, with flecks of gray on the side. He put back his spectacles, folded the handkerchief and slipped it into his pants pocket.

In contrast, Michio was dressed casually, as if he were off for a round of golf at a local country club, a white blazer, pink pants, a blue shirt with no tie. When she asked, he had shrugged and asked playfully in English: 'Why? Do you think I'm too scruffy?' Kazan was uptight. Michio was relaxed. Sara was a little lost. It was how it always had been.

The door to their father's room opened. Their mother waved her children in. Sakiya Kato looked more tired and shrunken than Sara remembered her. She was dressed as her station in life dictated. Sara had seen the conservative kimono before, a garment even older than Sara's, also made for a ceremonial occasion from the nineteenth century. Her mother barely looked at her daughter. Nor did she acknowledge her; it must have been nearly twenty years since they were together. Old anger and confusion that had wracked her adolescence tried to take over. But Sara pushed it away. Never again would she open the door of that dark mental closet filled with unresolvable anguish. Sara now felt sorry for her mother. She was unable to love her own daughter because she would have had the same treatment from her own parents. Standing in front her, beckoning the three of them to her father's side, was an obedient elderly woman whose life had been one of subjugation and suppressed emotion.

Jacob Kato sat in a wheelchair, dressed impeccably in a tailored dark suit bearing the Kato family crest. An oxygen tank was hooked to the back with its tube latched under his nose. Liver spots covered his crinkled face. Chemotherapy had rid him of hair. A drip fed into his left hand. Despite his frailty, his eyes were alert, settling on each of his children before shakily lifting his right hand and beckoning Sara to him. Suspicion clouded her face. She hesitated. Michio touched her elbow for her to go. She stepped forward. It was her father's hostility and absence that Sara had been unable to shake off. If she could win her father's love, she had thought many, many times, then her mother's would naturally follow.

'I make no apology for treating you harshly, Sara.' The strength of Kato's voice belied his infirmity. 'Nor for sending you away, for ignoring you, for allowing you to think you had a father who did not love you.'

Their mother put a hand to her mouth, unaware of what her husband was about to say. Kazan seemed unsure, too. Michio's expression was unchanged. Jacob Kato's diction was decisive and commanding. 'Because of how I treated you, my daughter learned to think and act independently. I gave you only an education. Not love. Not security. Not money. Not context as to who you are and where you belong. For that, you found your own way, and you have done it well because you are a Kato, and you are my daughter.'

Trailing the drip tube with him, he held out both his hands. Sara's eyes filled with tears. She loathed him. For all those years she had tried to shake off the bond of his parentage, free herself, and she had failed. She craved his acceptance, his respect. She clasped and unclasped her hands. Sunlight from the garden played on her face. She let him hold her face,

a hand on either side. He stared at her, nodding, beaming. Was
it real? Or had the old man's chemo worsened his dementia?
Had Michio put him up to it? She couldn't hold back.
She found herself smiling, laughing, giggling like a child,
unable to conceal her happiness.

'Now come, Sara.' Kato let go her face and adjusted the
oxygen tube under his nose. 'We have an important meeting.
We must not be late.'

No one asked what meeting. Sara had not been told. Kazan
made a show of checking the gold watch in his waistcoat
pocket. He led the way out, followed by Sara and her father,
with Michio and their mother behind. There was a wide,
polished wood corridor leading to the double front door, open
with drivers waiting. Sara saw two vehicles, a black Toyota
van adapted for her father's wheelchair, and an old black Lexus
saloon that looked like the one her father had had when she
was a child. She thought she recognized the family doctor.
There were also a female nurse and a male paramedic who
stood by the back door of the van. The ramp was lowered to
take the wheelchair inside.

Kazan walked toward the van, expecting to ride with his
father. But, as his hand was on the door, his father said, 'No,
Kazan. You go with your brother and mother. I want to travel
with Sara.'

Kazan hesitated, looked around to check with his older
brother. Michio stayed back with their mother and Sara. A
flood of childhood family choreography swept back to Sara,
revolving around the rivalry between Michio and Kazan. Who
had the old man's attention? Who was his favorite? Who would
inherit the family empire? It was sure to be Michio, except
Michio told her he had made a mistake that had brought shame
upon the family. Maybe that explained why the brothers were
dressed differently; maybe that was why Michio had been sent
to bring Sara back.

Kazan turned toward the saloon, and her father explained,
'If my strength fails me, Sara and I can go home. You and
Michio are the important ones. You go on ahead. We must not
keep our Prime Minister waiting.'

TWENTY-THREE

The Kato family convoy pulled up outside the main gate of the Yasukuni Shrine where police had emptied the road of traffic. There was a clear blue sky allowing the sun to warm the dry winter cold. Set back from the road stood the bold First Shrine Gate, the Daichi Torii, made of circular gray steel pillars with a massive crossbeam and, to its right, was a stone pillar on which the shrine's name was engraved.

For much of the fifteen-minute drive, Jacob Kato appeared to be asleep, his head lolling. They would stop at lights or turn a corner and he would look up, smile at Sara, and doze off again. His first words on the journey were, 'I am glad you came back.'

Sara asked how sick he was, to which he replied, 'Sick enough. That is why we are going to Yasukuni.'

She remembered the shrine from her childhood Shichi-Go-San ceremony and understood how much it meant to her father. Even so, she pressed him. 'Why, Father. Why are we going there and why are you meeting the Prime Minister?'

'You will see. You all need to meet him.' Closing his eyes, Kato rocked back and forth with the sway of the drive. As they were pulling up, Kato said, 'Did I ever tell you that you were born seventeen minutes before Kazan?'

Sara held back from asking how could he have told her when he had barely spoken to her. They stopped behind the Lexus. Kazan pulled open the side door. He waited for Sara to climb out, then snapped, 'What were you talking about with Father?'

'Why don't you ask him?' Sara tilted her head toward the ramp being lowered to bring down the wheelchair.

'Why don't you tell me?' Kazan bristled, overdressed against the stream of tourists with his expensive suit and shiny shoes.

Sara stepped close to him and laid her hand on his arm. 'If you are to take charge of our family, little brother, you must learn to control your fear of the unknown.' She smiled, making fun of him like he had of her so many times before.

'I am not your little brother.'

'Father just told me you were born seventeen minutes after me.' Sara adjusted her obi, the band around her kimono that was so stiff she could barely breathe. Their mother walked across. She fussed about a scuff on Kazan's shoes. She pushed Sara's hair behind her ears. She had a hairpin between her teeth but nowhere to put it, and muttered, 'Why do you girls cut your hair so short?'

Jacob Kato's wheelchair reached the ground. A paramedic pushed him off the ramp. Kazan squatted to speak directly into the old man's ear. Michio spoke softly to Sara. 'Kazan is telling him we should drive in. This is too public, too long a walk.'

Jacob Kato splayed out both arms as if symbolizing his certainty. 'No, Kazan. You are wrong. Our family has been working in the shadows for too long. Japan needs to learn about the contribution I have made to my country and to know who will be carrying on after I am gone. I am in my final days. Our nation must know.'

Sara glanced inquisitively at Michio, whose slight move of the head confirmed changing dynamics. 'I don't know exactly what's happening,' he said. 'The plan had been to go into the underground car park and take the elevator straight to the Yūshūkan War Memorial Museum where we would meet the Prime Minister. For some reason, Father has changed his mind.'

He wanted to see the whole shrine, thought Sara. To honor it. That was why she was wearing an antique kimono. To show off his family.

'It's too dangerous, Father,' objected Kazan. 'People should not know who we are.'

A smile spread across Kato's worn, sick face as he pointed to an approaching convoy of government vehicles. Two security cars went around the Kato vehicles. Escorts stayed back, and Sara recognized the black armored Lexus carrying the Japanese Prime Minister. It must have been a while since a Prime Minister had visited the Yasukuni Shrine. Sara remembered being asked at school if she was angry about it because the shrine commemorated war criminals and people still thought she was Chinese, not Japanese. There had been outrage and more demands for Japan to apologize for war atrocities. Sara had read up on Yasukuni then. Among the two and half million war dead honored were fourteen convicted war criminals. Some had even been elevated to the status of a Shinto god. The Yūshūkan War Memorial Museum presented a version of history abhorred by many around the world: Japan conquering Asia as liberators against Western imperialism, not massacres and brutality. Sara had never been sure how she felt. Part of her was ashamed for her country. But a big part was proud, like now, as excitement rippled through her.

Squat and bespectacled, the Prime Minister stepped out of the Lexus and brushed down his dark navy pinstripe jacket. In the same vehicle were the ministers of Trade, Foreign Affairs and Defense, all similarly dressed. One by one, they stood in front of Kato and gave a long bow, indicating deep respect.

Sara could not play down the thrill. Her father would be in full view for all to see as he was wheeled through the Daiichi Torii arch, past the statue of Ōmura Masujirō, the founder of the modern Japanese Army, through the second shrine arch, then the Shinmon main gate, with its chrysanthemum crest of sixteen petals, and into the area of cherry trees whose blossom would be magnificent barely a month from now. With the Prime Minister and his senior cabinet colleagues, the journey would be publicly chronicled. Security would be in place. But the shrine had not been closed to visitors. The frailty and sickness of Jacob Kato would be for all to see, and to photograph. It was a scene of weakness and of power that injected Sara with an unfamiliar feeling. She had a place in the world. It was here, exactly where she was now, with her family.

The Prime Minister acknowledged Michio, ignored Sara, touched Kazan's sleeve and said, 'Kazan. Walk with us.'

A paramedic stepped aside for Kazan to take the wheelchair. Her father signaled that they should begin. With the Prime Minister on his right, and other ministers on his left, Kazan pushed his father along the symbolic route into the Yasukuni Shrine.

Sara, Michio and their mother followed at a distance. As they watched, Kazan turned back toward them. To Sara, he looked afraid and alone.

TWENTY-FOUR

Washington, DC

Rake last went to the White House with Harry Lucas to see the former President in the small sitting room attached to the Lincoln Bedroom. It was there, in a late-night meeting, that Lucas had been instructed to set up a special task force to track extreme threats posed by international criminal networks. Rake had been assigned from his home unit at the Alaska National Guard for the duration – what they called 'serving at the pleasure of the President'.

This meeting was daytime, in the ground-floor office of National Security Adviser, Nick Petrovsky. His background was CIA. Rake didn't know him. New administration. New people. Lucas told Rake to be in uniform. The only one he had was full dress, smelling of mothballs, medals coloring the chest; what Carrie called his show-pony clothes. He had shaved and cleaned up as best he could. There was nothing he could do about the bandage on his hand and bruise at the back of head from the fight outside the Åland Islands hut. Lucas wore a freshly pressed dark suit and dark blue patterned silk tie. Rake had only seen him so formal in photographs from when he was a politician.

They went through the pedestrian entrance and were shown immediately into Petrovsky's office which, given his influence, was small, with a dark wood desk, a suite of pastel sofa and chairs, high windows on two sides and a glass-topped conference table where Petrovsky told them to sit. 'I kept it to the three of us because something's come up. You need coffee?'

'No,' said Lucas. Rake shook his head. There were notepads and water bottles on the table.

Petrovsky brought up a screen from the end of the table with a still image of half a dozen men in dark suits gathered on a wide sidewalk. Black vehicles were parked on the road behind them. 'The Japanese Prime Minister, Foreign, Trade, Defense. Their meeting place is the Yasukuni Shrine which honors Japan's war dead. You both understand the symbolism. Imagine Germany having a shrine to honor Hitler and Nazi war heroes. Yasukuni is Japan's tinderbox, the unlanced boil, the tumor that refuses to die.'

'I thought these visits had stopped,' said Lucas.

'You and me both. They slowed because we rapped them so hard over the knuckles, not to speak of China, South Korea and any of those countries colonized by them.' Petrovsky flipped to an elderly man in a wheelchair. 'The Prime Minister bows deeply to this old man.'

'Jacob Kato.' Lucas's palms were flat on the table, pressing into the glass.

Petrovsky switched to a different shot of Kato with a young man, formally dressed, standing behind his wheelchair, ready to push him. 'That is Kazan. Sara's twin. Looking at the choreography, he could be the chosen heir.'

Kazan pushed Jacob Kato to the shrine in his wheelchair, flanked by the Prime Minister and his Cabinet colleagues. Petrovsky turned his gaze to Rake, opened the screen to a wide image and asked, 'Recognize these ones, Major?'

The street surveillance footage was not the best. Light skewed across faces. The older woman would be wife and mother. The younger one was unmistakably Sara, dressed up like royalty. She was composed, assured, disciplined, nothing like the expressive, outgoing woman he thought he had got to know.

'Sara Kato,' said Rake.

Petrovsky shifted the camera angle to show Michio, dressed less formally, near Sara. 'This is Michio, the man you've been hunting.'

Rake studied the lean, relaxed face. Michio's eyes were cast toward Sara, watchful, filled with humanity, not cruelty. Sara gazed forward, looking uncertain about where she was. Her head must be filled with childhood memories from the shrine, and being back with the family that had rejected her.

'I ran Michio Kato through Saito Habiki, my National Security counterpart in Tokyo,' said Petrovsky. 'It took a sackfull of favors to get an answer. Almost two years ago, Michio went off radar. Word was he had done something that shamed the family, and he was at a Buddhist retreat. But he was actually training under a false name with the Japanese Special Forces Group.'

Lucas and Rake exchanged glances. It rang true. Petrovsky continued, 'Michio Kato vanishes and reappears. A Japanese Prime Minister pops up at the Yasukuni Shrine. The most powerful crime boss in Asia, not seen in public for a quarter of a century, is with him. Any ideas, Harry?'

'Japan has never succeeded in separating Yakuza operations from those of government and legitimate business,' said Lucas. 'It's partly our fault. We haven't muscled them enough. The executive order we discussed named the Yakuza as a threat to American interests. It helped increase budgets, focus intelligence gathering, but it didn't dent their operations. There is no secret about who runs the networks. They have business cards, titles and offices.'

'That executive order got me posted to Tokyo for a year,' said Petrovsky. 'The FBI bought the line. The CIA wasn't convinced.'

'Different missions,' countered Lucas. 'The FBI looks after American soil, the CIA American interests.'

'Implying?' Petrovsky tensed.

'CIA's interest is to keep a rock-solid relationship with Japan to ensure US supremacy in Asia. If that involves turning a blind eye to organized crime, so be it. They're not Islamic State. They're not the Chinese Communist Party. Japan is one of the good guys. Work with them. Think nine/eleven. Saudi nationals knock down the Twin Towers. The CIA's job was to protect our relationship with the Saudi government.' Lucas let out a loud sigh. 'Let's agree that both you and I know this stuff.'

Petrovsky pushed back his chair. 'Things have changed since then.'

When he walked in, Rake had detected open tension between Lucas and Petrovsky. That began to loosen, but he couldn't read how it would play out: whether Lucas would be willing to share all they had gathered on Kato and risk burning contacts and information; whether he trusted Petrovsky or John Freeman enough.

'The executive order named four criminal networks,' said Lucas, 'dangerous to the United States, entrenched in the operations of foreign governments and the international financial system, weakening democratic institutions. That's a direct quote. The Brothers' Circle is a loose network of Russian and European operations, not structured in any meaningful way. The Camorra is an Italian, Naples-based Mafia operation, well-structured. Los Zetas is a Mexican drug cartel, ruthless and disciplined. The surprise was the Yakuza, meticulously structured and embedded within Japanese business, government and society.' Lucas twisted off the top of a water bottle and took a sip. 'Kato's crime family goes back to before Japan's Meiji Restoration, when they threw out the Shogun military rulers and installed a teenage Emperor as a figurehead. Kato family influence grew in parallel with a modernizing Japan and peaked in the 1930s as Japan colonized Asia and Jacob Kato was born. Then came Pearl Harbor and we beat them.'

'And built a democracy,' interjected Petrovsky.

'People like Jacob Kato never accepted defeat, never stopped doing what they felt they were born to do. He runs one of the best-managed crime operations anywhere in the world, and we've just seen the evidence from the Yasukuni Shrine.'

A sharp female voice burst through on the internal intercom. 'The President needs to see you, sir, in the Oval.'

Petrovsky stood up, his expression creased, arranging his thoughts, glancing at the snow out of the window. 'Grizlov? Is Stephanie with him?'

'Just arrived,' answered Lucas.

Petrovsky brushed his right hand over his face, as if he wanted to put on a mask. 'I have to see the President and don't even have a clean shirt in the office. Freeman is obsessed with Russia. Barely knows where Japan is.'

'Get me into see Freeman,' said Lucas.

'Do you know what's happening here, Harry? Because if you do, just spit it out.' Petrovsky unhooked his suit jacket from a stand next to his desk. Rake expected Lucas to reveal something, even if it were something obvious and straight-forward like the link between Kato's Yakuza and the Russian Big Circle. But instead of responding directly, Lucas said, 'I'll check with Stephanie when might be a good time for the President to make a condolence call to Grizlov.'

TWENTY-FIVE

Stephanie's motorcade sped through Moscow's winter streets with siren and wipers clearing snow, mud and ice splashed up onto the windshield. She had called from Washington and fudged why she was coming to Moscow. President Sergey Grizlov hadn't asked. He wanted to see her and sent cars to the airport.

The vehicles entered the Kremlin through the Borovitsky Gate in the southwest corner, the main vehicle thoroughfare, and pulled up outside the yellow and white Senate Building with its circular terrace of white pillars, home to the presidential administrative offices. She was shown straight into Grizlov's empty, austere office in the Senate Building.

The door closed and Stephanie was left alone. She had been in the presidential office once before when ambassador to Moscow. Grizlov had been with her, and she had been seeing his predecessor, to try to unwind mounting crises between Europe and Russia. Unlike most world leaders who enjoyed putting a personal stamp of authority on their offices, Grizlov had barely changed a thing. There were dark wood-paneling walls with the crest of the double-headed eagle in the center, behind a functional leather-embossed desk. There were two chairs for guests on the other side, a small table in between, heavy draped curtains, a glass crystal chandelier and a suite of sofa and chairs. That was it. Bleak, colorless and, frankly, bloody depressing.

She ignored her vibrating phone. Harry again, pestering her for a result, which meant the White House was panicking, which also underpinned that new kid President John Freeman understood little about diplomatic nuances, not least when breaking bad personal news.

Grizlov had retained the charisma Stephanie had admired for decades from when they met in Moscow, he a young chancer determined to make his fortune, and Stephanie a kid escaping the drabness of south London and chasing dreams. Grizlov taught her how to work systems; he did it better than anyone else she had ever met since. 'You never know when you will need your enemy,' was one of his doctrines as they stumbled together through the pitfalls of post-Communist Russia. 'Never make a demon out of your adversary.'

They liked each other, had fallen in and out of bed and he cut her into his deals, made sure she stayed safe and made money. While her friends in London struggled with student debt and mortgages, Stephanie banked millions. At one stage, after leaving Moscow and heading towards politics, she had hired a lawyer to go through her businesses. He proclaimed them all legal. Cleverly so. Grizlov had protected her, made her rich, made her laugh, and had been an occasionally attentive, sometimes distracted lover. They stayed friends and hadn't slept together for thirty years.

Grizlov had fought the presidential election on an unashamedly pro-Western ticket. 'Do you want to see a Broadway show or yawn through a Chinese opera?' he had asked voters. 'We are not the West. We have our own souls. But why make an enemy of our friends and neighbors?'

This line had caught the attention of the US President, who had now made friendship with Russia the cornerstone of his foreign policy. Stephanie and Grizlov had not seen each other since he had become President and, before that, when they were both Foreign Ministers. It had often been awkward.

Grizlov came in from a side door at the back, unescorted, all smiles and embraces. Stephanie returned them, her stomach churning, as he hugged her, held her shoulders, looked at her, kissed her on both cheeks, hugged her again. It was no act. He was genuinely pleased to see her and had no idea that his son had been murdered.

'Thank goodness you got fired,' Grizlov joked, warmly squeezing her arm. 'I could not have met the British Foreign Secretary like this on the spur of the moment.' He led her to the large L-shaped sofa and asked if she wanted coffee or anything. Water was fine. He poured them each a glass of sparkling.

'I have to tell you, Steph, I really think we may have cracked it. Not Gorbachev. Not Yeltsin. Not Putin, God forbid. But an easier rapport with the West.'

Stephanie let him talk while looking for an opening. He asked her about her life as an academic, about her cantankerous and funny father embedded in the extension to her London house, then teasingly about her love life, to which she shrugged and smiled and shook her head. She couldn't just jump in. There was too much to explain, like how did she know and he not. She steered the conversation back to politics and the US, and he said, 'Have you met Freeman? There'll be bumps between us and they'll last more than one term. Is he the type of leader who will see it through?'

Grizlov sat beside her on the sofa. Stephanie took both his hands and said in a stern tone, 'I'm here because Freeman sent me.'

Grizlov gave a quick smile. 'I know you, Steph. He sent you with bad news?'

She nodded. 'But personal. About Yuri.'

Grizlov's eyes danced with confusion. 'How do you know about Yuri?'

Stephanie held his hands tighter and made sure her eyes were locked onto his. 'There's no easy way to say this, Sergey. Yuri has been murdered.'

Grizlov's eyes flared. He drew his hands away, pushed himself back. 'Yuri. You are talking about—'

'Yuri. Your son. Yes. I am so, so sorry.'

'You know about Yuri?' He was on his feet.

'Yes.'

Grizlov paced to his desk and back to Stephanie, to the desk again, where he turned and faced her. Their two crystal glasses of sparkling water stood on the table. Suffocating Russian symbols of flags and plaques hung around them. 'From the beginning, Steph.'

'Yuri was at a conflict resolution conference in Finland, the Åland Islands. He was invited because of a paper he had written on the Kuril dispute. He was killed there.'

'When?'

'Yesterday.'

'Who?' Energy drained from Grizlov. He leant on his desk for support. 'Who did it?'

'It was professional.' Stephanie stood up and held out her arms to him.

'An assassination?' Grizlov stiffened.

'Yes.'

'Why don't I know?'

'The Americans were there and tracking. There were delegates from the Middle East and Africa. They discovered who Yuri was and kept the lid on it. It went to the President who went to Harry who asked me to come here.'

Stephanie wanted to hold him, give comfort, as the truth sank in. But Grizlov did not respond to her outstretched hands. His voice became taut, commanding. 'Then show me. Steph. Don't just tell. Show.'

'Here.' Stephanie laid her tablet on the table and brought up the file Harry sent through. 'It's not nice.'

'But is it true?'

'Yes.'

Grizlov picked up the tablet, flipped through the pictures quicky, sat down next to Stephanie, put the tablet between them and went through it again. Stephanie had acquainted herself with the twelve shots so that when she came to show them to Grizlov she could keep her own composure. The images were mostly straightforward police procedural, unemotional, the corpse, the cut across the throat, the red-soaked sheets, Mishkin's face, blood drained, eyes closed by the paramedics. There was also Mishkin's portrait shot, used on the conference brochure, and a couple of pictures from the bar of Mishkin talking in a group, then separately to Sara

Kato. Mishkin was laughing, his eyes inquisitive, alive with horseplay and, with Sara, openly flirtatious. *Not good for the situation*, thought Stephanie. Color drained from Grizlov's face. He moved jerkily, his hands unsteady, his fingers shaking over the screen. As he spent time on each picture, his confidence returned, his survival instincts fighting to find a way through. He enlarged Mishkin's face, tracing his finger over its shape, turning some images to monochrome then back to color. His right hand stayed with the tablet. His left hand reached for Stephanie's. 'Why?' His voice was barely a breath. 'We had only just found each other.' Grizlov's brow tightened. 'That paper on the Kurils was my idea. Something to keep him busy. He was kind of lost.' He sat back heavily. 'An assassination to get at me. Yuri was a playboy. No one important. Who would do that?'

'I don't know. Harry's looking.'

Grizlov let go of Stephanie's hand and leaned forward, his elbows on his knees. Stephanie stayed quiet, allowing Grizlov to talk and go with it wherever he needed. 'Six months. Less. He wanted to know who his father was. That's all. His mother knew the danger. She tried to stop him. She asked me to stop him. But I was, I don't know, dumb, selfish, lonely. Yuri insisted. He died because of who his father is. I killed him.'

'Contract killers murdered Yuri. Not you.' Her tone was empathetic, firm and unhesitant.

Head on her shoulder, eyes closed, he stayed quiet for long minutes. The moment needed to play itself out in Grizlov's time. At some stage, Stephanie would get an update from Harry. At some stage, if Grizlov did not say it, she would spell out that Yuri was murdered to weaken Grizlov and Russia. The President of the Russian Federation shivered, holding her hand, seeking sanctuary on her shoulder, a world leader depleted and confused. She was convinced Grizlov would recover. Her friend was made of steel when it came to survival. What she couldn't predict was his determination for justice and revenge, whether his mantra of not demonizing adversaries would hold through to resolving the murder of his son.

'Thank you for being here, Steph.' He squeezed her hand,

kissed her lightly on the forehead and stood up. 'I can't think in this place. Come to my house.'

He stood up abruptly, brushed down his suit, and reeled off instructions through the intercom on his desk. Prepare the car. Cancel the rest of his appointments. Fix a call with the Deputy Speaker of the state Duma. There was no hint in his voice of any trouble.

In the armored limousine, he sat close to Stephanie, keeping hold of her hand, discreetly under their heavy overcoats. When not working his phone, he stared at snow, traffic, and red and blue escort lamps bouncing off the vehicle windows. He initiated two conversations, speaking in English – light, small talk stuff about a new opera at the Bolshoi and an upcoming soccer match between Chelsea and Manchester United. Both petered out quickly.

Grizlov's house was in Barvikha Village, an expensive western suburb where he had bought an ostentatious mansion long before he went into politics. Once, when Stephanie teased him about it, Grizlov argued that anyone wanting to be taken seriously in Russia needed to own a monster house. This was Russia, not the countryside of the English Cotswolds. Every leader of any note had had a place in Barvikha Village – Lenin, Stalin, Putin, so why not Grizlov?

Stephanie had been there several times over the years. Most of the house was set up for formal entertaining, with oil paintings, finely knotted carpets, ceramics, rare editions of Tolstoy, Pasternak and Dostoyevsky, the play-sheet of Russian power bling. Then there was a smaller south-facing wing that Grizlov had turned into his private apartment, with posters of his favorite rock and movie stars like the Rolling Stones and Clint Eastwood, with light, pastel colors and relaxed furniture, a sense that if you spilt wine it wouldn't cost a million dollars to clean up.

Stephanie stepped out of the limousine onto a smart red weather-proof carpet, embossed with the Russian flag. It ran toward steps leading up to double-fronted main doors. Grizlov got out of the other side, trod through snow to take Stephanie's arm and walk her up. His grip was light, hesitant. He needed her support more than she his.

Four agents, wearing black uniforms of the Presidential Security Service, led them through the property. They carried holstered pistols. Two had submachine guns slung around their chests. They stepped back as they reached the main library where a bookcase concealed the door to Grizlov's apartment.

TWENTY-SIX

Grizlov punched in a code, which activated iris and handprint scans. He told the agents he was not to be disturbed under any circumstances, and showed Stephanie in. The steel front he had put on melted away. He took Stephanie's coat, their eyes meeting, his heavy with sadness and beginning to tear up

He fetched two glasses of water from a cooler at the corner of the room, which was almost unchanged from her last visit. Still a poster of the Rolling Stones in concert; still a colored psychedelic poster from the seventies, asking, *Suppose There Was a War, and Nobody Came*; still paraphernalia collected in his youth and never shed. The change was the photographs of Yuri: one with friends on horses; one at a conference with a Eurasian logo in the background, and the main one with Grizlov, father and son, standing in the garden of the Barvikha mansion. There was nothing public because Yuri remained a secret.

'Show me those photographs again.' Grizlov sat on a firm white leather sofa and patted it for Stephanie to come next to him.

'Are you sure?' Stephanie sat down, keeping her tablet in her shoulder bag.

'Do it, Steph. Then I decide what to do.'

They looked through the murder photographs once more. As Grizlov moved from a shot of the bloodied body to a smiling portrait of his son, Stephanie's phone vibrated, the encrypted and hardened one given to her by Harry.

'It's Harry.' Stephanie balanced the phone in her hand. 'He'll know more.'

'Is the line secure?'

'Yes.'

'Put him on speaker.'

Stephanie weighed options. It was better to talk than not. She was cocooned anyway. Things were as secure as Grizlov wanted them to be. She lay the phone on the table next to the tablet. 'You're on speaker, with myself and President Grizlov in his private residence in Barvikha Village.' Harry would know her location from the tracker. Stephanie needed Grizlov to know he knew.

'Sergey,' began Harry. 'I am so, so sorry. I don't know—'

'Who killed him?' Grizlov cut in, accusing, anger flaring against Harry.

'We think two.' Harry's tone hardened to match Grizlov's. 'Alex James Hunter, aged thirty-four, from Lancaster, Ohio. He is a former US Marine, highly decorated. His co-conspirator is Simone Nancy Tallick, twenty-nine, from Little Rock, Arkansas. She served alongside Hunter in the same unit in Afghanistan. How much do you know about the location and the—?'

'Why don't you just tell me?'

'I've filled in the setting,' interjected Stephanie, putting herself between whatever rage flowed from Grizlov to Harry.

Harry kept his answer detached and factual. 'They posed as delegates alongside Yuri and were registered as members of opposing American groups. We believe they were hired to kill Yuri.'

'Who hired them?'

'We don't know yet.' Harry spoke in a soft, measured, tone.

'But you have leads?'

'Yes, and motives. People who want to weaken your presidency by weakening you.'

Grizlov slid the photographs on the tablet back to the wide shot from the hotel surveillance camera. 'Were Hunter and Tallick among the group drinking in the bar?'

'Tallick is the black woman,' said Harry. 'Hunter standing next to her.'

'They are yours. Americans.' It wasn't a question. It was an affirmation of what they all knew and its implications.

'They are in custody in Helsinki. They're not talking, and the Finns are being protective.'

Grizlov moved the photographs back and forth like worry beads.

Harry said, 'The perpetrators have a video of the murder. We're doing everything we can to keep it buried.'

Grizlov kept staring at the pictures of his son.

'Yuri's topic was the Kuril Islands,' said Stephanie. 'Is there anything going on that might be linked?'

'A snuff movie of my son's murder and you try to move us onto the Kuril Islands.' Grizlov's eyes blazed, this time at Stephanie. 'You fucking people! No wonder the world hates you.'

Stephanie had seen Grizlov's temper many times, part heartfelt, part targeted to get what he wanted. She had never done family with him, never seen him snap like this before.

'I don't know, Sergey. I'm sorry. It's just the Kurils—'

'Japan wants them back and it isn't getting them.' Grizlov's anger quietened, as if he realized he was not speaking to an invisible voice on a phone line, but in the room with Stephanie, his friend, and she was on his side. 'Yes, I suggested Yuri look into the Kurils. He was drifting, sleeping with too many women, obsessed about getting to know his father. He needed it all at once. It got difficult and I had to reassure him we would work it through. He needed direction and an anchor, and I wanted to be part of his journey wherever he was going.'

'While keeping secret who he was and that you had a son,' nudged Stephanie softly.

'It was safer, and Yuri and his mother agreed.' Grizlov looked down, studying the floor. A calmness enveloped him. When he spoke next it was to Harry, 'The Kurils are harmless because they're going nowhere. Everyone's learned to live with it.' Grizlov pointed his forefinger in the air. 'The Japanese refuse peace. If every country acted like that because of territory lost in war, there would never be peace anywhere. Russia and Japan remain in a technical state of conflict because Japan does not accept it lost the war.' He tapped his middle finger against the right side of his skull. 'Besides, waters around the Kurils are ice-free in the winter, which we need to get to our bases in Sakhalin and Vladivostok. We're not giving them back, and if your President thinks he can befriend Russia and then put muscle on us over the Kurils to sweeten Japan, then tell him from me, Harry, that won't work. And if that's part of Yuri's murder and Americans are involved, then fuck the President and all around him.'

Stephanie tried to hide the anxiety running through her whole body. This was a precarious moment. Grizlov was emotionally raw. The killers were Americans hired by Japanese mobsters to trigger exactly this response, to fuck everyone. For the moment, Harry was keeping Japanese involvement out of it. But that couldn't last.

She tested gently, 'And you had no idea Yuri was in Finland?'

'I didn't. Maybe he wanted to get a Kuril solution and present it to me to make me proud.' Grizlov shifted to the photograph of Yuri's body, the most graphic and bloody one. He addressed Harry again. 'You sent Steph here to persuade me to keep quiet.' He finished the glass of water, swallowing fast and hard. 'I can do that. I want to do that.' He walked across the room and refilled from the cooler. 'For a few hours. Until the morning. You nail this, Harry. Bring in the murderers.'

'It might take—' began Harry.

'And in the morning, this tragedy will be fed into the Russian system, and we will take control because a Russian citizen has been murdered.'

'Sergey, we'll need longer,' began Stephanie.

'No, Steph.' Grizlov shook his head. 'I have a duty to tell Yuri's mother. I have a duty to warn Russia, and Russia will not tolerate such a catastrophe being run by a hostile foreign power.'

'Not hostile, Sergey,' objected Harry. 'The President's whole initiative is to end—'

'The President's fucking initiative. It's always about America, isn't it, Harry?' Grizlov drained his glass of water again and wiped the back of his hand hard across his mouth. 'This President might be gone in three years, and you won't want us anymore. You'll be sleeping with the Chinese again, making up bullshit stories about shared values and making a demon of Sergey Grizlov.'

Grizlov picked up the tablet and moved to the photograph of Yuri Mishkin and Sara Kato laughing in a corner of the Åland Islands bar. He turned it around like a placard. 'Who is this woman with Yuri? She has to be Japanese.' He looked tersely at Stephanie. 'Steph, tell Harry which shot I'm showing you.'

'I can answer,' said Stephanie. Grizlov was honing in. Stephanie needed to pre-empt. With Sara Kato identified, he could run an immediate straight line to the family. 'Her name is Sara Kato. She is an activist for the Ainu, the indigenous people of Japan, hence her interest in the Kuril Islands. She paid for Yuri to go to the conference.'

'Did she kill him?'

'No,' said Harry.

'Did she hire those two who killed him?'

Harry stayed quiet. A tough call. To say she didn't but her brother did wouldn't do the business.

'Still checking are you, Harry? You know and you're not saying. You have until morning, Harry. I will stay quiet to help you sort out your shit. Then I unleash my intelligence services onto Sara Kato, Yuri's killers, the Finns, the Americans, and anyone else who thinks they can get in Russia's way.'

Grizlov picked up the phone, ended the call and dropped it onto the sofa. He sat down next to Stephanie, took her hand and pressed it against his face.

TWENTY-SEVEN

On their way back from the Yasukuni Shrine, Sara Kato rode with Michio in the sedan, while Kazan, their mother and their father traveled in the wheelchair-adapted van. The traffic was heavier. They moved slowly, stopping and starting.

'As soon as I get back, I'm putting my jeans back on.' Sara

shifted in her seat to get comfortable. The many layers of her great-grandmother's old kimono rubbed irritatingly against her waist.

'Ride with it,' Michio smiled. 'The day is not yet over. Father wants to do more.'

'More what?' The very public walk to the dreary military museum at the Yasukuni Shrine had lasted longer than the meeting. Sara shuffled along, the kimono skirts wrapped tightly around her ankles. Security agents kept tourists back but allowed them to take photographs, which would be all over social media. Sara hoped the kimono would disguise her from her friends, at least for a few hours.

Her sick father, the Prime Minister and his glum, black-suited ministers had gathered under the wing of a fighter aircraft from the Second World War. Sara, Kazan and Michio stood to one side with their mother while a pompous man spoke about the origins of the museum. It had opened in 1882, suffered an earthquake in 1923, got wrecked by bombing in 1945 and reopened again in 1986. It was now preparing for celebrations of National Foundation Day – the creation of the Japanese nation on 11 February.

The snatches of Japanese war history she saw around her contradicted what she had been taught at school in England. Like the Nanking Massacre in 1937 had never happened. Like tens of thousands of killings and rapes. At the museum entrance, they walked past an old steam engine from the Thai–Burma railway. Thousands of prisoners of war had died building it. What bullshit! A crazy craving came to her to have a cappuccino on an English high street. England had bullshit, but a different kind.

The Prime Minister gave a speech about paying respect to the spirits of the deceased. One by one, the siblings were summoned. Michio went first, bowing to his father and then to the Prime Minister. Kazan stepped forward to go next, but Jacob Kato sharply told him to hold back, and beckoned Sara forward instead. Of course. Dumb twin brother. She was seventeen minutes older and, for some reason, in the old man's mind, men and woman had suddenly become equal.

'Do exactly as I did,' whispered Michio.

Her bow wasn't enough for her father. He took her hands and held them as tightly as his frailty would allow. His skin was transparent and silky smooth. He let her go and shooed her toward the Prime Minister, who had his arms by his side as if on a parade ground. Sara had been trained on how a woman's bow was different to that of a man. She moved her hands and arms to her front as was traditional. They bowed together. 'Thank you for your contribution to our nation's strength,' said the Prime Minister.

She walked back, and Kazan hissed, 'I warn you, silly sister.' Sara shushed him.

Kazan's ritual was less elaborate. A perfunctory nod to his father and a shallow bow to the Prime Minister, who did hold Kazan's gaze. He straightened his colorful bow tie as he walked back. As he took his place beside Sara, he checked his pocket watch and stared out ahead.

There was one photographer attached to the Prime Minister's office. That was it. Unlike the walk through the shrine, there would be no social media. By now the vehicles had been driven into the underground car park. They went down. Jacob Kato told Sara to ride with Michio. He would travel with Kazan and their mother. They had headed out into the midday Tokyo traffic.

Sara loosened the cords that held her obi in place, took Michio's hands with both of hers and switched to English. 'Come on, big brother. Isn't it time to tell your little sister what the bloody hell is going on?'

A pall fell across Michio's face. He kept hold of Sara's hands and used English so the driver and bodyguard would not understand. Sara's accent was English upper class. Michio's was American East Coast. The language had a psychological impact, bringing to them both a Western and not a Japanese mindset.

'It's got more complicated than I ever imagined,' said Michio. 'Father is undecided about who should take over. I messed up on something a few years back and he says I brought shame on the family.'

'What was that?'

'For later.' Michio stared out as light rain streaked against the window. 'Father began training up Kazan. But your twin brother carries too much of his life on his sleeve, his joys, his doubts, his self-admiration, his self-hatred. He puts it out there for all to see. You cannot run the family like that. He doesn't understand the concept of a cause greater than himself. It is a tragedy. That is why I suggested that we bring you back.'

'You suggested?' muttered Sara.

He let go her hands. 'And how the hell did you get mixed up with that mess in Finland?'

They had barely spoken of the Åland Islands. Sara shrugged. 'I was doing my Northern Territory, Ainu, thing. I find this Russian guy then, guess what, he's the son of the Russian President, although he doesn't say who he really is and tells me he doesn't have any money. I find enough to fly us both to the conference. He comes. He's cute and funny and he ends up getting murdered. There's an American there who's meant to be a speaker, mentor, that kind of person, except he's not. He's like one of those wild survivalists from a TV show and ends up shooting his way out and taking me with him.'

Sara sucked in her cheeks to stop her eyes tearing as the memory flooded back. *What was all that about?* she asked herself. She didn't analyze things enough, didn't ask herself enough questions. She just went for things. She wasn't thoughtful like Michio, whose gaze stayed firmly out the window with the weather and traffic. She pulled his arm to get his attention back.

'How come you were there with the police and all those people?'

'Like I said, I needed you urgently because of Father and that's where you were. I insisted on seeing the commander, told him I was your brother and to get me to wherever you were. My job was to get you back here.' He rubbed her arm caringly. 'Which I did. So, mission impossible became mission accomplished.'

'Loved that movie.' Sara smiled. 'So, what more does Father want today?' She spoke with a playful lilt. Michio had made her feel better. He always did.

'He wants to finalize the handover. He thinks he only has

a few days left. I don't know exactly how or what, or where you fit in.'

'But I don't want it, Michio. Who wants all this crap hanging around their necks?'

'Alas, little Sara. That is not the point. Neither do I. I wanted to stay in the US and get into the movie business.'

'You did.' Sara turned to him with a chuckle.

'I would have made *Mission Impossible* ten times better.'

'You never told me that.' She punched him lightly on the arm.

'But we're all wrapped up in the Kato legacy. So, ride with it. Do what he asks, then I'll help you melt away when you can.' Michio tapped his forehead, as if he had forgotten something. 'You don't have a boyfriend, do you? I should have asked.'

'I do not. I'm going to marry an Ainu warrior.'

Michio looked at her with a sternness, which prompted her to punch him on the arm a second time. 'Only kidding. There has been a boyfriend and there will be again. But, as of now, none.'

By the time the car pulled up in the Kato compound, Jacob Kato, her mother and Kazan had gone inside, and the wheelchair ramp was being folded back.

'Showtime.' Michio unclipped his seat belt.

Sara got out. It was quiet. She could hear a faint trickle of the waterfall from the back garden and a hum of traffic from outside the compound wall. The rain was light and refreshing on her face. Michio's lips were pursed, tightly locked. Maybe she had missed it earlier, but he looked worried in a way Sara had never seen. He walked toward the front door, held open by one of the old house servants. As Sara followed him, she heard a sharp, frightened scream from somewhere inside the house. The voice of her mother.

TWENTY-EIGHT

'Wait here.' It was a command from Michio, and Sara was grateful. Her mother's cry was more of a yelp, an unpleasant surprise. Her childhood home was alien to her. Her mother had been distant, fussing about her food and dress, reprimanding, never asking how she felt and, God forbid, never asking about her daughter's dreams and ambitions.

Michio left her in the front hallway, with its polished wood floor and an old carved and lacquered table against a wall of glass bricks, again embedded with the family crest. The table was the only piece of furniture in the vast entrance space. Her father liked austerity and emptiness.

Michio sprinted along the corridor toward their father's room, but turned just before that into the extension with the mementoes and kamidana shrine.

There was quiet in the hallway. With the door closed, the waterfall and traffic sounds had gone. Sara heard a whirr of air conditioning or heating. She had never learned what her father did exactly. She had boasted to the American soldier about hotels and banks and golf courses. In reality, she had scant idea, because she had never cared for his power and his wealth. She had two focus points in her family. Michio she loved more than anyone else in the world. And Kazan, who had tried to undermine her for as long as she could remember. She didn't hate him. She wanted him to stop. She wished she could love him. She did love him. He was her twin. But she didn't know what sort of love it was.

Two men stood by the doorway of the house, like Secret Service agents in an American movie. Another came up the stairs, standing on the top step as if to stop Sara going down.

Sara imagined her father would have gone to his private sanctuary. His Yasukuni meeting over, business done, she thought, had his body given up, prompting her mother's scream.

Regret trickled through that she had not got to know him
better. But, how could she? Her father was an impenetrable
pillar, barely human. Even today, she was in tears when she
had thought for a moment that he loved her like a father, only
to find he wanted someone to help run his bloody company,
and only because Kazan was so bloody useless. If he had
wanted her to join, to understand, why send her to that plum-
in-its-mouth boarding school in England? Weird Japanese
cultures had become alien to her. Her father was unfathomable.
She was angry and sad and, more than anything, so dog-tired
that she found she was digging her thumbnail into the side of
her hand, as if that would make sense of it all.

Michio came back, walking along the corridor toward her.
'Sara, you need to come.' He was stern, that commanding
tone. He turned for her to follow which she did. She noticed
he was carrying Kazan's pocket watch in his right hand. Michio
slid back the wooden door to the right. Her father's shrine
room was much as she recalled. There was no view out into
the garden. Natural light came in from high horizontal windows
between the wall and the ceiling. Portraits and photographs
were there with family artifacts, tapestries, old guns, the
Japanese flag, and swords in exquisitely filigreed sheaths
passed down through the Kato generations. Sara recognized
three types from childhood, the tanto, wakizashi and tachi,
which was a long-bladed sword, and each had a name:
Kusunagi-No-Tsurugi, the Grasscutter, Kumorigachi, the
Broken Cloud, Inazuma, the Lightning Strike. There was a
photograph of the old man with the Prime Minister they had
just seen.

Jacob Kato, a hand on each side of his oxygen tube, was
in his wheelchair on the right side of the altar. Her mother, a
tissue crumpled in her hand, sat on an embroidered red tatami
cushion on the other side. Next to her in the corner was a
small cleansing basin with two wooden cups and a silver
dragon-shaped water tap.

Sara's eyes locked onto Kazan, who knelt on a tatami mat
in the middle of the room. Michio took her by both shoulders.
'Father has insisted you be here,' he said in English. 'I told
him, "No." He overruled me.'

Kazan was shivering. His hands were pressed onto the floor, his head lowered.

'What is happening?' Sara asked in a whisper. There was a horrible atmosphere in the room, created by her father. 'Why have you got Kazan's watch?'

'It's from the early Meiji period. It belongs over there,' muttered Michio, pointing to the display on the wall.

'Did he steal it?' Sara sank to her knees in front of Kazan. He looked up, eyes bloodshot. She held him gently by the shoulders. 'It's only a bloody old watch,' she joked. 'Here, get up with me.'

Kazan ignored her hand. Sara tried again in English. 'Forget running the family firm. Let Michio do it. You can travel the world shagging beautiful women.'

'Help me,' pleaded Kazan. 'For God's sake, help me.'

Michio squatted down next to them. He removed Kazan's hand from Sara's and asked him, 'Can you do it? Will you do it?'

A trembling took over Kazan's whole body. Michio looked at their father.

'Sara, come here.' It was her mother. Tears gone, scream silent, she spoke with a strong, decisive voice that Sara didn't recognize. Michio held Sara's elbow. She got up. Her mother patted a cushion next to her for Sara to sit. Two security guards walked in and slid shut the door behind them. Sara shouted across to her father, 'What's going on, Dad?'

The old man said nothing, didn't even acknowledge her.

'Sit.' Her mother again. Sara obeyed. Her mother stood behind with both hands on her shoulders, pushing down with considerable strength. The room was claustrophobic, cluttered with people, myths and bad history. For some reason, an antique watch no one cared about had turned her twin brother into a shuddering mess. She had to get out of here. Take Kazan with her. Michio had to get them out of here. They were all grown up. They didn't need this, three siblings locked in a room waiting on the command of her father. Christ, how she hated it. 'Michio, please.' She stuck to English. 'We don't have to put up with family ritual crap. Let's go.'

Michio's face knotted. The security guards stood either side of Kazan. They held his shoulders just as her mother held hers. Michio moved, quickly, efficiently. She stared, paralyzed, as he drew a sword from a black glossy sheath bound by a red ribbon. Michio cut through his brother's white linen dress shirt with the blade; tore it apart exposing his bare skin. 'Can you do it?' Michio coaxed softly. With his right hand, he held the sword, its blade an inch from Kazan's body. With his left, he lifted each of his brother's hands and placed them with his around the handle. 'Honor is more important than life. For Kato honor, it is better, that it is you. I will be your Kaishakunin, your second.' Kazan was motionless, staring ahead, not resisting, not reacting. '*Nooooooo!*' Sara screamed. She struggled to free herself from her mother, smashed her hand onto her mother's arm. A security guard roughly took her wrist and held her in place.

Michio pushed the sword into Kazan's belly, drew it to the right and then left. He twisted it until blood gushed like from a geyser, splashing onto Michio. Kazan slumped forward, folding in on himself. Michio stood up and stepped back. He bent down and drew out the sword. There was gold and red in the black handle. It was the small one, the Inazuma or Lightning Strike, its blade mixed with the bright red arterial blood fresh from Kazan's heart. Michio handed the sword to a security guard. He walked across to their father and bowed deeply. The old man pointed to another longer sword on the wall display. Michio drew it from the scabbard. He stood behind his trembling, dying brother whose hands were uselessly clasped around his bleeding stomach. Michio lifted the blade and plunged it horizontally into the middle of Kazan's neck, severing the spinal cord and giving instant death. The traditional task of the Kaishakunin was to behead the one who committed ritual suicide. Michio has chosen a neater, faster way. He turned to his father who clasped his son's bloodied hands in his. The security guard rinsed the two swords in the cleansing basin. He wiped them dry, returned them to their sheaths and replaced them on their wall hooks.

'Come,' said her mother. 'We'll go and have tea.'

Sara had to steady herself as she stood up, too weak to do anything except obey. Her mouth was dry. There was no scream

left in her. It was as if she was unconscious or watching
television. Her mother held her arm. Kazan's blood pooled on
the mat. Michio pushed their father around it. Their eyes met
at the door. All Michio's layers of personality had gone. His
eyes were flat and dead. Sara glimpsed a cruel killer and she
was terrified. 'You go first,' Michio told her in Japanese.

Sara could barely put one foot in front of the other. 'Why?'
she said in English.

'Later, for God's sake,' Michio snapped.

The body of her vindictive twin brother was slumped, his
innards spilling out, his flesh cleanly cut open. She knew the
bullshit Japanese death ritual, the shame crap, the suicide crap,
the family honor crap, the emotionally cretinous father crap.
But not this. She didn't know this. She couldn't handle it.
Voices screamed around her head. There was no time for
voices, for thinking, for feeling. She needed to work things
out. She had to hold herself together because what happened
to Kazan could happen to her. Until she got the hell out.

Her father and Michio went ahead. Sara walked side by
side with her mother who held her daughter's arm in an
affectionate way she had never done before. They reached the
hallway.

'We should all change.' Michio held out his bloodied hands,
as if they had got sullied changing oil in the car.

Sara's room was on the top floor, next to Kazan's and
Michio's, overlooking the back garden and the street. She shut
the door firmly behind her and looked for a lock which wasn't
there. Posters from old animated children's television shows
were pinned to the wall above her single little girl's bed. She
had barely used it since she was ten, a child's room with a
couple of backpacks from the Åland Islands out of place on
the same pink floral bedspread that had been there for as long
as she could remember. She had arrived, showered, and
changed straight into the bloody kimono. She angrily ripped
off the obi strap and hurled it into the corner of the room. The
knotted cord ends slapped noisily against the wall. She was
about to hurl something else when she froze herself. She
couldn't lose control. Get a grip. Her teachers' favorite phrase.
She picked up the obi cord and folded it neatly. She stepped

out of the kimono and lay it on the bed, and then the other layers. She put the kimono on the floor and began to fold it, step by step, precise folds, trying to calm herself by checking her memory that she was doing it right for her mother to pack away again. She went to the shower and kept the water warm and let it cleanse her. She scrubbed with a coarse sponge, imagining she was scraping off layers of herself, of what she had seen and turning it into a nightmare that never happened.

Get a grip. Then what? In a few minutes she would put on her jeans, find a clean shirt from her luggage and go down to those murderers and have tea. No, Sara. Don't think like that. She needed to make sense of it. She cut off the shower. In the quiet, without water splashing, the image came right back to her, high-definition, vivid, fresh and real. There was nothing to listen to. Nothing Michio could explain. A wild thought came to her. Stupid, maybe. At least she would be doing something to rebalance her sense of powerlessness.

She reached into her jeans pocket and pulled out the hard black steel phone the American soldier had given her. It wasn't like a commercial phone. She turned it on. There was full battery, full signal. Her thumbprint worked. That green light flicked on. The passcode. Four numbers. Her mind went blank. Nothing. He said it must be easy to remember. But she couldn't. Not her birthday. She felt shattered. She had to keep things together. She laid the phone on the bed. Let herself calm. Slow down. She began slipping her foot into the jeans. It caught on a loose thread. The leg got tangled, and she pushed irritably, propelling the jeans out of her hands onto the floor. She had got them at TK Maxx on Kensington High Street, the first shopping day after one of the Covid lockdowns. Years ago. She took a long, deep, steady breath and the code came back: 0607. Her and Yuri's room numbers on the Åland Islands. She picked up the phone and was about to punch them in when there was a knock and the door opened. 'Can I come in?' It was Michio.

TWENTY-NINE

Rake was in the Oval Office with President John Freeman when his phone screen lit with an alert of an activation of the phone he had left with Sara Kato. Lucas, barely six feet away, got the same message. His gaze met Rake's as Freeman stopped spinning a pen on his desk, looked up from it and asked, 'Major Ozenna. You were there. What is your assessment?'

Rake and Lucas were either side of the marble mantelpiece, at the back of the room, standing under portraits of past presidents. More than a dozen officials stood between them and the President. Nick Petrovsky had insisted they come to the meeting, but to stay quiet, to give their reading afterwards. Everyone was on their feet apart from Freeman, who had asked a lot of questions but not yet come to a decision on when to call the Russian President and what to say.

Under discussion was the impact of Yuri Mishkin's murder on US–Russia relations. This was the type of meeting no one wanted, but everyone needed on their résumé because it could be a defining moment of history. Lucas had briefed the room about Stephanie being with President Sergey Grizlov, who had agreed to keep the murder of his son quiet for only a few hours. After that Russia would know and all hell could break loose. Principals from State to Treasury, through Defense and Homeland Security, had offered advice, all of it circling around the future of America and Russia. Some were hawks, some doves, many veterans of the Ukraine crisis. Some referenced the China threat, none Japan, a given that it was a locked ally and irrelevant to this meeting. On Lucas's advice, Sara Kato's name was not on documents.

Sara's phone had been set with a one-time activation, which meant that once used another number would be automatically allocated. Sara, or whoever had the phone now, would be the only person with this number. Lucas moved toward Rake, edging past the FBI director and an assistant Treasury secretary. His phone was lit up, lying flat in his hand, and said, 'We have to take this, now.'

'Harry Lucas,' interjected Freeman. 'My question is to Major Ozenna. You need to let him answer in his own way.'

'Apologies, sir.' Lucas held up the phone. 'With your permission. This is relevant to our meeting.'

Rake had never seen Freeman close up in person. A few months shy of fifty, he looked older. Gray flecks streaked through his dark hair and a double chin hung from his jaw. Less than a hundred days in, the campaign smile – the beaming projection of purpose that had scraped him enough votes to win the Oval Office – had gone. The President was sharp and irritable and, more than that, Rake knew by an instinct that had saved his life many times that this was a man he could not trust. But that didn't mean he would not work with him.

Those in the room followed Freeman's gaze, turning around to face Rake.

'Gloves off,' Lucas muttered, brow knotted, as he pushed open the door that linked to the Chief of Staff's office and left.

'Ozenna,' prompted Freeman.

Rake wasn't sure what Lucas meant by 'gloves off'. He was a soldier, not a politician. He wasn't seeking high command. He was heading to his island home in Alaska. He had skin in the Kato game, but not skin in this room.

'Yuri Mishkin was the victim of a professional assassination,' he said. 'The person who invited and funded Mishkin's trip is Japanese. Her name is Sara Kato. She is the daughter of a family that controls a global transnational crime network named in Presidential Executive Order 13581. I was there to establish if Sara Kato could become our asset in determining to what extent Kato and affiliated operations posed a threat to our national security. Forensic evidence found Mishkin's bloodstains in Sara Kato's room. The evidence was fabricated. At that point, I was instructed to get her away and keep her safe.'

'Which you did?' Freeman picked up his pen and jabbed it onto a pad in front of him. 'Without querying the order?'

'Yes, sir.' Rake met his gaze head on. 'That is how we are trained.'

'And you kept her safe?' Freeman pressed the pen harder into the pad while eyeballing Rake.

'Until my orders changed, sir. My final order was to leave Sara Kato behind and board a helicopter to Sweden.'

'Mr President, if I may?'

Here we go, thought Rake. He recognized Clive Gold, director of the CIA. The inter-agency turf fight was playing out in the Oval Office with himself, a National Guard major, as the football.

'Sure, Clive. Go ahead.'

'Major, could you confirm that you did all of this without any cross-reference to the CIA or our colleagues at Japan's Cabinet Intelligence and Research Office.' Gold made a point of spelling out the CIA's Japanese counterpart. One current foreign policy fight going on was about Japan's partnership with the Five Eyes intelligence-gathering network. The question was a trap, but to hesitate would show a weakness, and Lucas had instructed him to take off the gloves.

'CIA liaison is outside my brief and above my pay grade,' replied Rake. 'The authority for my work comes from the previous administration and remains until it is withdrawn.'

'How do you know it remains?' challenged Gold.

'I am on secondment from the Alaska National Guard. I have not been recalled to my unit and I have seen nothing to show that the authority has been rescinded.' Rake paused, but in a way that the room knew he was not yet finished. 'The reason that agencies such as yours, sir, were kept out of the loop is with the President.'

Faces tightened. Lips curled. Heads tilted. Feet shuffled. Hands clasped and unclasped, Rake had laid down a direct challenge to the US President and CIA director. His dark green uniform, black hair and leathered skin stood out against the pastel wallpaper and gray-white marble of the mantelpiece. There were people in the room who had seen plenty of action. But they were now manicured executives. Rake wasn't. He did not need Freeman on his side. Yet how each responded to Rake's challenge could determine the rest of their careers.

Eyes shifted from one to the other. Who was an ally, who an enemy? People checked artwork around the Oval Office.

They looked anywhere except at John Freeman, who kept his searchlight focus on Rake.

'Come up here and explain yourself, Major.' The President ran his finger down a tablet on the desk.

Freeman was either giving him a boost or setting another trap.

THIRTY

Rake maneuvered through the room. Most edged aside, keeping their eyes away. Two laid a hand on his shoulder, showing support. As he approached the front, Nick Petrovsky staked his own future by firmly shaking Rake's hand and gripping his right elbow. Turning to face the room, he saw worried expressions. Too many felt out of the loop. Rake spoke directly to CIA director Gold. 'Sir, you were kept out because you would have shared with your Japanese counterparts where it would have been compromised.'

The director opened his mouth to object. Freeman raised his hand to stay quiet.

Rake continued, 'The previous administration had given former Congressman Lucas a specific and highly classified brief. His reporting line was to individuals, not institutions, and had not yet been adapted to this administration. Security threats do not take note of our electoral cycles, which is why many of you did not know what we were doing.' He spoke without emotion. It was as it was. He had no view one way or another.

'President Merrow tasked us to investigate transnational crime networks that posed an extreme threat. I was seconded on agreement from the Alaska National Guard. Confidentiality is needed because all governments use private transnational networks to execute parts of their foreign policy. That includes our own. The separation of state and private differs from country to country. In China and Russia, the private sector is beholden to the state for its existence. In Japan, it is blurred because of culture, tradition, and weak legislation surrounding organized crime. That Japanese blur in recent years has become dangerous—'

'Mr President,' interrupted the Secretary of Defense. 'Japan is our closest ally, the bedrock of our dominance in the Indo-Pacific. I am not sure where Major Ozenna is going with this.'

'Then let Ozenna go there,' said Freeman.

'You are correct, sir. Japan is our closest ally in Asia.' Rake looked straight at the Secretary of Defense. 'But there is regional friction. Japan and China over their bad history; the same with Japan and South Korea, and Japan and Russia over the Kuril Islands or Northern Territories, which stopped them signing a peace treaty to end the Second World War.'

'You're kidding?' exclaimed Freeman.

'I'm not, sir.'

Freeman rolled his eyes. 'No one tells you these things.'

'Bad blood slows trade,' said Rake. 'Crime networks move in to fill the vacuum.'

'Mr President, sir.' CIA director Gold again. 'Major Ozenna's emphasis is wrong. Yes, there is organized crime in Japan. But there is no threat whatsoever to the United States. Our relationship is rock solid.'

'Sir?'

'Go ahead, Frank,' said Freeman. Frank Marshall was the FBI Director. Rake had not logged him, barely recognized him. He had a tough, stubby face, narrow eyes, high forehead, dark cropped hair, short neck, and the look of a bulldog.

'The FBI has found patterns similar to that outlined by Major Ozenna.' Marshall made a point of moving his gaze between Freeman and Rake. 'The more crime becomes entrenched, the harder it is to distinguish between criminal and legitimate entities. The more sophisticated a group is, the less visible it becomes.'

'And you have this evidence, Frank?' Freeman laid down the pen. He was interested.

'Yes, sir. I have evidence that – if left unchecked – Japanese crime could impact negatively on our own financial and democratic systems.'

The President spoke to the CIA, director. 'Clive, your response?'

'The Japanese have bought in laws. Yakuza numbers have plummeted. Frank, you're talking about setting up prostitution and gambling rackets, not the kind of threat—'

Frank Marshall cut in, 'Wrong metric, Clive. People are no longer declaring syndicate membership because that is illegal. But they stay on the payroll. Numbers are increasing. They have name cards, offices and three-thousand-dollar suits. These are not night-club bouncers.'

'Such as,' challenged Gold.

Marshall raised a hand, asking for a moment to decide on what or how much to reveal.

'We don't have all day, Frank,' interjected Freeman. 'Either you have it at your fingertips, or you don't.'

Marshall spoke directly to Freeman. 'We have evidence of racketeering and two homicide charges against Kazan Kato, sir. The Japanese government are being slow to cooperate.'

Lucas walked back in, and Freeman said, 'Did you know that, Harry? The FBI and Kazan Kato, the younger brother?'

Surprise washed through Lucas's expression. 'Kazan. I did not.' He swung his gaze to Marshall who said, 'We didn't share, Harry. Same reason you didn't.'

'Seems I'm in one of my first Oval Office inter-agency dogfights,' said Freeman. 'Harry, do I need to know anything from that call you took?'

'Not yet, sir.' Lucas slipped his phone into his jacket pocket.

'Then, come up here and help us resolve a disagreement. Can we trust Japan?'

'Over Kazan Kato, sir, or—'

'No. Big picture. Japan is our most important ally in the Indo-Pacific.'

People stepped aside to let Lucas through. 'Our troops are there. It's a democracy. It is our main military ally as we face Russia, China, North Korea – hostile forces we know a lot about.' Lucas reached the President's desk and turned to face the others. 'Japan is on our side. But we don't know enough about it, and Japan could have threats within itself that leave us exposed.'

Freeman's eyes were on his pen, which he picked up again, spun around and hooked between the fingers of his right hand.

The room waited for his cue. They didn't get it. 'That'll be all, everyone,' he said. 'Thank you for your time.'

'Mr President, sir.' An unfamiliar voice.

'Later, Max. That's it for now.'

The abrupt dismissal of so many senior figures took on a ripple effect, like heavy rain across a lake. The meeting was inconclusive, its participants' stature weakened or fortified on a presidential turn of phrase. They filed out in silence, a mix of uniforms and suits, through the door to the right that led into the area with the President's secretary and other staff. Rake moved to go with them, and Freeman said, 'Harry, Ozenna, Nick, a moment more.'

Freeman flipped up his pen to hold it between his fingers. It was black with gold rims and Rake saw the logo of a Florida golf club. Worry was still there, but he looked more in control than when Rake had been watching him from the other end of the room. The Oval Office door clicked shut. Freeman said, 'What you got, Harry?'

'Sara Kato—'

'The mobster's sister from the Finland mess.'

'Yes, sir.' Lucas noticeably flinched at Freeman's blunt encapsulation. 'She used an encrypted phone given her by Ozenna to try to make contact. Her location was the Kato family home in Tokyo, less than an hour after the family returned from the Yasukuni Shrine. It's safe to presume Sara was in that meeting with her father and the Prime Minister.'

'Your conclusion is that something in the meeting prompted her to reach out?'

'More than that. There would have been a dozen people she could have called. She barely knows Ozenna. What she saw or heard must have a direct bearing on the Åland Islands and Yuri Mishkin's murder and, of course, our future path with Russia.'

The reference to Russia made Freeman's eyes light up. 'Then we need to get to her, and what the hell is this you've been doing with this Kato family, Harry?'

Rake wondered how much Lucas would reveal. Congress wouldn't understand it. The news networks even less. A multi-agency turf fight on national priorities risked blocking any chance of fixing things before it was too late. Lucas was noncommittal. 'It could be a lot of issues, sir,' he answered. 'I don't want to mislead. Once I get back into my systems, I can crunch it down.'

'Get it done, Nick,' Freeman instructed Petrovsky. 'Whatever Harry had before, give it back to him.'

In two brief sentences, Lucas had got his security clearance fully restored and trashed whoever had advised Freeman to shut him down.

'I've had another call.' Lucas portrayed his phone like evidence in a courtroom. 'From Moscow, Mr President. You need to talk to Sergey Grizlov. You need to do it now.'

THIRTY-ONE

Stephanie woke feeling Grizlov's warm, smooth skin and his leg hooked over hers. He lay wide awake, hands behind his head, staring toward the ceiling and barely moving. She leant across and kissed him on the lips, full and sexual, to let him know that she had not spent the night with him out of sympathy.

Exhausted and dulled in a way that only came with the finality of death, they had talked randomly and personally, mixing grief with politics with anger and thoughts of revenge. There had been no good way to spend those hours. She had microwaved them borsch soup from a cupboard in the small kitchen: They hadn't wanted staff in fixing them a meal. Neither had drunk.

'Stay with me, Steph,' he had said.

'Of course.' She pointed to another door. 'Is there—'

'I mean really with me, like the old days.' His hands clasped around hers. 'Or I'll have to get staff in to make up another bed.' His expression was half joking and half pleading. He didn't want to be alone, even if she was just a wall away in another room.

She looked at him, confirming, but saying nothing. They

had been lovers, and he needed love. She had forgotten how
much she craved intimacy. In bed with him, she realized
how much she missed it, the need to fix that empty part of
her life. They knitted together like old friends, bodies more
worn, skin looser, his hands moving over her as they had three
decades earlier, kindly, attentive, remembering her buttons to
push, and those buttons held up surprisingly well. It was all
right that his mind had been on his son and not on her because
that is what intimacy and friendship was about.

'How are you?' He kissed her back. She could tell he was
staying with his thoughts: You don't get to be President of the
Russian Federation by taking your eye off the ball. No notepad,
no tablet, Grizlov would be planning the next few hours and
keeping the finest details all in his head.

'You want to talk to Freeman?' She unhooked his leg from
hers.

'Yes.'

'Coffee?' She sat up and stretched.

'Thanks.'

Stephanie quickly showered and put on a white toweling
robe hanging on the back of the door. Her clothes were folded
neatly on a small green armchair in the corner. Drying her
hair with a towel, she walked barefoot to the kitchen, fired up
the coffee machine, called Harry and said he needed to get
Freeman ready.

'Is Sergey still going to go public?' Harry asked.

'Unless Freeman can talk him out of it, and I doubt he'll
succeed.'

'Why. What's he said?'

'He can't do it any other way,' she said. 'He can't let the
Americans run the investigation into his son's death. Not for
himself. Not as President. Unless Freeman has any bright
ideas.'

Harry began speaking about organized crime and Japan, but
Stephanie cut in. 'Yuri was killed by Americans.'

'Hired by Japanese.'

'You don't have that.'

'Not yet.'

'We don't have time for "not yet", for Christ's sake. If

Freeman wants it to work, he'll have to pledge support for Russia, even if Japan is implicated.'

'Japan's not implicated.'

'So, fix the call, Harry. Get them talking. We're running out of wriggle room.' She ended the call, put on her clothes and went back with two black coffees. Grizlov was up and dressed, no suit, a black T-shirt and jeans, the attire he used for his tough-guy leader photographs. He looked good, grief vanished from his expression.

'Harry's setting up a call.'

Grizlov held the small cup in both hands. 'I'll do it in the secure area in the main house.' He took a sip of coffee. 'And thank you for last night.'

'It wasn't out of sympathy.' Stephanie ran her hand lightly down his arm. 'I liked it. So, thank you.'

'Grief narrows the world. You helped stop that.' Grizlov put the cup on the low table on his side of the bed.

Stephanie smiled. 'What's that thing they say about grief being the price we pay for love.'

'But I barely knew him, Steph. I loved him because he was my son, not because of who he was. I was filling a space for love and that's a confusing thought. But, for today, with Yuri, the politics supersede the personal.' He took a dark blue blazer from the wardrobe, hooked it over his shoulder and brushed his right fingers like a comb hand through his salt-pepper gray hair. He kissed Stephanie on the lips. She tasted of coffee and toothpaste. He held her tight and close to him. 'Come.' He stepped back. 'There's someone I want you to meet.'

Not a good time for surprises, thought Stephanie. Grizlov led them through to the main room, where the sofa was creased and cushions rumpled, and the smell of a borsch soup hung in the air from the evening before.

Grizlov ignored the mess and opened the apartment door. A tall woman with long loose gray hair walked straight past him with no greeting. She wore a dark business suit, was about Stephanie's age, and she showed no astonishment at seeing her.

Standing ramrod upright, she deftly pulled off her snow boots, one at a time. Grizlov took her coat, hung it up and said in Russian. 'Tatania, this is Baroness Stephanie Lucas from London. She is an old friend. Stephanie, this is Dr Tatania Mishkin, who is deputy speaker of the state Duma.' Grizlov gave Stephanie a long, slow, commanding look. 'But that is not why she is here. Tatania is Yuri's mother.'

'I've heard about you, Lady Lucas,' said Tatania dully.

Stephanie had ridden a career of curve balls and precarious turns of events. This one gave her a bad feeling. Grizlov could have warned her, and he hadn't. Tatania's hair was pinned back. She wore no make-up, no jewelry, giving her a mannish look. There was no visible self-doubt, either. She had a hard, don't-mess-with-me expression. Stephanie recognized it. She often wore the same.

Grizlov had deceived Stephanie by not telling her Tatania was coming, and she understood what he was doing. The American mindset would immediately side with a man unable to withhold from the mother news of their son's death. But Yuri's mother was also a senior parliamentarian. If Tatania Mishkin wanted to go public, Grizlov could not gag her.

'Stephanie.' Grizlov's voice was strong. 'Could you tell Tatania exactly what you told me about Yuri's murder and show her the photographs?'

Stephanie inwardly recoiled at Grizlov's new mood and what he wanted her to do. She had seen enough of those sickening photographs. She lay the tablet on the low coffee table, just as she had before. To her surprise, Grizlov left her to it. He returned to the bedroom. She sat with Tatania, running through the photographs, while hearing the low murmur of Grizlov's numerous phone conversations.

Tatania gave no reaction as Stephanie explained the Åland Islands, Sara Kato, the way the conference was meant to work and the different conflicts. When she came to the gruesome police procedural shots of the body, there was not a flicker of change in Tatania's expression. She did not ask Stephanie to pause on one particular image. She listened, watched and when Stephanie fell quiet, she got to her feet, stood in front of the bedroom door and folded her arms, waiting for Grizlov to finish. When his conversation fell into a lull, she said loudly, 'Sergey. Stop and come here.'

Grizlov stepped back in. Tatania slapped him hard across his right cheek and with equal force on his left with the back of her hand. His eyes squeezed shut. His face reddened. He did not move. He kept his hands lowered, as if to say: hit me as much as you want.

'Who did this?' she demanded.

'I don't know yet.' Grizlov shrugged, a signal to Stephanie that he was prepared to hold back on detail.

'I raised him by myself,' Tatania said. 'I sheltered him from you because I knew your ambition.'

'I am sorry. I am so, so sorry.' Grizlov kept his gaze on her. Tatania swung around to Stephanie. 'Did he tell you I am a virologist? Did he tell you that I study our melting permafrost? Did he tell you that some things are best left frozen because of diseases that lie beneath? Did he tell you how I begged him not to see Yuri, to leave things frozen and harmless?' She turned back and jabbed her finger at Grizlov. 'They found out he was your son and they killed him because they couldn't kill you.' Like swinging a rifle, she pointed at Stephanie. 'Why is she here? Why is she telling you this and not our own people?'

'Dr Mishkin.' Stephanie needed to protect the imminent conversation with Freeman. 'The Americans made the identification of exactly who Yuri was through their intelligence databases. Because of that, they asked me to break the news. All three of us understand the significance.'

A sharp Russian voice came through a speaker somewhere. 'The President of the United States, sir.'

'I have to go.' Grizlov took Tatania's hand and brushed his lips over it.

'Promise me,' insisted Tatania. 'Yuri's death will not go unpunished.'

Those who seek revenge should dig two graves, thought Stephanie, a quote from Confucius. She stayed quiet. Emotions were raw, hidden and dangerous.

'I promise.' Grizlov turned to Stephanie. 'You both need to stay here.'

Tatania reached up to touch Grizlov's cheek, affection after anger. 'Those who killed Yuri are trying to destroy Russia. We must destroy them first. No compromise, Sergey. You will bring to justice those who used a knife on our son, and to those who paid them to kill, to any who aided and abetted his death. Do you understand that, Sergey? The murder of our son was an attack on all of us in the Motherland.'

THIRTY-TWO

John Freeman stood in front of the Oval Office desk, Lucas and Petrovsky on one side, Rake on the other. A screen above the mantelpiece showed the empty chair that Grizlov would take. His people said he didn't need an interpreter. The conversation would be short, informal and conducted in English.

Grizlov appeared looking fit, alert, and dressed in a dark blazer over a black T-shirt. He sat down, pulling a silver microphone toward him. 'John Freeman,' he began. 'Our first meeting is shrouded in unfortunate circumstances.'

'I am so sorry, Mr President,' said Freeman. 'All our thoughts are with you. I know you had been estranged, but—'

Grizlov broke in. 'That is immaterial. We are leaders of our countries.' He looked straight into the camera, no trace of personal tragedy on his face. 'You want to turn the relationship around. I think that is a good idea. Now we have this.'

'Of course. I understand.' Freeman's face was tight. He had not been in office long enough to experience the nuances of a leader-to-leader conversation. He shifted on his feet, keeping his expression stable, but showing irritation at the way Grizlov was taking a lead.

Grizlov continued. 'You need to share with us all the evidence you have. We will be asking the Finnish government for access to the American citizens in custody.'

'Sergey, if I may—'

Grizlov ignored him. 'We will be asking Japan to share details of the organization that funded my son's trip to Finland and the woman he met there.' Grizlov put his hand on the base of the microphone and pushed back in his seat.

'There's a lot there, Sergey. Why don't you—'

'Who ordered the murder?'

'We would like to work with you on that. We need to set up systems.'

Grizlov tapped the top of the microphone, sending a thud, thud, thud down the line. 'You have two hours and I'm going to give you an unwelcome home truth. No country needs America anymore. If they once thought they did, they are finding ways around it, and realizing they are better off without you lecturing and breathing down their necks. Whether you're an Afghani, a Ukrainian, a Russian or a Japanese, you don't stake your future on friendship with America.'

'Sergey, I can assure you—'

'You can assure me nothing, John. Whatever deal you and I might be signing, it could get blown away four years from now when a new President comes in. We view the murder of my son as an attack on Russia itself. Our SVR will be making direct contact with the CIA and cooperation will flow from there. Let's get this done.'

The screen closed to black. The speaker spat out static until a technician shut it down. Freeman wiped his hand across his brow, turned to Petrovsky and asked testily, 'What the hell was that?'

'Strategic belligerence to mask his grief,' suggested Petrovsky.

'He meant it,' countered Lucas. 'Grizlov will do exactly as he says.'

'How much can we share?' asked Freeman.

'We can't, sir,' conceded Lucas. 'Not everything, and if we hold back, Grizlov will know.' Lucas ended the sentence abruptly. Rake detected hesitation; Lucas asking himself if this was the time to tell what they knew about the threat posed by the Kato family. As much as Lucas distrusted John Freeman, he was the President of the United States.

'Harry, you look like you have more to say,' challenged Freeman.

'Yes, sir.' His mind was made up, Lucas's vacillation vanished. 'Your predecessor tasked me to keep a track of missing nuclear material that could be used in weapons programs.'

'We already have that,' interjected Freeman. 'We spend billions on it.'

'This was different.' Lucas held up a hand to press his point. 'I was to examine transnational crime networks with strong links to their national governments. This is why we did not share with other agencies.'

'Why? Explain?' Freeman sat in the high-back leather chair behind his desk.

'Because of the risk of leak, sir.'

'So, spill it.' Freeman looked at Petrovsky who stayed impassive, giving Harry no support.

'We believe Japan may have built nuclear weapons in a program supported by elements within the British and American governments.' Lucas paused, allowing for a response. Freeman rolled his Florida golf club pen back and forth over his desk. Petrovsky stood, arms folded, gazing at the carpet.

Lucas continued, 'Since the mid-seventies, highly enriched plutonium and uranium has been syphoned off in the US, Britain and Japan and stored in facilities in Japan. There is enough stockpile to build fifty or so warheads.'

'Bullshit,' muttered Petrovsky.

'Not bullshit, Nick,' said Lucas calmly. 'Some of it has reached the press. Small amounts of unaccounted-for nuclear fuel has become so routine in our industry here that it is listed under an acronym MUF, Material Unaccounted For.'

'All right, Harry.' Freeman stopped his pen in mid-roll. 'The whole thing. A to Z. Spell it out.'

'We didn't share because we didn't know who or what in the US was involved. There is growing belief in Britain, the US and Japan that the world would be a safer place if Japan were a nuclear weapons power. None of this is new. But it is constant. Way back in 1975, the *New York Times* reported plutonium missing from a plant in Oklahoma, as well as from at least fifteen other facilities. In 1987, two hundred kilograms of plutonium, that's twenty-five warheads, went missing from the Tokai nuclear reprocessing plant, northeast of Tokyo. The government said it was a result of miscalculation and measuring mistakes. Nothing was done about it. In 2005, 29.6 kilograms of plutonium went missing in Britain, enough for around seven warheads. The government waved it off, saying there was no real loss of plutonium.'

'What do we know about this?' Freeman snapped at Petrovsky.

'This is all public record.' Petrovsky opened his arms to show exasperation. 'Like Harry said, the *New York Times*.'

'So, what's new, Harry?' Freeman pushed back his chair and looked distractedly out of the window to the snow-laden Rose Garden.

Lucas said, 'What's new is that this material is not under the control of the Japanese government as we thought, but of the Kato family, which began the program after we lost Vietnam in 1975.'

'That's half a century ago.' Freeman swung his gaze back inside. 'Go on.'

Lucas had his attention. 'In June 1975, two months after the fall of Saigon, Tozen Kato, the father of Jacob and grand-father of Sara, initiated a plan to protect Japan in the case of American retreat. Uppermost in his mind was that, after losing Vietnam, the US would fail to fight for Japan should China or Russia attack. Kato's sentiment was not unlike that which rippled through many governments after Afghanistan in 2021.'

Freeman raised his hand for Lucas to pause. 'This Kato family?'

Lucas picked up seamlessly. 'The family became what it is through Tozen Kato's father. He was the old samurai class, fallen on hard times. Tozen was smart enough to befriend street kids, show them respect, and he molded them into a gang that broke through to control a district of Kobe. Over the years he expanded his operation and set up in Tokyo. His son, Jacob, was born in 1939. He recreated stories about his family being part of a long lineage of Japanese aristocracy stretching back centuries. We don't know how much is true. Jacob was educated at the best Japanese schools and took on the Yakuza mantel with a flourish. During the boom years of the 1970s and 1980s, he built what has become the Kato empire, while continuing with his father's goal of giving Japan its own independent security umbrella. In 1975, he reached out to the British, American, French and Canadian governments. France and Canada refused. Britain and America agreed. Jacob is now dying. His oldest son, Michio, was the heir apparent, but his younger brother, Kazan, now seems to be in the frame. Kazan's twin sister is Sara Kato, who has effectively been excluded from the family since being sent away to an English boarding school aged ten.'

'Jacob, not a very Japanese name?' said Freeman.

'On the nail, sir,' agreed Lucas. 'Seeing the writing on the wall about American power, Tozen gave Jacob a Western first name and Jacob did the same to his children. Their names are interchangeable with other cultures. Michio, Sara – and Kazan isn't even a traditional name. It literally means volcano: fiery, powerful, unpredictable.'

Rake hadn't known that, hadn't thought much about it. But the way Lucas and Petrovsky fell quiet indicated they shared his thoughts. Fiery and powerful and a nuclear weapons program. Maybe Kazan had been the heir apparent all along, until something went wrong.

Petrovsky picked up, 'Do we know where the missing nuclear material is?'

'Partly. Stockpiled in Japan's reprocessing plants. But we don't know if it's all there or who controls it. The Kato family are entwined with the country's nuclear industry, from weapons research to bricks-and-mortar construction to security around nuclear facilities.'

Rake listened while thinking through logistics, running possible triggers for Michio Kato to launch a nuclear attack. And if there was one, what would be his target? The killing of Yuri Mishkin would be aimed at wrecking Freeman's attempt to befriend Russia. It was timed to precede the family's visit to the Yasukuni Shrine and that would have taken some planning, the date set weeks, maybe months ahead. There was no coincidence. Even while Freeman was talking, Rake pulled out his phone and spooled through dates that could have made February significant. There were Arctic Eagle military exercises in Alaska that took place every year. Russia was holding its Vostok exercises in Siberia. Not enough. Something wider. To expand his crime empire, Michio would want to weaken America's ties with Japan and bolster his own influence.

'Major, are we boring you?' said Freeman. 'Or do you want to put that phone away.'

The obvious lit up on Rake's screen. 'The eleventh of February, sir?'

'What about it?'

'Japan's National Foundation Day. If the threat is imminent, this could explain the timing of the Yasukuni Shrine meeting.'

Freeman let out a short laugh, part jeering, part nervous. 'I think you're simplifying, Major, to grab a speculative date out of the air.'

'Our enemy is the Kato operation. And our best, quickest way in there is through Sara Kato. She has just tried to call us.'

Freeman shook his head. 'And putting so much relevance on this one woman.'

Freeman's Chief of Staff peered around the door to his office. 'Sir, you have the Majority Leader. We can't afford—'

'Yeah. I know.' Freeman waved the Chief of Staff away and turned his attention back to Rake. 'If you were in my seat, what would be your plan?'

'I would send a team to Tokyo to find Sara Kato. Stop the Kato threat. Revive your initiative with Russia.'

'And how are you going to do that?'

'We attack the threat at source. Sara Kato is his sister. She will lead us to Michio. As the saying goes, Mr President, we cut the head off the snake.'

THIRTY-THREE

Tokyo

'It's not as if I haven't seen my sister get dressed before,' said Michio, walking into Sara's bedroom. He closed the door, pushing a tautness on the hinge to make sure it clicked shut. He had showered and was wearing denim jeans, a casual blue shirt and a faint musk-smelling aftershave. He carried a plastic folder, acting as if nothing had happened, giving Sara the smile that had reassured her since she was a little girl. He looked as if he were about to sit next to her on the bed. Sara stiffened completely, felt herself going rigid like a concrete post, in a way she had never done with anyone. Total rejection. Total survival mechanism. Michio noticed and chose a small blue velvet armchair draped with her clothes. 'This OK?' he asked.

No, she wanted to shout. *Get out. This is my space. Don't come anywhere near me. Don't smile. Don't explain.* She couldn't speak. No words. No voice. She could barely explain it to herself. She had been a Japanese child raised by foreigners in a faraway land. How much she had cried and craved to come home and be with her family. How often she had dreamed that Michio would come and get her because he loved her and would make sure she had a home in her country. He had come eventually, but with no love, only some kind of sick evil. She fought to keep her composure.

Michio moved her clothes and lay them on the end of the bed. Sara put her all into keeping her hands steady as she buckled her jeans, feeling the pocket to make sure the American's phone was there. Terror mushroomed that Michio would find the phone and kill her, stab her, rip out her guts like he did with Kazan. She felt the dryness of her mouth.

'That was horrible. I am so, so sorry you had to see that.' He covered his face with his hands and pushed hard against his chin. When he took them away, his eyes were red and teared. 'It was horrible.' He held out the folder to Sara, his hands shaking. She didn't move. Couldn't move. Pretended she was tightening her belt buckle.

'Please, Sara.' He switched to English. 'Please. I need to share it with you.'

The folder was strong transparent plastic from her father's office. Inside, were single-sheet papers in a mix of English and Japanese. There was a report with the circular Federal Bureau of Investigation logo on the letterhead; another from a private psychiatric practice in New York; another in Japanese from the head of security at one of her father's companies. The final document was made up of two sheets stapled together, in Japanese. Sara recognized Kazan's handwriting. She glanced through, unsure of what she was seeing and why. She shot

Michio a heated, hateful look. She shook her head violently back and forth.

'God, this room is claustrophobic,' he said. 'Let's get out of here. I know this great place in Shibuya.' Michio waved his hand toward the window and began to get up.

No. Not outside with him. Pull yourself together, Sara. The English boarding schoolteacher's command took over. Get a grip. She opened the file, felt resolve take hold and said, 'We're going nowhere until you explain.'

'Father is asleep. Mother is resting,' he whispered. 'We're family, Sara. We have to stick together.'

'I'm not moving, unless you want to kill me like you did our brother.' Sara collated the sheets back into the folder, kept it on her lap, stared at Michio. They stayed in silence for a long time. Michio sat upright, his hands firmly on the arms of the chair. Sara leant forward, elbows on her knees, hands covering the folder. An image of Kazan's final seconds leapt into her vision. She squeezed her eyes and gave her brother a look which dared him to harm her.

'I didn't want to do it, Sara. I pleaded with Father. I pleaded with Kazan. They both insisted it be me. For the honor of the family. For the future of the family. For you, Sara—'

Sara slammed her right hand down on the folder. 'No. You shit. Don't you fucking dare.'

'All right.' Michio raised two trembling hands. 'Kazan was wanted by the FBI.'

'What for?'

'Racketeering. They were pinning organized criminal activity onto him. He had been shooting his mouth off and was about to be arrested here for extradition to America.'

'So, you killed him?' It was challenge, and she wanted to say so much more, to tell him to go to burn in hell for cutting up their brother like a piece of raw meat. But she was frightened of him, the house, her parents, all the men guarding them.

'It was our father.' Michio's voice dropped so as to be barely audible. 'A few years back I was involved in something in Europe that went wrong. Father went crazy. He ranted about family honor and shame and insisted I step aside. I was shaken, naturally, and went to a retreat in Hokkaido. I lived with the

mountain priests. I walked in mountains and bathed in icy
waterfalls. I did fire purification, some Bōjutsu, staff fighting.
A lot of stuff like that. I learnt to master my emotions. I wish
Kazan had done the same. Then, Father called me back and
told me Kazan was causing problems.' He pointed to the folder.
'The FBI have two murder cases against Kazan.'

'But Kazan's not a murderer.' Sara bit her lip.

'No. But they have audio of Kazan boasting. Father said
we could not allow him to be arrested.' He shook his head
sadly. 'Kazan knew too much, and he would never have shut
up. It's hard. It takes mental rigor to be head of a family like
ours, and Kazan doesn't have it.'

'Didn't have,' corrected Sara. 'He's dead.'

'Yes. Didn't. Past tense. Sorry. Kazan had a choice of life
in an American prison. He would have turned informer and
we would have had to have dealt with it. Or he faced an end
here, at home, with honor and with his family.' Michio stepped
across to the window where clouds and late afternoon winter
light cast a gloom over the cityscape. He faced Sara, backlit,
looking down on her. He repeated exactly what he had just
said about honor and family in Japanese. It was a clever thing
to do. In English, it sounded stupid and defeatist. In Japanese,
it made sense. In some crazy way, it sounded obvious.

'Father thought he had arranged it well. Kazan would be
seen publicly with the Prime Minister as the heir. Then, he
would disappear, like I did.' Michio pushed his hands against
the arms of the chair and began to stand up.

'No.' Sara put both arms out, blocking. 'Don't you touch me.'

Michio's confidence faded. His face became shadowed with
a sad, quizzical look, as if he couldn't understand her. 'He was
meant to do it himself.' His tone was pleading. 'But he chick-
ened out. Father insisted that I did it and that you watched.'

'And you just obeyed him?' Sara formed her outstretched arms
into a cross, blocking her brother mentally and physically.

'I've lost Kazan. I don't want to lose you, Sara. I can't.'

'So why involve me? Did you know . . .' Sara fought to
keep her voice low as she remembered her thrill at seeing
Michio outside the hut. 'Did you know you were bringing me
back to witness Kazan's murder?'

'It was the right thing to do.' Michio's voice was low but seemed to shift from regret to certainty. He reached out both hands. Sara didn't move. 'I couldn't have done it alone.' His lips were tight, his expression vulnerable. 'I needed you with me. I needed your support in taking over this shitty family.'

'I don't understand,' Sara managed. *To kill our brother* echoed around her head.

'The family is more important than any single life. I know it's different in England. But that is how it is here. My duty is to clean it up, to leave our father a legacy, and I need you by my side, Sara. I need to work with you.'

Sara half listened to Michio continuing his justification. She tried to work it out, her Japanese and Western values battling against each other. This fucking shame thing! No way would she be part of it. She must escape, get far away from her family, Tokyo, Japan. She believed Michio. Trusted him in a way, was grateful for his honesty. But as her brother, he was gone. His mind was fucked up, dressing Kazan's murder as a necessity. And the way he did it, so easily, so fast, with no hesitation. She needed fresh air, a street, a train, an airport, an exit.

She handed the folder to Michio and stood up. She took a breath, braced herself and hugged him. He wasn't expecting it. She smelled his freshly laundered shirt, taken aback by how his warmth comforted her. What the fuck! Fight it, Sara. He could kill you. She let him go and took a jacket and scarf from the back of the door. 'You're right,' she said. 'Let's get the hell out of here. Take me to whatever that place is in Shibuya.'

THIRTY-FOUR

Fresh air injected energy into Sara, but not enough to penetrate the cascade of reactions, her grief, her anger and her fear of her older brother. She needed emotional discipline to maintain the façade that she supported the vile thing he had to do. She kept the smile. She touched his arm when speaking as they drove to Shibuya, tactile, in a very un-Japanese way. She was chatty, looking up at skyscrapers draped with sparkling advertisement. She gazed at pedestrian walkways flowing with people, a fluttering sea of colored umbrellas, stretched across wide, busy roads like bridges over rivers. Shibuya made London's Piccadilly Circus feel like a sleepy village. Sara squeezed her eyes shut, craving scrappy little London more than anything.

When she said she needed money, Michio tried to give her yen. When she pressed to get out and go to a cash machine, Michio came with her, surrounding her with his goons. He insisted on showing her around, taking her along narrow streets where bar and café owners bowed and scraped. She heard how their father and grandfather had helped them set up their businesses. Michio was proud and wanted Sara to be proud too. They went through a counter bar where three elderly men sat on stools. Michio led Sara into a wide stairwell, smelling of new paint. One floor up was an elevator with an old gilt-framed mirror inside and a dark blue velvet bench. An attendant wore a white uniform with gloves. Michio talked about a bygone era. They stepped into a large airy space with a view over Tokyo, a marble mantelpiece, a mirror encased in red velvet and a long, curving wooden bar, so highly polished that it glittered with reflections of a chandelier. An overweight manager greeted Michio. When the bowing was done, he led them to a table that looked as if it was made from a slab of thick wood, the type Sara imagined an English Tudor king having for banquets.

'It's our newest joint.' Michio slid into his seat. 'Let's savor it before we move on. Order something really special.'

Part challenge, part grasping for the old Michio, Sara ordered a Chitose Ame, the red-and-white striped candy that Michio had given her during her upsetting Shichi-Go-San at the Yasukuni Shrine.

'They don't sell that here.' Michio raised his eyebrows in surprise. 'That's for kids.'

'I know. It reminds me of the seaside red-and-white rock sticks you get in England.' She shrugged with an apologetic smile. Michio didn't remember his gift at the shrine. 'I'm not really hungry. I'll just have a lychee ramune.' That was the soft drink he had given her.

'Something more substantial, surely.' He looked at her strangely.

Sara shook her head. Michio matched her and ordered a kukicha tea, made from twigs of the shrub. 'We're like a couple of monks,' he quipped. 'We should celebrate.'

'I'm not celebrating,' Sara snapped. 'Our brother is dead. We grieve.'

Michio's eyes hardened. She had never felt fear like this, and her anger put her in more danger. She had lost two brothers today, but she had to keep going. She trailed Tokyo with him, sometimes walking, sometimes taking a short car ride. When she went to the restroom, someone was there. When she said she needed fresh air, they went out and to another place. He talked at her, and she kept saying she understood. He pointed out to her the greatness of Japan in one nightclub, where many young women wore kimonos. He yelled through the music, 'See, they are rejecting Western fashion and ideology because it has only brought Japan humiliation.'

In a quieter place, sitting at a counter bar, hands wrapped around a glass of Japanese single malt whisky, he said, 'You and I were born into something, Sara. The way to deal with it is not to ignore it but to adapt yourself to make it work.'

'Sure. Good point,' she said. *Adapt myself to become a killer. Fuck you.*

She tried again, not expecting success. She told him she was fading and would get a hotel, bringing out her phone to scroll through and find one. But, of course, he already had a hotel lined up. When they got there, Michio's security was everywhere. It looked like they had the floor, luxurious rooms with fabulous views – a prison. Deep in her jeans pocket was Rake Ozenna's phone. She would try again with a message. Her memory of Rake was sharp. It was natural to trust a brother over a savage-looking guy with guns you had just met. But now that brother was not who she thought he was and, deep inside, she trusted the American, Ozenna.

She crawled under the bedclothes so Michio's surveillance cameras couldn't see her, pulled out the phone, did the thumbprint and passcode numbers and was ready to go. She typed H-E-L-P, thought again, and made it more specific. R-A-K-E O-Z-E-N-N-A. H-E-L-P M-E P-L-E-A-S-E.

THIRTY-FIVE

Anchorage, Alaska

R ake shielded his phone screen from glaring overhead lighting to read the message. The location indicator put Sara Kato at a luxury hotel in central Tokyo. He was inside the hangar he had been allocated at the Elmendorf-Richardson base in Anchorage, Alaska. Outside, an F-35 warplane roared in takeoff. Inside stood the C-37A military Gulfstream that had flown Rake, Harry Lucas and Carrie Walker from Washington. They were stopping over to collect Rake's team and then heading for the massive US naval base at Yokosuka in Tokyo Bay.

The hangar, newly renovated, opened onto the busy north–south runway. Air hung thick with smells of aviation fuel and fresh paint. Labels dangled from cladding around pipes criss-crossing the ceiling. Ladders and chairs were wrapped in plastic. They would need it for a couple of hours at most. It was fine.

Rake was working at one end of a long metal trestle table, designing a snatch squad to bring Sara in as soon as they got there. For a city snatch, the weapon configuration would be different to Rake's usual pattern: smaller pistols, shorter knives, everything hidden, plus civilian tools like tasers and cuffs. He and Lucas had gone back and forth over the skills needed. Rake had insisted on a sniper marksman, to which Lucas had exclaimed, 'In Tokyo city?'

'We don't know where it will lead,' insisted Rake.

Lucas kept testing Rake's choices. Soldiers who performed well on the Alaskan tundra, decorated for combat in Islamic wars, might not be suited for the jammed, concrete jungle of

Tokyo. They needed to coordinate in unfamiliar civilian terrain. Their task was to identify Sara Kato, assess her security, and get her with minimum disruption.

They agreed at least two Japanese speakers would be needed. Rake called Taki Umeda, whom he trusted completely; he was three months out of Japan's Special Forces Group and had been with Rake on an operation in Myanmar to free kidnapped Japanese and American journalists. Taki's logic and planning had impressed Rake so much that he had persuaded the National War College to bring him across for a couple of lectures. Taki was brilliant, a hard-fighting son-of-a-bitch of a soldier who spoke like a professor. On the call, Taki had agreed in seconds. Rake asked him to find one more Japanese speaker and meet them at Yokosuka.

They had talked about taking Michio Kato and decided against. They needed him to show them the threat and for Sara to lead them to him. Michio would have put measures in place. If they captured him they would lose the trail.

At his end of the table, Harry Lucas had a map laid out in front of him while cross-referencing on two tablets. He liaised with Petrovsky's people in the National Security Council, clearing permissions where needed while ensuring other agencies were kept out of the loop. Carrie stayed on the aircraft to work undisturbed. Her task was to use her psychological trauma knowledge to get inside Sara Kato's head.

After leaving the White House meeting with John Freeman, Rake had called Carrie asking, 'Can you leave within the hour? We need to go to Japan.'

'Something tells me this isn't a hot Rake Ozenna date,' she answered.

'I need a medic and a psychologist. You're both. You're here. We've worked—'

'Save the sell. Ronan's arriving, if you remember.'

Rake had forgotten. More like, he had never really logged it. To escape a fabricated rape wrap, an orphan kid from Little Diomede was flying in to carve the mammoth tusk stored in his apartment for the Smithsonian Museum.

'It's OK,' said Carrie. 'Mikki's with him. He can handle it.'

Except, Rake needed Mikki with him. He knew no better

marksman and combat fighter, a soldier who could decide in a nanosecond whether to kill or let live. Rake's plan wasn't just to get Sara out. He would also go after Michio Kato and avenge the deaths of two children in Portugal. For that, he needed Mikki Wekstatt at his side. 'Mikki's with us,' said Rake. 'I'll ask Henry if he can come.' Henry, Rake and Mikki's adopted father, had also raised Ronan.

'Where in Japan?' asked Carrie, as if he had booked a downtown restaurant for dinner. Her question was her agreement.

'Tokyo to get Sara Kato,' Rake answered. 'I need you to tell me her state of mind.'

His next call was to Mikki, who had just flown in from Nome with Ronan. They were changing planes in Anchorage to come to DC. Rake told him what was needed and asked him to bring Henry in for Ronan. Mikki asked nothing, said he would handle Ronan, make sure he was safe until Henry arrived, and would meet Rake at the base.

Rake stepped across to Lucas, who held a pen between his teeth while his eyes flitted between his tablets and the map. Rake showed him Sara's message. Lucas picked up his own phone and saw the same there. R-A-K-E O-Z-E-N-N-A. H-E-L-P M-E. P-L-E-A-S-E.

'Can we trust it?' he asked.

'No. But we can't ignore it.' They needed intelligence on whether Sara could be taken from the hotel, or if her security cordon was too tight. Whether she had been forced or had sent the message herself. Either way, they needed to get her out. It was just past midnight in Japan. Flight time would be seven hours to the Yokosuka base forty miles south of Tokyo. Once there they would head to wherever Sara Kato was. The message meant they needed to speed up their departure.

'Wheels up in thirty,' Rake shouted to everyone in the hangar. The pilot gave a thumbs-up from the cockpit. The C-37 was designed for VIP military personnel and had a pressurized luggage compartment accessible from the cabin. The advantage was they could check and assemble weapons in-flight.

Two minivans drove into the hangar and pulled up next to the Gulfstream. Doors slid open. There was one unfamiliar face. The others Rake knew well.

Jaco Kannak and Dave Totalik were marksmen, superb with rifles and pistols. Eric Wolf and Tommy Green were all-rounders and trackers, who had proven themselves equally in packed streets and on remote tundra. Wolf was officially attached to Delta Force, but happened to be with the Guard on cold-weather training. Mark Roller, Rake had not met, Mikki had brought him in from Nome. Roller flew planes, helicopters, gliders; anything that could leave the ground.

Rake beckoned Carrie over. He needed her advice before responding to Sara. Should he acknowledge the message and, if so, how? Say what? Should he ignore, track the phone and take Sara in whenever they could? Lucas joined them. Carrie checked her watch. It was just past seven in the morning in Anchorage. 'What is it in Tokyo? Seventeen hours ahead? I can't do the math.'

'Midnight,' prompted Lucas.

'We do nothing,' said Carrie. 'We have all night.'

'Explain,' said Lucas.

'Let's assume she sent the message of her own volition. Sara Kato was abandoned as a child. Aged ten, she was sent to boarding school in a foreign country where she did not speak the language. That could create a sense of rejection by her parents, which causes attachment anxiety, an inability to form relationships, not knowing whom to trust. This state of mind may have led her toward activism. The Ainu minority cause is a natural home; people from her land, which she wanted to be part of and loved but excluded her. Her fellow activists befriended her and gave her an emotional home.'

'Which she has never had,' said Lucas.

'Correct. Her twin brother, Kazan, humiliates and bullies her. Her father never speaks to her. Her mother is cold and distant. Her only sanctuary has been her elder brother Michio. If he has now turned against her, Rake would be the last person she had felt safe with. We can't ignore the recent trauma from her discovery of Yuri Mishkin's body. There's bound to be visual and emotional impact, especially if she went into Mishkin's room to slip into his bed. Anger. Depression. Fear. Guilt. We all know the patterns. I've been watching footage of her at protests and giving speeches. Sara is a tactile person. She thrives on human contact, meaning she must feel really vulnerable now. We can't exclude her putting two and two together and suspecting Michio of orchestrating Mishkin's death. She must know something of how her family operates.'

'Nor can we exclude her working with Michio,' added Lucas.

'Avoid getting into a text chat with her. We'll be there soon enough. Keep track.'

Rake wasn't convinced. If he were Sara, and he got no answer, what would he do?

'The hotel data is in.' Lucas swiped up the screen of his tablet. 'She's booked in on the thirty-fifth floor with security in the corridor, in the lobby and outside. The phone is in her room. The hotel is a Kato joint. No way we can go in there.'

'Are we inside the hotel surveillance?' Rake asked.

Lucas shook his head. 'Some of their security comms. Visuals on the exits. Facial recognition.'

'We get Taki to stake out the hotel in person. He sticks with her wherever she goes.'

'One guy,' said Lucas. 'Not guaranteed.'

'Nothing's guaranteed and eight hours is a long time.'

'Your op, Ozenna. You decide.' Lucas walked back to the end of the trestle table, leaving Rake and Carrie together. Rake put the phone into his pocket. He clipped up the straps of his rucksack and found himself in the unusual position of being undecided.

'Do you have an issue?' asked Carrie.

'She needs to feel we're there for her. If we don't respond, she can't.'

'If we do it's operationally risky.' Carrie was telling Rake what he knew. It was a matter of balance. Rake ran a knife through a lightly oiled cloth, slid it into a sheath and sealed it in a rucksack side pocket. He imagined switching Sara for someone he didn't know, didn't like, hadn't promised to keep safe. Yes. He would follow Carrie's advice. But with Sara it had become personal.

'I know you like her,' Carrie gave him a sideways glance.

'You're right. We don't respond.' He tried to push that side of Sara out of his mind, as he snapped shut the buckle of his rucksack and hoisted it onto his shoulder. 'We need to get going.'

He was turning toward the aircraft, and Carrie stopped him, her hand firmly on his left forearm. 'Did she come over giving her all to you? Interested in you, liking you because you were her sanctuary? And you liked it. You liked her. You felt an affinity because your parents abandoned you.'

'Stop there.' Rake pulled his arm free. They were under the fuselage of the plane, and they needed to be out of anyone's earshot. Something had happened to Carrie in Brooklyn. She had never brought their private relationship into their work in the field. 'Don't mix it, Carrie,' Rake said angrily. 'Maybe stick to doing trauma medicine and forget the psychology.'

'Or what?' challenged Carrie, stepping back from him.

'Or get a plane back to DC.'

'Jesus, Rake!' She swiveled sharply away from him.

'Whatever's going down between us, we can't afford anything personal to interfere with the next twenty-four hours.' Rake secured the rucksack over his shoulder and walked toward the steps.

'I'm doing my job,' Carrie fell in beside him. 'Sara's wounded. She may not know her mind. I need to be sure you know yours.'

THIRTY-SIX

Sara woke to the bleeping of the hotel phone. She was deeply asleep and opened her eyes to dawn splaying through the windows. Her pillows with fresh white cotton cases were in a mess around her, scrunched, pushed away and turned during the night. The room was awash with soft yellow. She was fully dressed, her shirt tight on her armpits. Her mouth tasted stale, her teeth in need of a brush.

As she lifted the receiver, the horror of yesterday unfolded, pushing the worst to the top. She saw Kazan, eyes terrified, in the moments before he died. She picked up the phone.

'Morning, Sara.' Michio spoke breezily in English. 'Sleep well?'

'Fine. Thanks.' How could he put on such a front?
Imprisoning her. Threatening her. Yet . . . If she thought too
much she would collapse. She propped herself up and took a
sip of water from a glass by the bed.

'Sorry to wake you so early. There's something I really
want you to see.'

'Sure. Give me—'

'Is an hour OK?'

'An hour is fine.'

'There's a tray outside your door. Coffee, continental
Western breakfast. Enough to keep you going.'

'Thank you.'

'A change of clothes.'

'Where are we going?' Sara ran her hands down the side
of her jeans, feeling for the American's phone. The pockets
were flat. It was gone. She drew a breath, feeling the skin
around her mouth quiver.

'Yokohama? You'll love it. It's very special.'

'Yokohama. Great. See you soon,' she managed, ending the
call. She jumped from the bed and tore the covers back. She
ran her hands over the sheets to make sure her eyes weren't
tricking her, a black phone on the white sheet. Nothing. She
stepped out of her jeans, running her hands down the seams,
and folding them tight. Nothing. She was about to tackle the
pillows when a voice inside screamed for her to stop. *Hold it,
Sara. Think. Play back. Remember. The phone was with you in
the bed. You sent a message. You tossed and turned during the
night. It must have fallen out. It will be in the room. They are
watching you. That's why you went under the covers. Get a grip.*

She walked calmly across to the door. In the corridor, on a
low wooden table, was a tray with grapefruit, croissants, orange
juice and a pot of coffee. Next to it a dark green carrier bag
with the hotel logo leant against the wall. She took all into the
room, put the tray on a workstation by the window and tipped
the clothes from the bag onto the end of the bed. They came
from her luggage in the house, a blue winter dress, a cream
pair of jeans, socks, underwear, gloves, a woolen scarf, a couple
of T-shirts and her toiletry bag. She undressed, stepped into the
rain shower, closed her eyes and, straight away, the dying Kazan

flashed in front of her again. She shut off the water and spent time on her teeth, yellow and red dental brushes, flossing everywhere and brushing and brushing, meeting her own face in the mirror, the same Sara, the same short hair, no creases showing grief. She smiled at herself and saw her energy and youth undiminished. The contradiction made her want to cry out.

She put a spring in her step as she walked back into the room, wrapped in towels. If they were looking, she wasn't letting them ogle her. She spread the new clothes across the bed, moving pillows and covers, which is when the phone fell out of a fold in the sheets. She covered it with a wet towel. He legs went weak with relief. She sat on the side of the bed, reining in her runaway mind, beating herself up for panicking. But she had the phone. She allowed her breathing to slow, then got dressed, putting on fresh underwear and shirt, but keeping the jeans because of their deep pockets.

She lay on the bed, pulling covers over her as if she were cold, enough to check messages without them seeing. Nothing. Hers had gone and been received. Like before, it was a long shot. She waited for despair to subside. She needed to retain hope. She typed a second message Y-O-K-O-H-A-M-A. She pushed the phone far into her pocket, pretending to doze, giving it ten minutes. She swung her legs off the bed, fixed a second coffee, drank the orange juice, tore chunks off the croissant, which tasted good.

When she opened the door to leave, Michio was outside. He kissed her on both cheeks and hugged her. This was the American Michio acting in a very un-Japanese way, like he was needing her more than threatening her. They rode in the same car again, Michio mostly quiet, a contrast to his chattering the evening before. There was heavy rain with the beat, beat, beat, of wipers. Traffic was smooth along a wide highway with steel bridges, greenery, housing developments, an airport, never really leaving Tokyo before getting to Yokohama, Japan's second biggest city. They kept driving.

'Yokohama. Aren't we stopping?' asked Sara.

'A little further.' Michio kept his gaze out of the window. Her muscles clenched. One moment her mind told her she was safe. The next it pummeled her with terror.

'Come on,' she tried playfully. 'Not more surprises.'

'A little further,' Michio repeated. They stayed on the highway, running along the coastline, which became a port with container ships, hotels, factories. Sara read signs for Yokohama Hakkeijima Sea Paradise, which she remembered was a tourist place for sea life. There was a park to the right and a university to the left. They turned into a compound just before a bridge and pulled up outside a low, two-story building which ran down to the water. A ship with the Kato logo was moored there, together with two speedboats.

Outside the main entrance stood a greeting line of men in dark suits, behind them staff in blue uniforms with immaculate white gloves, holding umbrellas with the same logo.

'You go first,' said Michio. Sara stepped out of the car, hearing the patter of rain on the umbrella which a young woman held for her. She walked the short distance to the door, where she was faced with a life-size model of a gray humpback whale, mounted against a seascape backdrop of islands and choppy water. The area behind covered the whole building. The left looked like a laboratory, with freezers, microscopes, and people working in smocks, clinical coats with visors and gloves. To the right was a control room with keyboards, wall screens, maps, charts. Blinds covered the windows.

'Welcome, Sara, to our cetacean research center,' said Michio proudly. 'Cetaceans are sea mammals, whales, dolphins, porpoises.'

'I know what cetaceans are,' retorted Sara testily. She had had enough of Michio's pride and surprises.

'Of course. Many people don't. The project here is looking at the impact of global warming on the cetacean population in the northern Pacific.'

Sara walked into the center, taking in the diagrams, charts of changing temperatures, images of mammal sea life, looking for the reason that Michio had brought her here. He was at her side. 'Like I said, Sara, I wanted you to see the other things we do. Big things. The millions of families we help every day.' He turned toward a screen that filled a wall. People stood up from their desks and stepped back from workstations. They gave a low cheer, then, on cue from a manager, a round of applause.

Sara recognized a map of the Northern Territories. Russia occupied two islands: Kunashir, which nestled up close to Hokkaido, and Iturup further to the north. Russia controlled the whole chain running northeast to the mainland at Sakhalin. On Michio's map, the red sun symbol of the Japanese flag stood on the two disputed islands, accompanied by the Ainu flag; a deep blue represented sea and sky; a white wavy symbol denoted snow and a jagged and sharp red shape showed the Ainu hunting spear or arrow. At work, Sara looked at this flag every day. This was her mantra, her reason to get out of bed in the morning. She was seeing the same flag on every island between Japan and Russia, on land that had been home to the Ainu for thousands of years. He put his arm around her, and she did not resist. She was scared of him. She also liked his warmth, the familiarity.

Beaming, Michio held the remote like a wand and moved an arrow up the screen to the third island called Urup. 'And here, Sara, is where we will build the headquarters for our Marine National Park, vital research into the future of our oceans.'

Russia controls Urup, she thought. The bloody island is volcanic. No one lives there. He's talking crap.

'Are you beginning to understand?' asked Michio.

'Yes. I am.' She met the gaze of the man who had murdered her twin brother. Adrenalin rushed through her.

'Will you support me?' pressed Michio.

'Yes,' she mumbled. Through the denim of her jeans, she felt the vibration of the American's phone against her right thigh.

THIRTY-SEVEN

Rake's message to Sara was straightforward, 'Need you on street.'

Yokohama gave him an advantage in that it was only ten miles from the US military base where they would take Sara Kato. There, she would be safe from any tentacles of the Japanese government or its organized crime affiliates. To get her, she needed to be outside, so Rake's team could assess and deal with Michio's security.

He would use a diamond formation that he had improvised many times in different theatres; a fast, offensive snatch, with layered responsibilities, extraction, protection, cordon and transport out.

Rake's team was assembled, together with Taki Umeda and the second Japanese, Haru Goto. Mikki and Haru Goto would distract Michio's immediate personal security. Rake and Taki Umeda would snatch Sara, Rake standing directly in her eye line, so she recognized him. Eric Wolf and Tommy Green would make up the second layer to handle threats from extra security. This method would be close-contact, similar to a mugging; no weapons unless Sara was directly threatened. The two marksmen, Jaco Kannak and Dave Totalik, would cover from a distance and use weapons if necessary. Eric Wolf from Delta Force would be at the wheel of the vehicle, and the pilot, Mark Roller, in the air for helicopter extraction if needed. Harry Lucas and Carrie Walker were monitoring from the Yokosuka base ready to receive Sara.

Rake was in a van with Taki Umeda in a parking lot across the road, with line of sight into the compound. Mikki was with Haru Goto in a vehicle nearby. Rake formed the plan in his head as he had so many times before. Except, he had not anticipated the landscape he saw before him. Sara was inside a two-story brick building, set back in a compound overlooking the water, and wedged between a university and a nine-hole golf course.

He detected no extra security, a small guardhouse on the right of the driveway entrance, a man inside dressed in the light blue uniform of the research facility. A red and white metal barrier covered only half the driveway. A runner or a motorcycle could easily get through on the other side. Surveillance cameras were routine, nothing special. The area around was built up, roads, businesses, houses, marinas, a total urban development. But there were no people, no bustling street, no wide-open landscape. Rake hadn't done it like this before. He had rarely worked in a place so developed but so empty. He needed Sara on a street. But how? There was no shopping center, no attraction, no reason to go anywhere except in her car.

Rake worked through ways of moving into the compound itself for when Sara stepped out of the building, the same methodology. But they would be hemmed in, and Michio's half-dozen security guys would have back-up in the building. The alternative was to play it safe and trail Sara to wherever she was going next. That pushed against his every instinct. Losing this initiative increased the risk of failure.

'They're coming out,' Lucas's voice in his earpiece. 'Three front. Michio, Sara. Three behind. Can you see the vehicles?'

'Affirmative.' Rake looked straight at a three-vehicle convoy of two Toyota vans and one Lexus saloon. Either Sara had not got his message, or she had changed her mind, or it was too dangerous or too impossible to walk out of the compound.

'Michio and Sara in the Lexus,' said Lucas.

Rake judged distances and timings and decided to go in. They would need to make the grab inside the compound and get to Sara before she and Michio were in the vehicle.

Rake switched channels to speak to the team. 'It's the compound.'

'Got it,' answered Mikki.

'Mark?'

'Here,' answered Mark Roller from the US military Bell 429 helicopter ten thousand feet overhead, an altitude which did not attract attention from the ground.

Mikki and Haru Goto went ahead, crossing the empty road toward the compound. Rake with Taki Umeda gave a few seconds then followed. Others took up positions.

Inside the compound, the double glass entrance doors slid open. Staff filed out and formed a line to say goodbye. Rake counted fifteen, seven of whom were fit, young men, any of whom could make a mess of what he needed to do. Umbrellas went up against the light drizzle. He hadn't factored in a farewell ritual.

Mikki would have no hope against Michio's security and the staff. Without that diversion, Rake's chance of getting Sara was slight. The operation had become too risky. He was about to abort when he got sight of Sara, and it didn't look right, unless it was play, which he had to hope it was. She wore no fear in her expression. She was animated and excited, holding Michio's arm, looking up at him affectionately, lively, chatty, in blue jeans and green trainers and a warm dark blue down jacket. Michio was a tall, slender, figure, dressed in a well-cut suit and a bright yellow tie that carried some company or club logo. Yes, this was the man Sara had embraced on the Åland Islands, the killer Rake saw walk out of a house in a Portuguese vineyard, where a dozen people including two children had been shot in cold blood. The greeting line ran in front of the vehicles, headed by a slim figure in a dark suit, no tie, no coat, presumably the manager. The line cascaded from the suits to the laboratory coats to the gatepost guard who ran to get in the photograph.

'Hold,' instructed Rake.

Keeping her left hand on her brother's right arm, Sara pointed toward the gate. Michio hesitated, then smiled and shrugged. His security men spoke on radios. Vehicle doors opened and drivers got out. The guard ran back to the gatehouse. Three security men spread across the driveway. Sara led her brother out of the compound.

'Street?' said Mikki.

'Street,' repeated Rake. 'On my signal.' They melted back into the environment, with skills honed from the Alaska coastline to the deserts and mountains of America's different wars. An empty suburban street in Japan was not easy. Rake and Taki Umeda walked casually back toward the parking lot, feigning deep conversation. Mikki and Haru Goto moved north where buildings gave way to trees. They would watch to see which way Sara took them.

THIRTY-EIGHT

n a restroom cubicle, a female staffer keeping watch outside, Sara read the American's message. 'Need you on street.' With a jolt of excitement, those four words clarified her jumbled emotions. He was here. He would get her out to a life she understood. Michio was bad. He was bullshit. The American was straight. She understood what she had to do. She put on an act for Michio, persuaded him to go for a walk with her. Just the two of them. No staff needed, and he agreed. Outside the compound, she turned them left and headed south. Across the road was a golf course. On the other side was a small marina with sail and speedboats, and straight ahead a rail bridge cut across the highway. She let go of Michio's arm, walking briskly, turning around and around like a kid and pointing toward the water.

'Come on, Michio,' she shouted in English. 'Let's look at the boats.'

Sara took his arm again. She sensed the American was somewhere, but she couldn't see him. Maybe her instincts were playing tricks and Rake Ozenna was not there.

'Great idea,' said Michio. 'Fresh air will do us good.'

She gripped his arm too tightly, terrified that he might turn against her like he had Kazan, so suddenly, so efficiently. In seconds, he could cut her up here on the street. But she had to keep smiling, putting on the act. She felt she was losing trust in her own mind. She wanted things to make sense and they didn't. Couldn't. Not after Kazan. They were getting wet in the rain. She let go of his arm and raised her face skywards to feel cold drops of it on her skin. 'Come on.' She broke into a standing jog. 'Let's run.'

She got ahead of Michio, beckoning him on. Once separated from Michio, she knew Rake Ozenna was there. She looked around and saw nothing. Two women with two pushchairs along the sidewalk. A taxi rank way up ahead with nobody there. A golf course across the road. Nobody there either. This was a desolate urban landscape. He would be here, she told herself. She forced herself to believe it. He was that type. He had asked her to get onto the street and she had done it. Terror of Michio was eating her up. She couldn't go back. She would have to run.

Then, out of nowhere, two men took down the security guards behind them. Just like that. In a second. Another three held Michio so he couldn't move with tape across the mouth to keep him silent. Sara spun back round, to see guards in front attacked in the same way, which was when straight ahead she recognized the American soldier, clear as daylight. He was not tender like Michio, nor tall. Maybe shorter than her. Solid like a tree. He was there, and Michio was being carted off.

She broke into a run toward him, wiping rain from her eyes. As she got closer she saw the hooded eyes, cropped black hair, craggy skin. Without warning, her mind did a somersault. She didn't want to be anywhere near him. He was violent, just as Michio was. He could turn on her, just like Michio. With all his guns. Shooting that policeman. They both sickened her. They were as bad as each other. She wanted to be free, not controlled by any man, free to grieve for her murdered brother, free to go back to her old life in London.

She slowed, her arms hanging listless by her side, her fervor of a few seconds ago suddenly stunted by fear and a sense of total helplessness. She had nowhere to go. She was trapped. Overhead came a loud clatter of a helicopter engine. A black van pulled up beside her, its sliding door open. She felt a jolt from behind as she was scooped up like a feather by another man, not Rake, who carried her toward the van. Strong hands pulled her in. There were three other men, all in black face masks. The front was sealed off by a metal screen. Sara sat on a bench seat, holding a handle on the side to stay steady. Rake got in, and the van moved at a snail's pace, turning a lot, right, left, U-turns.

'Are you OK?' asked Rake.

She nodded. She tasted the bile of fear in her throat. She couldn't speak. Didn't want to. She needed to let her panic subside and tell herself she had been rescued and was safe.

The van went faster. The helicopter overhead became louder. Window blinds were pulled back, and light flooded in. They were driving along the coastline. They slowed at an entrance where two barriers were raised to let them through to what looked like a university campus or hospital grounds. The helicopter settled down at an H-marked landing spot right on the water. Rake slid open the door, got out and took Sara's hand to balance her. He led her to the helicopter. Its roar made it impossible to hear. He indicated she should step on the skid and use the handle in the cabin to get on board. Sara did as he said.

THIRTY-NINE

R ake pointed to the headset next to Sara on her seat. Taki Umeda shut and secured the door and gave a thumbs-up for Mark Roller to take off. Sara fitted the headset, pulling the microphone close to her mouth without moving her eyes away from Rake. They took off in a rapid ascent to get above local air traffic.

'Well done,' said Rake.

Sara pressed both hands against the ear coverings.

'We'll be there in about ten minutes. We can talk properly then. It's a US military base, somewhere completely safe.'

Looking down through the rain-streaked cabin windows, Rake saw a cluster of people in the compound of Michio's maritime research offices and the flashing red light of a police car.

'Where's Michio?' Sara saw the same.

'Michio's fine. He thinks you've been kidnapped.'

'Have I?' She wrapped the headset wire around her forefinger.

'No. This way, the family will never suspect you asked for my help.'

'I want to leave. Just get out. Go home.'

Rake said nothing. Sara unwound the wire and let it drop on her lap. 'And how are you, American soldier?' Exhaustion streaked across her face.

'Things went to shit. We need to keep you safe.' Rake raised a finger to signal a pause as he switched channels to speak to Lucas.

'There's activity around the Kato family home. The old man might have died. We now have surveillance from the meeting in the Yasukuni Shrine. Sara was in the Yūshūkan Museum. She would have heard what was said. And Grizlov is playing hard ball. He wants total sharing, his people to interview Sara.'

Not going to happen, thought Rake, switching back to Sara's channel. 'Is your dad OK?'

'Sure, except he's dying. If that's OK.' Sara looked away from him. Rake sensed she was holding something back. If the family knew Jacob Kato was hours from death, they would be at the bedside, not down in Yokohama. Rake needed to know that he could trust Sara and, if they were going to turn her into an asset, her psychological state had to be intact. He wasn't convinced. He left it because they were beginning their descent which was fast and vertical like a bumpy, speeding elevator. Unmarked, the helicopter had filed no flight plan, a detail that Lucas would handle later. Sara's face went white. She gripped both sides of the seat.

The suburban landscape below gave way to the Yokosuka Naval Base, home to America's Seventh Fleet. Sara shifted closer to the window to look at the rows of gray warships against bleak concrete jetties, the reds, whites and blues of the Stars and Stripes, the shopping malls with McDonald's and the rest.

A squall hit Sara's face as she climbed down from the helicopter. She couldn't decide whether to tell Ozenna about Kazan's murder. It was horrible. It was personal. The Japanese side of her was screaming about loyalty to the family. A green minibus was there, door open, a man in uniform standing upright. She saw massive ships, even an aircraft carrier. Wind whipped up little white waves on the water. They were on an American military base, just as Rake had said.

'Can we walk?' She stood, arms by her side, her right hand on the strap of her bag.

'Sure.' Rake was unfazed. Not that he had much expression in his face. Eskimos were like Ainu, trampled by outsiders, knocked about by the weather, not given to swings of emotion, like she was. She loved it about herself; hated it about herself. She didn't want this strange American Eskimo to agree with her. She asked to walk because she expected him to say No. She wanted to have someone to push against her spinning mind, to help her get her thoughts in order.

'Just walk,' she repeated. 'No more vans. No umbrellas. No more men controlling me.'

'Head along the road,' he said, walking to the edge of the helipad to show her. 'Keep going, past the gas station, past the Kentucky Fried Chicken and those stores, and around that curve you will see a motel called Pacific Lodge. That's where I've booked you a room. You still got that phone?'

She pulled it out of her pocket. Rake ran through some settings, worked the keypad and gave it back. 'I've put in my local number. Faster connection.'

Sara took it loosely. 'Can I just . . .' She trailed off, locking her eyes into a faraway helicopter landing on a warship, then picked up again. 'Just leave? Will they, will you let me walk out of here? Catch a plane to London?'

'Sure, you can.' Rake took off his cap, shook the rain out of it and held it loosely in his hand.

'Sure, but what?' She zipped up her jacket against the wind. 'But bloody what, American soldier? I can't leave, can I?'

'Michio will find you. You need protection.'

'Protection what? Until he's dead, too.' Her eyes flared too much. Blood rushed to her face. She was thinking of Kazan, but Rake didn't know about Kazan. He noticed and stepped back, giving her more space. 'Here, in the base, you can be alone. You're safe. We can pick up again at the Pacific Lodge. Whenever you're ready.'

She moved around him and stood legs apart, arms folded, facing him. She wanted an argument, a fight, somewhere to unleash, somewhere to shout about Kazan and her family. About watching her brother cut open, about finding Yuri murdered; two young men, two killings, too much blood.

'Or you want to walk with me, go over things?' Rake said.

'Yes,' she answered straight away. She didn't want to be alone. Either the dim, gray sunlight hit Rake's face from a lighter angle, or something inside made her see him less as soldier and more as friend, protecting her.

'It's been a hell of a few days.' His expression was less stone-like, more human.

They started walking. Rake told her stories to take her mind away, fill her imagination with better things. She managed to half concentrate. He picked up where he had left off in the hut that seemed so long ago, about his island on the Russian border and a crazy little stepbrother called Ronan who could carve walrus tusks like Michelangelo. He told a story about shooting a polar bear in the middle of the night and waking the whole village to cut up the carcass for food. That brought a smile to her face. They slowed to let cyclists pass. Joggers ran by. There were big American cars and buses filled with military people. She liked his wild, faraway island life and didn't want him to stop. He told how, as a kid, he had fallen through a crabbing hole in the ice. The way he spoke, flat, few words, made it sound so funny. He told her how his mother and father had vanished. He didn't make it sound a good or a bad thing, not like she did, letting her family churn and churn in her mind. Rake said he would find them one day. She saw the sign for the Pacific Lodge hotel. Rake kept talking because that was what she needed. She pictured his beautiful island. She looked around the base filled with warships. As soon as the walk ended, family horror would violate her thoughts again. Michio would be back in her mind, and she would see Kazan die while his mother and father watched.

FORTY

Hands clasped behind his back, head bent slightly forward, Michio Kato paced back and forth, past the huge display of the gray humpback whale in his maritime research center. He focused his eyes on the crisscrossing floor pattern of white tiling and listened to silence in his earpiece. As he was being held, a phone had been rammed into his jacket pocket. Taped to it were bank details and a demand for ransom for Sara's release, a stupidly small amount, 600 million yen, five million dollars, like tipping a taxi driver, which showed how little Sara's kidnappers knew him. He would pay a hundred times that to get her back.

Outwardly, Michio appeared a figure of calm, waiting to hear that the ransom had been paid and Sara was on her way back to him. He wore a fresh blue shirt to replace the one bloodied and torn in the attack. He had refused a Band-Aid for the cut on his right cheek. His bruised shoulder was invisible under his dark blue blazer. His hair was combed back, damp from the shower that had removed the grit from his being roughed up.

Inwardly, Michio was raging. Sara was in danger, and it was his fault. He had used his sister to lead Yuri Mishkin to his death and had thought his plan would be watertight. He had fabricated blood trace evidence in her room because – until things had settled – she would have been safe in Finnish police custody. After that, he would have injected new evidence into the investigation that cleared her and he would have brought Sara to Japan. She would be free and grateful to him. As he took over the family, he needed Sara's trust and for her to be with him. He had already lost Kazan. He could not afford to lose Sara.

Anger rolled through him against his father over Kazan's fate. He despised himself for carrying out the murder. He mourned his younger brother while hating himself for allowing regret to violate his thinking. That made him question his own ability to head the family: Did he have the resolve of his father and grandfather? If the killing of his brother was the test, then Michio had passed. He had carried out the killings in Portugal with precision, too, even the children to ensure no survivors. But how much more death would there be? And was he tough enough to handle it? To keep killing. He breathed deeply to confine his self-doubt. Too much would destroy him, and he could not deny the rush and thrill he got when violently ending a person's life.

One test his father had given him, when he was working in New York, had been to find an informant in the American witness protection program. She was a woman he liked a lot, a little older than Sara, climbing the career pole of an international bank in New York. Michio was her handler, and Jacob Kato had secured her the job. She had an affair with her boss and revealed to him her background, thinking he would protect her. Instead, he turned her over to the FBI, who offered her immunity and witness protection in exchange for evidence against Yakuza families.

She took it and was given a job as a lecturer in finance and economics at Ohio State University. Michio was instructed to find her and kill her. She had a new name and history, of course. When he found her, he saw she also had a new personality. Her vibrancy was gone. She was drained. She walked between her home and the campus, looking for the danger that she knew was coming. She was hunted. There was no lover, no child, no real friends. She lived waiting for the end, because this is how Michio, as her handler, told her betrayal would end up.

He traveled there with a professional team, so he didn't mess up. She lived alone in a pleasant suburban house that belonged to the university, with a front lawn and set back from the road. He rang her doorbell shortly after she had got in from work. Her eyes lit up when she recognized him.

'Michio,' she said. 'Thank God! What's happening? Come on in.'

'We're taking you home.' He didn't want her to die without hope. 'Go back. Work her with our companies. Keep your head down for a couple of years and everything will be fine.'

'Really!' She walked into the small living room. Michio remembered a poster of Tokyo on the wall.

'Yes. Really.' Michio followed her inside and closed the door. Two men, already in the house, skillfully strangled her, zipped her warm corpse into a body bag and carried it out the back door into their vehicle. As Michio had watched, he wished it was he who had done the killing.

A week later there was a story about an American-Japanese university lecturer going missing. She had a history of depression.

Michio could not risk Sara confusing her loyalties like that, like
Kazan had done. He could never put his sister in that situation.
He didn't know how he would live if he lost her.

Harry Lucas watched and heard Ozenna's conversation with
Sara Kato. It was a smart move to take her mind out to his
Little Diomede island in the Bering Strait, far, distant and
unknown to her, yet familiar to her from her work on behalf
of indigenous island people. As Ozenna talked and Sara
listened, real-time analysis from voice and visuals showed her
extreme worry mixed with some attraction – not sexual, but
to the sense of security that Ozenna transmitted.

Harry had secured the back end of the Pacific Lodge's
ground floor, together with the rooms directly above. Sara's
suite opened onto a small, paved patio surrounded by a high
concrete wall, designed for visiting senior officers to get fresh
air and talk without the need for extra security. The room itself
was standard motel fare: green bedspreads and carpet, navy
blue walls and curtains, ice-white lampshades, a good-size
bedroom, even bigger living room, and an extra perk of a
Jacuzzi in the bathroom.

Harry had fitted it with audio and visual tracers and
neuromarketing sensors which would read Sara's heartbeat,
respiration rate, eye pupils and blood flow. From the results,
Carrie could create a more detailed psychological profile to
decide if Sara was telling the truth and if she would be up
to the job of becoming a spy against her own family.

Harry had cleared beds out of his adjoining room to create
his communications center. One link opened to Nick Petrovsky
at the National Security Council, another to Stephen Case in
London, who would work with Carrie on analyzing data. Harry
had also tasked Case to run political analysis on Japan. America
had been caught out too many times. Intelligence failures in
Afghanistan and the Middle East rippled. Failure to predict
the collapse of communism was taught in classes. He needed
to gauge the emotional behavior of Japan. Stephen Case, the
amoral, nerdish, eccentric, tech-obsessed English billionaire
was the best for that job.

He heard the click of a key fob on the door. Carrie walked

in unannounced, and Lucas asked, 'Is she making a play for him?'

'More like a cry for help. She's lost. It's natural.'

Carrie stepped across to the suite's coffee machine. She fiddled with it, turning an empty cup in her hand.

'Your take so far?' he asked.

Carrie put down the cup. 'Corroboration of my initial analysis. Sara has a sense of abandonment. Attachment anxiety compounded by all that's happening now. She is how any of us would be if we hadn't been trained.'

'Are you OK with this?'

'With what?'

'If her attraction to Rake becomes more than seeking safety.' Harry didn't know the details of Carrie's collapsed Brooklyn relationship, but he did know that she and Rake went way back and had broken up and gotten together again more times than he could count. He needed his team to be watertight, no room for the personal.

'Of course,' Carrie replied defensively. 'Rake and I are long ago.'

'I'll rephrase. How far should Rake take it to get what we need?'

'As far as it needs to go.' Carrie looked away. 'If you're asking my professional view on whether his sleeping with Sara would make her more or less reliable, I would advise that, in the short term, it would make her more reliable. Rake's good at growing trust.'

'Even if it stacks up to long-term emotional damage for her?'

'We're not doing long-term, Harry.' Carrie stood next to Harry, examining the screen. 'Look at her. The woman is torn ragged as is. Rake's telling her stories to keep her mind away from the really bad shit. We need the now. The next couple of hours. Afterwards, if you succeed in sending her back into the family and she ends up in a mental asylum or dead, then each of us will have to judge if the price was worth it. It's not only on your head, Harry. We're all here. That's how we work, and that's what you're asking, isn't it?'

'That's what I'm asking.' Harry's response lacked certainty.

He was becoming less convinced that Sara could do the job needed. Like Carrie said, the next couple of hours should decide. Rake and Sara were past the gas station and the small shopping mall, ten minutes away. Rake was telling a story about cutting holes in sea ice to catch crabs.

FORTY-ONE

Amur Bay, Russia, Sea of Japan

S even hundred miles to the northwest, a large fishing vessel, known as a super-trawler, eased from its berth in Golden Horn Bay, Russia, and headed out into the ice-free Sea of Japan. On the hills at the head of the bay lay the city of Vladivostok, home to the Russian Navy's Pacific Fleet and a busy and expanding cargo port pivotal to Russia's Asia-facing economy. Vessels of all ages and sizes docked cheek-by-jowl, sleek modern freighters against rusting, ramshackle tramp steamers, loading and unloading to service the country's commercial hub, feeding the supply chains of Northeast Asia.

It was little wonder that the brand-new 120-meter *Viktor Lagutov* slipped out barely noticed, its crew on deck working in below-freezing temperatures against ferocious northerly winds, bringing with them snow and hail which stung eyes and faces. The *Viktor Lagutov* had state-of-the-art technology to process five hundred tons of fish a day with a massive five thousand cubic meters of storage. The vessel had been built to trawl simultaneously for different species, its computers programmed to look for Pacific cod, Alaska pollock, salmon, squid, tuna and any other fish that could be sold to market. Below decks, crew prepared to receive the catches.

The hull and deck were built in Bolshoy Kamen, in a shipyard twenty miles east from Vladivostok across the Ussuri Bay. Its seafood processing, engine, communications and navigation equipment were made in China, South Korea and Japan. They were fitted at a small private shipyard near Rokkasho in the north of Japan's main island of Honshu. Asian governments hailed the *Viktor Lagutov*'s launch as a symbolic joint venture of friendship between nations. The bulk of the money had come from Russia and Japan.

Michio had brought in crime networks from other Asian countries to ensure that they all had a stake and all were with him. The vessel had been named after the former Russian President, ousted by Sergey Grizlov. Not all Russians supported Grizlov's love-in with the West. Most feared and resented it. Sensible ones placed their trust in Asia.

Only one man on the *Viktor Lagutov* knew details of the mission. As the super-trawler left the Vladivostok cityscape skyline behind, Captain Ito Goro took a call from Yokohama and heard for the first time his real destination. He said it would take him twenty-three hours to reach and waited a full minute for an acknowledgement. He was then told that the Oyabun thanked him and looked forward to meeting him soon. Ito smiled to himself at the use of Oyabun, an old terminology referring to the boss. If they were meeting soon, it would be with one of the sons, Michio or Kazan, not with Jacob, who was too sick.

When the two brothers had met Ito, Kazan, the younger one, spoke the most. Any sea captain worth his salary needed to assess a person in mere moments. In Kazan, Ito saw a young man filled with fantasy and impatience, wanting everything to be done now and blaming others for what had gone wrong. The quieter Michio gave Ito hard facts, assessed risks and calculated potential. Ito's family had been with the Kato network through generations. He saw himself as a Kobun, a foot-soldier or a child of the Oyabun, the boss or, the parent. He could never see Kazan as Oyabun. His type could not last in the real world. But with the calm and thoughtful Michio, Ito was more than happy.

From the bridge, the snow-swept *Viktor Lagutov* unfolded in front of him, with its shining blue hull, ice-white deck and yellow, spider-like cranes that reached down into deep holds. Ito would make his final decision once he met the new boss. If it were Kazan he would refuse, even if it cost him his life. If it were Michio, he would gladly go ahead. Michio understood the modern world. He was tough, cruel when need be, and clever enough to forge alliances with the dominant Russian, Chinese and Korean networks.

Ito was energized. He set his course east-northeast toward Japan.

FORTY-TWO

R ake, Lucas and Carrie watched Sara in her suite from next door. She rearranged things just as she had in the Åland Islands hut. There wasn't much to move in a motel suite. But she put a chair close to the door and pushed the small round coffee table away from French windows that led to a patio. She leant a Gideon's Bible from the bedside drawer against the television screen, as if in a bookcase. She rolled up the heavy green bedspread and put it on the floor.

Carrie explained the behavior as an anxiety disorder, of which there were many categories. Sara wanted to make a place her own because she had never had one, make it more secure because she didn't feel safe, and arrange stuff so she could leave in seconds if danger struck. Sara did not turn on the television as many guests do first thing as they step into a hotel room: she wanted nothing to distract from concentrating on her own survival and immediate environment.

They had left a maroon tracksuit, white T-shirt and under-wear on the bed, so she didn't have to stay in her old clothes. She ignored them. She went to the bathroom, locked the door and showered.

'When you go in,' advised Carrie, 'you need to get straight to the point. No more dancing around. No more funny stories.'

'There's a risk of flipping a trigger and she freezes,' cautioned Lucas.

'Rake can't play the nice guy forever,' countered Carrie.

'However safe he makes her feel, however carefully we test boundaries, the triggers remain.'

'We do two stages.' Rake fixed a barely detectable earpiece into his right ear. 'Straight in, hard, on what happened at the Yasukuni Shrine.'

Carrie picked up. 'Right. Then soften, build trust, test whether she's tough enough to send her back in.'

'Are you receiving, Ozenna?' said Lucas.

'It's good.' Rake tapped the earpiece

Sara came out of the bathroom, dressed in her old clothes. Having ignored the tracksuit, she also did not use the robe on the back of the bathroom door. She rubbed her hair with a white towel, looking around the suite for danger.

Stephen Case, in London, was getting a feed from the suite and matching it against other data he had for Sara. Mikki Wekstatt and Taki Umeda were across the corridor on standby if needed. Sensors were all over Sara's suite. Rake went out into the corridor and knocked on Sara's door. She opened it with the towel around her neck and her hair uncombed. Her expression brightened.

'Is it a good time?' he asked.

She moved back, leaving the door open. Rake stepped in and closed the door. 'Thank you for the walk.' She ran her fingers through her hair. 'But that's over. So, what now?'

'There was a meeting with the Prime Minister and your father at the Yasukuni Shrine.' Rake walked toward the French windows.

'Oh, my God!' Sara sat heavily on the end of the bed. 'Is that why you snatched me away? To interrogate me?'

Rake rested his hands on the back of an upright chair at the dark wood coffee table. 'Your family is dangerous or you wouldn't have asked for help. The end game is to get you safely back to London.'

'But you want me to tell you things about my family.' She pushed her hands down hard into the mattress.

'We have to do it right and, for that, we need to know what is going on.' Rake kept his tone detached, professional, unlike his friendliness when they were walking together. Sara unhooked the towel from her neck and threw it onto the cabinet by the television. 'You were at the Yasukuni meeting,' said Rake. 'What can you tell me?'

'I was there. Yes.' Sara shrugged. 'I tuned out.'

The voice of Stephen Case: 'She's leveraging. Increased determination. Survival. Yes. Manipulation. My money is that she has something she knows we need. She wants something in return, but she doesn't know what.'

'It's more about control,' suggested Carrie. 'She thinks she needs control for her own survival.'

Rake pulled out the chair from the coffee table and sat down. 'Who was at the meeting? The Prime Minister—'

'Cabinet ministers,' interrupted Sara. 'I didn't know who they were.'

'Your father, Michio, Kazan, your twin brother, who didn't come with you to Yokohama.'

'What the hell do you want from me?' Sara bit down on her lower lip and clenched her fists tight.

'You might not know exactly what was going on. But what did you hear? What did Michio say afterwards? What did Kazan say?'

'Holy smoke!' said Stephen Case. 'Emotions going crazy on the brothers.'

'I wasn't listening.' Sara's knuckles were white.

'A word? A date? A place? A phrase?'

'Can I go?' Sara unfurled her fists and pressed her hands down on the bed. 'I don't have to be here, do I?'

'She knows stuff,' said Case.

'Keep up the pressure,' said Carrie.

But Rake rowed back. He felt her vulnerability in a way that electronic sensors could not. 'You don't have to be here, Sara. You can walk. No one will stop you. But, once outside the base, you'll be back with Michio. We can't protect you. The police or Michio's people will pick you up. If you want that, go.' He gestured toward the door.

'And if I want to stay here, I have to tell things against my family.' Anger ripped across Sara's face.

'Natural conflict,' said Carrie. 'However afraid she is of Michio, there will still be a bond of loyalty. Let the contradiction play out.'

'Give me something.' Rake pushed his baseball cap back and forth around the polished top of the table.

'What sort of something? You're right. My family are not good people. My father is a real shit. Michio . . .' Sara stopped abruptly and lowered her head.

'The brothers,' said Case. 'Matching the sensors. Kazan and Michio ignite extreme trauma.'

Rake stayed with the meeting. 'The eleventh of February. Did they talk about that?'

She looked up straight at him. The specific date seemed to focus her. 'Yes. The eleventh of February was mentioned. But is it anything? It marks the foundation of Japan. Like talking about Christmas.'

'What context?' Rake pressed.

'My father said it to the Prime Minister. I didn't hear his exact answer.'

'Then what?'

'They started on the same old record. The war. Hiroshima. The American yoke.' Her eyes cleared. 'It's why I didn't listen. I hate it. I've been hearing this rubbish since I was a kid.'

'What did the Prime Minister say to you?'

'He thanked me for my contribution in making Japan strong.'

'Meaning?'

'Who knows?' She sat on the bed, less taut, arms wrapped around her knees and chin on her hands. 'For God's sake, even you can work it out. It was some nationalistic masturbatory jerk-off for my father for his final days. My dad with the Prime Minister and his family around him at the shrine. I know what you're thinking. My dad's a big Yakuza boss in with banks, politicians and businesses. But I don't know anything about that, Rake. I really don't. Remember what I told you about him throwing me out when I was ten. That's how it is. Maybe he's so evil he makes the Godfather look like a shoe-shine boy. But I don't know, and you have to believe me.'

'I do,' said Rake quietly. 'Have Kazan or Michio ever spoken of it?'

Sara said nothing.

'Did you get a sense at the shrine?'

Case said, 'High stress. A lot of anger. She's not being straight. Definitely holding stuff back.'

Sara shifted back on the bed, sat cross-legged, her hands tightly gripping her knees.

'Is Kazan taking over?'

'I don't know.'

'Is that why he took your father's wheelchair through the shrine?'

'Please. Stop.' Sara pushed herself fully onto the bed and stayed lying down. 'I had just flown in from our little hut. Remember. Why would I know shit?'

'Rake's dancing on a bomb,' said Case.

'We're on the edge of a trigger,' warned Carrie. 'Pupils dilating. Blood flow leaving the skin for the muscles and the brain. Hands trembling.'

'Can we rest?' Sara's voice was faint, pleasing. 'Please. Sit on the edge of the bed. Just be with me. Do what you said you would do and make me feel safe.'

'Do it,' said Carrie.

Rake perched on the corner of the bed. Sara folded her arms across her chest.

'Heart rate up,' reported Case.

'Regular fight or flight response,' said Carrie. 'The body preparing for danger, wishing for safety.'

'Will Michio be the new head of the family?' asked Rake.

Sara turned on the bed and reached out her right hand toward him.

'Respond positively,' said Carrie.

Rake shifted his position to take her hand.

'It's all right. I'm not hitting on you.' Her fingers curled hard around his. 'We all need touch, to be skin to skin with someone who is not going to harm us. Are you going to harm me?'

'I'm not.'

'Then hold my hand and let me sleep.'

'Do it,' said Lucas. 'We have time.'

FORTY-THREE

Sara slept. Rake eased himself away and slipped quietly out of the room. Next door, in Harry Lucas's suite, was an atmosphere of high tension.

Carrie stood up as he came in and gave him a quirky smile with an oblique glance. 'I'm taking a break. Have my seat. This stuff is outside my skill set.' She gripped his upper right arm, then quickly let it go. With that one touch, Carrie told him they were good, as if she didn't mind him thinking a lot about Sara, which he was. He wanted to be with her in some place with shorelines and wildlife and fresh winds, and no one around telling them what to do. He wanted more of her.

Carrie left. On the central screen was Harry's ex-wife, Stephanie Lucas, in Moscow where she used to be ambassador. On the right screen was Nick Petrovsky in Washington, DC. To the left, Stephen Case leant against the glass wall of his office, wearing a loose, floppy cotton T-shirt, looking totally absorbed in his own thoughts.

Lucas worked his keyboards until a green light ripped across his control panel. 'Nick, Stephanie, Stephen, we're secure and good to go. Stephen?'

Stephen Case stepped closer to the camera. 'The big question: Would Japanese voters support their country having nuclear weapons?' He tapped his green jade vape pipe against the palm of his left hand and brought up graphs. 'We see here, fifteen–twenty years ago, most Japanese said they loathed nuclear weapons because they had been on the receiving end of two. But surprise, surprise, the view shifted when there was a question mark about how much Uncle Sam would protect them. An increasing number of Japanese believe their country needs to take back control of its own destiny and find a way to look after itself.'

Case cleared the screen for a diagram made up of different colored lines moving in an upward trajectory. 'Here is a compilation of data from neuromarketing sensors. They tell us about the heart and not the head. If the Japanese woke up tomorrow to learn they were a defensive nuclear weapons state, eighty-five per cent would have feelings of increased relief, heightened dignity and a brighter view of the future. Once the bomb goes off it will be universally popular, what we call a vote winner.'

'We only have to look at how Indians and Pakistanis reacted when their governments declared nuclear weapons,' said Stephanie. 'By outsourcing its weapons program to the private sector, it can deny involvement and take over once the weapons are declared and prove popular.'

'How does the private sector declare a nuclear weapon on behalf of a sovereign state?' challenged Petrovsky.

'With the complicity that we saw at the Yasukuni Shrine,' said Harry.

'How exactly? An underground test?' queried Petrovsky.

'That's the nub,' Case answered. 'To secure those votes in today's political climate of nationalism, it would combine the bomb with an enemy. Our artificial intelligence scenarios suggest the enemy is Russia. Old man Kato wants to blast Japan out of its Pacific War defeat.'

'But that would prompt a merciless response from Moscow,' said Petrovsky.

'We would be obliged to weigh in on Japan's side,' said Lucas.

'Britain, too,' added Stephanie. 'Given the new Indo-Pacific alliances.'

'To what end?' asked Petrovsky.

Case let out an exasperated sigh. 'That is Kato's precise aim. War preoccupies governments and weakens structures. Crime moves into vacuums.'

'Germany after the Second World War,' said Stephanie. 'Russia in the 1990s. If Japan explodes a nuclear device against Russia, Sergey responds or gets thrown out of the Kremlin. Japan triggers its security treaty with America, putting the two superpowers in direct confrontation. That sets off the NATO treaty which states that any attack against one member is an attack against all. Europe would be drawn into the conflict. World wars have started on far less.'

'But we don't know a damn thing, do we?' Petrovsky spoke with his face taut, eyes closed, as if wishing clarity to burst through. 'This whole fucking conversation is speculation, and I cannot take it to the President. For Christ's sake.' He opened his eyes and jabbed his forefinger toward the camera.

'Sir,' said Rake quietly, speaking for the first time.

'Yes, Major,' snapped Petrovsky.

'At the Yasukuni Shrine meeting, Sara heard them speak of the eleventh of February – Japan's National Day. Jacob Kato has days to live, but he may make it until then.'

'The old man wants to witness his father's dream,' supported Lucas. 'It makes sense—'

The door to the suite opened, and Mikki Wekstatt walked in, followed by Taki Umeda.

'You need to—' began Mikki.

Lucas held up his hand. 'A moment, detective.'

'No, now.'

Before anyone could respond, Taki Umeda said, 'Kazan Kato was murdered yesterday in the basement of his house. His belly was cut open in a ritual form of killing we call Seppuku.'

'Seppuku is suicide,' said Petrovsky.

'You are technically correct,' agreed Taki. 'Michio Kato improvised. He forced Kazan to slice the sword into his belly. He then embedded another sword into the back of his brother's neck. In traditional Seppuku, Kazan would have been beheaded.' Taki grimaced. 'Michio Kato did this in front of his parents, Sara, and two men from security.'

'Sara's sensors went volcanic on Rake's mention of Michio and Kato,' said Case.

'The police and ambulance activity around the house,' said Lucas.

'We thought it was Jacob Kato. But it was Kazan.'

'You're sure?' checked Petrovsky.

'A hundred per cent, sir,' said Taki Umeda. 'A bleak underbelly of our culture.'

'What we don't know is why?' said Mikki.

'The FBI murder rap. They didn't share it with us. Kazan was on an extradition list.'

Rake played the timeline. Michio brought Sara back to her family in time for the meeting at the Yasukuni Shrine, where she heard the date of the eleventh of February. The same day, back at the house, Michio murdered Kazan, securing himself as head of the family. He took the terrified Sara around Tokyo. She contacted Rake when she had a chance. Sara was now safe. But she had not revealed Kazan's murder. As Stephen Case had said, she was holding back and the threat remained. 'We need to find the weapons now and neutralize them,' he said.

'If they exist,' said Petrovsky.

'We can't take the chance. The eleventh of February is three days away.'

Petrovsky stayed quiet. Case prompted him. 'If Michio lets off his bomb, the Japanese will cheer, and the world will become even more perilous than it is now.'

Petrovsky's eyes flitted around then settled on the camera. 'How, exactly, do you plan to do this, Ozenna?'

FORTY-FOUR

The click of the door as Rake left woke Sara from her light sleep. She had sensed him next to her, made sure he kept hold of her hand, and felt an emptiness with him gone. She turned onto her back, looking up at the white ceiling with a brown stain in the corner. It reminded her of the first night at her English boarding school, lying in a bed next to the toilets and unable to sleep. Her time clock was skewed because she had flown in from Tokyo on the other side of the world. She had barely known where she was and no idea why she had been sent there. Until that day, she had been looked after every moment of her life, her decisions made for her. But Sara had never experienced real family love. Michio spoiled her and Kazan was always horrible. Her mother reprimanded her, and her father ignored her. Staff fed her, washed her clothes, tidied her room and drove her around. At

school in Japan, because she was a Kato, she had been treated
with respect by teachers and classmates.

At the school in England, as everyone arrived for the start
of term, she sensed this was a hostile place. They called her
Chinky and slitty eyes, the boys especially, and no girl came
to defend her. They pushed into her as she stood in line for a
locker key. When she put her things on a bed in the dormitory,
three girls surrounded her and told her Chinks had to sleep in
the corner, that or go back to yellow-faced land where she
belonged. Sara did what they asked, all the time asking herself
how Michio would have handled it. Her elder brother was a
peacemaker. As for Kazan, he would have yelled and hit out
at them. But then, in Japan, nobody would have dared speak
to her like that because she was a Kato. England was different.

She lay through that September night drying tears and crushing
an instinct to run, because there was nowhere to go and no one
to go to. She cupped her hands behind her head, looking at
the high dirty-white ceiling with stains and cracked plaster.

Similar protective instincts enveloped her now. Over all those
years, however far away, Michio had acted as her fallback savior,
and she had found that comforting. Now, she was struggling to
understand her own feelings toward her family, her country, her
brothers. She could not pull herself completely away from who
she was. At first, when they called her Chink, she had stayed
quiet. When she gauged things better, she said she was from
Japan, not China. They didn't care. When she had mastered
the accent and the language, she added to it that Japan was the
country that made their cars. Then once, on the hockey pitch,
when they set on a Chinese friend, Sara smashed her stick onto
one of the bully's knees. As she blubbered, she said, 'I am Sara
Kato. I am Japanese. This is my friend, Adele Ying. We are
from Asia. You touch her again, and we Asians will eat you up
and spit you out to the ants.' Pride had flashed through her as
to who she was and how she could bring justice to the world.

She realized she belonged to something she hated but of
which she was proud. With Kazan's murder, she had witnessed
the true nature of her family, which was the product of her
whole bloody country. There was no easy way to sort
her emotional contradictions.

Nor was there anything easy about the rough-and-ready American soldier who had dropped into her life. In the movies he would be the good guy and Michio the villain. But real life and real love didn't work like that. She propped herself up, leaning back on her elbows. Yeah, she was struggling all right, which is why she hadn't told Rake about Kazan, because she was frightened and hopeful it would all go away, that he would put her on a plane to London so she could pick up her life where she left off. Stupid. With his guns and his special phones, Rake had the whole of the American government behind him and, if they wanted Michio, they would get him.

School had taught her stuff like that, knowing where power lay, knowing whose side to be on, not picking fights you can't win. She had to choose between Rake and Michio. No question. To survive and get the hell out, she would go with Rake. She should have done it when the helicopter came to the islands. But Michio had been there, and she didn't know shit then.

It had been a good half-hour since Rake had left. Sara was wide awake. With the decision made, she was impatient. She wanted to see him again.

As if on cue, there was a click and the door opened. Earlier, he had knocked. Yet he had a key all along, she thought. Rake stepped in, but not alone. Two guys were with him, rough men, in jeans and boots.

Rake signaled with his right hand toward the taller one. 'This is Mikki, my stepbrother from Little Diomede. And this is Taki Umeda. They helped get you out.' Taki Umeda was smaller and stockier.

Sara sat cross-legged on the bed again, hands cupped around her knees, pressing her fingers in hard. She had to say what she thought, tell Rake that she saw him as her ticket out of this hell, give him something and say it before anything changed her mind. Before Rake spoke again, she said, 'Michio murdered my twin brother Kazan. That must have been why the police were at the house.' She made her cheek muscles tight so she could swallow without showing it. She kept her eyes from tearing and looked straight at Taki Umeda. 'I saw it happen. Use me as a witness if you need to.'

'He's not a policeman,' said Rake. 'But thank you for telling us.'

Taki Umeda spoke to her in Japanese. He had a dark rounded face, honest, but battered like a piece of old wood. 'You know what your brother did, how he did it.'

'Yes. Michio tried to dress it up as Seppuku. But I saw him push the . . .' Sara stopped, looked away.

'Will you help us?' said Taki.

'Yes,' she said. 'Yes, I will.' Adrenalin kicked through her stomach.

'We need you to go back to Michio,' said Rake.

Sara put her hand to her mouth. A coldness ran through her.

'To help Japan,' said Taki Umeda in Japanese. Rake had brought these two guys so she wouldn't say no, she thought. 'It's necessary.'

'And afterwards?' She meant it to sound like an objection, but it came out as if she were asking for a full plan. She needed to picture the end.

'It'll be over,' Rake answered. 'You go back home to London.'

London. Stupid old London with coffee shops, weird politicians, red buses and her crazy friends. 'Y-yes,' she stammered as Rake was saying, 'If you don't do this, you'll be looking over your shoulder the rest of your life.'

'I'll go.' The decision calmed her. Her voice quietened. 'What exactly do you need me to do?'

'Your story is that you were kidnapped,' said Rake. 'Your brother has paid the ransom. You tell him you spent these hours in the black van. Your kidnappers were hooded. You never saw their faces.'

She nodded.

'Can you do that?'

'I can,' she whispered.

'Be with him. We will give you equipment so that we follow your every move.'

'OK.'

'You sure you're good with it?'

'Yes. I am sure.' Sara uncrossed her legs, swung them off the side of the bed and stood up.

FORTY-FIVE

Alone in the large entrance hall of the Maritime Research Center, Michio Kato paced from side to side, forty steps each way. The ransom was paid. Sara was about to be released. His security team was spread through the forecourt outside. He had put three men across the driveway at the gatehouse.

He had concluded that the kidnappers must be from a rival network, striking now because of his father's ill-health. They were sending him a message by taking Sara. His reply would be far, far more lethal than a kidnap negotiation. They and their families would experience violent deaths.

But, first, he had to meet the 11 February deadline. His father had chosen the date and in recent years had swung back and forth on whether Michio or Kazan would lead the operation and take the crown of the family. Michio's first choice had been to stay in New York overseeing legitimate family business. But that ended when he was pulled into a job in Europe which, through no fault of his own, went wrong. Jacob Kato had blamed Michio and his path to the top came to an abrupt halt. It was then, though, that Michio saw his father's blind spot for Kazan. He was not capable of running anything. Under him, Kato power would deflate, which was when, through anonymous channels, Michio brought in the FBI.

The family was now his for the taking. Its new power would be marked on 11 February when Japan commemorated the founding of the nation. In his mind, Michio replayed the plan, searching for weak points. Assembly of the weapon would be finished at the military base in Wakkanai. Then, it would be transported to a super-trawler. The weapon's delivery system was a Russian-designed hypersonic missile which, unlike a Cruise missile, would fly low, fast and undetected, taking five minutes and twenty-three seconds to cover the five hundred miles to a small military base in the far north of the island of

Etorofu which Russia called Iturup. Wind from the south would take nuclear fallout harmlessly up into the Sea of Okhotsk. The missile was so finely targeted that the dead would be limited to around 150 Russian conscripts and officers quartered there. Given the casualties during its usual wars, even in Ukraine, the deaths would represent barely a slap on the wrist for Russia. In the eyes of Japan, the troops were there illegally, and this would be a nuclear test over Japanese sovereign territory. Planning was meticulous.

Michio paced past the humpback whale and read through the names of the body parts, the flippers, the dorsal fins, the blowholes. His earpiece clicked as he was turning yet again, watching rain streak down the glass front doors.

Sara was free.

He took a bright red rain poncho from a row of hooks on the wall. He didn't want to be encumbered by an umbrella or a security guy holding it for him.

He stepped out into blinding rain. He walked fast toward the driveway entrance and broke into a run to get to the road. Sara was walking toward him, drenched, water glistening on her tangled hair. She saw him, wiped her face and sprinted toward him.

'She's in.' Rake watched from the back windows of the van in the parking lot across the road. Sara dabbed a tissue on Michio's forehead to soak up the rain and examined the cut on his cheek. She held Michio's arm as he led her into the compound and to the black Lexus saloon which had brought them from Tokyo. Taki Umeda translated. 'She's saying how she worried about him. Her kidnappers were hooded. She never saw them. She has been sitting in a van which drove around and around. They didn't speak to her.'

There was no sign of suspicion from Michio. Sara had her bag slung around her shoulder and she kept hold of her brother, not caring about the rain.

'She's holding it well,' observed Taki Umeda. 'We Japanese are good at layering our feelings.'

'Carrie? You reading?' asked Rake.

'She's doing OK.' Carrie had argued against sending Sara in so soon. Lucas and Rake insisted they didn't have time to wait. 'Her emotional reaction matches exactly that of someone going through her experience and being returned to family.'

Carrie was with Lucas in the Pacific Lodge hotel, reading data from sensors embedded within a pair of contact lenses they had given to Sara. The lenses were a joint invention between a private Silicon Valley giant and the CIA. Tiny solar-powered chips embedded in the lenses were able to send through very basic visuals and acoustics, as well as monitoring the wearer's biological changes such as blood pressure and raised levels of fear and excitement. They had been switched for Sara's real ones and custom-made on the base while she was being briefed in the Pacific Lodge.

Michio opened the back door of the Lexus saloon. Sara climbed in. Michio got in the other side. The lead car pulled out. The Lexus followed. The chase car took up the rear. The barrier swooped up. Men at the guardhouse bowed as the convoy moved onto the street and turned right toward Yokohama.

The car was the same but seemed different. The armrest was down between Sara and Michio. There was a smell of new leather she hadn't noticed before and only the driver, no bodyguard.

'Where are we going?' Sara asked.

'It was my fault. Father insisted, but I was stupid to let you be seen at the shrine.' Michio worked his phone. 'They threatened me to my face. Took you. Made me pay. They are putting down a marker and we will respond.' His gaze was on his phone's keyboard, not her.

'Why me? I'm a nobody.'

'Because they know you are my sister and that I love you.'

Instinctively she touched his arm, even though Rake had warned her not to let him prize open her feelings. The wipers pounded rhythmically, the rain so hard she could only see a blur of headlamps and backlights out of the window.

'They are people who don't want us to succeed.' Michio finished sending his message, pulled a bottle of water from the seat holder and took a long drink. 'But that's for later, Sara. You're safe. And that's the most important thing.' He gave her a caring smile.

Sara reached across to his hand. 'So where are we going, big brother?'

'Do you want to see Father again?'

'No.' Sara replied too sharply. Her heart began to race, and she drew a breath. 'I mean: Why? Not in that house, Michio. Please. I don't think I can ever go back there.' She leant her forehead against the rain-swept window to feel the cool of the glass.

'We are administering death with dignity to him at the end of the week,' said Michio. 'He has asked it to be for noon on the twelfth of February.'

'We don't have to be there, do we?' She stiffened at the thought and Michio noticed. Rake had talked to her. Taki Umeda, too. A psychologist called Carrie told her how difficult it might be. Don't fight it, understand it, Carrie had advised.

'You don't have to go. I do.' Michio's phone lit up with another message. He told the driver to change route and take them to Haneda Airport.

'Don't tell me, we're flying off to the Greek islands.' Sara gave a quick smile.

Michio took a folder from his briefcase on the floor. 'We're going to open a new Maritime Research Center the operations center for the national park we will create on Iturup.' He spread a sheet of architect's sketches across the armrest. 'Here, see? The northern tip of Hokkaido. Father bought this land around the old American air base. We have a hotel and golf course.'

He tapped his finger as he explained. 'Factories underpin the local economy. We've renovated the port for our fishing industry and it's less than fifty miles from the Sakhalin peninsula. Hokkaido, Sakhalin, the Northern Territories. Our grandfather, Tozen, ensured the family put down roots there. We are very strong in Hokkaido. No one can touch us. You will be totally safe.'

Michio was back with his phone. He made a call and said in a clipped tone, 'We're ready. How long will it take?' He listened to the answer while folding the sketches, his gaze sweeping back and forth outside the window. 'Good,' he finished. 'We're on our way.'

FORTY-SIX

The nuclear weapons engineer speaking to Michio Kato bunched up her shoulder-length black hair, covering it with a cap of thick blue cotton. She slipped off her black leather flat-heeled business shoes, stepped out of her skirt and put on blue overalls hanging in a cupboard of her small office. She turned off her phone, removed the battery and the SIM card and left them in the cupboard. She took a new phone from her stock, one that was embedded with a Geiger counter to measure radiation levels.

She left her office, locked the door and made her way through the maze of metal walkways and corridors of the Rokkasho reprocessing plant in Aomori prefecture on the northern edge of Japan's main island, Honshu. Her electronic swipe card, iris scans and palm prints allowed her full access throughout the sprawling facility. Managers knew she operated with the highest authorization. Only a handful of people were aware of her role

Protecting her face with a scarf, she went outside into a screaming wind whose chill factor took the temperature down to minus twenty or more. It hit her like ice from a shower, knocking away any dullness in her mind. The sheer force of the cold helped curtail elation and excitement of what she had to do. She was an engineer, not a politician or a visionary.

She took several tight breaths to acclimatize her lungs to the bitter weather. Rokkasho's forty snow-laden buildings covered more than a square mile. This was where Japan stockpiled enough plutonium for dozens of nuclear warheads. Most had come from Japan's own reactors. Some had been shipped from Britain and the United States. When building began at Rokkasho in the early 1990s, Kato companies were contracted for critical construction work. They provided security in a way that infuriated the Americans. There were no mandated staff background checks on the grounds that such intrusion would be against Japanese culture. Because of the country's strict gun laws, the guards were unarmed. There was barely any training on how to handle a terror attack on a nuclear facility.

Over the years, while studying weapons engineering, she had watched the mood of her nation change. There were growing movements to expel the American troops and more talk about forging a new, independent nation. She had little interest in the politics. But her father was obsessed, and her duty, as his daughter, was to contribute toward his happiness.

Rather than take the underground corridors linking Rokkasho's facilities, she chose to walk, hunched forward against snow driving in from the sea. The plant was built around an inlet from the Pacific coast, with separate sections for plutonium reprocessing, low-level nuclear waste, mixed oxide fuels from reprocessed material and, on the other side of the inlet, for uranium enrichment.

She headed for none of those. Her destination was a small warehouse on the edge of a recently added landing strip. From the outside, the warehouse appeared to have two large steel doors of fading red paint, secured by a regular padlock. Anyone who approached would be turned away by men looking like routine security guards. A closer eye would show that they were fitter and more alert than most guarding Rokkasho. An experienced eye would spot slight bulges in the tunics from concealed weapons.

Her swipe card got her through a side door to the main entrance, and into an antechamber where she went through electronic identification. Once through, two men, weapons visible, walked her through a large area used for the making of nuclear warheads and for computer-simulated testing. At the end, locked and strapped into trolleys of reinforced steel, were the nuclear pits, named after the hard core from stone fruits such as peaches and dates. This was the heart of the bomb, where detonation compressed a plutonium sphere, beginning a chain reaction that produced a force of destructive energy. Each was identical, measuring 43 centimeters high, 52 wide and 120 long, smaller than anything else around, like a parcel with a round lump at each end for the primary and secondary detonations. With long and painstaking work, she had succeeded in getting the weight down to 257 kilograms.

At their destination, the pit would be fitted into the warhead to become part of the delivery system. She had no idea if they would be launched from an aircraft, a ship, a submarine or a silo. Her business was only to get them there.

She signaled the technician in charge who confirmed the aircraft was in position. Security staff, trained many times in this exercise, wheeled the trolleys to an elevator which lifted them directly into the hold of the aircraft positioned on the apron above. The four-man transport team followed. Finally, she rode the elevator herself into the belly of an adapted Boeing 737. The trolleys were locked into the racks at the rear. She took a seat at the front with her team.

As they taxied for take-off, the pilot announced flying time would be one hour and seventeen minutes. He did not say where they were going.

FORTY-SEVEN

Sara's contact lenses struggled in dim light from the vehicle's darkened windows to deliver a clear image of the architect's drawing Michio was showing her. Harry Lucas needed to run them through pixelation-enhancing software to get enough definition to pinpoint the exact coordinates of his new maritime research center.

'It's around an old US air base and radar station.' Lucas's split screen allowed details to unfold in a column on the right. 'The Japanese took it back in 1972. Now it's operated by the Japanese Defense Force, the 301 Coastal Surveillance Unit and 2nd Defense Intelligence Division.'

Harry, Rake and Taki Umeda fell into silence, reading and assessing as details came through. A trash can was spilling over with pizza and sushi cartons, whose smell of pepperoni, soy sauce and wasabi, together with old coffee and male sweat lingered, not the best for clear thinking. The name of the city was Wakkanai, on Japan's northernmost edge.

'Fifty miles north is Russia's Sakhalin,' said Taki Umeda. 'Tides of war have tossed people there back and forth between Russia and Japan. Sakhalin was Japanese until the Pacific War.'

'And the base?' asked Harry.

'Listening and intelligence gathering on Russia,' said Umeda. 'The regeneration around it has been done by private developers.'

'Mikki's onto that,' said Rake. Since becoming a detective with the Alaska State Troopers, Mikki Wekstatt had proved skillful in pinpointing illegal operations by matching factories, airlines, company executives – whatever caught his eye – to establish criminal links. His rushed task now was to establish anything that linked construction and development to the Kato family.

'Fishing. The port.' Umeda pointed to the harbor a few miles south of the base. Statistics appeared on the column. Wakkanai was the top Japanese port for Russian fishing boats. Japanese companies also funded oil and gas exploration in Russian waters off the Sakhalin coast. 'Two parallels,' explained Umeda. 'Japanese governments become colder toward Russia. Trade becomes warmer, and in Hokkaido it's hot love.'

Rake saw that the US had a base at Chitose in Hokkaido. The team could fly there, commandeer a stealth Black Hawk, and Mark Roller could fly them to Wakkanai. By then Lucas should have collated real intelligence on what Michio Kato was doing. But that was conjecture. Michio might have been showing Sara innocent sketches and heading somewhere else altogether. Wakkanai could be a decoy.

'Taki, a moment outside.' Rake needed to know how far Umeda would go if Kato brought in support of Japanese troops from the base. Breaking the Kato family was one thing. Going face-to-face with the Japanese military was another. When they first worked together in Myanmar, Umeda's jet-black hair had been shorn to a buzzcut. Now it was thick, long, and tied back with bands to keep it out of his face. Outside in the corridor, Rake asked, 'How far does this go?'

'It goes everywhere. This is Japan. There are no lines.' Umeda gave a sharp, short smile. 'Kato is *Zaibatsu*, a family-led industrial and financial conglomerate. *Zaibatsu* were meant to have been rolled up after the war and replaced by the *Keiretsu*, business groupings like your American chambers of commerce. They worked well for a bit, but failed to get Japan out of its slump, move it away from American reliance, keep it ahead of South Korea and China. So, the *Zaibatsu* came back with people like the Katos. *Zaibatsu* was remembered as the nucleus of the system that had made Japan a great power in the 1930s. That is what so many here want to see again, a Japan with its own voice and strength. Like Yakuza, *Zaibatsu* never really went away. A strand runs from street muscle to the government. To get elected, a politician collects a debt of honor which keeps them in check.' Taki spoke, gazing down at the green carpet along the wide, dimly lit corridor. 'We're dealing with the proud institutions of my country.'

'If the threat comes from the port and the fishing industry?' asked Rake.

Umeda looked straight at Rake, knowing what he was asking. 'I'm very happy to fight Russian and Japanese gangsters.'

'From the base?'

'I'm out.' Umeda grimaced. 'I know you, Rake. It won't be quiet, and I will not betray you, but I will not open fire on my colleagues.'

Rake gave him a single nod. They had a deal. 'You gather your people up. I'll check with Carrie how Sara's doing.'

The team was spread through rooms along the corridor. Rake knocked on Carrie's door. 'It's unlocked.' When he walked in, Carrie said, 'Michio and Sara are taking a Gulfstream to Wakkanai.'

'You good to go?' Rake felt a stab of relief. The talking and guessing were over.

'Can we track Sara from the plane?' As always, Carrie was concerned about her patient.

'We can.'

'Then, I'm good.' Carrie's things, jeans, shirts, scarfs, woolen hats, toiletries, were strewn untidily across the bed.

'How is she?' asked Rake.

'Complicated.' Carrie gave him an inquiring look. Rake and Carrie were no longer lovers, but they could be again any moment. She cared what he thought about Sara.

'How complicated?' Rake needed Sara at two levels. The simpler one was to know Michio's location. The difficult one was to be sure she would stay the course on betraying her brother.

'The lens sensors are close to the brain, good at picking up emotional reaction. There are different pulses.' Carrie spoke straight, like a doctor with a bland bedside manner. 'There's stuff coming in that is different to a physical reaction.'

'Like?'

'She's bonding again with Michio. Family and familiarity.'

'Compromised?'

'Impossible to say. But we need to be aware.'

Lucas's voice came through his earpiece. 'Ozenna, I need you back here.'

'We leave in ten minutes.' Rake stepped toward the door.

'It's fucking freezing in Wakkanai.' Carrie opened her rucksack, picked up a pile of shirts to pack, then dropped them back on the bed. She took Rake by the hand and pulled him toward her. She kissed him confidently on the mouth, waiting for him to respond before tilting her head away. 'Look after yourself, Major Ozenna.' She pressed her hands against the roughness of his cheeks. 'You and me. We look after each other. That's what we do.'

FORTY-EIGHT

'The Japanese Prime Minister is about to relinquish power,' said Lucas as Rake entered the suite. 'Intel from Tokyo. No reason given. The favorite to succeed him is the Defense minister. If he screws up, it'll be Foreign or Trade, the three at the Yasukuni Shrine meeting.'

Things were going down as Rake anticipated. Prime Minister out. Vacuum. Kato strikes.

Mikki Wekstatt walked in, summoned, it seemed, as Rake had been. Mikki looked as if he hadn't showered in days, nor changed clothes. A long pale blue shirt hung loose around his slim, animal-like frame.

'We need to go.' Mikki drew a tablet out of a black Kevlar case and laid it on the workstation. 'A Japanese-owned, Panama-flagged super-trawler is three hours out from Wakkanai. Sailed from Vladivostok. The hull and deck were built in Russia. Electronics, navigation and interiors were fitted at a smaller shipyard near Rokkasho, owned by Kato-linked companies. Rokkasho is the site of Japan's biggest nuclear reprocessing plant. Construction and security contracts there have been awarded to Kato-linked companies and another family network from southern Japan. Kato funds a research and development laboratory at Rokkasho. Two years ago, an airstrip was added to the real estate there. Fifteen minutes ago, a freight-carrying Boeing 737 took off from that airstrip and is currently flying in the direction of Wakkanai.'

Lucas opened the line to the National Security Council in Washington. Nick Petrovsky was at his desk. High definition showed up his tiredness, the weariness of a man cooped up in an office for too long with insoluble problems.

'Nick, we need clearance into Wakkanai now. Anything from Tokyo?'

'Habiki's gone to ground,' replied Petrovsky, referring to the Japanese National Security Adviser. 'Same with State, Treasury, Trade, Defense. Hold on . . .' Petrovsky shifted to listen to a verbal message, then said, 'Wakkanai is a Japanese SIGINT and ELINT listening station. Ground interception facilities linked to long-range underwater surveillance, integrated with Japan's air and missile defense radar. Is that right?'

'Correct,' said Lucas. 'The network gives Japan information supremacy in Northeast Asia and shares with us.'

'Wakkanai's gone dark,' said Petrovsky. 'Black-out. They're citing technical issues.'

Rake picked up his rucksack. Mikki slid his tablet back into its hardened case. Lucas spun round in his chair, but Rake spoke first. 'Clearance our base at Chitose.'

'You got it,' said Petrovsky.

'Black Hawk from there to Wakkanai.'

'Done, Major,' said Lucas. 'Just go.'

'Rake. A moment.' Carrie was at the door. She leant heavily against the jamb, hand pressed against her forehead.

'Need to go.' Rake sliced his hand through air, pointing forward to underpin the urgency.

'No. Stop.' Carrie held him by the shoulders, distress streaked across her face.

'She's gone dark.' Dark. The same phraseology as Petrovsky used. Rake thought she was referring to the base. But he was wrong.

'Phone, watch, and it was like the lenses were ripped from her eyes,' said Carrie. 'We've lost Sara.'

Sara stood alone at the edge of an airstrip, watching an eagle with a bright yellow beak flying in rolls and swoops through the cold sky. She had never seen so much snow, fresh, white and piled everywhere, on the roofs of huts, covering vehicles, pushing up against fences. The eagle flew elegantly around steel towers, satellite dishes, and giant spheres shaped like white golf balls, which Michio said sucked in electronic messages from China and Russia and kept Japan safe. The eagle vanished, swept on a gust of wind.

There were two planes on the runway, the small private jet that she and Michio had arrived in, and a bigger cargo plane. Michio was talking to a beautiful woman who had just walked assuredly down the steps to the apron.

A truck carrying a dark green shipping container pulled up beside the cargo plane. Michio waved at Sara, indicating he would be a bit longer. He walked around the nose of the aircraft. The woman had her hand hooked into his arm. Sara didn't like it. They seemed too familiar. She kept her eyes trained on Michio and the plane. She was glad of her decision to work for Rake and dreaded that Michio would abandon her, no longer needed or wanted, like her father had. Or kill her because she knew too much. She tried to feel nothing, tried to use the cold to make her strong.

What Sara did not know was that electronic security at the base had picked up barely detectable signals from her contact lenses. Michio took a call and ran across the snow-packed apron to her. He wore a scarf over his face and a fur hat with ear coverings. His eyes were severe. He held her head hard in both hands. She smelt the leather of his gloves.

'Give me everything,' he commanded.

'Everything what . . .' A jolt of terror ripped through her.

'The lenses.'

'I need a . . .' She was numbed with fear, unable to think.

'Now.'

'The lenses? Why?' She challenged to stave off the terror thundering through her.

'Now. Sara. Before it's too late.' He let go his grip.

She pulled off her woolen gloves, pulled down her right eyelid, pinched the lens, and protected it from the wind as it fell in her hand. She did the same with the left eye. He took the lenses and wrapped them in a tissue.

'Did you know?' he asked.

'Know what?'

'Doesn't matter. Your phone. Your watch.'

She gave them to him.

'Anything else electronic?'

'No.'

Tightness vanished from Michio's shoulders. Harshness left his face. 'Say nothing of this to anyone. If anyone in authority asks, tell them to talk to me. I'll protect you. I promise.'

Spontaneously, she wrapped her arms around him in a hug, held him. Eyes closed, the roughness of Michio's jacket on her cheek, she saw Kazan's death again, just as horrible, but she was used to it now and it looked different, more fate or accident than a murder, a loss that both she and Michio were grieving.

'You were stupid or threatened.' Michio brushed snow off his face. 'We will talk about it later. When we have time. We are family, Sara. We love each other. We protect each other. Nothing will break that.'

Troops surrounded the cargo plane and truck. Men wheeled
a trolley under the belly of the aircraft. Michio took her hand.
'Come. See what we're doing. See how we will take back our
land from Russia.'

FORTY-NINE

S tephanie Lucas stepped into freezing Moscow sunshine,
a rare day with pollution swept away by a strong south-
erly wind, a blue sky with barely a cloud. She climbed
into an armored SUV with two bodyguards and protection
vehicles front and behind. The convoy drove out of the British
embassy's secure diplomatic compound on the banks of the
Moscow River. As they hit slow traffic along New Arbat
Avenue, the driver said the journey to the Kremlin would take
around fifteen minutes.

Stephanie had spent her career trying to predict sensitivities
of governments and their reaction to bad news. She had learned
from childhood to tread delicately around conversations as if
all life depended on it. She was raised in a ramshackle apartment on her father's used car lot in South London. He taught
her the lies and deals you could get away with and the ones
which could rip you apart. She should throw into that mix,
too, her unstable mother, who had stormed out for a new lover,
thank God. Living on the hoof, you learn how quickly
solid things can collapse.

What might unfold in the next few hours was unimagin-
able. National leaders, however just their causes, however
morally upright they might be, could be pushed like feathers
in strong wind into choiceless corners where survival of
their nation became paramount. The Japanese government
had gone quiet on its greatest ally. There was mounting
evidence of its cooperation with non-state actors, a term
once confined to terrorists. The Kato family and its allies
were far from being terrorists. They were a deeply embedded
element of Japanese society, one that might have been quiet

for decades, but one that was about to emerge and take back control.

After speaking to Harry, she had called Sergey Grizlov on his private phone. The Russian President answered, listened, and told her to come straight to the Kremlin. Both knew exactly the consequences should Michio Kato be allowed to succeed. But that invitation was about to change.

'A message from the embassy, ma'am,' said the security officer from the front passenger seat. 'We are no longer to go to the Kremlin, but to the Military University. President Grizlov is attending an event there. It's north, the Garden Ring, only five minutes longer.'

Outside, gray-white exhaust fumes spewed from crawling cars. Dirty snow banked up on the sidewalks. By using the British embassy to communicate with Stephanie, Sergey was making their meeting public and formal, with a military institution as his choice of venue. His unscheduled meeting with Baroness Lucas of Clapham, former British Foreign Secretary, would be logged for all to scrutinize. The British ambassador would be notifying London but, knowing Whitehall nowadays, her message would get blocked until someone worked out what spin to put on it. Downing Street had a new Prime Minister whom she barely knew and didn't much respect.

They eased through on the multi-lane city highway that circled central Moscow, traffic bumper to bumper, moving at walking pace. The Military University was less than half a mile ahead; plenty of time to call Stephen Case in London, the strange, androgynous neuromarketing expert whom she had come to deeply respect. He was skilled at drilling down into what people thought. He carried no scruples or moral compass, and Stephanie was convinced he was on their side.

'I don't take non-visual calls.' Case's voice was playfully reprimanding, carrying echoes of a speakerphone in a large office. 'Even from a real baroness. I insist on seeing the whites of your eyes.'

'I need you to look into something very fast, Stephen.'

'For Harry, I would dry oceans and flatten mountains. Baroness Lucas of Clapham might be on the A list of the

Garrick Club, but not on the client list of my Future Forecasting clublette.'

'The Garrick doesn't take women members, and it's for Harry, Stephen, so no time to fuck around.'

The speaker clicked off, and Case's voice became clearer. 'Then shoot, darling, and I shall perform.'

Stephanie had no idea what level of security clearance Case had in Britain. He worked for Harry whose authority came from the former US President. She said, 'With your neurodata, could you determine the will of the American people should Japan attack Russia and Russia retaliate? Would they want America to get drawn into a war?'

Stephanie heard a tapping on the side of the phone, then Case said, 'No time for new data. I am running this through my AI babies on their existing knowledge.'

'Can you do it accurately?'

'It will not be precise. But it doesn't need to be. I can give you the general mood when that news breaks followed by media and social media reaction. What would be their thirst for war and what style of media campaign would curb their most primal savage urges.'

'Exactly.'

'Give me an hour.'

The bold emblem of the Military University of the Ministry of Defense of the Russian Federation came into view, a silver double-headed eagle fronted by a red shield showing a soldier on a rearing horse. The sign stood out against the university's drab, gray building that fronted onto the busy main road. The Presidential Security Service had cordoned off the nearside lane, allowing Stephanie's convoy to slip in from traffic and draw up outside the main entrance. Her security officer got out and opened her door.

'They're saying only you to go in, ma'am. We advise against.'

'It'll be fine.' The last thing Stephanie needed was to walk into a Russian military facility flanked by British government muscle.

'Ma'am, our instructions are—'

'Your instruction from me is to wait here.' Stephanie felt

the stinging cold and pulled her scarf around her face. 'I'm protected by Russia's finest. They won't dare touch me.'

She recognized a dark-suited young man walking toward her as one of Grizlov's staffers. Without a word, he led her through a bland foyer of flags and military photographs and out into a large open parade ground. A band played martial music. Cadets in dark green uniforms goose-stepped back and forth. Buildings around created a wind tunnel that pushed the wind chill down even further as snow slewed across the ground.

Grizlov stood by a podium at the center, where awards were being handed out. He walked across to her. This was no longer the beaten-down Sergey from the evening at his house. This was the President, in a snappy, well-cut suit, expensive hand-made shoes, no tie and seemingly impervious to the weather, no hat, no gloves, no flinching against a cruel wind.

'Baroness Lucas.' His voice was raised to counter the sound of the band. 'Thank you so much for coming.' He shook her hand, clasped her elbow, and finished with a light squeeze of her right shoulder.

'Thank you for sparing the time.' She pulled down the scarf so he could see her whole face.

Grizlov leant forward. 'They are filming, but can't pick up audio. With a bit of luck snow squalls will hamper lip readers.'

'I'll get my social media people to talk to your social media people,' she quipped. This public meeting was not what she wanted, a former Foreign Secretary meeting the Russian President hours before a global crisis erupts. She was beating herself up for not anticipating it. But she needed a face to face, and it was Grizlov's choice.

'Any changes?' Grizlov asked.

'No. But if it does happen, Sergey, please. You know how brittle everyone is.'

'Sergey agrees with Steph a hundred percent. But the President of the Russian Federation does not agree with Baroness Lucas of Clapham, unofficial envoy from America. Russia will respond in a manner that is proportionate and neutralizes the threat against us.'

'It's a non-state actor, Sergey. Look what happened to the US when it elevated Bin Laden and Al Qaeda to—'

Grizlov raised his hand for her to stop. 'We're not here for a debate, Steph.' He drew a folded sheet of paper from his jacket pocket and opened it out, its edges flapping in the wind. The staffer, keeping his distance, stepped forward to help. Grizlov waved him back. 'Take this end, Steph, and I'll explain.'

Stephanie held a corner with each hand and looked at a map of Japan, Russia's Far East and parts of Northeast Asia. 'Let's say they go for the Kuril Islands or Sakhalin,' Grizlov said. 'We will respond with tactical nuclear strikes on all Japanese military bases north of Tokyo. We will not target the US bases. We will also take out the Japanese nuclear reprocessing plant at Rokkasho.' He looked up to meet Stephanie's gaze. 'I know. You're thinking contamination. But we destroy and seal. Check with Harry, he'll know the method.'

'And this is set?' Stephanie couldn't hide her surprise at Grizlov's detailed and disciplined preparation so soon after his son's murder. The conversation with Petrovsky and Harry about whether or not to alert him had been way behind the curve.

'It is,' said Grizlov. 'We are the US equivalent of Defcon Two. Your intelligence is sharper than ours, but they match. Should the US respond against us through its security treaty with Japan, we will target American bases there with conventional weapons. We will also move into the Bering Strait and seal off the border with America. Should NATO trigger Article Five . . .' Grizlov looked down with a thin smile. 'Well, it's literally off the map, Steph. No one wants to go there.'

'Don't. Please even start.' Stephanie shook her head. The horrific scenarios she had been through numerous times during summits and war games were hours away from being real. 'You can't, Sergey. From Sakhalin, you hit Sapporo, and they hit Vladivostok and America comes in and, before anyone can stop it, it's Moscow, St Petersburg, London, New York, Philadelphia, Berlin.' Drum beat and brass band music rolled across the square. 'You have a hundred dead in the first strike. A day later, it's a million. Nuclear, cyber. Everyone throws everything they have at this. You know it. I know it. I'm begging you.'

Grizlov stared across at the band. 'If I do not respond exactly like this, the gangsters of Vladivostok will take Russia. The gangsters of Tokyo will take Japan and China will show them the way because it is already run like a Mafia state.'

'Are you telling Freeman?'

'No. You tell him. Tell him to fix it.' Instead of folding up the map and putting it back in his pocket, Grizlov held it up, fluttering in the wind, for the staffer to take. Cameras would pick up the classified document, the targets and the missile bases.

She feared how the visuals would look, her studying a battle plan next to the Russian President while his troops goose-stepped in the background. The staffer folded the map.

'You're landing me in the shit again, Sergey.'

'Think of it as a favor. I'm making Britain relevant again.' He signaled to the people at the podium that he was on his way back.

'Anything?' Stephanie tried. 'Any wriggle room?'

'They murdered my son.' Grizlov's face went taut and dark. 'They killed Yuri. They fucked with Russia.'

'Yes, to create exactly this chaos.' Stephanie was shouting, tremors of helplessness shivering through her with the cold. 'The weaker the governments, the stronger they are.'

The staffer handed Grizlov a thin leather briefcase. 'Give it to Harry,' he said.

'What is it?' Stephanie took it. The black leather was new, embossed with an emblem of the Russian eagle. It was heavy. Stephanie unzipped it an inch and saw wads of paper inside.

'Harry will know what to do with it. Tell him to do it quietly. Best for all of us.' Grizlov turned to head back and asked, 'Does he have a team on the ground?'

'Rake Ozenna's heading there.'

'Good. You need to stop it, and fast. For that Ozenna is your best bet.'

FIFTY

Rake opened the door of the Black Hawk, bringing a brutal wind into the cabin. His night vision showed deep snow a few feet below swirled up by rotor blades. There was still no word about Sara. Taki Umeda was on the ground with three snowmobiles. Posing as a tour guide, Umeda had gone ahead on a civilian flight to arrange vehicles and check access to the port and the base. The base would not work. If they were to stop Michio, it would be at the port, the location of the weapon.

Rake jumped, sinking into snow so far that it propped him up. Umeda grasped his wrist to pull him out. Mikki came next. The others followed. Mark Roller took the Black Hawk up, its stealth technology hiding it from radar detection. The howl of weather dampened the throb of the engine.

They were on high ground amid heavy snowfall. Through his night vision, Rake saw a single civilian container truck driving out of the military base toward the coast. With it came four snowmobile escorts. The truck briefly headed north before turning into the main gate of the fishing port, where barriers were raised to let it in without stopping. It continued a short distance to by far the biggest vessel there. 'Confirmed destination the *Viktor Lagutov* super-trawler,' came Lucas's voice in his earpiece.

'Copy,' acknowledged Rake.

'The Russians are sharing some intel. The *Lagutov* is carrying a hypersonic missile based on the Russian 3M22 Zircon.' A Zircon flew at twenty times the speed of sound, so fast and so low that it would be near undetectable and impossible to intercept. 'The design of the *Viktor Lagutov* allows for a concealed silo in one of the holds. The pit has been flown in from Rokkasho. The launch mechanism is compressed steam.'

This was a traditional surface and submarine launch, like pressure pushing up the lid of a kettle. Once the missile cleared the vessel, its rockets would ignite. Any launch was a labyrinth of physics and engineering where a hundred things could go wrong. That didn't mean they would. Claws from the trawler's hoists gripped the sides of the green metal container lifting it from the truck. It slowly moved across the trawler's deck and was lowered into a hold.

The job needed the missile itself to be physically disabled. It would be designed so that if Michio was taken out, another could pull the trigger. Rake could kill everyone on the ship and someone on the other side of the world could still press the launch button.

The team had been on the ground just over a minute. It would take less than five to get to the port. They mounted the snowmobiles. Rake rode with Umeda who drove. Mikki with Tommy Green. Eric Wolf had stayed with Mark Roller in the Black Hawk. Jaco Kannak and Dave Totalik, the marksmen, took up the rear. Lights were off, engines kept quiet. They glided along lightly packed new snow, Umeda knowing a route that would avoid the surveillance cordon around the base.

They stopped halfway down the hillside, where scrub protruded from snow. Rake instructed Kannak and Totalik to set up a sniping position here overlooking the port. They were six hundred meters from the *Viktor Lagutov*, a straightforward clean shot, if they could get it, if the clear weather held.

The two Alaskans could judge cold-weather shooting better than any he knew. From winter boyhood hunting along the Alaska coast, they had learned how environmental conditions, wind speed and direction, humidity, temperature, and gravity drop impacted the journey of a bullet. If any could neutralize Michio with a single shot, it was them.

As the other two snowmobiles continued down to the road, Umeda received a message which he relayed to Rake. 'They're taking the civilian crew off and putting in guys from the Special Forces Group.'

Rake knew what it meant: Umeda and his team would not be with them. He had to calculate fast whether to keep going or abort. From a fighting force of around twenty, he was suddenly down to three. Taki Umeda's team was out. Totalik and Kannak were on the hillside. Roller and Wolf in the Black

Hawk. Mikki, Tommy Green and himself at the port. To abort on fresh intelligence was a professional decision. But abandoning Sara to Michio was mostly personal. He would not pull out, knowing she had been exposed and was at risk of her life. Except, she might already be dead.

Umeda slowed to take them down a sharp slope. A strengthening wind whipped up flurries of snow.

'They've flown in a specific unit of the SOG, one heavily infiltrated by nationalists,' Umeda continued. 'They are not nice people, but I won't go up against them.'

Rake said he understood, which he did. He gave himself a moment to assess if Umeda could be trusted not to warn his colleagues. He had given his word and Rake needed to trust it. The tell would be getting into the port.

Umeda drove through a street of residential houses, snow drifting against fences, icicles hanging from gutters, small bright-colored cars parked in driveways. They crossed the main coastal road where there was no traffic, then went back down a snow track by the port. Two men were slumped, unconscious against a gatepost to a side entrance. Umeda stopped and cut the snowmobile engine. Haru Goto, Umeda's partner, was there. He handed over a large, loose sack. Inside were six sets of dark green cold-weather gear. Sewn into the jackets and pants were the emblem of the Special Operations Group, JGSDF, a dark blue square, with a national flag and a yellow wings and parachute, the uniform of the men now boarding the super-trawler.

Rake, Mikki and Tommy Green put on the pants and jackets. Umeda handed them each a yellow armband for identification if things flared up. He tapped his earpiece. 'I'll stay on comms until you're on board. They have blacked out the port CCTV for the loading. Walk straight on. Any questions and you're under the command of Colonel Ichiro Watanabe.'

Rake nodded, not mentioning that none of them spoke Japanese.

Umeda pointed to the unconscious guards. 'They're sedated. They'll come around in about ninety minutes. If you're not done by then, you'll be dead or captured and I'll swear we never met.'

Umeda and Goto left on foot.

'Anything on Sara?' Rake asked Lucas.

'Negative.'

'Jaco, Dave,' Rake asked the marksmen on the hillside.

'Clear, no target,' answered Totalik. If Michio Kato stepped into their line of fire, he would be dead.

'Collateral?' Kannak asked: could they kill anyone else to get to Michio? If he was in a group. If he was obscured by another person. If he were holding a hostage.

Rake pictured Sara. Was she there? Was she terrified? Had she gone back over to Michio? He thought how it would be if he gave the orders for the shot that killed her. And how a devastated world might look, a week from now, if they failed.

'Collateral acceptable,' he answered.

'Good luck.' It was Carrie. With Lucas. She would have heard that and she would understand.

Rake checked cloud formations, the angle of moonlight, darker weather moving in from the north, the way the port lamps bounced off the ice on the ground, reflections from the steel of the fishing vessels. He worked out the short walk to the *Viktor Lagutov,* one that kept them in the shadows, between vehicles, forklifts, port paraphernalia on the jetty and the towering hull of the trawler which they needed to board.

FIFTY-ONE

The *Viktor Lagutov*'s gangway was lit like a shopping mall, its back-and-forth movement in the slow swell barely detectable. Around the hull, huge chunks of ice floated in sea water, white, blue and gray, as they picked up moonlight and reflections from the sea. Thick ropes running from each side of the hull secured the super-trawler to bollards on the jetty, in the same way ships had been moored for centuries. No technology had ever bettered this system. Two ropes came from the bow and two from aft. Midway along, just above water level, there was a door in the hull, half open, light seeping out onto a metal walkway lined up on the jetty to connect. This would be where stores were loaded, or a pilot taken on to guide the vessel out to sea. Somewhere midships was the silo holding the missile that had been vertically lowered in and was now encased in reinforced material capable of withstanding a launch. This was what Rake had to penetrate.

'Numbers?' Rake asked the sniper team on the hillside.

'So far, eleven civilian crew leaving. Four coming.'

Rake watched the four in Japanese Special Forces Group uniform walk across the jetty toward the gangway, relaxed, trained, disciplined.

'Any sighting of Michio?' asked Rake.

'Walking onto the land-side wing of the bridge,' replied Kannak. 'Two women with him.'

'AFR coming in,' said Lucas. AFR was automatic facial recognition which could make identification in seconds. 'One is Sara. The other is . . . hold . . . firming up . . . yes . . . the other Dr Niko Yimagi, a graduate of the nuclear physics program at the Massachusetts Institute of Technology, with a masters and doctorate from Yale and the rest. That adds up. She worked on the weapon. She's the kill, but do not implement in port. Nor Michio.'

What the hell! 'What do you mean, no kills in port?'

'No action on Japanese territory.'

'Spell it out, Harry?' He understood part of it, accepted it made part sense. Hitting just Michio could prompt Dr Niko Yimagi to trigger the weapon. But that applied anywhere. 'Does that mean we have to get twelve miles out?' The standard sovereign maritime territory was twelve nautical miles from a nation's coastline or continental shelf. Beyond that lay international waters.

'No,' clarified Lucas. 'On this strait between Russia and Japan, it's three miles to allow our nuclear-armed vessels to transit in international waters.'

'We can only hit them, then?'

'Correct. *Viktor Lagutov* is a Panama-flagged vessel. We can do what the hell we want with it in international waters.'

From casting off, the super-trawler with its modern engines would take fifteen minutes to travel three miles. With turn-around time and getting underway, Rake estimated less than fifteen minutes. It was just past eleven thirty. If he were Michio Kato, he would go for a launch just beyond the three miles line and on a stroke past midnight.

'And it gives us time,' added Lucas. 'Nick Petrovsky's made contact inside Japan. We're hoping for a political fix.'

There were no checks that Rake could see for the four Japanese soldiers boarding. The crewman at the top on deck stood aside to let them pass. Rake was close enough to recognize the spring in their steps. If tonight were a success, any soldier involved would want to have it stamped on his career résumé. He studied their body language, the way they carried their weapons, spoke to each other. They were not expecting a fight. But they were trained and tough. Any surprise advantage he had would last no more than three or four seconds. Once on board, Rake's plan was to damage the blast door, the lid on the silo, so it would not open. Simple, but effective.

'Hold back.' Umeda's voice, hard and urgent. 'Do not board. Repeat, do not board.'

Rake stopped. They had cover from the hull. Piercing wind careered around the bow in a low, pulsating shriek. The crewman on the gangway put his hand to his earpiece. The skipper on the bridge signaled with a 'T' motion, right hand horizontal on his left, a message that the job was done.

'The colonel's told the captain they have the full complement of men,' Umeda said. 'They're about to cast off.'

'You need to get the hell away, Ozenna,' said Lucas.

No, thought Rake. Not now. Not with Michio free and Sara in danger. He didn't answer. There were two ways in if they were fast enough. One was the jetty-level door, mid-ships, which seemed unattended and ajar. As if reading his thoughts, a hand reached out and closed the door.

Rake needed a Mikki with him and Tommy Green at close quarters on the jetty to cover. Green was younger, but Mikki Wekstatt was a lethal machine in a fight. He could construct firing patterns that made his enemy think there were five men and not just one. His grenade throws were long and more accurate than a basketball slam dunk. Rake closed Lucas's channel and cupped his hand over his mouth to speak directly to Green. 'Mikki and I are going on board.' He pointed to a white pick-up truck at the end of a line of five parked vehicles. 'Set up there and cover us.'

Green checked the position and nodded. Rake said, 'Once we're on, get the hell away.'

Rake and Mikki sprinted back to the bollards, where ropes secured the bow to the jetty. Rake clipped two knives onto his belt: the Ontario Mark 3 six-inch double-edged stainless steel on his left, and the slimmer and longer, seven-inch Fairbairn-Sykes on his right. Both were good for throwing. He screwed a suppressor onto his SIG Sauer and slid it into a holster on his right hip. Around his chest he slung a submachine gun that he had picked up at the Yokosuka base. He loaded it with a twenty-five-round magazine and slipped a seventeen-round one in the top left-hand pocket of his jacket. He latched grenades to his belt. He lifted the rucksack onto his back. Fifty pounds, sixty pounds dead weight. Didn't matter. He needed it, particularly the heaviest item, a small, black satchel filled with C4 explosives, which would unleash many times the destructive force of the four hand grenades nestled around it.

The ropes from the super-trawler were too thick to grasp with one hand and were covered in a film of ice. They ran up through a feeder hole in the lip of the hull to winches on deck. Sharp, jagged icicles hung from the lip. The climb would be ape like, arms locked together, with the feet propelling the body upwards and the thread of the rope supplying some kind of foothold for leverage.

'Good?' Rake asked.

'Let's roll this crap shoot,' answered Mikki.

FIFTY-TWO

Rake took the mooring closest to shore, locking his arms on the rope, right hand around left wrist, feeling the coarseness of the twine through his gloves. As he cleared the concrete of the jetty, ice floes in the water brought the air temperature way down. The wind cut sharper into skin exposed on his face. His boots found edges that held long enough to push him up. He went well for a few yards. Then, the angle steepened. He hauled up his bodyweight and the dead weight of the rucksack. He drew sub-zero air deep into his lungs. Still his blood was not oxygenating enough to give him the muscle strength needed. He would have to slow. He looked to his right. Mikki was the same, and Mikki had ten years on Rake. As tough as hell. He looked left and could see nothing around the white pick-up. But Tommy Green was there. Green could hide himself on carpet of white sand if he had to.

The lights above were static, not suddenly darkening and throwing out shadows, suggesting no one was yet moving up on deck to cast off. Rake hauled himself up the next few inches. He had forgotten his wound from the Åland Islands. It burst with pain, from a low awareness to screaming agony. He gripped tighter, making it worse. He had an urge to let go, fall onto edges of jagged ice. A couple of minutes earlier, at the start of the climb, the water and lumps of ice would have acted as a cushion to a fall from a low height. Not anymore.

To his right, Mikki was pacing him. Or he, Mikki. Like two competing kids in a playground running race. Mikki wore a huge grin. Rake caught snatches of a song in the wind. He recognized the rhythm and the beat. Mikki was pulling himself up with tribal music from Little Diomede, wasting his oxygen on his voice, the fool, but he was doing fine, as good as Rake, maybe better.

A low hum emanating from the vessel's generators changed pitch. The rope jolted and grew taut, lessening its steep angle so Rake could move faster. The oval gap in the lip of the deck was large enough to climb through. Good. He would not have to haul himself over the top. High on the hull, he spotted rungs of steps running up to the hole in the lip. The steps would give him stability to take off the rucksack, climb to the gap, push it through, then follow.

He climbed higher. A wind gust skidded around the hull with a force that tore off icicles and slammed them into Rake's rucksack like spears. He waited for it to subside, then reached out with his good left hand, first to knock icicles from a rung on the steps, then grip it and test that his hold was good. Only then did he separate himself from the mooring rope, briefly bearing the whole weight in a single left-hand grip. He swung himself around to grab the rung with his right and find ones below for his feet.

At exactly that moment, there were three cracks of gunfire above. Ice splattered up from the bollard rope. Then came a shrill sound of metal on metal as a weapon hit the deck, and the dull thud of a man falling. Either Tommy Green or the guys on the hillside got him. A hell of a shot. But he wasn't dead. He crawled forward until Rake had a clear view of his bloodied face. He was wearing blue overalls, an orange hard hat, and a hi-vis yellow jacket, technically a civilian. Then why the weapon? He looked as if he would be dead in minutes, but a dying man could inflict much harm in those last seconds of life. Rake shot him with the SIG Sauer, a quiet whisper of a single round as the suppressor did its job.

Mikki hauled himself onto the deck. He ran toward Rake and pushed the body overboard. It twisted in the fall, blood trailing from arterial bullet wounds. The corpse crashed onto an ice floe and slid into the water. Rake lifted his rucksack high enough for Mikki to take through onto the deck. He stepped from the highest rung and pulled himself over the blood-smeared rope. The area was flat, wide and dark. Mikki carried both rucksacks to a bulkhead where there was a dark, triangular area, free from moonlight and lamps from the trawler or the port. Above was a smaller deck which stretched back to the bridge. Mikki also had the radio from the dead sailor, which was silent. Both men rearranged their weapons, putting extra magazines in pockets, clipping more grenades to their belts. Rake strapped the satchel of C4 explosives to his back, ensuring the two-step detonation was in place so a careless knock did not set it off.

Deep vibrations of engine-powered propellors rippled through the hull. A searchlight swept around. Rake checked his headset. 'Great shooting, guys,' he said. 'Did the job.'

'Anytime,' Kannak answered from the hillside. 'Looks like you're leaving and the weather's whipping up.'

Mikki watched across to land-side. He signaled for Rake that they needed to move.

'Can you identify launch silo?' Rake asked Jaco.

'Above you. The deck running from the bridge. Blast lid slightly raised, like a drainage manhole. You're at the right spot.'

'Two men toward you starboard side,' Kannak's voice tensed. 'Losing visibility from the weather. Go port side. There's a life raft. Next to that, looks like a storage cupboard. You need to move. NOW. Port side clear. Repeat, port side is clear.'

The ship was moving slowly. Rake and Mikki sprinted out from the cover of the bulkhead across the deck to a patch underneath the large orange life raft. Moonlight and changing shadows made it look more like an airplane fuselage. Crew moved around to cast off. The spot would be good for a few seconds at best. Rake stepped out to test the light blue metal door to the storeroom. It opened. Inside was empty. Lamplight through the door illuminated random patches of its stainless-steel walls. There were hooks and workbenches, nothing else; no cameras that he could see. Mikki followed and locked the door from the inside. They were concealed, but they could not see out. They needed to hold for fifteen minutes at most, until they were outside of Japanese territorial waters.

It was twenty-two minutes to midnight and 11 February. The super-trawler would have a crew of around a hundred. Rake didn't know how many had been ordered off. The crewman they killed had been armed. How many of them were there? And there were seven or more Japanese special forces. From Mikki's pocket, the dead sailor's radio crackled. 'Les, where the hell are you? Get to the starboard winch. Do you copy?'

The voice on the radio was not Japanese or Russian. It spoke in clear American English, military style. Meaning that Rake had not killed a civilian crewman, but a mercenary from his own country, playing the part of a crewman. They would be working for Michio Kato, probably drawn from the same group hired to kill Yuri Mishkin. Then why had the Japanese soldiers, technically under government control, boarded at the last minute, taking even Taki Umeda by surprise? Had they been deployed to keep Michio Kato in check, or so that the government could seize the nuclear launch as its own? There was no time for the ins and outs. Rake and Mikki were now up against two separate combat units.

'Copy,' Mikki answered, disguising his voice, keeping it low, dulled by the enclosed surroundings. A fist thumped on the steel door, shaking the walls around it. 'Les, you in there? Get the hell to that winch.'

FIFTY-THREE

The storage room door had a single hand-wheel lock which moved bolts top and bottom. Rake stood by the wall at the end, Mikki to the left, where he would have a line of sight onto the deck once the door opened. The best scenario would be for their visitors to move on without checking inside. That would give a few minutes before Les the dead crewman's whereabouts were confirmed as unknown. Michio Kato would not hold up the departure to look for a hired gun who had become an inconvenience. If they did open the door, it would have to be a kill. Their Japanese Special Forces Group uniforms would give them a few seconds' grace, their Asiatic features a second more.

The hand-wheel turned. The door bolts drew back. A blade of light came through as the door edged open, followed by a cry and a thud.

'The fuck that come from?' Fast footsteps. Men hunting cover, coming under fire.

Jaco's voice. 'One down. Two out there, edge of range.'

An American voice over the radio again, 'Les, you there?' Mikki held the radio. Rake shook his head. Don't speak. Add to their confusion. The vessel rocked and swayed as it left the jetty. There was more footfall outside the door, the dragging of a fallen man to safety.

'Les, where the fuck are you?' Half question, half frustration. Rake and Mikki kept their positions. Static. Silence. Then, 'Jed, Jezza, get Paul to the medics. How is he?'

Paul would be the second one they shot.

'Karl, do Les's winch. That fucking rope is dangling and dragging.'

The radio channel clicked off. Karl, Jed, Jezza and the guy on the radio. And two down. That made six. Rake's best guess was the hiring of three US Marine units of four, making twelve in all. Then there was the Japanese Special Forces Group, pushing enemy numbers close to twenty. He should factor in any of the genuine civilian crew and Michio, who had been special forces trained. Not great odds.

The door opened full on, a flashlight beam turning inside, bouncing off the metal floor, coming up directly into the eyes of Rake, who fired two shots into the man's head. Mikki pulled the body inside and closed and locked the door.

From the bridge of the *Viktor Lagutov*, Michio Kato watched lightning streak silently across the night sky to the east. He was processing the short conversation from the head of the team of twelve mercenaries, hired for the mission. The American's tone had been a blend of anger and shame in informing him that one man was missing and another shot, he thought by a marksman on land. Was it from the base, Michio wondered, a sniper tasked to stop the mission, or a Japanese attacking a Russian super-trawler because it was on his sovereign territory?

Michio had brought in the Americans because he couldn't be sure all the Japanese would hold course or, in the chaos that he had constructed, that their orders would stay unchanged. He contracted them from the same company he had used for the killing of Yuri Mishkin, a job they had done well.

Sara was at the control panel, transfixed by the vessel leaving port, by ice floes on the water, staring toward the darkness out at sea. Michio loved his sister's innocence. She had the scatterbrain mind of a child's colored windmill on the beach, whirling this way and that, depending on the breeze, letting her feelings spin around with it. In time, she would come to understand, to love him again, to trust her brother as she always had.

The captain in command of the Japanese Special Forces Group agreed that the sniper shot could have come from an

area around the base. He would check. He advised doing
nothing: mission and timing were everything. He and his men
were in the aft section. The Americans were 150 meters away
at the bow. The *Viktor Lagutov* was gaining speed and would
soon be sailing east at fifteen knots. It was getting close to
midnight. In a few minutes Japan would begin celebrating its
National Foundation Day. The blast hatch would slide back,
giving the missile a clear path out.

'I need to hear it direct from the President.' Harry Lucas stood,
legs astride, leaning on his hands, knuckles down on the
scratched steel desk in a communications room he had moved
to from the Navy Lodge, deep underground at the Yokosuka
Naval Base, near Tokyo. Petrovsky had called in to tell Harry
that American warplanes would sink the *Viktor Lagutov* as
soon as it reached international waters.

'You're hearing it from me, Harry, and I'm his National
Security Adviser.' Petrovsky's eyes drilled, laser-like, into the
camera.

'Why now? Why did we send in a team? The *Viktor Lagutov*
is casting off.'

'The President's decision. He's in the Situation Room.'

'It's a Russian vessel,' objected Harry.

'It's a Panamanian-flagged vessel,' countered Petrovsky.
'And before you object too much, Freeman has spoken to
Grizlov who's agreed.'

'And the Japanese?'

'Screw them. They let this happen. I can get Indo-Pacific
Command in Hawaii to confirm if it makes you feel better,
but it's happening.'

'Ozenna is on board. Wekstatt is with him. Fuck you to hell
if this goes ahead.' Gripped with anger, Harry refused to hold
back. Screw diplomacy.

'I know. The Commander in Chief knows. I'll repeat, Harry,
he's given the order to take out the *Viktor Lagutov* as soon as
it leaves Japanese sovereign territory.'

FIFTY-FOUR

The weather change was abrupt and harsh. By the swell of the super-trawler, the circular sway in the small storeroom, Rake could tell it was only going to get worse. The vessel dipped back-and-forth in heavy waves, the sea current pushing it from side-to-side while being buffeted by savage wind. In calm seas and clear moonlight, men would be on deck. In these conditions, unless ordered otherwise, they would be in shelter, if not inside, under a roof somewhere, their line of sight diminished. Rake estimated they were less than ten minutes from international waters. They needed to get out and use the weather as their friend.

Harry Lucas had found the design plans of the *Viktor Lagutov*, ones from the Russian shipyard. Ladders attached to bulkheads on both sides led to the upper deck and the blast door of the missile silo. The rain and swell would make the upper deck treacherous. There were rungs on the surface which would help. The distance from the storeroom to the ladder was about thirty meters. Between the two was a large semi-circular covered area, with a door leading inside. If Rake were deployed to watch the deck, this is where he would shelter. This is where the enemy would be.

Mikki turned the hand-wheel. The two locks slid back. He pushed the door open wide to give an immediate wide arc of vision. Rake felt the chill of a sub-zero wind. Its roar dampened all other sound. The moon was dimmed and blurred from a night sky scudded with black clouds. Lines of white water rolled through the sea. Flecks of rain hit his face. Rake faced aft. Nothing. Mikki toward the bow. Nothing. Apart from deck lights that distorted and reflected crazily, visibility was cut to a few feet,

Rake steadied his footing against a roll of the super-trawler. He could make out figures on the bridge, the rain too heavy to identify or even count. It was good. They were safer. He signaled

Mikki to move to the bow. This would take them past the alcove where the American mercenaries might be sheltering. Rake edged with him, keeping vigil behind them. A blur of a man stepped out into their path, shining a flashlight on their faces and over their uniforms. He spoke into his microphone, 'Friendly.'

He listened to the response, half raised a hand to let them pass and stopped. He realized, exactly when Rake and Mikki did, that his orders were also coming through the radio Mikki carried from the dead crewman.

'Copy,' answered Mikki, the wind concealing his voice.

The mercenary was confused, making him far too slow to bring up his weapon. Rake was on him before he could make a sound. They fell heavily onto the deck. Rake held him down, pressing his left hand on his mouth while drawing with his right the Fairbairn-Sykes with the longer blade. A knife was better than a pistol muzzle flash. The mercenary tried to lash out but had fallen into a bad position with no leverage. In most circumstances, Rake would have been less lethal. But time was critical, the environment too uncertain, and there was no surrender in his opponent's eyes. He was white, thirties, buzzcut, and his weak response exposed him as a former soldier who hadn't kept up his skills. Rake cut his throat. Painless. Quiet. As he stood up, rain washed away blood.

They waited a beat and kept walking toward the ladder that took them to the upper deck. The trawler rolled hard to starboard. The mercenary's body slid and hit the frame that held the orange life raft. He was face upwards, eyes open, lashed by rain on a patch of deck lit by a bright static lamp, spotlighting the corpse as if on stage.

Gunfire erupted. Flashes lit up the deck. High-velocity rounds sparked off metal. They sprinted into the alcove where the mercenary had been. Gun noise cracked above wails of the wind. Rake spotted three men, carefully positioned, half exposed, half protected by derricks and railings.

'Hold fire, we're bringing in the wounded.'

Rake took the radio from Mikki. 'He's dead.' Rake emphasized his own American accent. 'Quit now.'

'The fuck are you?'

'US government. Throw down your weapons. Then walk out.

Three seconds to decide.' Rake was sincere about the surrender
offer. He doubted it would happen. There was no time for a
fuller explanation. The gunfire was fifteen seconds old. More
seconds and the Japanese special forces would be here.

No weapons clattered to the deck. Rake judged Mikki could
get two, not kills, but hits. He was about to signal a go, when
two laid down cover fire. A third ran fast down the deck to
their dead colleague. It was a distorted moving target, enough
for Mikki to take his legs away, half a magazine, slow and
steady, to catch the limbs on the run. The man's cry carried
back on the wind to his colleagues. One broke cover and Rake
shredded his neck, turning the streaking rain red, soon lost in
the gales.

Gunfire stopped. Rake's feet stayed steady on the heaving
deck, his face like a rock dripping with water. He calculated
five seconds of open ground to reach the ladder leading to
the upper deck. Fifteen seconds to climb. Once there, he could
crawl to the blast door but would be exposed. Perhaps. A
moving target on a night like this on a vessel diving and rising
in an angry sea could last a minute or two. Mikki would need
to stay where he was, where he could cover the lower deck
and the two wings of the bridge. In whatever way Rake
structured the next few minutes, the odds were bad. He needed
at least a platoon of good men. They were a fighting force
of two.

Mikki tapped his watch. Less than three minutes to
midnight. The *Viktor Lagutov* would be on the edge of international waters. Mikki took a position across the deck by the
body of the dead mercenary. Rake waited for his signal. As
if in an art form, Mikki designed cover to protect Rake in his
ascent. The roll of the vessel intensified as it careered through
the waves. Its bow plunged down, sending spray over
onto the deck. Rake's face stung with cold. Mikki pulled the
pin from a grenade and rolled it toward the bow. A second
grenade flew through the air toward the back. Harsh yellow
and white flashes lit both ends of the vessels. There were
crashes and sparks as shrapnel hit metal. Mikki stepped out
and opened fire on both wings of the bridge, half a magazine
to port, half to starboard. High-velocity rounds ricocheted off

bullet-proof glass. He couldn't hit them. Nor they him, unless they exposed themselves, which only a fool would do. Mikki's assault was Rake's cue to climb.

FIFTY-FIVE

On the bridge, sitting on a stool at the back of the control room, Sara Kato was terrified and close to vomiting from seasickness. She shivered with chill and dread as she saw flames leap up from an explosion on the deck. The captain stood silently in the center of the control panel, his gaze shifting from the destruction outside to the screens and monitors embedded in gray and green panels. He delivered calm orders. Put out fires. Check damage. Hold course. Michio spoke angrily on his phone. He had ordered Sara to stay quiet and close to him at all times. He had said nothing about what they were doing.

Sara had asked once and he told her to shut up and not leave his side. There were the plane, the truck, the loading of the container, the uniformed soldiers coming on board, that date of 11 February that Rake Ozenna had referenced, and now explosions outside. Michio's flags over all those islands gave her an idea of what he planned, and it was Rake's job to stop him. Rake would be outside. She sensed it. She had seen how he did things on the Åland Islands. He wasn't a safe man. Probably not a good one, either. She needed to find a way out and she couldn't see one.

Michio ended his conversation. 'Where are we?' he asked the captain.

'One minute we'll be across the line.'

'Get them to prepare the life raft,' Michio instructed.

'What,' shouted Sara. 'Why?'

Michio swung around, glaring at her. She looked away, unable to counter the fury in his stare. She looked out at surging white water where the ship plunged and rose, carried up and down like a twig in the valleys and mountains of the sea. She retched, tasting vomit and bile at the back of her throat. To keep it down, she swallowed and kept her eyes wide open, focusing on thick drops of rain glistening in lamplight. She tried to ride with the sway of the ship, back-and-forth, side-to-side, like a rocking cradle. She didn't want to be there in a life raft. There was a soldier outside on each wing of the bridge.

What was happening? Why were they leaving the ship? She put her hands against her brow to block out light so she could see outside better. On the deck directly below, she thought there was a sack that hadn't been there before. Then it moved. It was a person. An arm came out, grabbed hold of a deck rung, and pulled toward the center where there was something that looked like a drain cover or a trapdoor.

Michio saw it, too. He gave orders to the soldiers on the wings of the bridge. The one on the right peered over and stood higher to shoot. His head vanished. It seemed to evaporate. Just like that, bits of it flying off in the wind with his blood. The man on deck kept crawling. The other side of the bridge erupted into a massive explosion that tore up the wing and cracked the bullet-proof windows. Wood splintered and metal twisted.

Michio barely moved. 'Launch,' he said. 'Launch now.'

Rake was four feet from the blast door. The flare of light from Mikki's rocket-propelled grenade lit up the deck around him. Its grip handles worked well, pulling his body weight, using the gravity of the swell to get him to his destination. Mikki's cover was keeping him safe. But it wouldn't sustain. In a firefight, even Mikki could only hold off so many men for so long.

Rake would place the satchel of C4 on the forward side of the blast door, which contained its opening mechanism. The explosion would have ten times the force of a grenade, more than enough to damage the mechanism or set off electronic sensors that would stop the launch. He would set the detonator for thirty seconds to allow his escape.

The *Viktor Lagutov* lurched backwards. Rake's gloved hand kept grip of the rung. He saw Sara's face pressed up against the bridge window. The vessel pitched forward. Rake used the momentum to get him to the blast hatch. At exactly that moment, the lid of the silo smoothly slid open. Rake found himself looking at the nose of a missile decorated with the bright red circle of the Japanese national flag.

A door at deck level swung open. A shaft of light spread across. Michio Kato stood there with Sara, no more than twenty feet away. The wind was too violent to hear anything. Michio wore a wet-weather cape, nothing more. His hair hung soaked. Water streamed down his face. His hands were ungloved. He held a pistol at Sara's throat. He hooked her damp hair behind her ears. Her face was drenched with rain and terror. Two Japanese soldiers stepped out on either side, their weapons on Rake. Two more appeared on the surviving wing of the bridge. Mikki kept his guns silent. He had no angle to the deck. The trawler hit a wave that skewed into a sudden lurch. Sara was unsteady on her feet. The soldier on the left had to readjust his footing. There was a difference between training to a high level and fighting to high level with long combat experience. Apart from a very few like Umeda, Japanese troops didn't do combat.

Mikki's voice in his earpiece. 'From Michio. You have thirty seconds to surrender.' The message would be coming through the dead mercenary's radio. Why give him any time at all? The blast door was open but the missile was doing nothing. Was it still not ready for launch? It used a compressed gas ejector system to propel it away from the vessel before the rocket thrust took over. Rake should be feeling pre-launch vibrations. There was none.

Rake pushed himself onto his knees. 'Tell them we're beaten,' he said to Mikki. He grabbed the side of the blast hatch to steady himself and held open an empty right hand to say he was giving himself up.

FIFTY-SIX

Pre-launch vibrations started up. Rake gauged the roll of the vessel and the cycle of wind gusts. He lifted his hand off the blast hatch to get fully to his feet, his arms rising up in fake surrender. As he began to stand up, he flipped the detonator on the satchel of C4, waited fifteen seconds, then dropped it into the silo. He fell onto the deck and slid away as there was a single explosion and violent vibration. Flames and heat shot skywards and, just as quickly, flopped back down, revealing the missile nose unscathed apart from black soot smeared across the red Japanese rising sun. The rocket, its fuel tank and the warhead would be encased in material strong enough to withstand the blast. But the launch mechanism was destroyed. Michio's dream of Japan's declaration as a nuclear weapons power was dead. Rake looked up toward Michio and saw that Sara was still alive. Michio, the monster who murdered children and his brother, did not have the courage to kill his own sister. She stared ghost-like through the rain. Her hair hung soaked and flat against her forehead. She had no wet-weather gear. She shivered helplessly.

Rake slid the Fairbairn-Sykes long-bladed knife into an attack grip on his right hand and hurled it at the Japanese soldier on the right. At twenty feet, it missed the exact target of a neck artery, but it hit the face below the cheekbone. Startled, confused alarm spread across Michio's face. The second Japanese soldier fired on Rake. He was way off, and had little time to take a second aim. Rake, more familiar with the conditions, shot him with the SIG Sauer, the head and legs, avoiding the bullet-proof vest.

Gunfire came toward him from the surviving wing of the bridge. Mikki struck it with a rocket-propelled grenade. A massive explosion, ejecting white and yellow flames, hurled the two men into the air. Fire leapt off their clothes and trailed along hot, buckled metal before fading into the rain as the men tumbled toward the sea, their cries riding on wind that shrieked around Rake's ears.

'Michio wants to talk.' Mikki's voice. 'He's coming out to you. I'll cover.'

The Japanese gangster held his balance well in the swell. As far as Rake could see he was unarmed. Rake rested the SIG Sauer on his left wrist. He let Michio get close enough so they could yell and hear each other, then shouted, 'Far enough.'

Rake detected no anger, no frustration, no beating himself

up, none of the usual reactions of a defeated enemy. Michio
knocked rain off his jacket shoulder as if it were loose fluff
on a well-cut suit. He briefly shone a flashlight in Rake's face.
'You look Asian,' he shouted. 'Not American.'
'I'm native Alaskan.'
'Ah!' Michio even smiled. 'Like Ainu. That's why Sara has
such a crush on you.' Michio looked far from defeated. He
still had Sara. He had men under his command, guns quiet
for these few minutes on his orders. 'But you would have let
her die. You are a warrior, Rake Ozenna. You should come
and work for me. We could do great things together.' Michio
cast his gaze to the left. Lights went on around the life raft.
It was bright orange, long and round, shaped like a bullet and
positioned on a free-fall frame that would drop it into the
ocean. He looked back at Rake. 'I need you to understand
this, Ozenna. If I die, Sara dies. I am her protector. When I
am gone, what's left of this family will hunt her down wherever she is and kill her because, through you, she has betrayed
us. I need to know that you understand.'
'Yes,' yelled Rake.
'Take out your earpiece.'
Rake did what he asked. The vessel reeled sideways.
Michio held his position and raised his hand, beckoning Sara
to join them. Two soldiers helped her, bad news for Rake.
He couldn't see a way to take them on without risking Sara.
Michio shone the flashlight in Sara's face. She squinted. She
wore only a shirt. That was his game. There was a limit to
her survival in this weather and temperature. Fear stretched
across her face. Her eyes lit on the sight of Rake. She moved
to get closer to him. The soldiers held her back. Rake tore
off his jacket, held it out with his left hand and leveled the
SIG Sauer at Michio.
'Put it on her,' he instructed.
Michio took the rain-sodden jacket. 'See, Sara, he loves
you so much.' He hooked it around his sister's shoulders and
whispered something into her ear. Sara looked up, part startled,
part pleased. Michio took her arm and walked with her to
Rake, closer this time, and Rake allowed it. Michio let go of
her. Sara flung her arms around Rake just as the vessel was

buffeted by another strong wave and swayed suddenly, forcing
Sara to hold on more tightly.

Michio said, 'Did you tell him how Kazan died?'

Sara stiffened. She unfurled herself from Rake, kept hold
of his arm to steady herself.

'Did you tell him?' repeated Michio.

Fear turned to distress. Eyes pleading. Looking to Michio
and then to Rake and back again. Energy bled from her. Her
shoulders slumped. Unsteady on deck, Michio took her arm.
A flashlight came on from the door that led to the bridge.
Rake couldn't see who was there. He didn't sense added threat.
That would come from the Japanese soldiers, whose colleagues
he had killed and wounded, but who would act under orders.
On the deck below, the crew was climbing into the life raft.
Mikki Wekstatt was hidden down there, too.

'Yes.' Sara wiped her face. 'I told him that you murdered
our brother.' Distress turned to fury. Her words cut through,
fast, hard, full of hate. 'You cut Kazan in the stomach. You
did it because you are too weak to go against our sick father.'

'Did you tell him why our father needed Kazan dead?'

'No.' She faced Rake directly. 'Kazan was weak and spiteful.
He was damaging the family.'

'Well done, Sara.' Michio spoke as if she was a dog who
had just performed a trick. A woman appeared beside him.
Her jacket was torn on the sleeve. She had a fresh cut on her
left cheek and walked with a limp to her right leg. Rake
recognized the weapons engineer, Niko Yimagi, hurled about
by the force of the C4 blast. Rain splashed across her face.
Michio came closer, his face inches away from Rake's. 'Join
me, Ozenna,' he said. 'You are a fighter. You are a leader.
Marry Sara. Become my brother-in-law. We can do great things
together. Governments are dead. Look at them. Corrupt.
Disloyal. Weak. And democracy. What a fucking joke. I am
the future. I can buy, create, destroy, sell.'

Rake didn't move. As if through a cloud of weather, Mikki
appeared from below at the top of the ladder. He had a
submachine gun leveled at Michio and a pistol in his left hand.
Two grenades hung from his belt. His advantage lasted only
seconds. More figures, armed and dripping with rain, appeared

from the door leading to the control room. He and Mikki were
outnumbered. For some reason, they were still alive.

'You know nothing, Ozenna,' said Michio. 'We're leaving.
In an hour, I will be drinking sake in Wakkanai.' He pointed
to the life raft, then jerked his thumb toward Mikki. 'There's
been a deal: Russia, Japan and America. You and your
bloodthirsty sidekick are about to die. Your President has
ordered that the *Viktor Lagutov* be destroyed. There is no need
for me to kill you.'

Rake's expression didn't change. He believed Michio. The
way his orders kept going back and forth made him think that
Freeman was that type of President.

'Unless you join us, Ozenna,' jeered Michio. 'Name your
price. Just you. Not that murdering thug.'

'We'll stay,' said Rake. 'You need to look after Sara.' Sara's
best chance of survival was with Michio. To achieve that, he
should do nothing. Michio signaled Niko Yimagi, who limped
closer to give him a small square black box. Michio handed
it on to Rake. 'My parting gift to a warrior. Perhaps it's for
the best that you stopped the launch. That was my father's
wish. My style is more discreet. On that drive are details of
our weapons design. Japan is a nuclear armed state. We no
longer need American protection.' The box was military grade
steel, smaller than a phone. 'Seal it in a pocket,' continued
Michio. 'They'll find it if they retrieve your body, and you'll
get a posthumous medal. You were good, Ozenna. But we
have many missiles like this. No one can stop us.'

The control room on the bridge was lit but empty. Its
destroyed wings hung like mangled car wrecks. The moun-
tainous sea below formed a crush of white and black whirlpools
and waves. Rake tasted salt on the rain. The life raft was filling
up with people. Michio gripped Sara hard on her right arm.
He turned toward the door to the control room, which hung
open, swinging back and forth in the ship's roll. 'I salute you,
Ozenna. Your bravery and your honor.'

If governments had cut deals, there was nothing left to fight.
Rake didn't move. Around him was a mix of dark areas and
unfamiliar lights and an atmosphere of high mistrust, like in
a hostage exchange; no one sure if nerves would crack and

triggers get pulled. Rake had seen that happen a few times. Sara needed to get off the ship. Michio Kato was right about how Sara would be hunted down for the rest of her life if Michio died. That's what these people did, how they protected themselves. Rake's mission was to neutralize the missile. Job done.

Rake watched from the upper deck as Michio, Sara, Yimagi and those with them climbed into the life raft. Sara looked back at him like she had on the Åland Islands. He looked for confusion, wanted to see self-doubt. Instead, he saw certainty. Michio was safer than Rake. He pushed out his hand, hoping she would see it, telling her to go. It was fine. The right thing to do. The passengers would be secured by chest and waist belts, in seats designed to absorb the G-force of the fall. The raft's hatch came down and was sealed. The launch frame tilted back to give it angle and it was released like a funfair slide. Its bullet-shaped nose hit the water, sank in, then righted itself, rolling hard, the motor kicking in to keep it as steady as could be in the storm. It would be choppy and stomach churning, but they would live. Through rain and mist shone lights from some kind of vessel coming to pick them up, most likely a Japanese coastguard cutter.

Rake reinstated his earpiece. There was static, white noise, then a click, a clear signal and Lucas's voice: 'Get the hell off that ship. NOW.'

Michio was right. He knew what Rake had not known. Rake called in Mark Roller in the Black Hawk.

'I have your position,' replied Roller. 'Twenty-eight minutes out.'

'I cannot reverse the order,' shouted Lucas.

'Whose order?' Twenty-eight minutes was too long.

'You need to get off that ship,' repeated Lucas.

Rake cut Lucas's channel.

'Let's check out of here,' said Mikki.

FIFTY-SEVEN

Sea heaped up against the hull. Water tumbled and crashed, spreading foam and throwing up spray that cut Rake's vision as he climbed to the lower deck. Water temperature would be around freezing. Survival time maybe an hour if lucky. The drop was forty feet, sixty if they went in on a down swell. Waves rolled with overhanging crests of white. They climbed and crashed, sending up walls of water that no one could survive. In short moments when the moon shone through, there were different chaotic, restless patches of blue. When there was no moon, the water turned black and swirling, as if it would suck anything that tried to touch it. A surge heaving in from far across the Sea of Japan crashed into the bow of the ship, smashing Rake against a steel bulkhead. Mikki was there. Rake pointed down, Mikki, too, both hands positioned like parallel arrows toward the water. An air strike with the modern Naval Strike Missile would obliterate the *Viktor Lagutov* in seconds. If they waited for the sound of aircraft, they would be dead. They needed to jump.

Mikki handed Rake a rope which they fastened onto their belts to link them with a rapid release if one was dragging the other to his death. They unloaded anything heavy. Rake kept his knives and the pistol, into which he clipped a fresh magazine. Mikki looped his right hand around in the air, a signal that Rake had seen so many times in so many treacherous places.

Let's do it.

Rake hit the water hard on his shoulder. A wave threw him over onto his face. The current drew them both deep into the sea. He kicked, pushed up with his arms. Mikki was hurled against him with such force that he blanked out and came around thrashing, thinking only of survival and air.

Mikki's dead weight pulled him back down, wrenching him to one side and then the other. Rake wanted to choke. But if he opened his mouth, water would flood in. He felt ice cold. Trembling. His heart pounded through his ears. Darkness swirled. His eyes were soaked with salt water. There was no light, no air, the violent movement of the storm-churned sea twisting and tearing him, turning him over and over like a piece of driftwood. Mikki knocked into him, then was gone, then back again. Was he dead? Unconscious? Rake's lungs were squeezed tight. His body searched for the last trace of oxygen. So, this is what it was like, those seconds before death. His throat burned. He kicked to propel himself and was sucked down. Suddenly, Mikki came to life. Rake kicked again, Mikki propelling him up instead of dragging him down. A crush of water hurled them to the surface. Rake opened his mouth, drew in air, heard the scream of fighter jets and saw streaks of red and white light as missiles were fired from their wings.

The back and front of the *Viktor Lagutov* erupted into a spray of white, yellow and purple flame. Lethally hot waves of energy sped over Rake and Mikki, protected by the water. High explosive ripped the bow into jagged metal as if it were a plywood model. Water poured in, frothing, running as if through rapids. The ship lurched as the aft broke open, flames, explosions, the crafted, strong hull torn into a waterlogged void. The super-trawler tilted forward, then back, then leveled as water, front and back, weighed it down. The pilots came around and fired again. There was no need. But that would be their orders. Make sure. Certify destruction. Missiles hit the bridge, parts of the deck still above water. At the same time, a rolling wave, its strength gathered over many miles, smashed into the massive fishing boat which, shuddering from the impact, listed further. Second later, with its nuclear warhead still on board, the *Viktor Lagutov* vanished beneath the surface like a stone.

Rake rode with the swell. He watched the sea close over it and the lights of the vanishing aircraft. He spotted the distant light of the coastguard cutter. As the sea dipped, he saw the lights of Michio's life raft, a large orange steel tube rolling back and forth on the water, the occupants strapped into their seats like on an airplane, sealed safely inside. A blade of white water enveloped him. Cold salt sea rushed into his mouth. He choked hard to prevent it getting to his lungs. Mikki was at his side. The lip of a wave crashed onto him, and the sea wrenched him back.

The life raft was close, in control even in these waves. Michio had left Rake and Mikki to die on the ship. It made no sense that he would come to save them now. The life raft was being skillfully maneuvered in the brutish sea, close enough to throw them a lifeline. The hatch opened. Michio, strapped securely in, leant out. Rake's pistol would fire. But at what? He would have no accuracy. The best defense would be a grenade. But to get there, what chance of aiming it through the narrow entrance? And what of Sara? Rake could not work out if Michio was there to kill them or save them? He had offered Rake a job. He had given warning of the strike. He had delivered a hard drive of Japan's nuclear weapons design.

Rake knew rough water. He had been raised around a freezing sea. He had learned when dealing with an unpredictable unknown and thin on choices, it was often best to do nothing. Tread water. Stay afloat. Concentrate on the body fighting the cold. Michio stared down, face drenched, expression flat, mouth closed, eyes unflinching despite the rain, focused on Rake, hands holding the edges of the hatch. No lifeline came out. No invitation to come on board.

Amid the crashing of the sea and the wind, Rake picked out the engine of a helicopter. Mark Roller. Michio heard it, too, and looked skywards. Maybe he was watching out for them. Rake expected the door to close again. Michio sucked in his upper lip as if making a decision. Water splashed into the life raft. Michio reached back and dragged his sister to the narrow entrance. Her face was torn with horror. She looked at Michio, pleading. He pushed Sara into the freezing sea and shut the hatch.

FIFTY-EIGHT

Two months later

It was spring in Washington when Rake flew into Andrews from Manila, summoned by Lucas for a meeting at the White House. After his debrief in Japan, he hadn't wanted to go back. A kidnap rescue assignment in the southern Philippines had come up. Lucas got him on it, and it worked well.

After the rescue, as he had time to process things, Rake found he was unsettled in a way that was unfamiliar to him. Thrown out of the life raft, Sara had choked and choked, the freezing water sucking warmth from her unprotected body. Trained and familiar with cold water, Rake and Mikki's survival time might have been an hour. Sara's would be fifteen minutes before irreversible damage set in. Together, they held her up, head as clear as possible from lashing waves. They sandwiched her between them to give what warmth they could, keeping her alive until Mark Roller arrived. They winched her to warmth and safety in the helicopter. Physically, Sara recovered quickly. Carrie assessed her emotional trauma and set her up with counseling in London, where she was now, back at her job with her friends. Rake had heard she was all right. She had sent him a thank-you message and said she wanted to see him again. He wasn't sure.

Lucas had not explained why the President had ordered the destruction of the *Viktor Lagutov*. A sense of dread had fallen over Rake on going back to his rented apartment, just one floor down from Carrie in a city he didn't much like. The orphan kid – Ronan, the ivory tusk sculptor – was lodging there, entangled in his own challenges. He didn't plan to see Carrie until he knew where they stood with each other. He had done enough deployment returns to know that before stepping back into any old life, he needed to decompress. Rake craved the cold and the wild, a yearning to get back to his island where the ice would have two or three months to run. He got Lucas to book him into a hotel near the White House, where he found his full dress uniform hanging in the closet waiting for him.

Sun was warm on his face with only the slightest chill in the breeze as he walked through Lafayette Park toward the White House. No, he didn't like it here. Least of all the White House. Lucas had instructed Rake to wear the uniform and to leave his weapon behind. He was not to enter the White House until a call had come through from Leo Virtanen, the detective Rake had met handling Yuri Mishkin's murder investigation in Finland.

Rake leant against a tree enveloped in pink and white cherry blossoms. Sara had spoken about cherry blossoms, a beautiful sight in Japan that made her love her country. His phone vibrated with the call from Finland. 'Detective Virtanen here. I've been told to pass a message through you.'

'Major Ozenna here, Detective.' Rake did not know why Harry Lucas had been speaking to Virtanen, only that Lucas was with Petrovsky in the White House and couldn't take the call.

'It's good that it's you, Ozenna.' Rake detected respect in his voice, cop to soldier, professional stuff. 'I owe you an apology. My orders kept changing. We had an election coming up.'

'My orders, too. We had a new President.' Rake began walking toward the White House. 'What's the message?'

'Tell them it's done,' said Virtanen.

'It's done. That's all.' This had to be connected to Yuri Mishkin's murder.

'That's it.'

'Did they screw you, too?' He remembered Virtanen going quiet as Sara ran to Michio on the Åland Islands.

'You and me both,' said Virtanen. 'Governments all over are acting strange, not sure where they're at.'

Rake brushed loose tree bark off his uniform. 'Hope we get to work together again one day.'

'I would like that, Major Ozenna. I really would.'

Five minutes later, Rake was inside Petrovsky's corner office in the White House West Wing. He had no idea what Virtanen meant by 'it's done', the same way he had no idea of who or what was behind all that had erupted around the Kato family. He sensed that Harry Lucas was about to reveal it to him. Petrovsky's desk was cleared, his personal things stacked in a couple of plastic crates. The National Security Adviser was leaving his job but he didn't have the air of a man who had been fired.

'This was on the drive Kato gave you.' Lucas pointed to a screen showing an intricate engineering diagram. 'It's their nuclear weapons design and it checks out. We had it reviewed at Los Alamos and Oak Ridge.' These were two of America's leading nuclear weapons establishments.

Petrovsky said, 'Michio Kato gave you a step design and test simulation. Since then, a similar but not exact replica of that was sent through the dark web to Harry. The two corroborate that Japan is now a nuclear weapons state. But a covert one, thank God, because you, Major, stopped the missile launch.'

'Like Israel,' expanded Lucas. Israel had produced nuclear weapons since the 1960s, but never admitted it.

'Yes. Like Israel.' Petrovsky put a cap on his pen and stood up. 'At least, the Japanese have shared details with us.'

Rake pointed to Petrovsky's boxes. 'You've quit or been fired?'

'Quit, and I asked Harry to get you here, Major. We owe it to you, and thank you for bringing confirmation from Leo Virtanen.' Petrovsky gathered up documents on his desk and slipped them into a transparent plastic folder. 'We're going to the Oval, and I'd be glad if you joined us.'

Rake followed Petrovsky and Lucas into the busy corridor. The Oval Office lay at the diagonally opposite end of the West Wing. They passed harassed figures walking fast and purposefully, speaking quickly, laminated ID cards hanging from their necks, their job to ensure the will of John Freeman's administration. Petrovsky and Lucas walked in front, two middle-aged white guys in suits. Eyes fell on Rake, a younger Asian-looking guy, in military uniform with medals. The way they quickly looked away again told Rake he must be carrying one of his meaner expressions. Reeling through his memory were the flames, the missiles, the raging sea, and fighter jets sent in to destroy. He had moved on, but he would never trust or forgive this President. Two Secret Service agents fell into step in front of them and led them past the secretaries' desks into the President's office.

John Freeman did not look up when they entered. His jacket hung from the back of his chair. He wore a white shirt with a loosely tied dark blue tie. He took his time signing a document which he handed to a staffer, who left. He pushed himself back in his chair. 'What can I do for you, Nick, Harry. I can give you three minutes.'

Rake logged the lack of his name check and Freeman's irritated expression. The President's focus was on scrolling through his tablet, a signal that anything was more important than the people in the room.

Petrovsky lay the folder on his desk. Freeman shot him an impatient glance. 'Spit it out, Nick. I don't have time.'

'This file was given to Baroness Lucas by President Grizlov, sir,' said Petrovsky. 'It is evidence of your complicity over many years in the illegal transfer of nuclear materials from the US to Japan.'

Freeman pulled the file toward him. 'From Russian intelligence?' He fiddled with the flaps to get the documents out. 'You've got to be kidding. Put it in the trash.'

'The information has been corroborated by CIA, FBI and other agencies.' Petrovsky continued. 'As chair of the Senate Committee on Intelligence and head of Homeland Security, you repeatedly blocked investigations into missing plutonium. But more than that—'

'No. Not more of anything.' Freeman was on his feet, pressing the call button to his outside office.

Petrovsky stepped toward the desk, holding freshly printed photographs.

'Not a step closer,' shouted Freeman. Then to the intercom. 'Need the Secret Service in here.'

Rake hadn't been briefed, but he knew enough to know the photographs were evidence against Freeman that needed to reach their destination. Sensing Petrovsky might waver against

Secret Service agents, he took them from his hand, walked up to Freeman and lay them on the desk, fanning them out like a deck of cards. He folded his arms and stood directly in front of the President.

Petrovsky said, 'These are photographs of you with the Yakuza gangster Jacob Kato, together with his sons Michio and Kazan, and of the Kato families violent track record. In the Senate, you went out of your way to back Kato developments, hotels, golf courses, shopping malls. You name it.'

'Nothing unusual in a political career.' Freeman's defiance softened. He looked toward the door. No Secret Service. 'Besides, like I said, this is a Russian dossier.'

'That's the thing, sir,' Lucas interjected. 'It's not a Russian dossier.'

'Make up your damn minds.' Freeman's hand slid under the lip of the desk to press the emergency call button.

Lucas said, 'It was given to the Russians by Kazan Kato, the younger son whom you met and who has since been murdered by the family.'

Blood flushed from Freeman's face. His gaze stayed on the door. No help was coming.

'You need to sit down, sir,' said Petrovsky.

Freeman shook his head. He leant on his desk. Rake remained in front of him, eyes unflinching. The President looked down, unable to meet anyone's gaze.

'The file from President Grizlov prompted us to look more closely at your business operations outside of politics,' said Lucas.

'Waste of time, Harry.' Freeman pushed his hand through the air. 'They're all in blind trusts.'

'The killers of Yuri Mishkin came from a private security company you founded during our forever wars,' said Petrovsky. 'That same company infiltrated the Finnish security services at a high enough level to fabricate charges against Sara Kato and prevent her escape with Major Ozenna. There was an earlier fabrication of evidence against Kazan Kato leading to the FBI's involvement which meant he could not lead the family. He was murdered by his brother, as you had planned. And veterans from that same company were hired for the attempted missile launch from the *Viktor Lagutov*. Major Ozenna stopped it and saved thousands, maybe millions of lives.'

Freeman's eyes began flitting up toward Rake but didn't make it.

Petrovsky continued. 'We got the NSA to trawl the electronic traffic surrounding this. Your people have been liaising with Michio Kato throughout.'

'Bullshit. And you know it.' Freeman became more rigid. Rake recognized fear and self-justification, signs of a man who could be on the cusp of physically lashing out.

Lucas stepped in again, 'And you were fully aware, Mr President. In the Situation Room, you did not give the order to sink the *Viktor Lagutov* until you had been informed that Michio Kato's life raft was safely off the vessel. You knew the missile was neutralized. The only reason to sink it was to make sure Major Ozenna and Detective Wekstatt didn't make it out to tell the story.'

Only now did Freeman look straight at Rake, who had rarely seen such hatred in a man's eyes. Rake stepped up to the desk. He separated out two photographs from the pack and slid them directly under Freeman's gaze. They were pictures he had taken of the two children shot dead in Portugal. Rake stepped back, and let his arms hang loose by his side while he worked out the best short-distance knife-throw angles for a fast kill on the President's neck. Not that he had a knife, but it helped toughen his expression. Freeman glanced at the photographs and quickly looked away.

'Mishkin's killers have been talking, John.' Lucas used his first name to try and soften tension. 'The Finns have now handed them over to the Russians.'

That was what Virtanen's 'It's done' message was about.

'It's the right damn policy.' Freeman slammed his hand down on the folder. 'Don't you idiots see that. I'll do whatever it takes to get it done. We need a nuclear armed Japan. The more we keep American troops there, the more we put them in harm's way.'

'By working outside the law with murderers,' said Petrovsky.

Freeman pushed his golf club pen back and forth on his desk.

Each roll was slower, with less energy. 'That was them. I didn't know any of that.' He threw the pen hard across the room.

'You covered up. You kept going. You tried to kill my men.' Lucas looked across to Rake.

Freeman stared at the embossed leather of the desk.

'Go quietly, John,' said Petrovsky. 'We all want to keep a lid on it. Give yourself a chance to control the narrative and the consequences.'

The Chief of Staff walked in. Freeman's face lit up. 'Where the hell are the Secret Service?'

'Sir, the Vice President and the House Speaker are here with the Chief Justice.'

Freeman pushed Petrovsky's folder so hard it slid off the desk onto the floor. Rake was glad Lucas had called him in. He was watching a masterclass in Washington combat. Lucas gave him a glimpse of a smile. 'Are we good, Major?'

'We're good, sir,' said Rake.

Three men whom Rake only recognized from the television walked into the Oval Office to take Freeman's resignation and swear in a new President.

FIFTY-NINE

By the time Rake walked from the White House to his seventh-floor apartment on Virginia Avenue, news was out of President John Freeman's stepping down for health reasons. The Vice President was being sworn in. He called ahead and told Carrie he was heading over to his apartment.

'You got anything to do with this White House shit-show?' Her voice rippled with excitement.

'No more than you.' Rake felt it, too. 'Is Ronan there?'

'Technically. I'll head down and check it's not too much of a mess.' Carrie was friendly, relaxed, not judgmental, not rushing. Carrie sounded nice. Rake wanted to hang out with her a bit. They had tried to talk afterwards, in Tokyo, on video calls back and forth. On the surface, conversation came easily. But both seemed to run scared when the conversation risked going deeper. Rake thought Carrie's trauma psychology might be complicating things. Carrie dreaded him going on another dangerous assignment, or heading back to his island as a tribal elder, and her lover's instinct told her he wanted to see Sara again. Complicated stuff. Both knew they would not fall easily back into bed together, which is how they usually sorted stuff out. He liked Carrie a lot. One day they would again. But not yet.

Lucas had just told him of a job, leaving straight away. There was no need even to call in at his apartment. But he was. That indecision again.

The door was opened not by Carrie but by a teenage woman with green-hair wearing a bright pink T-shirt whom he took a moment to recognize. His tenant was meant to be Ronan, the ivory tusk sculptor. This was June, who had accused Ronan of raping her. That fight must have gone away as fights often did. The main bedroom door was open, bedclothes crumpled, a purple and yellow T-shirt draped over a pillow, both sides of the bed slept in.

'Hell of nest you've made here.' Rake embraced the young man, who was a younger stepbrother to him like he was to Mikki. June stayed back, head lowered. 'Come here.' Rake hugged her and she whispered how sorry she was.

'Don't matter. We all do stupid, crazy things that hurt people.'

'It was the, you know, the mess I was in.' She kissed him on the cheek and took Ronan's hand. Carrie stepped out of the kitchen and handed him a cup of coffee. 'Sorry about the clutter.'

'No problem.' The coffee tasted harsh and strong. Carrie knew how he liked it.

'Was it Freeman?' she asked.

'Yes. His masterplan for world peace.' Rake couldn't read Carrie's signals. He looked around at the untidiness of his apartment, Ronan's drawings scattered around, unwashed cups and glasses, clothes draped over chairs and, in the middle of it all, the mammoth tusk sitting elegantly in its cradle.

'It'll be gone soon,' said Ronan. 'They found a space there for me to work.'

'Stay as long as you like.' Rake sipped his coffee.

'Rest up in my place.' Carrie gave him a quick smile.

'I'm heading to Andrews.'

'You're really going.' Carrie's face tightened, but the way she said it suggested Harry had told her something.

'You know?'

'You never know everything with Harry.'

'I'm going. Harry thinks it's a good idea.'

Carrie led him into the small kitchen. She kissed him gently. 'I know you don't express feelings much. But I know you have them because if you didn't, I wouldn't love you.' She held both her hands against the roughness of his cheeks. 'Be careful, Rake Ozenna. Feelings are like war; they have a habit of ripping people up without warning. With Sara Kato, be very careful.'

Rake followed Stephanie Lucas down the steps of the Gulfstream 280 which had picked her up in London on the way to Vnukovo International Airport near Moscow. Stephanie was dressed formally in a black greatcoat with a bundled gray scarf and a fur hat with flaps over the ears. Rake had on a dark suit and a black cold-weather jacket. The apron's white snow was streaked by the tracks of vehicles and aircraft. The terminal shone through the afternoon darkness like a theater stage.

A convoy of three black SUVs, staffed by the Russian Presidential Security Service, stood by the aircraft steps. Back doors opened either side of the middle vehicle for Rake and Stephanie. Sergey Grizlov had asked specifically that Rake come. He gave no reason.

The convoy drove north with flashing lights, highway lanes cleared in advance. Rake had never been to Moscow. He tried to get his head around this vast country that stretched all the way from Europe to his home on Little Diomede in the Bering Strait.

Stephanie broke his thoughts, saying, 'Carrie wanted me to tell you something.'

'Sure.' *Why didn't Carrie tell him herself*, he thought.

'Harry's asked her to work for him. She wants to know what you think, and felt it better if I asked you.'

Good call, Carrie. And that's why Lucas had told her about Moscow. The idea gave him a warm feeling. He didn't want to lose Carrie. He liked her in his life. They ended up working together so often it wouldn't make much difference. Then again, with another new President, Rake could be assigned somewhere else, away from Harry Lucas. 'It's good,' he answered. 'Tell her to go for it.'

'That's it?' Stephanie looked around at him, her brow creased, offering a smile to coax him to say more.

'What's there to think?' Rake watched chaotic traffic, hunched people in thick coats around bus stops, shopping malls, and churches with gold domes. 'That's it. It is as it is.'

'You are a strange one, Rake,' laughed Stephanie. 'No wonder you drive Carrie crazy.'

They drove off the road, down a snow-packed lane and into the driveway of a church with a blue dome and a gold cross. There was security everywhere. Sergey Grizlov walked toward them. Doors opened, and he and Stephanie got out. There was no wind, no snow or rain, just a freezing stillness under a blue sky. Choral chanting came from inside the church. Outside, earth was piled up by a freshly dug grave. Grizlov embraced Stephanie, then moved to Rake. 'Thank you for coming, Major. It means a lot to me, and Russia owes you a debt of gratitude.'

Grizlov shook his hand. Rake returned the grip.

'Thank you for asking me, sir,' said Rake.

'Forgive me.' Grizlov gave him a sharp, quizzical stare. 'I asked our spies to look into your records.'

Rake's record was not good. He had killed Russians and fought them. Had he been stupid to come? Was he being set up for a fall? He cast his gaze expertly around, checking for ways of escape.

Grizlov noticed. 'No. Not those sorts of records. As a child you came to Russia looking for your father and failed to find him. But you still think he might be here.'

'Yes, sir.' Rake felt his heart rate quicken. Finding his father had become an obsession when he was a teenager, driving him down. Mikki saved him by pushing him into the army.

'We'll open up our files to you. Go look for him in Russia,

wherever the search takes you.' Grizlov turned as pall-bearers carried Yuri Mishkin's white coffin from the church across the snow to the grave. 'Come. Yuri has been too long in the morgue. It is time to bury my son.'

The coffin, covered in wreaths, was lowered in. Rake counted twenty-six people. Very private. He saw no cameras. Grizlov stood next to the Deputy Speaker of the state Duma, who was Mishkin's mother. Stephanie was close. A priest spoke at the graveside. The choir stepped out from the church, chanting, their breath creating a cloud of music around them. Mishkin's mother scooped earth and snow from ground and dropped it on the coffin. Grizlov did the same. One by one, mourners followed.

Rake sensed more than knew that Sara Kato had edged her way next to him. 'Thank you for coming.' She wore a long black, warm coat and fur hat. Either the cold or the occasion was tearing her eyes.

'Are you OK?' asked Rake.

'Better for seeing you.' She dabbed the edges of her eyes with a tissue. Putting her gloved hands on his right arm, she looked at him, then looked away. She was vulnerable. Her eyes had lost energy. 'Thank you for saving my life,' she said.

'Michio leave you alone?'

'Yes. Nothing.'

'Any problems let me know.' One day Rake would deal with Michio.

'Thank you.' Sara held him tighter. 'It's good we have closure together.'

'Yeah,' replied Rake. 'It's right.' *Be careful.* Carrie's voice came into his head. *Feelings have a habit of ripping people up.*

Rake didn't know what his feelings were. They were as they were and his mind was on finding his father.

'Come,' he stepped forward, loosening her grip. 'We need to throw Russian soil onto Yuri's coffin.'

AUTHOR'S NOTE

Thank you so much for reading *Ice Islands*. I hope you enjoyed it as much as I did the research and writing. Thanks to all those, too, who have recommended the Rake Ozenna series and to the booksellers who have promoted it in their stores. Word of mouth remains the most powerful way to build an audience.

Many helped in constructing the backdrop to the story. My thanks to Betsy Glick and her anonymous FBI colleagues who guided me through that murky nexus of transnational crime and politics. Grant Newsham from the Japan Forum for Strategic Studies was superb in drilling down on the nature of Asian organized crime and the political instability it might cause. The threat of the Yakuza to the United States is no figment of this thriller writer's imagination. *Ice Island*'s unnamed presidential executive order is drawn from Executive Order 13581, published on 25 July 2011. It cites the Yakuza as one of four international networks which, it says, 'constitute an unusual and extraordinary threat to the national security, foreign policy, and economy of the United States.'

I am grateful to Susann Simolin and her colleagues at the Åland Islands Peace Institute for guidance on their great organization's values and mission. As far as I know, it has never been involved in the bloodthirsty intrigue encountered by Rake Ozenna. The Åland Islands stand as a model of how conflicts can be settled without war.

My thanks to Duncan Bartlett, Yuka Morita and Lesley Downer for reading through the sections inside Japan and advising on everything from kimonos to body language. I am in awe of Lesley's knowledge of Japanese swords, and highly recommend her historical novels, *The Shogun's Queen*, *The Last Concubine* and others.

A Zoom and lunch with Shihoko Goto of the Wilson Center in Washington, DC was invaluable in understanding the disputed territories between Japan and Russia and how they impact the politics of Northeast Asia. Thanks, too, to Greg Poling and Michael Green at the Center for Strategic and International Studies, John Hemmings of the Asia-Pacific Center for Security Studies, Sally Leivesley of Newrisk Ltd, Karin Landgren at Security Council Report, Harlan Ullman at the Atlantic Council, Ian Bond at the Centre for European Reform, Charles Parton of the Royal United Services Institute, Bill Hayton at Chatham House and James Rogers and Matthew Henderson at the Council on Geostrategy. They and others who prefer not to be named contributed to my creating the canvas on which Rake Ozenna and his team could operate.

Unlike other books in the series, Rake's home island of Little Diomede on the Russian border did not feature as a location. But Rake's heart is in this rugged and beautiful place and my thanks to Opik Ahkinga, John Ahkvaluk, Frances Ozenna, Robert Soolook, Henry Soolook, JoAnn Kaningkok and all the Little Diomede islanders and Tribal Council for their hospitality and kindness during my visit. JoAnn takes the most stunning pictures of island scenery and across the water into Russia and posts them on Facebook.

Candis Olmstead and Dana Rosso of the Alaska National Guard have been generous with their time in sharing insights into their incredible work. Operating in the vast and hostile environment of Alaska, the Guard keeps communities safe and supplied. Also, alongside the North American Aerospace Defense Command, the Guard secures America's western border with Russia.

Thanks to Teri Hendriks of Visit Anchorage for showing me around; to Robert Gillam for explaining the growing trade routes between Alaska and Northeast Asia; Bob Sherill and his volunteer colleagues at the Alaska Veterans Museum with its story of the only American territory ever occupied by a foreign power; the thoughtful staff at the Hotel Captain Cook; and Matt Worden of Go Hike Alaska who took me on a walk of a lifetime through the Chugach Mountains which overlook the Elmendorf–Richardson military base. There is little better than a day out in the wilds with Matt.

Once again, in Washington, DC, I borrowed the apartment

of Nancy Langston for Carrie's studio and gave Rake a two-bedroom place in the same block. Thank you, Nancy.

Writing may be a solitary task. Being an author is not. No book would work without its support team. A big shout to Deborah Swain of Lit Web Studio who keeps content rolling into my website, updating day on day. Sergio Davison and Rob Falkner at Data Dial fine tune the engine running below decks. Kasim Javed of Creative Marketing has been with me from *Man on Ice*, coming up with designs, images and videos. Publicist Mickey Mickelson of Creative Edge ensures that Rake reaches a wide audience through interviews and podcasts, and Catherine Saykaly-Stevens of the Networking Web cracked the whip on social media marketing.

It is my privilege to host The Democracy Forum monthly debates, which puts me in conversation with some of the finest thinkers in global affairs, and to be a presenter of Goldster's Inside Story book show, where I meet authors and publishing industry executives and keep up with the buzz of the trade.

Crucially, there are those who knock a book into shape, decide on great covers and get it out to readers. Don Weise has honed Rake Ozenna's first drafts from the start. Liz Jensen, Adam Williams and Kei Lundqvist gave time in strengthening characters and motives. Great thanks to Joanne Grant at Severn House for her eagle eye on editing the manuscript, her team for designing compelling artwork and seeing through production, and to Kate Lyall Grant for commissioning the series from the beginning. David Grossman has been my agent since my first book in 1997. Thank you, David, for your wisdom, sharp mind and support over all these years.